CRITICS PRAISE CHARLOTTE HUBBARD!

ANGEL'S EMBRACE

"This loving series, reminiscent of the classic home-spun, Americana novels of the '80s and '90s, hits a soft spot. With her latest, Hubbard moves her series from inspirational to mainstream historical romance, but there's still a strong dose of inspiration in this lovingly crafted, yet gritty, story of small-town America."

—*Romantic Times BOOKreviews*

"*Angel's Embrace* is a very moving tale, and Ms. Hubbard does an excellent job at constructing relationships between her characters."

—Romance Reviews Today

JOURNEY TO LOVE

"Ms. Hubbard brings to life a spoiled, selfish young girl who has many lessons in life to learn, and learn them she does through the telling of *Journey to Love....* The romance is sweet and the conclusion a happy one, though it doesn't come without much soul searching and spiritual growth. Enjoy your journey of love with the reading of this novel."

—Romance Reviews Today

"This is an interesting historical romance that show-cases how different society was just under a hundred and fifty years ago as the sixte̶ẹ̶n̶ ̶ heroine hopes to mar̶ ubbard provides rea̶ ̶ ̶teenth century journ

—*Review*

A TIME FOR TRUST

"Maybe now that I've told *you* a secret, you could share some with me. I wouldn't tell a soul, you know." She whistled to Rex, and then walked resolutely across the lawn without looking back.

Gabe sighed wistfully. Best to keep his own counsel, as far as revealing anything about his life with Letitia. What would a young lady like Solace know about such things? Did he want to discolor her rosy assumptions about love? About what it meant to marry for better or worse?

She's wiser than you know. More mature than Letitia... less concerned about maintaining appearances.

He laughed aloud. Solace Monroe was anything but concerned about fitting society's mold! But it was too soon. She held too many innocent assumptions.

Would she confide in you if she knew the truth? About how your wife died rather than bear your child?

Gabe's smile faltered; his happiness drifted away on the evening breeze. Some secrets were too onerous to lift up to the light of day.

Other *Leisure* books by Charlotte Hubbard:

ANGEL'S EMBRACE
JOURNEY TO LOVE
A PATCHWORK FAMILY

Gabriel's Lady

Charlotte Hubbard

LEISURE BOOKS NEW YORK CITY

For Rhonda and for Laney,
who prove love can be absolutely stunning the
second time around!

A LEISURE BOOK®

May 2008

Published by

Dorchester Publishing Co., Inc.
200 Madison Avenue
New York, NY 10016

ISBN 10: 0-8439-6008-6
ISBN 13: 978-0-8439-6008-2

10 9 8 7 6 5 4 3 2 1   616338741

AUTHOR'S NOTE

The characters in my "Angels of Mercy" series discuss Negroes and colored men and Indians, because in the 1800s such terminology wasn't derogatory or demeaning. It simply *was*. The Malloys pray and discuss their faith in public, too, because a strong belief in God was the foundation these homesteaders built their lives upon.

So, at the risk of writing a politically incorrect story, I have told a more authentic, historically accurate one. I applaud my editor, Alicia Condon, for supporting me in this.

"Life is either a daring adventure or nothing."
—Helen Keller

"What the caterpillar calls the end of the world,
The Master calls a butterfly."
—Richard Bach

Psalm 23

The Lord is my shepherd; I shall not want.

He maketh me to lie down in green pastures: he leadeth me beside the still waters.

He restoreth my soul: he leadeth me in the paths of righteousness for his name's sake.

Yea, though I walk through the valley of the shadow of death, I will fear no evil: for thou art with me; thy rod and thy staff they comfort me.

Thou preparest a table before me in the presence of mine enemies: thou anointest my head with oil; my cup runneth over.

Surely goodness and mercy shall follow me all the days of my life: and I will dwell in the house of the Lord for ever.

Prologue

St. Louis, Missouri. June, 1880

"I now pronounce you man and wife. You may kiss your beautiful bride, Mr. Getty."

Gabe Getty thought his heart might fly out of his chest like a wild bird set free—even though the delicate face before him represented a whole new kind of commitment: settling down into a new life. New family. New responsibilities.

He fumbled with the wispy veil that floated like a cloud around Letitia Bancroft—now Letitia Getty, his wife!—and raised it over her golden upswept hair. "You *are* beautiful, Letitia," he whispered, "and I love you so much I-I can't find the words."

"So kiss me, Gabriel. It's what everyone's waiting for."

Letitia's blue eyes closed and her soft face radiated a surrender that made him want to gulp her down and swallow her whole. But they were in church, being observed by dozens of St. Louis's most influential lawyers and captains of industry. Not to mention Arthur and Henrietta Bancroft, his bride's protective parents. He dared not challenge propriety during this sacred, long-awaited moment.

Letitia's lips parted. She gazed up at him. The tiny hands on his shoulders relaxed. He felt her pulse racing with his . . . inviting him into that primal mating dance with all its mysteries, for which he'd waited so long.

He kissed her eagerly, spanning her tiny waist with his hands. So fragile she felt in his embrace, despite the rigid bands of whalebone beneath her white dress. Gabe set aside thoughts of peeling away her layers of clothing . . . .

Letitia's lips slipped from his too soon. When he opened his eyes, her face looked deathly pale beneath her rouge. When she collapsed, he had to grab her.

"Letitia!" he rasped. "Somebody—"

Gabe glanced anxiously at the minister, and then at his best man, Billy Bristol. "She's passed out! I don't know what to—"

A frantic cry rose from the first pew as Billy steadied Letitia's dead weight. "Better lay her on the floor to get some blood back to her head," he murmured. "Then we'll loosen that—"

"Letitia!" her mother squawked. "Wake *up*, sweetheart!"

Gabe winced at her shrill voice, and at the matron huffing up the chancel steps. The church filled with whispering as the minister spoke out.

"Just a case of the jitters," he announced with a chuckle. "Happens quite often, actually, so—"

"You must *not* put her on the *floor*!" Henrietta Bancroft topped the steps and bustled toward him. "We can *not* soil that exquisitely expensive gown by—she can't bend at the waist, you fool! What do you think smelling salts are for? If you weren't so eager to satisfy your *animal urges*—"

Letitia's mother plucked a small bottle from her reticule and doused her handkerchief with a foul-smelling liquid. Then she held it over her daughter's nose.

Gabe's eyes watered from the camphor fumes, yet he could see Billy trying not to laugh . . . could feel waves of indignation rolling off Mrs. Bancroft's substantial body as she wedged herself between him and his unconscious bride.

Letitia coughed like a sick kitten.

"Wake up, darling!" Henrietta cooed. "Show everyone how a young lady of your upbringing *carries on* after a lapse of—Lord, it's a hundred and ten degrees in here, Reverend Stilton! And *you*, Mr. Getty, are squeezing the breath from Letitia's poor lungs!"

"Mama?" Letitia's eyes widened with mortification. "Oh, my stars—Gabriel, don't you dare let me fall! I'll never get up!"

"Easy now. We've got you covered," Billy said. "Find your feet and take a few deep breaths to make the room stop spinnin'. Gabe would never let you fall—or let you down, either. Some punch and cake'll bring you 'round, so's all these folks can congratulate you, Mrs. Getty."

"Oh, I couldn't dream of eating—"

Letitia realized then that dozens of eyes were focused on her. Dozens of ears followed her every halting word. So she rose to the challenge: stood upright and lifted her head in that fetching yet determined tilt Gabe had always found captivating.

"You're right, Mr. Bristol," Letitia whispered. "I *am* Mrs. Gabriel Getty. I should act the part."

She took a deep breath—as deep as her gown would allow, anyway—and focused her blue eyes on her hundreds of admirers. "I'm fine now—really I am! Thank you all for your concern," she said in a lilting voice. "Shall we proceed to the reception?"

As Gabe flashed a grateful smile at his red-haired best friend, the organist struck up a triumphant recessional. Billy had the same way with skittish women as he did with the Morgan horses he raised; the same down-to-earth, unruffled manner he'd had when they were kids.

Gabe had a sobering thought as he slipped his bride's tiny hand into the crook of his elbow: what would he do once it was just himself and Letitia, and she had one of her fainting spells? Or if she refused to eat? What if he couldn't tease her out of her dark moods when things didn't go her way?

Mrs. Bancroft urged him forward with a jab of her finger.

"Oh, Letitia, you *swooned* at his kiss—"

"How romantic that he caught you and—"

"You look like an absolute *queen* in that gown! And he'd better treat you like one every single day!"

Gabe smiled at these remarks from beside the punch bowl, a safe distance from Letitia's highly excitable bridesmaids. He'd known them all at Miss Vanderbilt's Academy for Young Ladies, where he'd lodged while serving out an apprenticeship in Arthur Bancroft's law practice. He could've chosen any one of them as his bride, but Letitia had caught his eye and captured his heart from the beginning.

"Congratulations, Gabe." Billy's husky voice broke into his thoughts. "Won't be long before you're actin' like an old married man and chasin' after your kids. Just like me."

"You've always made that look so easy, Billy. You're a hard act to follow." His best man cradled a redheaded baby on his shoulder as though it were the most natural thing in the world. Meanwhile, his eyes seldom strayed from his four-year-old daughter Olivia, who whirled in a gleeful circle to make her new dress billow out around her legs.

"You'll do fine, Gabe. Gotcha a good job and a nice house. Pretty bride to make life worthwhile." Billy sidled closer, nuzzling his son's temple. "You've done right well for a kid who lost his family to Injuns and grew up in a two-room log house. Who'd've ever dreamed you'd be practicin' the law and hobnobbin' with the likes of *these* folks?"

Gabe smiled at the roomful of tuxedoed gentlemen and bejeweled ladies. He was indeed a fortunate man. "Agatha Vanderbilt handed me the opportunity of a lifetime when she introduced me to Arthur Bancroft," he agreed. "I-I just hope I'm ready to—"

"Oh, you'll never feel *ready*," Billy teased. "You gotta jump in feet first and pray a lot. Somehow, it all works out."

As though he already recognized the wisdom of this, little Owen raised his downy head to flash his daddy a toothless grin. Billy chuckled back, totally enthralled by the son who looked just like him.

Something tightened in his chest, and Gabe glanced away. Such love was written on his best friend's face, he envied Billy Bristol in more ways than he could count. And yet, when he glanced back at the gaggle of young women around Letitia—his wife, and the beginning of his own dreams come true—he wondered if he would ever share that all-engrossing devotion so evident between Billy and Eve Bristol. They'd married in turmoil: Eve had birthed Olivia out of wedlock because Billy's outlaw twin had abandoned her. Yet they made a shining example of how love could climb the highest mountains.

Maybe it was wedding-day jitters making his stomach roll . . . maybe his bride was still shaken from fainting at the altar . . . so maybe she wouldn't always depend on that little silver flask she'd just tipped to her lips. Once the wedding was behind them . . . once they settled into their fine new home just four doors down from Letitia's parents, everything would be all right. Wouldn't it?

From a few yards away, surrounded by her matronly friends, Henrietta Bancroft glared at him. Did she never intend to smile upon his happiness? How was it that even in this reception hall abuzz with happy conversations—two hundred people come to share this day—he felt singled out for Mrs. Bancroft's disapproval?

Gabe pasted on a smile. It was time to take his place beside his bride—to let her delicate perfume tease him while she still wore that voluminous gown of virginal white. In a few hours, he could finally tell Letitia how much he longed for her. He could tell her how lovely and wonderful she was, without parental ears or tattletale domestics listening in.

"Excuse me while I steal a kiss," he murmured to Billy.

He caught his bride's gaze—so elegant she was, with her blue eyes and creamy complexion . . . golden hair he longed to unpin. Letitia graced him with a flirtatious grin and his heart soared. He surged toward her, barely aware of the couples who stepped out of his way with their raised punch cups.

With lips pressed together and a protective lift of her eyebrow, Henrietta arrived at her daughter's side first. "Come along, dear! We mustn't ignore the ladies from the

Literary Club, who so graciously hosted your shower last week."

Letitia glanced at Gabe, her smile wavering. "Yes, Mother. You're right, of course."

"Didn't Letitia look *lovely* in that gown? So perfect she could've been a doll!" Ten-year-old Grace let out a languid sigh, pointing her pinkie as she sipped her punch. "I'm going to look that beautiful when I'm a bride, too!"

Solace Monroe rolled her eyes at her youngest sister, forking up the last crumbs of her cake. "Hope you'll let Asa or Temple make your wedding cake, though. This may be fancy fare, but it's got no taste."

"Solace!" their sister, Lily, hissed, "you shouldn't make such remarks where the bride or her mother might hear you! We're fortunate to be here, and to be considered Gabe's family."

"Say what you want, but I'll *never* truss myself up so tight I pass out! Matter of fact, I never intend to wear a corset at all!" Solace announced. "Letitia didn't even taste her wedding cake! Embarrassed poor Gabe—and worried him, too—when he tried to feed her a bite and she turned away."

Lily, looking like a princess in her frilly pink frock, raised an eyebrow. "You'll change your tune if somebody as handsome as Gabe looks your way! You're so caught up in your horses—"

"You'll have to change *completely* to interest anyone like Gabe!" Gracie chimed in. "Me, I'll be the perfect wife someday! Daddy says so!"

Solace bit back a retort when she saw their mother coming. Why did Gracie do her lessons and household chores so effortlessly, at ten, and get away with telling everyone how wonderful she was, too? And Lily had always looked picture perfect—like that parlor portrait Billy's wife had painted. Her singing had distinguished her, too, since she was even younger than Grace.

Solace whirled on her heel. Once again she felt dowdy and outdone, like a sparrow among swans. Once again her sisters' words had stabbed her like spears. She threw open the social hall's back door to escape to the small garden behind the church. The shade of the old maple trees and the nickering of the horses, tied beyond the carriages, brought welcome relief from the savage inner pain that welled up without warning these days.

As she drew a deep breath of the hot June afternoon, the door opened behind her. Solace sighed, willing away her tears.

"Are you all right, dear? I was just coming over to say how proud I am of my three pretty girls and the way they've behaved—"

"Mama, you shouldn't lie. Especially in church." Solace kept her back turned, detesting the way her throat tightened in anticipation of her mother's little talk. Why couldn't people just leave her alone when she felt this way?

"What do you mean? You girls seemed to be having such a nice time—"

"Yeah, but that was before Saint Grace reminded me that I'll never be smart and lovable and *perfect*, like her," she retorted. "Then Princess Lily turned up her pretty little nose as though I'd stepped in some horse hockey. They act like no man'll have me because I'm socially unacceptable and so—so *ugly*!"

Mama stopped behind her, laying a hand on her shoulder. "Did they come right out and *say* those things, Solace?"

"No, but a deaf idiot couldn't miss their meaning!" She swiped at a tear. "Just standing in the same room with 'em makes me feel homely and worthless, Mama! I wish I could live at Billy's, so's I could help train his horses without those—those *paragons* telling me how rude and crude I am!"

Mama gently turned her around. Here it came—another mother-daughter talk that was supposed to make her feel special. But such advice made her bite her tongue nearly in two, trying not to argue back. Life would be so much easier if she'd been a boy!

Mama gazed at her. She started to smooth back a wavy lock of hair that had escaped her ribbon, but thought better of it. "You probably tire of me saying this, Solace, but every time I look at you I see your father. And though I never let on in front of the others, I feel such an overwhelming love I nearly cry with pride."

Her mother blinked rapidly to clear her large brown eyes, and her smile softened. "While I love Lily dearly, she's not my true daughter, as you and Gracie are. And while Grace is a joy—and yes, constantly reminds us of that!—she'll never have your practical way of seeing things and solving—"

"And she'll never have troublesome hair or wide, bulky shoulders, or—"

"That's because her daddy's a slender man. And nobody's prouder than Michael that you have a strong, steady hand with the horses, Solace, just as your father did." Mama cleared her throat before she could go on. "And nobody's prouder than I that you look and act so much like Judd Monroe."

Her mother, a brown-haired beauty in her own quiet way, squeezed Solace's shoulders. "I never realized you felt so uncomfortable around your sisters, honey. You've always reveled in your horsemanship and your independent—"

"But what if they're right?" she blurted. "What if no man'll give me a second glance because I'm bowlegged from riding bareback and—"

"I predict, dear Solace, that you'll attract the most wonderful, loving man of all my girls, simply because you won't chase after him," Mama declared in a low voice. "You'll just be yourself. Not a woman molded by society's whims."

"Or corsets," Solace muttered. "It was my swearing to never wear one that made Lily and Grace insist I'll never—"

"Sweetheart, you're only eleven! You have plenty of changes to go through—and you'll handle them on your own terms. And maybe, now that Lily will be attending Aunt Agatha's academy, you won't feel so—"

"Ugly? Boyish?" Solace remarked bitterly.

"*Unique*," Mama insisted. "In this world of pinched-in waistlines and ladylike details that exasperate you, you stand head and shoulders above every young lady I know."

"Now you're saying I'm too tall!"

"I'm saying you're *you*, Solace. I still marvel at how Asa knew to name you that, for you've truly been my comfort— my reason for going on—during the trials of my lifetime."

Mama cupped her chin and gently raised her face. Solace was again reminded how very, very special she might feel if she could just believe what her mother said.

"You're created in God's likeness," her mother murmured. "You're the very image of your handsome, loving father, as well, and no one will ever take your place. No one will ever fill your shoes or follow in your footsteps, because you'll always blaze your own trails."

Mama leaned closer now, so they stood nearly eye-to-eye. "That's an exciting way to live your life, Solace, and I hope you let *no* one talk you out of it. Someday soon you'll realize how blessed you are—and how beautiful—because of *who* you are."

Dang it, now she wanted to cry because Mama had made her feel better! Was there no getting off this emotional seesaw? "Th-thank you, Mama. You really don't have to go on and on about—"

"I'll do whatever it takes to make you feel worthy. If you want to go to the academy with Lily—"

"I wouldn't last five minutes tryin' to figure out flatware placement."

"—or consider an apprenticeship in town to learn merchandising, you've certainly got a head for that."

"I want to be a trick rider. A sharpshooter like Calamity Jane."

Just saying those words made her blood pump hard through her body—even though her mother let out that same sigh every time. The ostrich plume on Mama's pretty lavender hat quivered when she laughed softly. "You've been reading too many of those dime novels."

"But at least I'm reading! And you've *heard* Billy invite me to help at his horse ranch, so's I can train my own mounts to—"

"We'll see, Solace."

She let out an exasperated sigh. *We'll see* generally meant *not in this lifetime*. But it wasn't a flat-out no!

Solace fixed a smile on her face and stood taller. "I really do feel better about things now, Mama," she said primly, "and if it's all right with you, I'd enjoy a few more minutes of this shade and fresh air. Some of those ladies are wearing so much perfume I can hardly breathe."

Her mother's lopsided smile said she wasn't fooled, but at least this conversation had come to a satisfactory end. "Being the middle daughter—being your age—isn't the easiest thing, honey," she said as she turned toward the door. "But whatever you choose to do—even if you never find a man worthy of your loving, trusting heart—I'll always love you more than life itself."

Once again heat welled up into her cheeks, but Solace smiled bravely. After all, Mercedes Malloy never uttered a word she didn't mean. When her two sisters rubbed her like a badly fitted pair of chaps, she could count on Mama to champion her cause.

As the church door drifted shut behind that elegant dress and the purple feather of her mother's hat, a waltz teased her. Solace grinned. Though she wasn't as dainty as Lily or Grace, she had a natural sense of rhythm that made her shine at anything physical. She slipped a small rock into the doorway so the music would soothe her as she stood in the shade.

And, because no one was there to make fun of her, she swayed to the three-quarter beat while the chamber orchestra played a song she'd heard Lily practicing on the piano. By an Austrian composer named Strauss, she thought.

Not that it mattered. All Solace cared about was being able to move without everyone watching her.

Smiling broadly, Solace stepped back with her right foot and then sideways with her left. "*One*-two-three," she mumbled with each measure.

As the waltz grew louder and more dramatic, she dipped and swayed to match its mood. Her eyes closed . . . and as she lifted her arms to where her partner's shoulder and hand would be, she allowed her imagination free rein. She saw Gabe Getty in her mind's eye, just as he would be leading Letitia in this grand dance right now. . . .

His eyes would be shining as he smiled down at his bride, and Letitia would gaze adoringly up at him as they circled the dance floor in graceful perfection. She might not cotton to all the frippery that went with being female, like corsets and frilly underthings, but Solace still dreamed of dancing with a man who admired her, and who wanted her to dance only with him.

As the music played on, she lost herself in an imaginary world where life went well no matter what she did or said. In her daydreams, her dance partners and the men who rode their fine horses alongside her complimented her courage and strength . . . accepted her for the way she trained a horse, rather than expecting her to sew stylish clothes and make inane conversation with other ladies over tea and prissy little cakes.

And then it was Gabe she danced with in her imagination . . . dipping and gliding gracefully while Lily and Grace gawked in envy from the chairs along the wall!

At least the three of them had agreed on *one* thing: their longtime friend Gabriel Getty had grown into *quite* a handsome catch while he'd been away, studying law with Mr. Bancroft. He wore his dark brown hair clipped shorter now, although an occasional curl still dangled over his spectacles. He dressed well, too, as befitted an up-and-coming man of the law, and his voice sounded low and controlled. Gabe sported sideburns now, along with the shadow of a beard where once his skin had been as smooth and bronzed as her own.

Maybe he won't like your sun-browned skin. He chose a hothouse flower for a bride, didn't he?

She dismissed such a thought, because it was *her* story and she could write it any way she wanted. In her mind, Gabriel Getty delighted in dancing with her even though he was married now. Even though, after today, she might never have reason to see him again.

A crescendo signaled the finale of the grand waltz, so Solace threw herself into a series of dips and turns that made her skirts billow. High on her toes she spun, delirious with the thrill of executing these moves so effortlessly, because Gabe was such a skillful dancer that . . .

"Whoever your partner is, he's a lucky man."

Her eyes flew open. She'd been so caught up in the music, she hadn't heard the door open. Now Gabe *was* smiling at her, but this was no daydream! Solace dropped her arms. Her face flushed ten shades of red as polite applause filled the hall at the song's end. "I-you probably think—"

"I think you're an exceptional dancer," he assured her. "I'm glad you're enjoying the music, but why are you waltzing out here instead of—"

"Stuffy in there."

Gabe blinked. Solace Monroe had always had a quick, honest wit—a trait he found refreshing these days. "You've got that right," he murmured. "And we're not just talking about the summer heat, are we?"

Regret stabbed his heart, not just for admitting such a thing to Billy's kid sister, but for feeling this way.

Desperation had driven him outside after another trying incident, or he wouldn't have interrupted her play-acting. "I'm sorry I said that, Solace. I didn't mean to burden you with—"

"Something else go wrong? I-I hope Letitia's all right." She focused on him in that forthright way she had, as though she could see through his excuses. "Or is it her mother again? That woman can't be happy unless she's making everyone else miserable!"

Laughter welled up inside him, a release so powerful he hurried over to hug her. "Solace, I—don't you go running your mouth, now!—but I truly don't understand how Arthur Bancroft is still sane!"

"You're worried about her running your life, aren'tcha?"

Gabe inhaled fiercely and stepped away from her. How old was Solace now, maybe ten or twelve? Yet she'd summed up his situation as though it should've been perfectly obvious that . . .

After two years of courting Letitia, you didn't really believe you'd muzzle her bulldog of a mother, did you?

He cleared his throat, wondering how much he should entrust to Solace. He'd stew his goose for sure if any part of this conversation made it back to Henrietta's ears. "You were always a straight shooter, Solace. I'm glad to see that hasn't changed."

"You dodged my question, Gabe."

Her heart pounded furiously at her own impertinence. This situation was none of her business, even if she *had* known Gabe Getty all her life. Was she acting particularly rude because he'd caught her dancing alone? Or was she flustered because this handsome man in the dove-gray frock coat and trousers had stepped out of her daydream to hug and compliment her? His spectacles twinkled in the sunlight as he studied her.

"I'm sorry I said that," she murmured. "Please forgive me for being such a—"

"Nothing to forgive, squirt. You were stating the obvious."
He took in her stiff new dress and realized how uncomfortable *she* was today. He also realized it was a pleasure to
hear someone else apologize. No whining or bossing or
manipulating—not from this sun-kissed kid with the dark,
sparkling eyes.

"Too bad young ladies don't go into the law, Miss
Monroe. You've certainly got the sharp mind and agile
tongue for it."

Solace blinked. Had he said she was smart? Called her a
young lady? "After the chat I just had with Mama, I'm sure
she'd rather see me be a lawyer than a trick rider in the
circus. But it's all I've ever wanted to be."

"No reason you can't amaze audiences with your riding
and sharpshooting," he mused. "But I'm sure Michael and
your mother would prefer . . . a safer kind of life than a well-
raised, attractive young woman would find among roustabouts and carnival barkers."

Had he just called her attractive, or was she still
daydreaming? Solace nodded, not sure why she felt . . .
giddy, standing in the shade with this man of the world—
*who's really just Billy's best friend in a frock coat, talking in
a deeper voice these days*, she reminded herself.

"No doubt you're right, Gabe. Many's the time I've
wished I was a boy, so's I could get out and do what I'm truly
good at!"

"And what a shame that would be. If you were a boy,
that is."

Where was that *sentiment headed?* he wondered. Though
he could easily imagine the fetching woman Solace Monroe
would grow into, he probably shouldn't encourage her to
join the circus. She was just willful and bullheaded enough
to do it!

He'd have hell to pay if Letitia or her mother found him
out here. Even though he and Solace were just seeking some

sanity in the shade. Even though he was what? Ten years older than she, and a lifelong friend of her family.

Gabe sensed he could admit the whole truth to Solace, that after his bride had nearly fainted again, during the first dance, Henrietta had whisked Letitia away to settle her frazzled nerves: bed rest in a cool, dark room. And it was not a cool, dark room in his house, even though Letitia was now his wife.

As the orchestra struck up another waltz, he tamped down the resentment and pain he could have safely expressed to Solace. She was a kid, but she already had him figured, didn't she? She wouldn't judge him or lecture him about getting lost in the luster of Letitia's blond hair, blue eyes, and her daddy's law firm. She would state the obvious and let him kick himself.

The music soothed him. It conjured up visions of elegance and romance, the kind Solace had been imagining, judging from the exquisite smile on her face while she'd danced alone. She was swaying to the three-quarter beat again, and not even aware of it.

To hell with what Henrietta would think! It was *his* wedding day, too, and he would dance to that orchestra's music even if his bride had been snatched from him! Why not enjoy one waltz before he subjected himself to the obligatory dances with Henrietta's friends?

Gabe cleared his throat and gathered his courage. Solace had the power to crush him with her rejection—or laughter—even though she didn't know it.

"May I have the honor—the pleasure—of this waltz, Miss Monroe?"

Solace's jaw dropped. The handsome man standing before her had said that without batting an eye! *May I have the honor—the pleasure—of this waltz?* If she lived to be a hundred, this moment would shine like a diamond in her mind!

Somehow she curtsied without tripping over her stiff new shoes or saying something stupid. "I would be delighted, Mr. Getty," she replied in a whisper.

And just like that, all the pretty pictures in her mind became real. She was circling the small garden with Gabriel Getty! He could've asked a hundred other ladies—Letitia's friends from the academy, or wealthy clients' wives—but he'd chosen *her*!

Hold yourself tall! BACK-two-three, UP-two-three! Smile and make pleasant conversation. Show your partner you're enjoying his company.

These instructions evaporated like the dew on summer flowers as she gazed up at him. Gabe was grinning at her, as though he were having a grand time instead of humoring Billy Bristol's kid sister.

She laughed, in spite of how improper that might be. Why hadn't she paid more attention to the social niceties Mama had tried to impress upon her? Any minute now, she'd step on his foot, or . . .

"It's nice to see someone smiling at me, Solace. Thank you." Gabe led her down the brick walkway in a series of simple pivots. When had this little girl grown so tall that she ducked to spin under his arm? But spin she did, and confidently, too.

"When you came outside, Gabe, it was *you* I was dancing—" Solace's cheeks flared, but it was too late to back out of her revelation. "*All* us girls were talking about how lucky Letitia was to catch you. I never figured it'd be *me* you'd dance with today, or that it'd be so much fun!"

Fun. He hadn't thought about fun for a long time. Gabe chuckled at her confession, not taking it too seriously: this was Solace, the outspoken one, after all. Yet he was glad he'd asked her to dance. The other ladies would expect him to flatter their gowns, or they'd quiz him about Letitia and whether he should be looking after her—as though Henrietta would allow him to.

"Yes, it is fun!" he agreed. As he spun her toward the door, Gabe reveled in Solace's delight . . . in her strong, solid body and face glowing with health . . . in the way she gawked at him, as someone too young to understand the complexities of marriage. He recalled special times he'd spent with her blended family—how different they were from the Bancrofts!—and his heart swelled.

Was it from the pleasure he'd known in the Malloy home? Or the pain of impending regret?

That was ridiculous, of course: he and Letitia were madly in love. She would come around to her pretty, winsome self again after all the strain of this day was behind them. His agitation came from playing his part as the groom, in a well-heeled world he was just getting accustomed to.

Too soon the music came to a halt. Solace allowed herself one last gaze at his handsome face. "Thank you, Mr. Getty," she said in the most adult tone she could muster. "I've never enjoyed a dance so much."

"Nor have I!" Gabe squeezed her sturdy hands. Took a last look at thick, sorrel waves that escaped their ribbon to drift around a face filled with exuberance and delight . . . wide brown eyes that shone with integrity and innocence beneath long, dark lashes. He almost reminded her to behave herself and follow her heart—all those adult things one said to a friend's kid sister. But all he could manage was, "Well, squirt, I should go back inside, before—"

"I understand," she whispered. "Thank you again, Gabe. You made me feel very special today."

He nodded and entered the reception hall again. For all his years of experience presenting evidence to judges and juries, he'd been rendered tongue-tied by a tomboy's simple gratitude. Solace had made him feel special, too. He wondered, bleakly, if that would happen again anytime soon.

But here came Arthur Bancroft with a pointed gaze and a

handful of bankers. Gabe sighed; put on a smile as he extended his hand to them. Best to leave Solace Monroe in that land of her happy imagination.

And in his.

Chapter One

Six years later: the spring of 1886.

" 'Surely goodness and mercy shall follow me all the days of my life, and I shall dwell in the house of the Lord forever,' " the pastor intoned. "Ashes to ashes . . . dust to dust. Lord, we commit the body and soul of Letitia Bancroft Getty into Your eternal care. Amen."

Gabe felt the eyes in the solemn graveside circle focus on him as he took the spade from the undertaker. Slowly he scooped up some loose dirt. He winced as it hit Letitia's casket with a sorrowful, hollow sound . . .

. . . like when it was Ma and Pa and the girls in their pine coffins, when I was eight and so scared after the Indian massacre I couldn't speak for months.

A sob brought him back to the present. It could have been his own heart's mournful howl, but it was Henrietta Bancroft, swathed in black from head to toe. Those standing around the open grave shifted nervously.

"My baby! Oh, my beautiful baby—too young to die!" she wailed. "And how will I go on without her? *Why* should I continue to live, when—"

"Hush, dear," Arthur murmured wearily. He muffled his wife's outcry against the shoulder of his somber coat. "We'll get you home and—"

"But this should *never* have happened!" She jerked her head from his hand. "She was in the dew of her youth! Had Gabriel not *insisted* on having his way—wanting children despite her fragile frame—"

Arthur flashed him a rueful grimace, still gripping his wife's girth. "Darling, you're too upset to remain here—"

"Of *course* I'm upset! He killed my only child—my splendid Letitia, for whom I'd die at this moment—"

Something inside him snapped. Somehow Gabe restrained the wrathful reply he wanted to spew at this spiteful, manipulative woman.

"I'm sorry," he muttered, aware that the other mourners were following every nuance of this provocative exchange. "I'll be out of your lives—out of the house—by week's end. Nobody loved Letitia more than I."

He turned sharply, avoiding the curious gazes of clients and friends of the Bancrofts. The hearse and several black carriages lined the cemetery's path . . . Gabe felt too agitated to take someone else's vehicle, so he strode as fast as his legs would carry him.

Not a solitary soul followed, which made his situation for these past six years all the more obvious: he was still the outsider. He'd played the parts of husband, partner, and son-in-law but he'd never been considered *family*. Or worthy of Letitia—not that any man could live up to her parents' expectations. He'd come as a lowly legal apprentice from the plains and had struck it lucky, and now his luck had run out.

Across the street he stumbled, crying openly. Not caring that passersby gawked at him on this otherwise beautiful Saturday afternoon. His feet knew where to turn, what streets to follow, while his mind spun in too many dismal directions to guide him to the fine house he'd shared with his wife. He ran up the front stairs as though Letitia's ghost chased him, entered, and then fell back against the door. He'd seen this day coming with every furtive tip of her silver flask . . . every afternoon she'd hidden in her curtained bedroom. . . .

Yet he still couldn't wrap his mind around the finality of it. How many times had he begged her to lay aside the laudanum? Uncivilized as it sounded, his wife was an opium addict, pure and simple. Her mother had been her accomplice at covering just how serious Letitia's problem was. Any disruption of her limited world sent her into hysterics—a condition she considered properly feminine.

For six years he'd pleaded with Letitia to live her own life—with *him,* rather than at her mother's whim.

For six years he'd endured Henrietta's insults and insinuations.

For six years he'd tolerated the domestics the Bancrofts had hired, in this ostentatious house that had never felt like home.

Total silence rang around him. For the first time, he was there by himself, because Mrs. Kirby and Cranks, the butler, were still at the graveside. Gabe swiped at his eyes and started up the grand oak stairway. No time like the present to pack his few belongings.

Time to cut all ties here and be your own man, dammit.

Sighing bitterly, he entered his room, where his staid half-tester reminded him how little conjugal joy he'd known. Something made him pivot on his heel and cross the hall, to the flounced, floral-papered room that still held the scent of Letitia's perfumes . . . and her secrets.

When he yanked out the drawer of her elegant rosewood night table, not one flask but four rattled like bones. How much of that stuff had she hidden around the house? How many times a day had she sipped—or guzzled—when she thought the sky was falling?

More often, after she learned of the baby.

His face contorted with the gut-wrenching pain of knowing—as only he and her parents had—that Letitia had taken his unborn child to the grave. Grief drove him to open the doors of her armoire, to glare at gowns that emphasized his wife's nineteen-inch waist—the envy of all her friends. And in her chest of drawers, where the delicate scents of her sachet bags wafted up, he found those blasted corsets that had maintained her perfect profile.

Gabe yearned to rip them apart with his bare hands . . . but that would only prove what a demanding madman he was, wouldn't it? What a despicable bastard he'd been for sharing his wife's bed—how often? Why, he could count the times on his fingers . . . nights of wifely duty followed by days of cold loathing.

Was that a carriage clattering up the drive? He quickly shut the drawer and then the doors of the armoire. As he reached toward the night table, however, instinct told him to claim a last memento of his marriage: her diary, with a cover of deep green velvet and a lock that mocked him. Gabe retreated to his room, still wondering why he had to sneak around in his own house . . .

But it was never really yours, was it? They merely allowed you to sleep and take your meals here.

The sonorous chiming of the doorbell surprised him. The domestics always entered through the kitchen, while Arthur and Henrietta would never have rung the bell because they had a key. Certainly no one had come to offer him condolences—he'd made few friends who weren't connected to Letitia's parents.

So who could it be? Should he pretend he wasn't home? By all rights, he should still be at the cemetery accepting words of stiff pity.

"Gabriel? Gabriel, are you here, dear?"

The familiar female voice ascended to his room as surely as its owner would if he didn't answer. He slipped the diary into his top dresser drawer and gathered his courage: accepting the sympathy of his few real friends would be the most difficult part of this ordeal. Best to greet the headmistress of the Academy for Young Ladies and get past the awkwardness of this condolence call before they had an audience. How like Miss Vanderbilt to try the door; to give his grief a higher priority than waiting for the butler's return.

Gabe straightened his tie and stood taller: Agatha Vanderbilt was a stickler for a tidy appearance. But as he descended the stairs and saw her snowy upswept hair, prim gray suit, and compassionate gaze, formalities melted. "Miss Vanderbilt! How nice of you to stop by."

"That was the most ludicrous, indecent display of cruelty I have ever witnessed, Gabe." Her voice resonated sharply in the high-ceilinged vestibule as her expression softened. "I'm so sorry for your loss. And sorrier still that you've endured that woman's tongue and interference all during your marriage."

He stopped halfway down the stairs. He felt like a little boy who desperately needed his mama, and when the headmistress opened her arms, he rushed into them. She came only to his shoulder, yet Gabe felt this powerful woman's embrace filling him with her love and light and strength. He could certainly use those things. "Thank you so much. I—"

"Your room is clean and ready at the academy, should you care to live there again. For as long as you need to."

His mouth fell open. How like Miss Vanderbilt to know exactly what he needed, and offer it without wasting words or expecting anything in return.

"That's the best idea I've heard today." He tightened his arms around her, noticing how robust she felt compared to the woman he'd held these past six years. Such an unfair situation, that his wife had trussed herself so tightly . . . starved herself for approval and the kind of love he apparently couldn't give her.

"It was kind of you to come to the funeral. Letitia gloried in the years she spent in your school."

"Too bad she didn't learn anything that really mattered." The little woman sighed sadly. "Who cares that the table is perfectly set and the linens properly folded, if those in the home are constantly at odds. Or . . . unwell? This might not be the proper thing to say—"

"I've never heard you utter an inappropriate word, Miss Vanderbilt."

"—but as her teacher, I suspected Letitia had . . . habits that would take over her life. She was a sweet, biddable girl from a prosperous family, but she had absolutely no sense of herself." The headmistress sighed, carefully considering her words. "She was too concerned with pleasing her parents—or being the envy of her friends—to know who she was. Letitia thought of life as a mirror, and it was never herself she saw there. Always a reflection of someone else's expectations."

What an astute observation! From his perspective— always at a distance, even when she stood beside him—Gabe had imagined marionette strings attached to Letitia's dainty limbs and firmly fastened to her mother's hands.

Miss Vanderbilt sighed sadly. "Here I am rambling on like an old maid school teacher when you've had your heart broken and your entire life shattered. Forgive me, Gabe."

Her brown eyes gazed directly at him—there was never any sidestepping the headmistress. Though she hadn't been his classroom teacher, she'd been a guardian angel who'd seen his need for a professional apprenticeship when no one else could introduce him to the right people.

"Nothing to forgive," he replied. "You handed me the opportunity of a lifetime, recommending me to Arthur while providing a room—"

"I've often wondered if I really did you any favors, dear. Perhaps if I'd warned you about Henrietta's meddling, or Letitia's—"

"I wouldn't have heard you. I was too dumbstruck by her beauty to see the thorns that came with the rose."

She smiled ruefully. "Well stated. Letitia had an ethereal charm that enthralled us all, even when we knew it might be her downfall." Miss Vanderbilt gazed around the vestibule then, taking in the mahogany credenza and the prism lamps that glowed in the gilt-framed mirror. "Did I surmise correctly that you'll be leaving the law firm, as well?"

"I don't see any way to continue working with Arthur, when—"

"*His* loss. And his fault, too," she asserted with a nod of her head. "Had he stood up for himself—stood up for you!—and for your right to a real marriage, many unfortunate situations could've been avoided.

"You can think this over, Gabriel, as you'll have better offers, but I'd be pleased to hire you as an instructor at the academy," she continued firmly. "Your command of the language and the law would be a welcome addition to—"

"But only girls go there! And teach there!" Gabe pointed out.

"Perhaps that's an oversight on my part," she responded softly. "My girls would benefit from the presence of a strong, upstanding male during their formative years. A man who would teach them the academics and serve as a model for the kind of mate they'd best be attracting, as well."

"Why . . . thank you," he breathed. "I believe that's the highest compliment anyone's ever paid me."

"High time. But mind you, Gabriel, I'll understand if you'd rather remain in your profession than subject yourself to my students," she said warmly. "You wouldn't be among total strangers, however. Grace Malloy is one of our graduates this term—"

"Gracie? But she was just a little girl at my wedding!" He smiled for the first time in days. "Of *course* she's grown up in the past six years. I've done some of that myself."

Miss Vanderbilt smiled. "And after Lily graduated, she became my personal assistant at the academy. She's a wonderful chaplain and advisor for the girls. Close to them in age, yet a shining example of using one's God-given talents."

"Yes, Lily always had an angelic glow about her," he murmured.

Empty and forlorn as he felt, returning to his room at the academy . . . overhearing the twitter of girlish laughter and shared secrets . . . sounded like a party, compared to the oppression he'd known in this grand mansion.

But he had loose ends to tie up before he could make any decisions about his future. It might be awhile before he could offer students at the Academy for Young Ladies the sort of leadership they needed, for Miss Vanderbilt's school maintained a high academic and social standard. If he decided to teach, there'd be no pulling out to practice law again. "I can't thank you enough for such a kind offer."

"I never proffer positions out of *kindness*, Gabriel. It benefits no one if I create positions that don't improve my academy and curriculum." Her smile warmed his weary heart as she grasped his hands. "Take your time. With the current term near its end, you wouldn't be assuming your duties until fall.

"And no matter what you decide," she went on softly, "I hope you'll allow yourself time to grieve and recover from Letitia's untimely passing. You've endured more than any of us can imagine."

As the door closed behind her, Gabe caved in to emotions he hadn't foreseen: anguish, yes, but relief and hope, as well! Having someplace to go—worthwhile work in his future—made dissolving his partnership with Arthur Bancroft far less excruciating. More importantly, he'd be surrounded by compassionate friends who truly cared about *him*. While living this life of social and professional privilege had seemed like a promotion from his humble youth, Gabe craved the companionship of everyday people. People who lived simply and loved deeply.

Mopping his face with his sleeve, he returned to his room to pack. Except for his clothing and books, little in this house really belonged to him. Letitia and her mother had chosen the furnishings, the china—all the accoutrements befitting the home of a coddled daughter. He emptied his armoire quickly, dropped his personal effects into a valise, and then gathered his legal tomes from the small study adjacent to his room.

Such a modest pile of boxes and two trunks . . . so little to show for six years of marriage and his partnership with Letitia's father. Yet it felt good to walk away unencumbered. Beholden to no one.

He loaded his belongings into the smallest carriage and silently thanked Billy Bristol for teaching him how to hitch up horses when they were kids. As the last rays of afternoon sunlight streaked the manicured lawn, Gabe Getty pulled away with a tired sigh. He stopped the horse at the end of the driveway for a final look back.

"Good-bye, Letitia," he whispered, choking on those words. "You'll never know how different things might've been . . . how I loved you so much I wanted to die right along with you and our child. I . . . I hope you've found your peace at last."

Chapter Two

After dinner that night, Gabe excused himself. Miss Vanderbilt was polite enough not to mention his skipping vespers; she could tell from his weary expression and bloodshot eyes, perhaps, that he didn't need three dozen curious young ladies whispering about him during church.

He closed the door to his familiar little room. As he gazed at its pale yellow walls and the simple quilt on the bed . . . the same bookcases, now filled with his law volumes rather than student texts . . . he marveled that while this little sanctum hadn't changed, everything else had. When he'd lived here during his apprenticeship, his life had seemed neatly boxed and wrapped, like a present he would open: a box full of good times and dreams, which he would enjoy and fulfill as he discovered each one.

Now he just wanted to lock the door and never go anywhere again. Entomb himself, just as they'd laid Letitia to rest in that pristine white casket.

He reached into the valise beneath the bed . . . fished out the velvet diary. Just grasping its plush covers made his heart hammer. He had no business prying into this private journal; eavesdropping on an intensely personal conversation between his wife and her closest confidante—after her mother, that is. What she and Henrietta had found to discuss for hours on end eluded him—it was just another female mystery. Reading Letitia's diary felt like a betrayal he'd never envisioned committing.

But he had to know! This pretty book held the keys to his wife's life and death. And before Henrietta came here demanding it—she surely knew the diary was missing by now—he would indulge himself in Letitia's neat, pretty penmanship and her delicate turns of phrase.

Maybe he would read between the lines. Maybe learn secrets she'd never shared with him—hopes and dreams he'd never helped her realize, because she'd kept him at a distance with the raising of her pretty eyebrow. As a sign he'd crossed her limit, Letitia would signal *stop*! by pressing her delicate palm against an invisible gate she'd never let him pass through.

Gabe wasn't prepared for the faint scent of Letitia's perfume when he popped the diary's lock with his penknife. He hadn't anticipated how her ornate handwriting would wrench his gut. This volume began early last fall . . . before the emotional descent, when his wife had suspected she was with child. The writing was neat and regular, and she wrote of the holiday balls she and her mother were involved with . . . the crimson gown she was having designed to wear at a Christmas gala.

She looked splendid in it, too, he recalled fondly.

Gabe swiped at his eyes. He flipped through the delicate pages . . . accounts of how she and Henrietta suspected the housekeeper was dipping into the household till by overstating the tab at the butcher shop. Endless pages of *Dear Diary, I can't begin to tell you how exasperating my day was!* Even though, as far as he could tell, Letitia had lived the life of privilege she'd been born into. How exasperating could that be?

Once or twice he honed in on paragraphs where she mentioned him in passing—his work for the Anheuser-Busch brewery, for instance. But as Gabe skimmed her late-November entries, it occurred to him that this diary could have been penned by a woman who wasn't even married.

That struck him in the gut. He stood up. Looked out the window into the twilight, to compose himself.

Maybe he should tuck the diary away, before his feelings

frayed even more. So many details he considered social and petty—gossipy snippets about her mother's friends or the domestic help—always circled back to *her*. And while Gabe understood this—Letitia had written these entries believing other eyes would never read them—he felt even more inconsequential now than when she'd been alive.

He exhaled harshly. Yes, his dear wife had been good at making him—and everyone but her mother—seem extraneous. Merely present to meet her needs.

There was no reason to read more, to make himself feel even worse—except a mid-December entry caught his eye. Not because it concerned anything of consequence, but because Letitia's handwriting looked looser. Loopy and irregular. Gabe held his breath, skimming accounts of that Christmas ball . . . the holiday dinner at her parents' house, where his wife had burst into tears because the peignoir he'd bought her was so "indecent," she'd been embarrassed to hold it up in front of her father.

Her writing became erratic after that . . . reports of going to bed at midday . . . feeling overwhelmed by the burden of holiday activities and events.

It struck him like a lightning bolt: she'd conceived by then. Had she not known it? Or had she not told him? Letitia had always kept to her room so much, her condition in December was no more an enigma to him than it ever was. She went to bed early, before he'd read his newspaper, and arose after he'd left for the law office . . . had spent many days last winter completely shut away from him.

And once the doctor he'd brought home had confirmed her pregnancy, Letitia's emotional health—and her handwriting— declined noticeably. She'd fretted about needing bigger clothes. Showed no interest in preparing the nursery. He'd been terribly worried, but what could he have done? She confided only in her mother, so Gabe had left Henrietta to counsel her distraught daughter—it was best for women to handle this ultimate female mystery, wasn't it? All he knew about pregnancy was the excitement of becoming a father, at last!

Except Letitia became so distant she refused to speak to him. When her parents' or guests' presence demanded it, however, she acted as though nothing were amiss, to keep others from suspecting she and Gabe were at odds—and to keep them from guessing she was with child. And what a fine actress she'd been . . . . tightly corseted and artfully painted whenever she ventured out in public.

Gabe dabbed at his eyes to keep his tears from splotching the handwritten pages. By his rough calculation, this meant Letitia's pregnancy was at least five months along when she died—and no one outside the family had guessed! Why hadn't he asked someone for help?

But who? And why do you think she would've listened?

He came to the diary's final pages . . . several days often passed between entries at this point . . . and his wife's words looked as if a different woman had written them. His poor Letitia had been far more distraught than she'd admitted—and dammit, her mother had kept that from him, as well! It was the final entry, written two weeks ago, that nearly choked the life from him. His heart hammered as he deciphered the garbled sentences, but her desperate tone wouldn't let him stop reading.

Dear Diary, I am at wit's end. This simply must stop. Why must I sacrifice my very self—my very soul—for the infernal child growing within me? I never wanted it! I was powerless to prevent it, after a foolish failure to cleanse myself. Gabriel looks as happy as a lovestruck puppy, while I want to curl up and die! I shall never show myself in those loose, ugly gowns he bought me.

And she hadn't. Letitia had spent her last month barely getting out of bed, claiming her nausea flared at the least movement.

But she'd so despised his child . . . she'd wanted to curl up and *die*! Gabe let out a loud sob, and buried his face in his pillow. Then he composed himself . . . sat up again to read to the bitter end. He'd gone too far to stop, and only a few lines remained before smooth, empty pages filled the rest of the book.

I have ordered a packet of infallible French female remedy, and when it arrives I shall be done with this agony once and for all! Then I shall return to my life. I shall be happy again! Meanwhile, Gabe will mourn the lost child and I shall act properly dejected. Perhaps my salvation will come in the mail today.

Gabe stood up so suddenly the diary hit the floor. He was no doctor, but it sounded like Letitia had bought a mail-order abortifacient from a newspaper advertisement. And if she'd washed it down with laudanum—probably a larger dose than usual, so she'd sleep through any cramps or pain that would alert them to what she'd done. . .

Was Henrietta an accomplice? Had Henrietta suggested the "infallible French female remedy" to alleviate her dear daughter's turmoil?

He would never know. He wasn't sure he wanted to. Now that his wife was dead and buried, the matter was a moot point, wasn't it?

"You're very quiet this morning, Gabriel. May I help you with something?"

He glanced up from the plate of eggs he'd been picking over, into Agatha Vanderbilt's legendary, all-seeing brown eyes.

"Forgive me," he murmured, failing badly at a smile. "The full force of Letitia's passing has struck, now that the burial details and severed family ties are behind me. I-I didn't sleep at all last night."

"I can't imagine your pain, dear man." The headmistress stroked his shoulder with a trembling hand. "Perhaps you should talk with Miss Malloy. She listens in a way that uplifts and—"

"Begging your pardon, but I can't put myself through that right now. Lily so closely resembles my wife, I was struck dumb when she expressed her condolences yesterday," he confessed in a tight voice.

Miss Vanderbilt adjusted her rimless spectacles. "I . . . I never thought of—but you're absolutely right. The resemblance would be uncanny if Letitia had allowed herself another inch or two around the waist."

"Or if Lily became gravely ill—which we pray will *not* happen!" He turned his head quickly, even though it would be no disgrace to display his shattered feelings.

But he could *not* reveal what he'd read in that diary. To anyone.

"I'm going for a walk," he murmured, despising the self-pity in his voice. "The fresh air and spring flowers might bring me comfort."

"A much better idea than haunting these halls, avoiding the girls' curious eyes and questions." Miss Vanderbilt gathered their dirty dishes from the small table. "Things are very difficult for you now, Gabe. Please let me know when there's anything I can do for you."

He sighed and stood up. "You've already provided a place to stay—and a job offer so I could part company with Arthur Bancroft. I can't thank you enough for that."

"You're quite welcome, dear. Come and go as you please," she added, pulling a skeleton key from her skirt pocket. "This unlocks the service entrance in the kitchen. The girls' curfew hardly applies to a grown man, after all."

He gratefully slipped the key into his trousers pocket. And as he stepped outside the grand mansion's back kitchen door, where the alley lined in lilac bushes led to the street, Gabe sensed he wouldn't be at the school long: a teaching position wasn't really the answer to his deep, dark needs, was it? But the Academy for Young Ladies was at least a place to land. Any port in a storm.

He wandered down the street with his hands in his

pockets, feeling uneasy and lost. When had he last worn his shirt collar open, and left his suit coat behind? When had he strolled along a residential row with no destination in mind? Gabriel Getty, attorney at law, had been so busy making a name for himself—making a living for his wife and an uneasy peace with her parents—that he'd forgotten how to do absolutely nothing.

He ambled toward the park where he'd spent many a pleasant Sunday afternoon as a student. Maybe he'd find the same shady bench where he'd studied so avidly . . . pondered the cases and precedents in his textbooks, and practiced telling Arthur Bancroft he wanted to marry his daughter. A breathtaking array of red and yellow tulips bloomed on either side of him while purple lilacs scented the breeze. His feet followed a long-forgotten path: during their early courtship, he'd driven Letitia here with some of the younger girls, who'd conveniently scattered with their sketch pads to work on their art assignments.

He let his tears roll freely down his face. How Letitia had loved those afternoon strolls! How eagerly she'd slipped her hand into the bend of his elbow as they walked along . . . eyes like blue crystal had glistened up at him, in a face radiant with happiness.

Where did that happiness go? How, in six short years, had such a lovely young woman slipped into such darkness?

Gabe knew better than to torture himself with these questions . . . he knew no one else—not even her mother—had the answers, either. Just as he realized that their courtship at the academy had been the only time Henrietta Bancroft wasn't exerting her overbearing control over her daughter.

Letitia had gotten along just fine without consulting her mother about every little thing. She'd excelled at hostessing teas . . . had read poetry aloud with such expression, he'd bought her volumes of Longfellow, Poe, and Byron to hear her bring this literature to life.

He slipped onto his favorite bench beneath the same flowering crab tree he'd enjoyed years ago, swiping at his eyes. For the first time since her passing, he could hear his wife's voice in his mind, reciting her favorite lines of poetry: she'd loved Edgar Allan Poe's sense of drama and bleak hopelessness . . . had put special emphasis into such ringing phrases as " 'Quoth the raven, "Nevermore." ' " and the wistful ending lines of "Annabelle Lee."

Gabe sighed. Should he have realized her penchant for the dark and dreary even then? Should he have foreseen her descent into a solitary madness, much like Poe's drug-induced dementia?

But how she'd loved bringing those poems to life! How she'd relished the praise of her audience, who'd often sketched whatever came to their minds from the imagery Letitia lifted from the printed page. What horrible things would they have drawn, had she read aloud from her diary?

Stop this! You should've left the damned thing in her drawer.

Ah, but he hadn't. His perennial search for the truth—the motivation behind his wife's behavior—had backfired. It was one thing to analyze the written testimony witnesses gave during his court cases, and another thing entirely when he was the judge, the jury, and the man who'd just hanged himself.

He was startled out of his reverie by the sound of a sweet voice.

"Please tell me if I'm intruding, Gabe. I was reading my morning devotional across the way, and I saw you sit down." His heart clenched and the air rushed from his lungs. Here in the blinding sunshine, where her blond hair shone like a halo and she demurely clutched her book, it seemed Letitia had stepped out of his imagination . . . out of his fondest memories of her, to read him some poetry.

Gabe attempted a smile. This was Lily, he reminded himself, not Letitia. Lily couldn't help it she looked so much like his dear wife. "Miss Malloy. How nice to see you out enjoying this day."

"Please call me Lily," she said with a heart-wrenching smile. "We've known each other forever."

"Old habits die hard." Gabe squinted at her from beneath his hand. He desperately wanted her to leave—wanted her words of comfort and counsel about as much as he'd relish a verbal trouncing from Henrietta Bancroft right now.

But she was only being kind. Lily didn't have a mean bone in her body, and the glow of her smile might make him feel a lot better, if he'd let it.

"Please—sit down if you'd like," he rasped, gesturing toward the other half of the bench. "Forgive my lack of manners, not standing up to—"

"Nonsense. I caught you off-guard—and I really must return to the academy for the Classical Rhetoric course at ten, followed by 'The Bible as Literature.'"

He hoped his smile didn't give away his relief. "I admire you, Lily, for taking on such responsibilities as Miss Vanderbilt's assistant. You could be out making your way in the world."

"Oh, but I *am* following God's plan for me, Gabe." She nodded with the conviction of these words, her blue eyes ablaze. "Just as Billy's sister, Christine, made her mark by designing new uniforms for the school, I'm leaving a legacy of better Biblical understanding for—"

"Christine Bristol," he mused with a sentimental grin. "A spitfire who'd probably have wandered *far* astray, had it not been for Miss Vanderbilt. Last I heard, she was in San Francisco with her husband and family, designing fine gowns for the upper crust."

Lily tilted her head in that too-familiar way. "Have you told Billy about Letitia's passing? I'm sure he'd want to know."

"Hadn't even thought of it," he admitted in a small voice. "Just goes to show how wrapped up I was in the details of—"

"May I write to him? I'm sure that would be a painful

letter for you." Lily's gaze wandered to where his rolled-up shirt sleeve revealed a jagged scar. "I recall being somewhat horrified—but fascinated—as a child, by the way you boys cut yourselves to become blood brothers."

"We believed we could save the world. Rid it of the evil Indians and Border Ruffians who'd shattered our families," he murmured. His heart raced like a nervous bird's. How many heinous criminals had he convicted in the courtroom? Yet the prospect of writing to Billy Bristol struck terror into his soul. "Thank you for thinking of that. And, yes—if it wouldn't be too much trouble."

"None at all, Gabe," she replied warmly. "The telegraph office is just a few blocks away, and I'll go after classes dismiss. Billy would appreciate hearing the news."

Lily's face lit up with this new mission. "I really must get back," she insisted, "but take your time here, Gabe. I feel closest to God when I sit amid His splendid springtime flowers, in this park or in the garden back home. I'll see you later, all right? I hope you'll come to vespers this evening."

He nodded, not quite meeting her brilliant blue eyes. Lily Malloy harkened from a more angelic realm than he could ever aspire to, and she was obviously pleased to do him this favor. Someday he'd find a way to repay her kindness.

Right now, however, he sighed and slouched on the bench. Then he hunkered with his elbows on his knees, to avoid making small talk with passersby. In this position, he clearly saw the scar running up the inside of his forearm like a jagged bolt of lightning. What a fearsome thing it was when he and Billy first scratched these wounds open with a hired hand's knife! His Aunt Rachel's outcry still rang in his ears after these twenty years. His cousin Emma had rolled her eyes every time she laid eyes on it.

But his aunt had died a horrible death during the grasshopper plague. And after Billy left Emma Clark at the altar, she and Uncle George had moved away from the Kansas farm that had been his home after his family died . . . .

All were gone now: his birth family, and then the aunt, uncle, and cousin who'd taken him in, and now Letitia. Though Gabe detested dwelling upon such morose thoughts, it struck him that at twenty-seven he was once again homeless. Just as he'd been at seven, when his family was massacred by savages while he'd witnessed the whole ordeal.

He stood up too fast. His head thrummed with the return of that dark desperation—it had struck him mute back then, and by God it would *not* shut down his soul again!

Chapter Three

Four mornings later, Gabe looked out the window of his room feeling as black and bleak as the clouds that shrouded the city with a promise of storms.

He'd visited with some lawyers in this neighborhood and delivered letters of application to others, but he hadn't received a single job offer. Just lots of counsel about taking time to grieve his wife's untimely passing.

How long would this last? How long could he continue this claustrophobic existence, lingering on the details of his wife's demise? Soon he'd be reduced to reading newspaper advertisements and applying for jobs he didn't really want.

"Mail for you, Gabe."

Bless her, Miss Vanderbilt continued down the hall without quizzing him. He retrieved the letter she'd slipped under his door, hoping it was from a local law firm—except that irregular handwriting could only belong to one man. The miracle was how *quickly* he'd gotten this response to Lily's telegram—yet hadn't he known Billy Bristol would write to him immediately?

He ripped the vellum envelope and let the letter slide out. There was no letterhead—no formalities before getting to the point. It was just Billy speaking to him from the page, in a voice he fondly recalled from their childhood.

    Dear Gabe,
    When we got Lily's message about Letitia's passing, I was struck dumb. It's God's providence that you could

*return to your room at the academy so Aunt Agatha can
cluck over you.*

*I can't pretend to know how awful you must feel, so I
won't belabor how sorry we are to hear your sad news. Lily
didn't pass along many details—not that they would matter.*

*Consider coming here for a while, if that suits you. It's
been way too long since you and I spent time together!
Eve and I are doing well, but life is busy with Olivia,
Owen and now Bernadette to look after. Their smiles
would lift your sorrowful heart, because they won't ask
any of those bothersome adult questions!*

*Please come! Even just to escort Gracie here, to her
new position as our governess. Don't go thinking we've
taken on grand airs. Believe me, Eve needs help with the
three children so she can paint—and because Asa and
Beulah Mae aren't getting any younger.*

*We'd be so glad to see you, Gabe. You'd share Owen's
room, but otherwise you'd have the run of the farm. The
fresh air and spring flowers would make you feel a dang
sight better than the busy streets of St. Louis.*

Gabe smiled. Billy Bristol was a horseman to the core,
and would never appreciate the conveniences of living in a
large city. Still, the prospect of spending time with Billy's
family made him picture faces he hadn't seen since he
married Letitia . . . far too long, where good, solid friend-
ship was concerned. The only men he knew now were
connected to his law practice. And if he accompanied Grace
Malloy to Richmond, he'd be repaying Billy's favor ahead of
time, wouldn't he?

He read the last few paragraphs in a rush of anticipation.
He needed to learn when Grace would be leaving, and then
send Billy an immediate reply.

*Solace will get here middle of next week. She'll train
some of my horses, in exchange for the matched*

*geldings I gave her last year. She's never been one for
book learning, and with Lily and Grace at the academy,
I suspect she feels like a dried pea rattling around in a
shoe box there at the Triple M.*

Gabe smiled. From what he recalled of sturdy, exuberant
Solace, she was anything but a dried pea. She must be
what—seventeen? Eighteen? Why hadn't a rancher from
around Abilene courted her away from home by now? Or
perhaps they'd tried, and Solace had sent them packing. She
had a mind of her own, that one.

He blinked. When had his dark mood lifted? He suddenly
had plans to make—a place to go and people to see. Though
he'd never escape his wife's death nor the grief that went
along with it, the prospect of spending time with Billy,
among his horses and children, suddenly seemed like the
lifeline he'd been yearning for.

And how like Billy Bristol to toss it to him.

Gabe grinned for the first time in days. He stepped into
the wide second-floor hallway, listening for Miss Vanderbilt's presence. She usually taught in the mornings, then
caught up on correspondence after the noon meal, so she
could spend time among her charges during dinner
preparations and vespers.

Her door was ajar. Gabe heard quiet humming before the
next crack of thunder announced another round of storms.
He knocked only once before she summoned him into her
front parlor.

"Gabriel, how nice to see you, dear. I trust Billy's letter
has put that sparkle in your eyes?" She *knew*—just as she
always had! But wasn't that one of the reasons he loved this
little woman?

"Matter of fact, he's invited me for a visit. He wonders
if I might escort Grace to Richmond to become their
governess," he said in a rush. "When is the graduation
ceremony? I—"

"A mere week from today. Just time enough for your reply to reach Billy so they can properly prepare and so can *you*."

His laugh sounded out of practice. "I've never felt the need to be proper around Billy, but—"

"Which is the perfect reason for going."

"—I can't imagine living with three little children, and a wife who—"

"I can't imagine Billy living any other way. He *adores* children. I'm in constant awe of how easily he accommodates them. Did he mention his youngest, Bernadette, is mute? Grace has learned the manual alphabet and has done considerable extra study so she can teach the little girl to communicate."

Gabe's jaw dropped. "Billy didn't say a word about . . . oh, my. I can't imagine having a child who's unable to speak."

"But what better, more loving family for such a child to be born into?" The headmistress chuckled kindly. "Miss Grace will have her hands full, to be sure! And since *she* is accustomed to being the baby—the adored one—she'll have an adjustment as she assumes this position. But, as you've surely learned, Gabe, life is one lesson after another. When we stop growing and changing, we stop living."

Once again this wise little woman had pointed out the obvious: the compass he'd lost sight of in his recent grief. He nodded, eager to be on his way. "I'll go telegraph my reply, then. I'd like to talk with Grace after dinner, about her plans. Would that be all right with you?"

"It's more than all right, Gabriel," she murmured fondly. "It's the answer to my prayers."

When he returned from town, Gabe noticed Lily Malloy lingering in the shade of the academy's back garden. Once again she looked so heartrendingly pretty . . . so much like his dear . . .

Stop it! Go in the front door instead! Get to your room before . . .

But Lily's smile said she'd spotted him, and that she'd been awaiting his return. She walked toward him, looking serenely ethereal in her pink spring gown, and then extended her hand. "I understand you're escorting Grace to Richmond."

Gabe found himself mirrored in Lily Malloy's huge blue eyes, which left him speechless for a moment. "Yes, I—"

"Godspeed and God's blessings, Gabe." Her voice thrummed, low and intense. "We'll miss you! But you'll find healing and laughter with Billy. A new sense of yourself as you live among his children."

"I hope I won't be in the way."

"Fear not," she said, much like the angels in the Bible had prefaced their greetings. "I'd hoped to help you answer those soul-provoking questions about Letitia's death, but a change of scene will benefit you, as well. You'll be in good company with Billy and Eve—and our paths will cross again someday!"

Before he knew what was happening, Lily threw her arms around him. He hugged her back, of course . . . an embrace of longtime friends that held more meaning than all the funereal condolences he'd received put together. Once again he was aware of how solid and healthy other women felt, compared to his Letitia, and yet. . .

Did he sense an ulterior motive behind Miss Malloy's unexpected blessing? Pretty Lily had always seemed more mature than her age . . . had a mystical presence that left others in awe.

Was it *awe* that fogged his lenses? Or did this pretty blonde have something much more . . . personal in mind?

"Thank you," he rasped, easing out of her embrace. "I hope to see you again someday, too," he continued in a halting voice. "Just as you've found your purpose here, at

Miss Vanderbilt's academy, I hope to find what lies ahead for me while I'm at the Bristol farm."

Her smile radiated a purposeful warmth. "God's not finished with us yet, Gabriel. It's no coincidence that you were named for an archangel—and that I've kept company with angels all my life." With an enigmatic grin, she turned away.

God's not finished with us yet? What on earth did she mean by that?

Chapter Four

"Gabe! Gabe, it's so dang good to see ya! But I'm so—"

When Billy grabbed his hand, the grip stunned him because it was so strong from his years of working with horses, but also because it swung him into an unexpected hug. A choking sound made Gabe's eyes go wet; for the first time, someone *felt* his pain instead of just giving it lip service. Billy Bristol's arms clamped around his body like steel bands, yet he sensed that his friend—this blood brother of his childhood—would be the one to free him from his misery.

When the redhead stepped back, his blue eyes sparkled with unshed tears. "It's so good to see ya," he repeated, "I don't want to get to that other part. But it tore me up pretty bad to hear about Letitia. I'm real sorry for your loss."

Billy glanced toward the train then, where porters scurried to unload Grace's belongings at the encouragement of her pretty smile. The platform was stacked with an impressive number of trunks and boxes. "Good thing I drove my biggest buckboard," he remarked with a chuckle. "Can't thank you enough for escortin' Gracie, since any man with eyes'll try to sweet-talk her. And she so obviously hates that!"

Gabe laughed. "Yes, she could charm the socks off any fellow alive."

"Yeah, well it's what those fellas'll charm off *her* that scares me."

He stood back then, a rugged man in denim and homespun—clean but well-worn. *Comfortable* had always been Billy Bristol's way, in clothing and behavior. His hair had turned a darker shade of auburn and he wore it a little longer now. Gabe tried to imagine him as a desperado, like his twin brother had been, yet the direct gaze of those blue eyes bespoke a man of utmost integrity. A man who'd earned his place in the world by the sweat of his brow and the strength of those broad, calloused hands.

"It was a small favor, considering your generous invitation to—"

"Well, how *else* could I get ya here? Been way too long," Billy insisted. "It's a shame it took a situation like yours to get us together again."

He sighed. "Yes, well . . . situations happen, don't they?"

"And we'll hash all that out after we get you home and outta these fancy city clothes. Gotta say I like that derby, though. Never owned one myself." Billy plucked at the sleeve of his brown plaid suit. "Looks like you've done right well for yourself practicin' the law, Mr. Getty."

"It's what's beneath the suit that's taken the beating," he replied with a sigh. "Appearances can be deceiving, my friend."

"And I want to hear whatever you gotta get off your mind, but meanwhile it appears our new tutor is ready to load up." Billy grinned. "You were the perfect escort, Gabe. Professional, well-heeled air about ya—to discourage anybody else who might be givin' her the eye. And lots of practice at totin' a woman's trunks, I bet!"

"It's amazing how much luggage one tiny female requires. Where would any of them be without men for pack animals?"

For a fleeting moment he wondered how Cranks, the butler, spent his time now that he no longer accompanied Letitia on her shopping excursions. It was a good sign that such a thought didn't depress him today; a better sign that he could laugh at himself for ever depending on domestic help.

It felt good to shoulder those trunks with Billy; they'd worked together as boys, and it was only his bent for book learning that had sent him away from such a salt-of-the-earth existence. As he heaved Gracie's trunks up to the buckboard, his muscles told him he hadn't pulled his weight lately. Maybe this trip to rural Missouri would balance him . . . show him what he was made of, without stylish clothing and someone else's mansion to live in.

When they pulled into the Bristol driveway, lined with maple trees in their shiny spring leaves, Gabe's heart fluttered. It was still the home place he'd envied when he came here for Billy's wedding: the house glowed with fresh white paint and its pillars suggested Southern grandeur of a bygone era. Lilacs scented the breeze, and beyond the large red barn stretched miles of white plank fence. Beautiful grazing horses dotted the lush pastureland.

He couldn't have painted a prettier picture if he'd been Michelangelo.

A dog raced toward them then, white with distinctive markings around his eyes and ears. Some of his fondest childhood memories returned: Billy letting him pick out a Border collie puppy born in the Monroes' barn . . . their four dogs herding Texas longhorns that had cut across their Kansas farms. Those black and white collies were long gone, but Gabe still glowed, thinking about them. Everything about this family took him back to better days, and Gabe felt happier than he had in weeks. Maybe years.

"Rex!" a loud voice called. "Rex, you ornery mutt! We're not finished practicing!"

Billy halted the horses while Grace sat taller on the seat between them. "Don't tell me that's Solace, riding without—"

"Haven't you ever seen your sister practicin' her act?" Billy cut in. "She's trainin' her new dog, and he's a handful."

"Mama would be having a—time and again she's told Solace not to—"

"Which is why Solace loves to come here." Billy leaned his elbows on his knees to include Gabe in his grin. "You and Lily were cut from silk and satin, honey, and Aunt Agatha's academy was the place you needed to be. But while you were away, how do you s'pose Solace entertained herself? She *sure* wasn't perfectin' her needlework."

Gabe chuckled. He gazed at the approaching figure in rapt fascination, for she was standing barefoot on the back of a bay gelding that cantered alongside the driveway. Solace Monroe wore old denim pants and a red plaid shirt, and with her dark brown hair flying behind her—and a daredevil grin!—she seemed like something from a dream. She balanced so confidently on the horse's back that she appeared to be floating. Or flying.

And then, a few feet before she reached the buckboard, Solace dropped down to straddle her mount as though these acrobatics were second nature to her. Such effortless grace bespoke hours of practice, and Gabe wondered how many times she'd tumbled off—how many bones she'd broken—to reach this level of performance perfection.

"Gabe! Gabe Getty, it's been way too long!"

Her hands shot out and he grabbed them. A warm tingle of energy raced through his body when he felt the strength in Solace's sturdy hands. Her face was flushed from riding and her breath came in exuberant bursts as she grinned at him. The little girl he'd danced with at his wedding was anything but a child now.

"I was so happy to hear you'd be—" Her face clouded over then, but her brown-eyed gaze never wavered. "We were all so sad to learn about Letitia, Gabe. How horrible it must've been for you to—but you're here now! *Family* again, like when we were kids!"

His heart turned a cartwheel. When had anyone ever greeted him with such enthusiasm? Such all-embracing sincerity? He opened his mouth but it took a moment for the words to come out.

"It's good to be back," he murmured. Grace and Billy watched him closely, so he gave them the best smile he could muster. "The past few weeks have been sheer hell. The Bancrofts blame me for Letitia's untimely—"

"How absurd!" Solace had no need for more details. She believed without question in the Gabriel Getty she'd known all her life.

He swallowed hard. Her compassion nearly overwhelmed him. He wasn't sure he deserved such outright confidence in his innocence. Those bold brown eyes unnerved him, too, yet the glow on Solace's face drew him in and warmed his very soul. And she did all this as effortlessly as she'd ridden her horse standing up.

"Don't mind my sister, Gabriel," Gracie murmured. "She wants the best for you—as we all do. But she needs to rein herself in."

Anguish froze Solace's face, and then Gabe watched a play of familiar emotions: despair and betrayal . . . the sense of being an outcast in her own family. And in that brief moment, he heard the cry of a kindred spirit. How often had he himself felt despised and belittled these past six years?

"Now Gracie," Billy began, "you shouldn't doubt your sister's intentions about—"

"No, Billy, she hasn't a *clue* about what anyone else might think or feel," Solace huffed. "So nice to see you again, Saint Grace. How have we gotten along without you?"

Before Gabe could offer Solace encouragement, she whistled. Her dog leaped onto the horse, in front of her, and Miss Malloy wheeled her mount in a tight circle. Then she charged full tilt toward the pasture, but the gate wasn't open. He held his breath, wondering if . . .

As though the horse were a part of her, flying on her will alone, it leaped up and over the white plank fence to land proudly on the other side. The dog was still seated, and so was Solace, who urged the bay into a breakneck gallop. Had he not seen it with his own eyes, he wouldn't have believed it.

"Show-off!" Gracie muttered.

Billy's sigh suggested that this rivalry had tried his patience more than once. He clucked to the horse. "We're every one of us different, Grace," he remarked quietly. "But we're all created in God's own image. I know Solace's . . . *talents* try your patience, honey, but the kids you're about to teach will exasperate you, too. They'll need your grace and patience—just like your sister does."

The young lady beside him sat taller. Gabe noted the belligerent lift of her chin . . . the blaze of an untested mettle in her eyes. He'd seen this expression at the academy, when Grace Malloy believed she was *right*—and would prove it. While he was no expert on children, he sensed this young governess would be tested to the end of her tether once she took on the three Bristol kids.

"I hope you'll tell me if I'm in the way, Billy," Gabe insisted. "I'd hate to disrupt—"

Billy laughed warmly. "When *aren't* we bein' disrupted?" he replied. "If it's not Olivia tattlin' on Owen—because it's in his best interest, of course—Owen's pullin' some stunt that gets his mother in an uproar. This makes Bernadette whirl around in circles 'til she tips over and lands in a heap, usually bawlin' for attention.

"How long can you endure all that commotion, Gabe?" His chuckle deepened the lines beside his eyes. "Olivia informed us last night that Owen's found a pet garter snake, and he might slip it into your bed. So consider yourself warned—and welcomed."

Gracie sucked in a horrified breath. "If he pulls something like that on *me*, why, I'll—"

"You'll either faint or scream, sweetie. I've seen you with snakes." As he halted the horse in front of the wide front porch, Billy graced his new governess with a kind smile. "Ask Solace for help if that happens. She'll likely drop that snake down Owen's shirt and make him wear it awhile."

Gracie shuddered and clenched her eyes shut. After

leading a sheltered, privileged life at the academy, she had as much of an adjustment coming here as Gabe did. Grace Malloy had been greatly loved—sought out by Miss Vanderbilt's younger girls for her wisdom. None of them would have dreamed of holding a snake in front of her.

Such thoughts vanished as the front door opened for an old black man with sprigged white hair. "Now *here's* a sight to behold!" he said with a cackle. "Miss Gracie, it's good to have you here, honey! And Mister Gabe, we's glad you's come to visit, son."

"It's good to be here, sir." He stepped down from the buckboard, extending his hand to the man who'd seemed a hundred years old when he was a kid. Except for his whiter hair and stooped shoulders, however, Asa still seemed spry. "When I heard you and Beulah Mae had tied the knot—"

"That was the day my life began! A blessin' the good Lord sent me in a bossy ole woman who don't leave me no peace nor dignity!" Asa crowed as he pumped Gabe's hand. "I ain't never in my life been happier."

Asa's fingers felt like delicate twigs in Gabe's grip, yet the old man sounded as robust as ever. As delighted as he'd always been, no matter what life brought his way.

The door opened again and the object of Asa's teasing affections stepped outside. Beulah Mae held a little girl on her hip and wiped a floury hand on her sackcloth apron while she beamed at him. "Mister Gabe, it's mighty nice to see you again—and there's our Miss Gracie, too!" She planted a noisy kiss on the little girl's cheek, pointing and nodding with unabashed glee. "Bernadette, this here's your new teacher, baby doll!"

The little girl's red ringlets bobbed brightly as she followed the old cook's finger. Her impish grin stole Gabe's heart as though she'd grabbed it from his chest with her chubby hands. Bernadette was another redheaded Bristol with crystal blue eyes, and she threw her arms wide to jump into Billy's open arms when he hurried over to her.

The love between father and daughter burned so brightly, Gabe's heart clutched again. Envy, this time. He himself might have been favored with such a love, if only Letitia had . . .

That's behind you. These friends want to give you a fresh start.

He nodded, although the voice was in his head, unheard by anyone else.

"We's been keepin' dinner warm 'til you folks got home," Beulah Mae announced, "so I'll go put it on the table whilst you freshen up. Plenty of time to unload the buckboard later—after you fortify yourselves!" the old cook added playfully. "Mercy, but you's brought a lot of trunks, Miss Grace!"

Miss Malloy still sat demurely on the wagon seat. "*Some* of them belong to Gabe, you know," she pointed out. "And what sort of governess doesn't bring books, and materials for teaching the children, and—"

"You'll be a governess like no other." Gabe returned to the wagon to help her down, winking to reassure her. "These Bristols are an ornery lot, but their hearts are big enough to hold us all. We're both lucky to be here."

"You's said a mouthful there, Mister Gabe. Lemme show you to your rooms now, so's you can splash your face, if you've a mind to," Asa drawled. "Beulah Mae, she's cooked us up a feast."

"Is her food as good as yours?" he teased back. "I've *never* tasted pies like you made when Billy and I were kids."

"Still got my touch, yessir. As I recall, cherry was always your favorite, Mister Gabe." Asa's grin got sly as his ample wife caught the door with her backside to keep it from slamming. "Every now and again I tell her she's got me beat at the cookin', just so's I can live under the same roof with her. If Beulah Mae ain't happy, ain't nobody happy!"

There it was again, that wedded bliss that had eluded him . . . the give-and-take between two people who could laugh and make their way despite life's pitfalls. Gabe offered his arm to Grace, so she could climb the porch steps with the same determined daintiness his wife had always displayed. Why did everything either remind him of Letitia or call to mind his dismal failure to please her?

He forgot his despondent thoughts, however, when he stepped inside the house. Although the rooms and furnishings were the same as he recalled from Billy's wedding, the front parlor was now littered with doll babies. The doilies from the chairs had been arranged along the edge of the low table, and tiny teacups and saucers were set upon them. Heavenly scents of ham and hot biscuits wafted out from the kitchen, and Gabe was again transported back to meals with the Monroes and Malloys. Food had never smelled this good when Mrs. Kirby cooked for them in St. Louis, maybe because she was a finicky little widow who despised getting the kitchen messy.

Gabe stood in the front entryway, soaking up the aromas and the evidence of children . . . gazed at a portrait of those three little redheads, which Eve had painted when Bernadette was a baby seated in her big sister's lap. Asa and Beulah Mae—more family than hired help—carried the steaming bowls to an extended table set for ten. *Ten*! Letitia would have swooned had she been expected to accommodate so many.

A *whoop* made him jump aside. Here came Owen down the walnut bannister, sliding on one hip. At the large, knobby newel post, he hopped to the floor to flash Gabe a grin with a double gap in the front.

"Ya gotta sit by *me*!" the boy declared. "Too many danged girls in this house, so we gotta stick together!"

"Dang right we do!" Gabe replied as he grinned into that fresh, freckled face.

Where had *that* come from? He couldn't recall ever saying "dang," even when he was Owen's age. He refrained from rumpling that mop of russet hair, again transported back to happier times, when Billy Bristol had looked like this—and had invited him to be his best friend in the same exuberant way.

Dang! It was good to be home.

Chapter Five

Solace slid into the last empty chair at the table, between Billy and Gabe. Owen had already corralled their tall, lanky guest and sat grinning up at Gabe, idolizing him. Olivia, across the table, had commanded Grace's attention—no doubt to win her new teacher's favor before her brother could.

This is fine, Solace thought. Billy has Eve, Asa has Beulah Mae, so Bernadette can be *my* special friend.

Why she felt the need to pair everyone up was a mystery to her, as most things were these days. Now that she'd turned eighteen, it seemed important to have someone she considered her own special companion—aside from Rex and her two geldings, of course.

"Will you ask our grace today, Olivia?" Billy smiled at his daughter from the head of the table.

"Of course, Papa. Let us bow our heads," she said primly. Her shiny ringlets fell forward like a curtain of fiery curls as she pressed her hands together.

Solace smiled with her eyes closed. Miss Olivia was in top form, showing off for Grace—who would soon learn what sort of chaos reigned when this ten-year-old paragon antagonized her brother.

"Dear Lord, we ask Your blessings upon this food," the little girl began, "and we thank You for our new teacher, Miss Malloy—"

"Nuh-uh," Owen mumbled into his hands.

"—and we thank You for bringing Mr. Getty to stay in Owen's room so he won't torment me so much—"

Beside her, Gabe was shaking with the effort it took not to laugh, while Billy sat straighter, preparing to give his daughter some prayerful assistance.

"—and we ask You to fix Bernadette so she can talk to us, because we all love her so. Please and thank you, Jesus. Amen."

Solace blinked. Once again Olivia had circumvented a lecture about proper prayer requests. Everyone silently affirmed her wish when they smiled at the little girl who sat in a high chair beside her mother. Bernadette beamed back, delighted with their attention.

"I sure do want a big ole piece of that ham!" Owen piped up. Then he flashed his gap-toothed grin across the table at Grace. "After you help yourself, of course, Miss Malloy."

Grace smiled brightly. "What a pleasure to eat with children who pray so sweetly and have such commendable table manners," she replied as she reached for the meat platter. "I hope you children and I will—*oh*! Oh, my stars, that's a—"

Grace dropped the plate and lunged backward, nearly toppling her chair. She was pointing, breathing so hard she couldn't speak.

Beulah Mae moved faster than any of them had ever seen, desperate to get away from the table—but with the presence of mind to glare at the redheaded culprit. "Mister Owen, you is askin' for a smack across the backside for—"

Asa plucked up the little garter snake that had darted to safety under his wife's plate. As he held its tiny head between his thumb and forefinger, Gracie looked ready to have a seizure. Her eyes went huge and glassy. She grabbed for Olivia, who was entering the same sort of hysterical state.

"Mister Owen, I b'lieve you owes Miss Malloy—and the rest of us—an apology for disruptin' our dinner," the old man said sternly. The arm holding the snake shook, but his solemn gaze didn't waver.

"And when we've finished eatin', you and I will have a chat behind the barn, son." Billy stood up to give his boy a no-nonsense look that wiped the snicker from his lips. "It's one thing to play with snakes outside, but your mother's warned you time and again about bringin' 'em in the house."

"Oh, all right." Owen leveled his gaze at the three jittery females. "I'm real dang sorry my snake got loose durin' the prayer. He heard us blessin' the food and prob'ly figgered he could share it. He's one of God's creatures, ya know."

Two spots of color stained Eve's cheeks as she, too, glared at her son. She'd gathered Bernadette into her lap, ready to spring out of her chair if Asa dropped the snake. "This is inexcusable, Owen," she said. "You'll go to your room now, without dinner, and await your father's call for the rest of your punishment."

Owen sighed loudly, as though one measly snake wasn't worth all this fuss. As he clomped up the stairway, Solace sensed he was more upset about missing out on Asa's pie than he was about the whipping that awaited him—just as she realized Grace had left herself wide open for more of Owen's shenanigans. He wasn't a mean boy, really. Just ornery.

And a pretty good judge of what sends people into a conniption.

Solace saw the grin flirting with Gabe's face, and as Gracie and Olivia assured each other it was safe to sit down again, she leaned toward him. "You can see how things get pretty lively around here," she murmured.

"Yes, but how we cope with surprises—how we deal with unexpected disasters—says a lot about us, doesn't it?"

Solace met his brown-eyed gaze and felt momentarily stunned, not just by his provocative statement, but because his bottomless eyes looked into hers as though he could read the answer written on her heart. As though he really cared what she thought. *And Lord knows, he's endured his share of unexpected disasters.*

She swallowed and so did he.

"At any rate, Gracie, I'm really sorry Owen's started off on the wrong foot," Billy said as he resumed his seat. "It won't happen again."

After Asa took the snake outdoors, her sister sat back down, as did the cook and Olivia. They glanced warily under their plates and the serving bowls, until Bernadette clapped her hands together, crowing with a delight that put everyone in a better mood.

"Owen's a Bristol, through and through. All boy, just like you were, Billy," Solace remarked. As she reached for a steaming bowl of greens, she grinned pointedly at his younger daughter. "Takes more than a little ole snake to scare *us*. Right, sweetie?"

Bernadette shrieked with laughter, which made Solace wonder again how the little girl could make such a joyful noise when she didn't form words despite everyone's coaxing. It was good to see Eve's smile return, too, because this dear child's condition had aged her visibly. Billy's wife still appeared gracious and pretty—when she wasn't wearing her paint-streaked smock, anyway—yet she blamed her daughter's silence on the measles she'd contracted during her pregnancy. Blamed herself, in other words.

"Well, it weren't Mister Billy who pulled such stunts as a young un," Beulah Mae replied with a chuckle. "His brother Wesley—Lord rest his soul—had enough spitfire for the both of 'em. I tanned that boy's behind more than once for trappin' mice in my mixin' bowls, so's they'd jump out when I took 'em down from the shelf."

Olivia rolled her blue eyes and took a biscuit. "That was Papa's twin brother, Miss Malloy. Did you know my Uncle Wesley was an outlaw like Jesse and Frank James? And that Aunt Solace gunned him down before he could shoot Papa? And she was only Owen's age! Can you *imagine*?"

"I shot his horse out from under him, Olivia. I would *never* aim at a person," Solace corrected firmly.

The tense expressions around the table warned her that Olivia didn't know the whole story about Wesley Bristol . . . or which twin had actually fathered her. It wasn't a topic to bring up over dinner—nor was it her place to put Billy and Eve on the spot—so she gazed pointedly at Grace. "And you realize, of course, that Miss Malloy is my sister, just a year and half younger than I am. She was there that night, too."

"I only remember what people have told me about it," Grace chimed in carefully. "I was sleeping when all that commotion woke me up, but I recall how shocked and scared . . . and very sad for Billy everyone was, when his twin brother went on that rampage. He'd already set fire to a neighbor's new house and our barn, and scared away the horses my daddy raised for his living."

Grace reached for Olivia's hand beneath the table. "Sometimes I act appalled at how well Solace shoots and rides, but we're very thankful she saved your papa's life. He'd been living with our parents, you see. He held us when we were babies and treated us like his own little sisters, so we'd have missed him terribly."

"And we wouldn't have *me*!" Olivia said smugly. "And then you wouldn't have come here to be my teacher, and Mr. Getty wouldn't have Papa for his best friend. So God just worked things out for *everybody* that night, didn't He?"

"Yes, dear, He certainly did," her mother put in. "And with all this chatter, poor Grace—Miss Malloy, we should call her—hasn't had a chance to eat a bite of her dinner."

"Yes, Mama. I'll be quiet now." Beaming up at her new governess, Olivia imitated Grace's perfect posture by lifting her back away from the chair. Then she took a big forkful of her corn pudding.

The meal proceeded quietly then, until Asa's cherry and apple pies reminded Billy and Gabe of the old cook's desserts from their boyhood. "I can't tell you how much I've missed this," the slender lawyer said with a shine in his eyes. "Not just Mercy and Asa's wonderful food, but all the . . . the love it was served with. You couldn't go into that home without knowing you *belonged*. And I feel the same way here."

Billy flashed his friend a misty-eyed smile. "I'll show you around the place after I set my son straight, Gabe. We've got a lot of catchin' up to do. Lots to talk about from the past six years."

And secrets. Lots of secrets. Solace watched the two men leave the dining room, chatting as only boyhood friends knew how. Though she believed it was time for the Bristols to tell Olivia the circumstances of her birth, before someone around town let it slip, she also sensed Gabriel Getty was a man of sorrows they had no idea about . . . that he harbored pain and regrets he might keep to himself, even if it wasn't the best thing for his grieving soul. Men weren't much good at letting loose of such things.

But then, who was she to speculate about other people's secrets?

After the dishes were washed, Solace went upstairs to the room she shared with the girls. From the valise under her narrow bed she took her portfolio, her pen, and some ink, and then slipped down the service stairway at the back of the house. Olivia, Eve, and Bernadette were getting acquainted with their new governess, so it was a perfect time to go outside.

She'd found a swing beneath the huge old lilac bushes, which hid her from the house: a place to think and read and write, because sharing a room with two little girls didn't allow Aunt Solace much time to herself. When she stepped outside, Rex joined her immediately, his eyes bright with anticipation. Gabe and Billy were walking toward the barn, with a very somber Owen in tow, so she settled herself on the slatted seat.

The white paint needed freshening, but the chains made a homey creak with her weight . . . the swing curved to fit her

backside . . . her dog posted himself proudly at her feet as
though he'd been the one to introduce her to this hideaway.
As the evening breeze stirred the lilacs' perfume, Solace
inhaled deeply, grateful for these moments alone.

Then, with a huge grin, she slipped an envelope from
behind her supply of fresh paper. She'd read the letter's
angular script a dozen times, but it still made her blood race:

> *Dear Sol Juddson,*
>
> *We here at Beadle and Adams have read the
> adventurous stories you submitted to us, and we believe
> our readers will relish them every bit as much as we have.*
>
> *Please find your check enclosed for all three titles,
> which we will publish as full-length novels. Your "Smoky
> Hill Hide-Out" will appear in our Dime Library
> collection, while our younger readers of the Work and
> Win series will enjoy both "Captured by the
> Comanches" and "She Ran Her Daddy's Ranch."*
>
> *Thank you so much for stories that captivate the
> imagination and require very little correction. We would
> welcome any further tales you care to send our way, Mr.
> Juddson.*
>
> *Yours very sincerely,*
> *Horatio P. McElroy*

Solace sighed blissfully and tucked the letter behind her
paper supply again. She set the ink bottle beside her on the
seat and dipped her nib in it.

"Daddy Was a Desperado" by Sol Juddson, she wrote
across the top of a clean page. She closed her eyes and
squeezed the pen, and in that magic land of her imagination
she was seven again. . . .

The memory of Wesley Bristol charging from the barn on
a huge palomino, his sawed-off shotgun aimed at Billy's
chest, sent her mind into a full gallop. Vividly recalling the
taste of fear and adrenaline that night . . . the weight of that

forbidden pistol in her grip . . . the thunder of hoofbeats and the scents of leather and sweat and hot horse flesh, Solace lost herself in the sheer, solitary joy of blending fact with fiction.

As the words poured out of her pen, she chuckled smugly. Lily might be a princess and Gracie a saint, but *she* was a *writer*!

Chapter Six

"What a beautiful sight." Gabe gazed out over the pasture nearest the house, where sturdy Morgan horses grazed alongside sleek, slender bays with black manes and tails. Frisky Thoroughbred yearlings stopped romping to watch him, their fine, slender ears pointed skyward. The grass was coming in lush and green this spring, and when the afternoon sun struck the new leaves on the trees, he had to squint to look at them.

"Everything here is about new life. Fresh and hopeful . . . ready to go on," he remarked sadly. "I hope I'll feel that way, too, someday. But meanwhile it's good to be here, Billy. Good to see how you and Eve have made such a fine life for yourselves and your children."

Billy rested his corded arms on the top plank of the white fence, which stretched as far as they could see. "Hasn't been easy," he replied. "If Mike Malloy hadn't given me the breeding stock to get started with, I wouldn't have made it. Glad I went with his wisdom about raisin' horses instead of cattle, too. That market's cost a lot of ranchers their shirts lately."

He held out his hand to the nearest cluster of bays, whistling low to coax them over. "A man with any ground's always gonna need good horses," Billy continued, "and townspeople need reliable mounts. I'm thinkin' we could get into more trainin'—ridin' lessons, even—if Solace stayed on to handle that for me."

Gabe nodded. It felt good to rest against the fence, wearing old pants and an open-collared shirt, with no one expecting anything of him. Nobody accusing him. Not much likelihood of Letitia haunting him here, either, as her world had been so totally different from this one. He might finally sleep through an entire night.

As he stroked the muzzle of the bay in front of him, Gabe grinned at the contrast in textures: the velvety smoothness of its skin and the spiky whiskers, the glossy muscles of the horse's neck and the power in its sleek body. It struck him that he'd forgotten so many of the sensations he'd been familiar with as a boy.

"Handsome mount here," he murmured. "They're all so sleek and healthy—and I can't tell you the last time I saddled up. Cranks, the butler, drove me to the office or the courthouse each day."

Billy grinned. "This here's Owen's horse, Jesse. Named for the outlaw, of course."

"Boys find that profession fascinating, even in the city." Gabe glanced sideways, taking in the lean profile of his best friend and the way those blue eyes still sparkled. Years in the wind and weather had etched inroads around his brow and mouth, but Billy Bristol was a handsome man in his rough-cut way. He wouldn't look right with his auburn hair cut short or slicked back—not that the current styles in clothing or hair were of any concern to him.

"It hurt you to punish that boy," Gabe observed. "I thought you were going to crack with every slap of that paddle, even though I was standing too far away to read your expression."

"Good thing Owen couldn't see my face," Billy agreed with a pensive grin. "But I can't let him get the upper hand with Gracie—not the way Wesley did with our teachers, and with Mama. One hardened criminal's enough in this family."

"Must've been a horrendous shock, to have your own brother charge at you with a loaded gun." Gabe tried to envision that awful scene at the Triple M ranch, but his mind had undergone enough torture lately, so he let go of those images. "I missed out on a lot while I was apprenticed to Bancroft."

"Yeah, well, watchin' your long-lost twin turn on ya— seein' the cold cruelty in eyes just like your own—isn't an experience I'd recommend to any man." Billy let out his breath. "Hard to believe that's been ten years ago."

Gabe nodded. For a few moments they watched a pair of yearlings kick up their hind legs and challenge each other to a playful race. Only a matter of time before his best friend— his blood brother—asked the obvious questions about how he'd been doing since Letitia's death, so he posed a question of his own. It was a diversionary tactic that served him well in the courtroom. "Are you concerned that Olivia might find out Wesley was her father?"

Billy let out an undignified snort. "I wonder every single day if we've waited too long to tell her. Scares me half to death that if she finds out, she won't . . . won't want to think of me as her daddy anymore."

Raw emotion—naked fear—rarely welled up in his friend, but Gabe could feel the tug-of-war taking place in Billy's heart. "It's a wonder somebody hasn't already told her. Like your mother, perhaps."

"She and Carlton have hired a manager for the hotel, so we don't see 'em as much. But yeah," he said with a nod, "Mama says it's high time Olivia knew the truth. Eve's as wary of letting that cat out of the bag as I am, though. She's got her hands full, paintin' portraits and keepin' up with Bernadette while she rides herd on our boy. Olivia's always been as good as gold. We hate to upset her beliefs about who she is."

"You'll find the right way. The right time," Gabe assured him. "You're the kindest, most patient man I know, Billy, and I admire the way you've taken responsibility for so many people. Why, I couldn't even make a wife happy, let alone answer to so many other family members."

An odd expression overtook his friend's face. Billy straightened up from the fence and started walking; although he appeared to have no particular destination in mind as they strolled across the lawn alongside the white house, Gabe sensed they were on a private journey. A journey Billy couldn't share with just anybody.

As they approached a small cemetery surrounded by a spiked iron fence, Gabe tightened. A large river rock marked the grave of Billy's father, Owen Bristol, and the headstone beside it was his twin brother's, but Gabe hadn't expected to see two small stones with statues of lambs resting on top.

"Didn't know how to say this—and didn't know if it was any of my business," Billy said softly. "I didn't know Letitia, 'cept for seein' her at your weddin' . . . but my gut said she'd never be happy, no matter who she married. Partly on account of her overbearin' mama, and partly because she was just . . . fragile. Not long for this earth."

He slung a loose arm around Gabe's shoulders then, and his voice thickened with emotion. "I know you truly loved her though, and I'm real, real sorry you lost her, Gabe. I'm guessin' you've passed through a valley of the shadow like none of us'll ever know."

Gabe closed his eyes against tears that dribbled down his cheeks. When would he climb off this emotional seesaw? Would he ever hold a conversation about his wife that didn't make him feel the loss and guilt and torment all over again? His pulse thudded, much like that dull, hollow sound of the dirt hitting Letitia's casket in the grave.

"You're not the first to say that," he admitted with a sigh. "I-I knew she tippled too much from that flask of nerve tonic. Suspected her mother would interfere at every turn. But I thought I could accept those things. I thought if I could introduce Letitia to new interests—like starting our family—but she just—she just—"

"Too scared, prob'ly," Billy offered. "Didn't want to feel

fat and ugly. Didn't know how she'd handle a cryin' kid in the night. Didn't—"

Didn't want to bear my child. Gabe's thoughts mocked him for the hundredth time. But he couldn't tell Billy the awful truth he'd read in his wife's diary. Couldn't expose that deep, throbbing wound even to his closest friend.

"—wanna give up bein' a child herself. 'Cause once you've had a baby or two," he added with a fond shake of his head, "there's no gettin' around bein' a grown-up. No goin' back to bein' responsible just for yourself, or pleasin' yourself, when there's backsides to wipe and tears to dry."

Gabe sighed heavily. "I try to convince myself it was for the best," he muttered. "I can't understand what God wanted when He brought this situation to pass, because—because Letitia was about five months along, carrying our firstborn—"

His voice broke. He paused to compose himself. "We're taught that the Lord's working out His purpose even in the most painful, unexpected situations. So I try to believe that. I get no comfort from it, but I try to believe it."

"You can't tell me God gets any good outta one of His children dyin'." Billy's sigh sounded so forlorn, Gabe looked over—and saw two huge teardrops spilling out of those blue eyes. "Nearly killed Eve to have this little girl—Jennie, we named her—die in her arms just three days after she was born. We were thankful Bernadette came along shortly after, but then Matthias was stillborn."

"I'm sorry, Billy. I had no idea. I don't know how you and Eve can stand that agony." Gabe hooked his arm around Billy's neck and for several moments they stood in their silent sorrow, gazing at tiny tombstones that seemed cold and hard even when surrounded by the soft green grass and warm sunshine of a spring afternoon.

"Makes you grateful for what you've got, I can tellya that much." Billy swiped at his face with his sleeve and put on a smile. "But I didn't mean to heap more grief on top of yours, Gabe. You came here to sort things out."

"And I can feel it happening already. You can't imagine how oppressive that household in St. Louis felt to me," he explained. "It all piled up on me after the funeral . . . the house her parents gave us . . . the job as her father's partner . . . the two domestics hand-chosen by Henrietta. I earned a very respectable living, yet I didn't have a thing that truly belonged to me."

He sucked in a deep, cleansing breath. "I felt the pull of invisible strings dictating Letitia's every move—every thought—as if her mother were a puppeteer. Her laudanum bottle drowned out any inclination to think for herself, or to listen to my suggestions."

"Nasty stuff, opium. Hard habit to break, the way I understand it."

"You've got to *fight* to overcome its power and . . . Letitia had no inclination to give it up," Gabe said with a sigh. "She couldn't imagine a day without her 'tonic.' Got agitated when her supply ran low. I had no idea how many flasks she had stashed around the house. It was within her reach every hour of every day."

"She had every privilege, that woman did—and she had *you*, Gabe," Billy added staunchly. "I hope you'll let go of any notion that her death came from somethin' you said or did to her. Or somethin' you could've changed."

They were circling the crux of the situation again, as if Billy was slyly luring a confession from him. He'd used this strategy himself while arguing some landmark cases. As much as he wanted to, Gabe couldn't purge himself of his odious knowledge about the exact nature of Letitia's death. Not yet, anyway. The facts still felt too raw.

At the sound of hoofbeats out by the barn, Gabe's melancholy mood vanished. Solace, clad in pants and a tucked-in shirt, was leading matched bay geldings around the corral with halter ropes. She trotted backward as she talked to them—a feat in itself—and the horses followed her low voice with their ears pricked forward. Their gait became perfectly even.

"Good boys!" she crooned, still backpedaling. Off to one side, her dog, Rex, sat watching attentively. When his ears pricked up, his dark markings resembled a mask—or a butterfly.

"I can't believe what I'm seeing," Gabe murmured. "That girl—well, she's no girl anymore—and those animals are so in tune with each other—"

"You got that right!" Billy replied. "And you ain't seen nothin' yet! When I gave her those geldings last year—Lincoln and Lee, she calls 'em—I had no idea 'bout the performance they had in 'em. Always had a way with horses myself, but Solace makes me feel pretty humble."

Billy's face eased into a grin as the two bays circled the corral again in perfect, measured step. "It's like she casts a spell, and they'll do anything she wants," he remarked in a faraway voice. "Same way with Rex—and he's just a mutt, far as breedin' goes." This spectacle seemed to relieve his sadness, too, so the two of them stood in awed silence to watch Solace work.

When she looked satisfied with the horses' performance, she draped their lead ropes loosely over their necks. Then, with a snap of her fingers, Lincoln and Lee resumed their circling of the ring without her. Gabe had never seen horses keep in step so well—even teams who'd pulled wagons together for years had their occasional lapses. But the two bays continued to circle the corral with their ebony manes and tails flowing at the same graceful angle.

When Solace glanced over at her dog, Gabe grinned. "He's a lot like your Snowy and Spot, isn't he? I suppose Hattie and Boots are long gone by now."

"Yeah, it's been a few years, but they lived out happy lives there at the Triple M," his friend replied in a sentimental tone. "It was a dang good thing Emma left your two dogs behind, 'cause they were everything to Solace after I came back to this place.

"Good thing Mike found that ornery white dog makin' a nuisance of himself in town, too," he added with a chuckle. "Solace was heartbroken when our other dogs passed. And now Rex, he's the *king*. Just like his name says."

The small white collie—no doubt a border collie mixed with something else—slipped under the bottom rung of the corral at Solace's silent hand signal. Gabe nipped his lip, anticipating something wonderful. The dog's intent expression as he watched the two horses told him Rex was about to make his move.

Crouched like a small white fox, the dog let the horses canter past him. Without missing a beat, he fell into step with Lincoln and Lee, and then he leaped onto the inside horse's back.

"Holy cow! It's like having a circus right here in your own yard!" Gabe marveled in a whisper.

"Oh, it gets better." Billy's pride shimmered brightly in his eyes as he followed the geldings and the mounted dog around the corral. "Solace makes it look easy, but I can't tell ya how many hours she's spent bringin' her act this far. And there she goes—"

Solace, too, fell into the rhythm of those eight prancing hooves, while Rex spanned the short distance between the horses' moving backs. His tongue was hanging out and he appeared to be grinning at his mistress, urging her to join their game.

Solace lunged then, mounting the unsaddled inside horse by landing on its shoulder and swinging her leg over it. She sat for only a moment before drawing her feet up under her lithe body, while grasping the two ropes. Then she stood up on her mount's back, balancing without any apparent effort.

"This is too much," Gabe whispered. He wiped the lenses

of his spectacles on his shirt sleeve, shaking his head in amazement. "She doesn't even seem to be thinking about—"

"There's more. But it gets tricky here. We've gotta be ready to run over there if she slips."

Solace held the ropes so they dangled slightly, and then carefully—carefully—she stepped sideways so she had one foot on each of the two cantering bays. Rex had inched forward, to crouch low on his horse's shoulders—

And then Solace bent her knees and urged the two horses faster. And faster yet!

The look on her face held Gabe Getty spellbound. Her sorrel hair streamed behind her in waves that caught the afternoon sun, while her slender body flowed as though she were an integral part of the horses. Or were the horses an extension of her? With her face uplifted in a victorious grin, Solace Monroe was flying without wings. Soaring in ways few humans ever knew.

"This is absolutely incredible," he whispered.

She's a woman like no other. A woman you could love, Gabe.

Gabe held his breath. Where had *that* come from? As he glanced sideways at Billy, he had no indication his best friend had said a word, yet he had clearly heard a voice. These past few weeks had presented him with so many new decisions—so many unexpected directions—that he'd gone to bed each sleepless night in total confusion about what he should do next and where he should go.

But this voice had spoken directly to him.

He shifted, needing to change focus. Something felt absolutely wrong about having such thoughts of love for another woman so soon—let alone for Billy's kid sister!

Never mind that Solace Monroe was no blood relation to Billy, and that she was a young lady of eighteen now. It was unthinkable to look at her in a romantic light. He was twenty-seven. His years in St. Louis as a lawyer and a husband gave him nothing in common with this acrobat circling the ring—

"If you'll put your eyes back in their sockets, Mr. Getty, I'll have Solace show ya her *best* trick," Billy teased. "Believe me, after ya see the way she handles a gun, you'll wanna stay on her good side! Not that Solace would harm a flea," he added quietly. "And not that you'd care about which side of her you're on."

Gabe met his friend's gaze and didn't know *what* to think about that remark. But he couldn't miss the lights dancing in Billy's blue eyes as they walked to the corral.

Chapter Seven

"Lookin' real good today, Solace," Billy said as he clapped her on the back. "Someday, when you're rich and famous, ridin' in some fancy Wild West show, don't forget who set you in a saddle 'fore you could even walk."

Solace laughed. "I'll thank you forever for not snitching to Mama about how I was practicing behind the barn. And where would I be without Lincoln and Lee?"

"Oh, prob'ly sittin' in some ole rich guy's house, eatin' bonbons and bossin' the household help. That's what you were born to do, isn't it?" Billy ruffled Rex's head when the dog placed its front paws on his knee. He flashed Gabe a conspiratorial wink. "Lemme get you an apple, so's you can show our citified friend what you and this worthless mutt are really made of. Get your pistol, honey."

It was nothing unusual for Billy to brag about her, but Solace couldn't miss the undertone in his words. And as he walked to the root cellar for that apple, she noticed Gabe Getty's nervous grin. It flickered across his lips like lightning bugs on a summer night, as if he wanted to say something but the cat had his tongue. Imagine that, from a lawyer!

Rex let out an imperious *woof* and then held up a front paw.

"You're right, pup, I've forgotten my manners! This is Gabe Getty, Rex, and I've known him since I was—well, since I was no taller than you are!"

The dog's ears fanned out and he looked up at the tall man's face with bright, assessing eyes.

"And before Solace was that tall, I had a Border collie very much like you," Gabe crooned. "Except Hattie was mostly black—and while she was the best friend a kid ever had, she never rode a horse. That was some show you put on, Rex!"

Gabe then crouched to solemnly shake the dog's paw, eye-to-eye. When Rex placed both his paws on the man's shoulders, darting in for a quick lick on his cheek, Solace's heart fluttered. "That's a high honor, Gabe. Rex doesn't kiss just anybody, you know. We're choosy about the company we keep."

She was teasing, trying to make Gabe feel more at ease. Yet when his dark eyes focused on her from between Rex's fluffy ears, she saw an intensity she hadn't expected.

"The honor's all mine, Solace. I-I'm flabbergasted at the way you can ride and—"

"Well, we've gotta do what we can with what God gave us, don't we?" she cut in before he got gushy. "I sure didn't get any of Lily's talent for singing or Gracie's skills in teaching. So I ride horses and play with my dog. And maybe I can shoot a little, too," she added as Billy approached them.

"From what I can see, you're an extraordinary teacher, Solace. Don't sell yourself short, just because you don't fit your sisters' molds," he replied quietly. "Watching you just now has brought me more joy than I've felt in a long while. I can foresee a day when you'll amaze the hundreds of people you'll perform for. Right, Billy?"

"Yeah, well don't encourage her," his buddy teased as he handed her a big red apple. "This kid's been threatenin' to run off and join the circus since the first time she saw one, even though her folks've done all they could to tame her ambitions. We'll see who wins."

Nipping her lip, Solace trotted to the barn for her pearl-handled pistols. These, too, were a gift from Billy—a special honor, because they'd once belonged to his father. But she was used to Billy's playful praise and encouragement. It was Gabe Getty's eloquence that echoed in her head now.

Don't sell yourself short. . . . more sheer joy . . . a day when you'll amaze hundreds of people . . .

Could those be the words of a man who'd married a beautiful, wealthy woman? Solace heard more than just surface admiration between Gabe's lines. For a moment he'd forgotten to be anxious . . . had perhaps forgotten about losing his wife. He'd spoken straight from his heart about her talents and abilities.

And her heart had certainly heard him. She couldn't stop grinning as she took the more accurate of the two pistols from their case. For just a moment there, Gabe had looked, well—*interested* in her!

But she set this sentimental claptrap aside. Gabe was still grieving, after all, and she couldn't let a single stray thought distract her during this trick. Sure, she practiced it often with her faithful dog, but only one bad shot would end the love that sustained her. Long after Gabe moved on to a new job and probably a new wife, Rex and Lincoln and Lee would be her dearest friends.

"You ready, Rex?" she called.

His eyes lit up and his whole body wiggled.

"You know the rules, fella. Gotta sit tight—no panting, and no looking around to see if everybody's watching how wonderful you are," she reminded him. "We save all the congratulations for later."

When Solace stroked his silky ears, he gazed at her with devotion only a dog could know. She marveled again at the beauty of the markings around his ears and eyes . . . his muscled, angel-white body. Rex sat regally still, muzzle up, as she positioned the apple on the flat of his head.

"Real still now," she murmured. She counted back about fifteen paces, not thinking about Billy and Gabe watching . . . not allowing potentially fatal consequences to cloud her inner vision, or to distract her from the perfection this trick required.

Solace turned to face her dog. With slow, smooth moves

from hours of practice with tin cans on a fence, she inhaled . . . raised her pistol and sighted with one eye closed on that big red apple. She said a quick, silent prayer as she exhaled. She squeezed the trigger.

It took an eternity for the bullet to hit, no matter how many times she did this trick. She'd never missed, but she took nothing for granted. If a fly buzzed into Rex's ear, it was all over.

Thunk! The apple exploded into a hundred soft pieces.

Rex let out a victory yip and dashed toward her—leaped— and she caught him in a triumphant hug. "Yes, yes, you were spectacular, boy!" she praised the wiggling, licking, ecstatic dog. "You brought the house down with that one!"

Billy clapped wildly. He trotted over, throwing his arm around her and Rex to share their excitement, as he always did.

But Gabe Getty's reaction gave her pause. He yanked his eyeglasses from his pale face, as though he couldn't bear to witness her marksmanship ever again. "What if you— Solace, how can you look into that dog's eyes and fire—"

"That's rule number one, Gabe," she corrected. "I never look Rex in the eye, and I never think—even for a second— that I won't make the shot. One tiny doubt—one split-hair of hesitation—and Rex is out of his misery. It's *me* who's left to suffer."

The slender man beside Billy exhaled slowly, thinking about what she'd said. His hand went to Rex's back from habit. He'd missed having a dog, by the looks of it, and it pleased her when her pet gazed up at him with obvious adoration. Dogs were excellent judges of character, after all.

She didn't move her hand when Gabe's fingers brushed hers. He was stroking the dog, wasn't he?

"It's all about trust," she explained in a lighter voice. "I'm relying on Rex to hold absolutely still—he's learned to focus as completely as I do. And he's trusting me to do it right, every time. He lays his life on the line for me, Gabe," she insisted. "If I feel one iota of doubt, I call off the shot. Because if I hit him, I'll be putting the pistol to my own head next."

Billy clamped his hand playfully at the back of her neck. "Don't you *dare* leave me behind to tell your mother and Mike what happened! I'd never forgive myself if—"

"Why would you need to, Billy?" She hadn't meant for the conversation to turn this serious, yet there was no dodging its direction. She shifted Rex's warm weight in her arms, looking from one man to the other. "I've made my own choices about riding and shooting. I live with the danger of it every time I mount a horse or cock a gun, because it's what I'm *good* at. No need to blame yourself if I've lived by my own decisions."

Billy's brow furrowed. "Don't you go talkin' that way about—"

"Why? Because I'm a girl?" Her heart thudded in her chest, but she had to say this plain out. Wouldn't duck this issue just because it wasn't ladylike. Solace shoved her unruly hair out of her face to look at him straight-on.

"You risked everything to reclaim this place, Billy Bristol," she continued in a low voice. "I watched you talk your long-lost brother out of shooting you down—more than once he could've killed you and Eve, and he even threatened your mama! But you're here, because you believed in your *purpose*. Your birthright!

"So hear me out," she said, hugging Rex to her chest. "Believe what I say, Billy, because I see no point in going on if I can't live out my dreams, just like you have! It's the way you and Michael—and my daddy, Judd Monroe—have taught me to live."

She let Rex hop back to the ground. Had she given Billy more of an earful than he deserved? As she walked back to the barn, Solace squared her shoulders and breathed deep.

Thank you for being with me when I have tough things to say, Daddy. I just want to make you proud, and I sure wish you were here. Sometimes it feels like you're the only one who understands.

That evening at the table, Gabe was again transported to earlier, happier times when Billy stood up as the dishes were being cleared. Beulah Mae had fried chickens fresh from the hen house and had mashed potatoes from last summer's garden. Asa's peach cobbler, still warm and served with fresh cream, had demanded a second helping. He'd forgotten about such down-home pleasures while living in the city.

He leaned back in his chair, feeling full in many ways . . . trying not to steal glances at Solace as she scraped chicken bones and scraps from their plates. She'd eaten more at this meal than Letitia touched in weeks, yet she looked slender and strong. Tonight she wore a simple blue gingham dress and had tied her thick, wavy hair with a ribbon at her nape. Such an unsophisticated style, yet it suited her—called to mind her mother, Mercy Malloy—while in the depths of those bold brown eyes he saw her father, Judd.

"Did you get enough, Gabe?" she asked quietly.

I'll never get enough of the warmth that surrounds me here . . . . or the way your voice and eyes make me think about . . .

"Yes, thank you," he rasped, hoping he didn't sound adolescent.

She smiled as though she'd heard his inner thoughts and found his anxiety endearing. So *sure* of herself, Solace was—just as she'd been when they danced at his wedding. Why was he aware of her every move now? Thinking about the fit of her denim pants when she'd stood on her two horses, riding hellbent-for-leather?

"Tonight we're gonna continue our work on the Twenty-Third Psalm," Billy announced. "Seems a fittin' end to a fine spring day. And it's a passage that helps us through many a rough spot. Reminds us how strong the Lord's love is when we're feelin' too weak to carry our share."

His friend smiled at him then, and Gabe's gut tightened. While he certainly knew this Psalm, his recitation skills were rusty; he'd never possessed the heartfelt eloquence Judd Monroe and Michael Malloy brought to these devotional times. Surely Billy wouldn't ask him to—

"Each adult picks a child to say it with," his host explained, "so I'm hopin' my kids do me proud with their recitin' for you and Gracie tonight."

"Pick me, Gabe!" Owen piped up. "I know the whole thing by heart now! Well . . . mostly!"

His heart swelled as the boy clutched his hand and grinned at him with that gap in his front teeth. Across the table, Olivia gave her new teacher the same earnest look, while Solace had lifted Bernadette from her high chair. But this moment between him and Owen, when Billy's son had chosen *him* rather than waiting to be picked, touched Gabe deeply. This Psalm reminded him of Letitia's funeral, so he hoped he could say it with conviction rather than tears.

" 'The Lord is my shepherd; I shall not want,' " Billy began.

Around the table, voices young and old joined in. The words flowed in rhythm as they always had, to carry Gabe along with their soothing reassurance; the faith of many generations had gathered together in this room as dusk wrapped around them like a blanket.

" 'He maketh me to lie down in green pastures,' " Gabe continued, pleased that Owen's voice sounded confident above his own. " 'he leadeth me beside the still waters . . . . He restoreth my soul . . . . he leadeth me in the paths of righteousness for his name's sake. Yea, though I walk through the valley of the shadow of death, I will fear no evil; for thou art with me: thy rod and thy staff, they comfort me.' "

Where had his own voice left off and Solace's taken over? When the words threatened to undo him, Gabe mouthed them—as though listening for Owen to say the verses correctly. Beside him, with Bernadette in her lap, Solace was forming the words distinctly as she recited them . . . hoping the little girl would read her lips and be coaxed into saying them herself?

How did this family keep believing their curly haired Bernadette would talk someday? Not once had anyone made concessions to her muteness, or treated her as though she were to be pitied or coddled.

"'. . . surely goodness and mercy shall follow me all the days of my life, and I will dwell in the house of the Lord forever.'" Solace pulled the toddler close and smacked her cheek with an exuberant kiss to make her giggle.

Owen's eyes narrowed. "Don't do none of that kissin' on *me*, Gabe, or I'll—"

"Wouldn't dream of it. But I *will* say you did a fine job of reciting your verses, young man."

The grin he got in return did those same sad-and-happy things to him. *How it would feel to be hearing my own boy's voice? Holding my flesh and blood by the shoulders?*

All boy, Owen didn't stand still any longer than he had to. "Can we be excused—pretty please?" he pleaded.

"*May* we please be excused?" his sister corrected pointedly.

"Yes, you may," Eve replied as she stood up. "But since Miss Malloy and Gabe are family now, don't think you're excused from helping Asa and Beulah Mae with the evening chores. See if you can amaze them by being the quickest, most efficient helpers they've ever seen."

Chapter Eight

Gabe found himself waiting, watching . . . but for what?

For whom, came the reply, even though he knew the answer. While he loved being here among the Bristols, they all had their routines at the end of the day: the children did their chores; Eve had invited Grace upstairs to discuss her duties as the family's new governess; Billy had an account to prepare, for a buyer who'd claim his horses tomorrow.

So where's Solace?

And why should that matter?

Gabe's lips twitched. He felt like a kid again, eager to gawk at a pretty girl. But he was twenty-seven, too old for the unique young lady who'd grown up as Billy's kid sister. His life had taken too drastic a turn for him to be interested in *anyone*, yet when he stepped out into the evening shadows and the cool spring air, he looked for her. Solace had helped in the kitchen after clearing the table, but surely she was finished . . . .

And why would she want to see you? You're a fish out of water here, same as you were in Letitia's family. . . .

And so is Solace.

As this thought struck him, Gabe stopped beneath a weeping willow tree that glowed bright and green in the sunset. Why hadn't he seen it? Solace Monroe might handle a horse and a gun as competently as any man—*better* than most but—her talents set her apart from Lily and Grace, as surely as her staying at home had separated them when her sisters attended Miss Vanderbilt's academy. She looked confident riding in the ring and aiming a pistol above her dog's head, but Solace was every bit the outsider he was. Feeling the same sting of society's disapproval.

He saw a bushy white tail wagging near the lilac bushes behind the house; the object of his curiosity had sought refuge from the busy, noisy Bristol family, just as he had.

Gabe's pulse pounded painfully. Why couldn't this be easier? He was supposed to be sorting out his thoughts, planning his next professional step, getting his life in order—even if he felt like a shell of himself, so fragile he might crack at the least provocation.

Yet his feet went where they wanted to. Rex's bright eyes followed him as he approached the canopy of lilacs that waved in the evening breeze, wafting perfume like a lure he couldn't ignore.

He saw Solace's bare feet then, and about six inches of slim, sturdy ankle below her gingham dress. He heard papers rustling—she was shuffling something out of sight—and he chided himself for being so insensitive. Solace needed time to ponder and assess, just like he did, and he was intruding. "I—didn't mean to interrupt your—"

"It's all right, Gabe. Rex and I are glad to see you!" She leaned around the lilac bush to smile at him. "I love these Bristols dearly, but it's overwhelming to be in their midst sometimes."

"So I've noticed! They all have their own pursuits."

"And this is when Eve usually takes Bernadette to her studio. I don't want her to entertain *me*, when she needs this time with her little girl."

"She takes a three-year-old where she works?" He glanced toward the tall white house. The round window in the third-floor dormer marked Grace's new classroom, while the larger window on this side let in the light Eve needed for her work. "How does she get any painting done with Bernadette there? She's a busy little thing."

Solace smiled, patting the other end of the swing. "Bernadette may be mute, but her sense of form and color are extraordinary. Billy built her a miniature easel so she can paint, like her mama. Her brushes take off in their own directions, but she astounds us when she captures things she sees . . . and things no one else does."

Gabe perched on the edge of the swing, considering this. "How do you mean, things no one else can see?"

Solace rested her arms across a portfolio, as though protecting its contents from him. "She draws little winged creatures . . . sprites and fairies and angels. She paints extraordinary animals, too. She gave me a sketch of Rex that's priceless!"

Solace opened her portfolio and flipped through pages of firm, precise script that might be a journal or a . . .

Gabe looked away. He'd learned his lesson about reading diaries.

His gaze wandered, though. When she tugged out a piece of heavy drawing paper, he saw a page heading that said something like . . . "Daddy Was a Desperado."

That made no sense at all! So he took the sheet she offered and forced his attention away from those handwritten pages.

His jaw dropped. Anyone who'd seen the dog with the unusual markings would recognize Rex immediately, but in this picture, he'd grown wings like a butterfly. Gabe realized then that these wings matched the shape of his darker ears and the mask around his eyes.

It took more than artistic talent to complete such a portrait: it required a sophisticated thought process. "If I didn't trust your word that Bernadette painted this—"

"I was in the studio when Rex sat for her."

"—I'd swear Eve had." Gabe studied the picture again, shaking his head. "Incredible. Absolutely incredible."

Solace scooted closer to admire the painting herself. Rex hopped onto the wooden swing then, which meant his mistress was sitting so close to Gabe, her blue checked skirt edged over his leg.

He cleared his throat . . . . a futile attempt not to notice her nearness.

Solace smiled as though she knew exactly what effect she had on him. "Eve believes that Bernadette's artistic skills have developed to compensate for the fact she can't express herself any other way."

"To . . . relieve the frustration of not being able to talk." Oh, how he knew about frustration! It had been the hallmark of his marriage. . . .

Don't let it ruin the moment. When did you ever share such fascinating conversation with Letitia?

Solace nodded, which made the glossy brown waves around her face glimmer in the sunset. "If Bernadette doesn't get her time to paint each day, she's a holy terror! You've not seen a tantrum until you've watched that kid run through the house throwing everything in her path against the wall."

"Oh, my." Gabe considered this, partly because thinking was all he could do that didn't involve touching Solace more than he should. "Does she sketch what she's trying to say?"

"Sometimes. Bernadette gets so engrossed in her own little world . . . well, who knows what connections she makes?" Solace's brown eyes sparkled and a dimple winked in one cheek. "Gracie'll have her hands full. Part of her mission is to teach Bernadette—and all of us—sign language, to connect words with their meanings. The alphabet, and how to spell with it."

"A formidable task," Gabe murmured. He tried not to gaze into Solace's soulful brown eyes, or to watch her lashes brush her cheeks each time she blinked. It wasn't as if she was flirting with him—was she?

Solace laughed. "What is it they say? 'When the student is ready, the teacher appears'? I'm betting Bernadette makes those connections anyway—if she *wants* to," she emphasized. "That kid's so bright, I sometimes wonder if she uses her silence to get exactly what she wants."

Memories of Henrietta Bancroft's manipulation made him frown. "You think she chooses not to talk? You make her sound like a little tyrant—a very smart one."

"Not at all." Two warm spots glowed in Solace's cheeks, as though she wanted to share something from deep within her. "I don't discuss matters of faith as much as some in my family do . . . but I truly believe Gracie is here because Bernadette called to God for help, and He heard her prayers as no one else could. That probably sounds so far-fetched, you think I'm—"

"That's the most intriguing idea I've heard in a long time," Gabe breathed. "Only someone who loves Bernadette very much would see it that way."

Solace focused on his face. His spectacle lenses amplified her gaze until he swore his eyes might catch fire. His hand reached toward hers . . . .

And she grabbed his first.

Solace exhaled slowly, and in her eyes he saw his own confusion. The same terror, too. She licked her lips, which drew his attention to how soft they'd feel if he kissed her.

The portfolio slipped from her lap, breaking the spell. Solace sprang from the swing to catch the loose pages before the breeze carried them off. Gabe dashed after a few sheets, too, cursing when some of the ink smeared from the dampness of the grass. Again he saw the heading, "Daddy Was a Desperado," which sounded more like a story title than a journal entry.

"I'm sorry, but you can't—" Solace snatched the pages from his fingers, her cheeks aflame.

Isn't she pretty, blushing, with her hair blowing loose?

"This is something I do to—a way to pass the time when—"

"When you're lonely? And when no one else understands you?" His face felt hot. Gabe shifted his weight . . . stuffed his hands in his pockets to keep from doing anything stupid—like grabbing her shoulders to tell her she was wonderful.

Solace's heartrending expression told him he should've kept his mouth shut. Why had he presumed to put meaning to those pages full of neatly blocked paragraphs? She must think him the most rude, insensitive . . .

"Spoken like a man who knows what it is to be lonely and misunderstood."

She had him there, didn't she?

"If you promise not to tell a soul, can I show you something, Gabe?"

Now *there* was a request that could only lead to trouble! Yet Solace's expression showed no hint of flirtation. She looked like a young girl with a secret she just *had* to tell someone. And she'd chosen him.

"Looks like you have several pages of a story here. I'm sorry the ink has smeared."

"Do you want to see something *really* exciting?"

She reached behind the paper in her portfolio, and when she pulled out an envelope, her face shone so brightly Gabe prayed he wouldn't do anything stupid. The last thing he wanted was to jeopardize her trust in him. Or to spoil the excitement that sparkled in her pretty brown eyes.

He unfolded the letter. Glanced at the letterhead and then skimmed past the salutation to a Sol Juddson and . . .

"This man wants to buy three stories for publication in the Dime Library and Work and Win." Gabe gaped at her. "You're Sol Juddson! And these are *your* stories! This is the company that publishes all those dime novels in the stores."

Her head was bobbing with delight.

"My God, Solace! I've written dozens of legal briefs, but I've never known anyone who wrote *real stories*!"

"Shhh! Someone might hear—"

"Why are you keeping this a secret? This is so—" Gabe raked his hair with his fingers, searching for the highest compliment. "While I'm astounded by the way you ride and shoot, sweetheart, writing stories is, well—I stand in *awe*! Your family will be so proud! Lily and Grace have accomplished *nothing*, compared to this!"

Solace's lovely flush deepened as she glanced toward the house. "I didn't open this letter until I got here, so I wanted to . . . savor my accomplishment. What if people think I was wrong to take a male name? Especially since I rearranged my father's?"

He considered this. "You're not the first female novelist to do that, Solace. The English writer, George Eliot, took a male *nom de plume* so her work would be taken seriously by—"

"I didn't think Beadle and Adams would buy adventure stories by a-a girl," she explained.

Oh, you're way beyond being a girl. Who would've expected this literary effort from horse-racing, pistol-packing Solace Monroe?

"You're probably right about that," he said with a nod. "I hope you'll tell your family, though. Mike and your mother—Billy and Eve!—will be so proud of you."

Her deep dimple flirted with him again. "I've written myself into a corner, though. Maybe . . . you could help me?"

She could've asked for the moon and stars, and he would've delivered them. Gabe fought the urge to hug her: if she misinterpreted his intentions, they'd both be in trouble. "I'll do whatever I can, Solace. What seems to be the problem?"

"Well—" She searched behind the paper in her portfolio again, and pulled out a check. "The publisher has paid me. But if I take this to the bank in Abilene, the teller will know about my male name and it'll be all over town—"

Gabe nodded. Abilene had its gossips, and she was right to anticipate some negative reactions.

"—and here in Richmond, they don't know me from Adam," she continued earnestly. "So even if Billy comes with me—and even if I wear my pants and boots—it's obvious I'm not Sol Juddson. *Isn't* it?"

He choked on a laugh, because Solace was sincerely perplexed. "No male with eyes or ears could mistake you for a man, honey. But you're making good points. You've thought this through."

She nodded, some of her luster dimming. "I'm not even sure they can give me the money for it," she mumbled. "Sol Juddson doesn't really exist, after all. And if I ask my publisher to exchange the check, he might not buy any more stories."

Despite his better judgment, his hands landed on her shoulders. Her request for his help made Gabe feel ten feet tall. He doubted a bank would give her any trouble if he, Billy, or Mike Malloy accompanied her, yet he admired the way she'd considered all these angles . . . the way she'd written and submitted three stories. Most people with sense enough to string that many sentences together didn't have the nerve to show their work to anyone.

"I understand your dilemma," he murmured. "Give me a little time. The answer's somewhere in my law books, or I can inquire discreetly at the bank."

The tension left her shoulders. Solace looked very vulnerable and open to him and . . . he couldn't seem to take his hands from her. "Thank you, Gabe. I-I knew you'd help me!"

He wrapped his arms around her. How tall she'd grown! How warm and firm her body had become. Solace's loose hair teased his face, and sensations he didn't dare admit stirred within him. When she slipped her arms around him, her trembling—her trust—made Gabe swallow hard. Lord, how he wanted to bury his face in her soft waves and give in to a kiss.

Here in this lilac-scented hideaway, it would be so easy to indulge his lonely need. Evening was drifting in around them, and the night usually taunted him with memories that Solace's simple affection would ease.

Gabe stepped back with a sigh. "I should go inside, before my roommate comes looking for me," he remarked, glancing toward the house. "Something tells me Owen doesn't miss much."

"He'd tease us to high heaven—in front of everyone." Solace released him, and meticulously tucked her papers back into her portfolio. Her heightened color suggested the same sort of awareness he felt . . . the same longing. "I'll go on inside, so nobody'll think—well, it's not like we're sneaking around—"

"No, we're not." Yet his heart hammered at the way she'd said this. Did she want to be alone with him?

"—or like we have improper feelings for each other."

Gabe's rapid heartbeat said they did, but he just smiled. "Good night, Solace. It was a real pleasure to share your writing success. Congratulations!"

"Thanks," she murmured. "Maybe now that I've told *you* a secret, you could share some with me. I wouldn't tell a soul, you know." She whistled to Rex, and then walked resolutely across the lawn without looking back.

Gabe sighed wistfully. Best to keep his own counsel, as far as revealing anything about his life with Letitia. What would a young lady like Solace know about such things? Did he want to discolor her rosy assumptions about love? About what it meant to marry for better or worse?

She's wiser than you know. More mature than Letitia . . . less concerned about maintaining appearances.

He laughed aloud. Solace Monroe was anything but concerned about fitting society's mold! But it was too soon. She held too many innocent assumptions.

Would she confide in you if she knew the truth? About how your wife died rather than bear your child?

Gabe's smile faltered; his happiness drifted away on the evening breeze. Some secrets were too onerous to lift up to the light of day.

Chapter Nine

Solace's heart was pounding so hard she couldn't talk—and it wasn't from taking the back stairs too fast. He understood her need to write! Gabriel Getty, an esteemed attorney—the most educated man she knew!—was impressed and downright astounded by the fact that she was a writer.

Quickly, before her sister came to the room they would share, Solace slipped her portfolio into her valise and then removed the small framed picture of her daddy, Judd Monroe. She gazed at the face she'd never known—the dark eyes and curls and distinctive eyebrows she'd inherited—as she sat on the side of her narrow bed.

"Oh, Daddy, I can't believe it!" she whispered. "I took a chance on sending in those stories—just like you said! And when Gabe saw those loose pages, I acted on gut impulse and trusted him. And now he thinks I'm smart, Daddy! He thinks I'm special!"

Clasping the small likeness, Solace paused to let the evening's events sink in—and to consider what she'd just done. Was it wrong to talk to a dead man, even if he was her father? Would God think she was praying to Judd Monroe? If Gracie walked in, she'd be appalled: would never understand about discussing important matters with the father she'd never known.

Heck, Gracie doesn't talk to Papa about things even though he's alive, and a good listener, too. And Lily . . .

Well, Lily wasn't here, was she? And while the princess in pink had no idea who'd fathered her, she had her angels to talk to and her own ways of knowing how God worked out

His purpose. She'd always known she had a special mission and the gifts to carry them out. . . .

You have gifts, too, Solace. Never let anyone tell you different. I was proud of you today.

She exhaled slowly. It was a definite voice she heard at times like these. She couldn't explain it, and it scared her a little. But when she trusted this voice, believing it was her father's, things worked out the right way. When she followed his instructions in the corral, her horses behaved just like he said they would. And she never fired a gun without waiting for Daddy to say her aim was straight and true.

Though Michael Malloy had raised her as his own—had loved her without limit from the day he'd helped deliver her—it wasn't his familiar voice in her head and heart. Solace was afraid to believe God might be talking directly to her, so she attributed this wisdom to Judd Monroe. From what Billy and Mama and Michael said, he would've loved her this way. Would've stood by her, no matter what.

"Was it wrong for me to twist your name around?" she asked. "Seems like I've always been better at boy things than—"

Footsteps on the stairs made her slip Daddy's picture into her valise again. She stood up to look out the window, in case Gracie was in the mood for Twenty Questions. Her little sister could be mighty nosy when she suspected people were keeping secrets.

"Why are you staring outside? It's pitch dark."

Solace closed her eyes and reminded herself to be patient. When she turned, Grace had shut their door and kicked off her kid slippers. "I was thinking, that's all."

"About what?"

It was just like Grace to corner her with curiosity. She should've thought of an answer before she opened herself to her little sister's question. As Grace's light brown hair fell from its pins to tumble over her shoulders, she looked young and slim and pretty—full of bright ideas for teaching Billy's children.

"Thinking about how lucky Billy's kids are to have you as their governess," she hedged. "Olivia adores you already."

"Solace, you were *not* thinking about me," she interrupted pertly. "That look on your face is all about Gabe Getty. We saw you talking to him, out in the yard, so don't deny it!"

"Is that a crime? He has a lot on his mind, and—like me—he's at loose ends right now." Grace's arched eyebrow shot her a look of disbelief, so she kept talking. "We were talking about Bernadette, actually. About how she might be perfectly capable of speech, but prefers not to talk because it's to her advantage."

"That's absurd! Why would a bright little girl—" Grace perched on the edge of her bed to peel down her stockings. "I'm not even going to mention such a far-fetched notion to Eve. She's been through so much already. And besides— what would *you* know? You've had no education beyond what Mama taught us!"

But I've trained a few contrary horses in my day. And I've sold three stories! And I'm getting ideas for more characters all the time. . . .

"Just a hunch," Solace murmured. "I'm guessing Owen and Olivia will keep you busy, as well. Was the school room nice? Did you visit Eve's studio?"

As she'd hoped, Gracie's eyes lit up. "You should see all the portraits she's working on—as well as Bernadette's sketches and paintings! That little girl is amazing, the way she—"

Solace smiled to herself. As easily as she'd sidetracked her sister to avoid an inquisition about Gabe, Billy's kids would lead their new tutor through many a conversational maze to avoid doing schoolwork. But every new teacher had to learn that for herself, didn't she?

Gracie was still chattering happily when Solace tucked herself into the bunk across the narrow room. As she closed her eyes, she thought about the next section of "Daddy Was a Desperado," but Gabe Getty's lanky, bespectacled face kept floating through her mind.

Coming to Billy's suddenly felt like the right move . . . much less of an escape from her sense of stagnation at home. Maybe it was meant to be. Maybe God had brought her here because Gabe Getty needed a sympathetic ear. The way he'd watched her perform with Rex—the widening of his eyes as he'd read the editor's letter—stirred a promising warmth inside her. Though Gabe was far more sophisticated than she, he'd been sincerely impressed with her accomplishments.

Had she been too forward, suggesting he share his secrets? Most men never spoke of their troubles—especially to women.

But tomorrow would tell, maybe. And if not tomorrow, she wasn't going anywhere else anyway, was she?

Gabe gazed at the rivulets of rain running down the window. After Beulah Mae's wonderful flapjack breakfast, the children had gone upstairs with their new teacher while Billy, Eve, and Solace were tending their own tasks. Even with so many people engaged in so many pursuits, he felt at peace for the first time in weeks . . . well, *months*. Letitia had never inspired a feeling of tranquility. Her constant dramas had made the law office a haven of sanity, where he'd spent many extra hours because he had no one to talk to . . . or to share a life with at home.

He glanced at his valise, where his wife's diary beckoned him. Now that he had time alone, perhaps he could read her final entries with more clarity. Moving out of that dismal mansion had given him a sense of progress. The entries would upset him and reopen his wounds, but he'd come to Billy's to slay such emotional dragons. No time like the present.

The velvet covers of Letitia's private journal felt cool and smooth; a hint of lavender sachet and her pretty script bespoke her privileged upbringing. Much more elaborate than Solace's penmanship, it was, as his wife had always embellished her word endings with curlicues.

After only two paragraphs, he saw an aspect of Letitia that had escaped him before: her writing looked pretty on the page, but she said absolutely nothing of importance. It was all for appearance, without content—until those last two weeks, when she'd sent for that "infallible French female remedy" and eagerly awaited her salvation. Freedom from the fetus that grew within her.

Gabe tried very hard to set aside his dismay. How could any woman detest her unborn child so thoroughly? What struck him, however, was the vapid vanity behind this hatred—not to mention her total disregard for his feelings. She knew how eagerly he'd awaited a child.

Vapid vanity. Certainly not a description that applied to Solace Monroe. But why was he thinking about her? In his present state, he had nothing to offer her, nor should he burden her with his secret agony. Solace was young and had ambition. She was writing and riding and training her beloved dog. Her eyes sparkled with life and love—a *purpose*—that renewed her each day.

Gabe slumped on the edge of the bed. Letitia's words blurred, and once again he felt overwhelmed by the sad truth: his wife had never loved him—not the way he'd adored her. She hadn't possessed the capacity for that emotion because she'd never looked beyond her own whims and childish desires. He'd married her with such high hopes of giving her something worthwhile to build a life upon, but with each tip of her silver flask, Letitia had drifted further away from reality. And from him.

Why hadn't he confronted her about her laudanum habit? They could have afforded the best medical care. . . .

She lived for being sick. For being the center of everyone's attention.

He closed the diary. Gabe trembled once again, for all the

things he could have said or done and the way Letitia had
rejected his suggestions—and him. It was useless to walk
this hall of sadness again and again, but his heart didn't
know what else to do. His sigh escaped and then turned into
a sob. At least no one else would know of his failure or the
hopes and dreams that had faded long before Letitia
breathed her last.

He heard footsteps on the stairs . . . held his breath,
hoping no one would peek through the door, which stood
slightly ajar.

The energetic steps continued down the hallway and he
relaxed. His heart recited those heartrending words again. . . .

*I have ordered a packet of infallible French female
remedy, and when it arrives I shall be done with this
agony . . . I shall be happy again! Perhaps my salvation will
come in the mail today.*

Angrily, he wiped away fresh tears. Time to put away this
sad account of a woman and a life he would never really
understand, and find his own salvation. No need to burden
Billy with a situation his best friend couldn't fix.

Without knocking, Solace entered his room. With a
worried frown, she sat on the bed beside him and wrapped
her strong arms around his shoulders. She felt damp from
being out in the rain, and she smelled of horses. "Oh, Gabe,
you must be missing Letitia terribly—"

"I-don't understand," he rasped. "She didn't want the
baby. She took a powder and—"

Solace's horrified expression told him he'd crossed the
line: he'd blurted out the words he'd sworn he'd never share
with anyone. And he couldn't take them back.

Chapter Ten

Solace's stomach flip-flopped. "There was a baby?" she gasped. Here it was, that secret she'd perceived this melancholy man was concealing, and she had no idea how to make him feel better.

Gabe Getty looked ten years older; haggard and defeated. He sagged against her. Removed his spectacles to fidget with them. "I-I'm sorry," he mumbled. "Never meant to bother you with that."

"Bother *me*? My God, Gabe!" Solace held his dark gaze, trying to understand this delicate situation. "Are you saying Letitia deliberately . . . did herself in, to—"

"No, no!" he rasped. "She was ridding herself of something she never really wanted. I—"

"And you think it's your fault. You think you should've— *could've*—saved her life." Solace took a deep breath, frantically searching for words. The man in her arms sobbed softly against her shoulder as she stroked his rumpled hair. When he lifted his head, Gabe's pain made his velvet brown eyes look too big for his pale face. She saw, too, the abject humiliation of his admission.

Oh, Daddy what should I do? she prayed. *Lord, help me say something that won't make his situation even more unbearable.*

She took another deep breath, not wanting to rush. Gabe was calmer now. He looked almost peaceful, with his eyes closed and those long lashes resting against his cheek, and Solace sensed she was helping him in a way no one else could.

"Gabe," she murmured, "do you remember when we danced at your wedding? I was only a kid, and you were preoccupied with more important matters, but—"

"That dance brightened my whole afternoon," he admitted. "Weddings are fraught with emotions and unexpected difficulties, and Letitia was having a bad day."

"Even then, I sensed she'd have very few *good* days. Your bride was trussed up so tightly, she fainted at the altar," Solace recalled softly. "I vowed then never to wear a corset or let fashion enslave me." She cleared her throat, hoping she hadn't overstepped. "Letitia did that to herself, Gabe. She was on the road to self-destruction even before you married her."

The room rang with shocked silence. Had she really said that? Solace hadn't thought about Letitia's all-encompassing slavery to fashion since—well, since she and Lily and Grace had discussed it on the way home from the wedding. And now she'd just blurted out her opinion, as though she knew everything about Gabe's pretty wife while he had no idea what was going on.

"Please forgive me. That sounded very presumptuous."

Gabe inhaled deeply. "No, Solace. It's a very honest assessment of Letitia, and you said it in all sincerity."

He sighed, shaking his head. "I-I knew her need for perfection drove her to sip laudanum at the slightest ripple of agitation, yet I overlooked it. Hoped I could someday overcome her doubts. Perfectionism is a form of fear, you know." Slowly he reopened the velvet diary . . . flipped the script-filled pages that sounded as fragile as the woman who'd written them. "I was wrong to take this, but Letitia's diary revealed what my wife would not."

He gazed at her then, his face a mask of pain. "Solace," he said softly, "I've admired your honesty—your compassion— ever since that dance in the church yard. If Rex can let you shoot an apple off his head, I can trust you to look at these entries. I'll value your insights if you care to share them."

Solace's mouth opened and shut. She became fully aware that they sat on the edge of his bed, alone in this room. The air between them—the very breath they breathed—had become charged with dangerous sensations. Gabe Getty wanted her to delve into a secret so dark, so painful, that his marriage might be fully exposed to her. "Gabe, if it'll upset you more to—"

"Take a look—although I'll understand if you don't care about Letitia's thoughts and—"

"Oh, but I do!" she blurted. "I just thought I was too young, or that you'd entered a world so far beyond me that—"

"People are people, Solace. The Bancroft money didn't buy Letitia the happiness and health you've embraced all your life. Never, never underestimate yourself," he continued urgently. "You have the strength to defy social convention—to live life on your own terms. I'd do well to imitate you, sweetheart."

Again her mouth worked and no sound came out. When he smoothed the pages open and then placed the little book in her lap, Solace gazed down at the entry.

Letitia's penmanship was a work of art. This entry, from early in the year, described a Valentine's Day charity ball she and her mother were planning . . . line after line of detail about her ball gown, followed by a section where the script grew looser and lost its energy. Gabe's socialite wife bemoaned her boredom—the sameness of her days and their lack of meaning. She'd written a few gossipy entries then, but nothing about friends or anyone else other than her mother.

Nowhere did she mention Gabe. It was as though her handsome young husband didn't exist.

Solace blinked and swallowed hard. She felt wicked, peering into Letitia Getty's private life—and yet, what had the young woman revealed, really? Letitia's soul sounded as emaciated as her body.

In the last entries, the words wandered across the page like a drunkard. Letitia's desperation poured forth, and it took an effort to read to the bitter, tragic end. It might have been obvious to some folks, but Solace wasn't sure what Letitia was hinting about. Did she dare ask Gabe? This seemed like a journey deep into the female body and soul, and she wasn't sure he would want to discuss the subject.

"What's this . . . French remedy she mentions? I don't mean to upset you more by asking—"

"It's an abortifacient." Gabe squeezed her hand, smiling sadly. "A form of poison, fatal to the fetus yet supposedly tolerated by the woman who wishes to rid herself of an . . . unwanted child. This is an indelicate subject, so if—"

"I've witnessed the conception and birth of many a foal," Solace assured him. "Billy's taught me how to deliver them, and to assist the mare when problems arise."

Gabe's eyes widened. "Letitia would've fainted—or vomited—just *thinking* about animals giving birth. Thank you for understanding, Solace. You're an angel in my hour of need."

Who had ever said that to her? No one.

Who had ever gazed so deeply into her eyes, searching for answers and reassurance? Solace hoped she was providing those things for this wounded man, and that he would heal now.

She swallowed hard. Being a good listener in the face of such problems demanded a lot more of her than training Rex and her horses. Had Gabe placed his trust in her wisely? Could she handle such a responsibility, now that this older, wiser man had bared his soul. . . .

"My stars, what's going on in *here*?"

Grace scowled at them from the doorway, with her fists planted on her slender hips. Her cheeks were flushed with indignation. "You're more brazen than most, Solace," she rasped, "but I never dreamed I'd find you—well, in Mr. Getty's bedroom! On his bed, and holding him in your arms!"

Her finger trembled as she pointed it, and she looked very much like an old biddy schoolteacher. "I hate to bother Billy and Eve with this unfortunate discovery, but it's my duty—as the guardian of their children—to inform them about such a breach of propriety!"

Solace stood up quickly, her face red. "Must you always be the tattletale, Saint Grace?" she retorted. Yet guilt made her waver: anyone might draw the same conclusion her sister had. "I was offering Gabe condolences—"

"You were holding him so close, his face was in your—your *chest*!"

"I'm sorry I placed your sister in a compromising position," Gabe said in a tight voice. He stood up, gripping the diary. "Our intentions were perfectly honorable, and—"

"The road to hell is paved with good intentions," the young governess intoned. "You know that, Solace. You received the same solid Christian upbringing I did. Mama and Papa will be so disappointed in you."

"Only if you feel it's your *duty* to tell them." Without a backward glance, Solace stalked past her sister and out the door. Bitterness rose in her throat. Once more she felt like an outsider. Why was it, when she'd reached out to comfort Gabe Getty's broken heart, her efforts were perceived as inappropriate? *Brazen*, Grace had called her! How could her timing with animals be split-second accurate while she inevitably bungled her efforts with people?

As she hurried down the back stairs and out into the drizzle, Solace hoped Gabe would know how much she hurt for him—despite what anyone else thought about her feelings! How horrible, what that man had endured because his wife didn't want to bear a child! *His* child.

She ducked into her haven beneath the lilac bushes, oblivious to the rain that dripped through the leaves. Rex hopped into the swing with her, his tawny eyes shining with concern. He whimpered to get her attention.

Solace released the breath she'd been holding. Stroking

the dog's soft coat, seeing the love reflected in his expressive face, restored her perspective, just as the cool, rainy morning restored her soul.

"Maybe if I write him a story—" The drama was already unfolding in her mind. The intense emotions they'd shared made pieces fall into place as though this puzzle had been waiting for her to discover it . . . to make it all fit, so Gabe's sad situation made sense.

"I'll write it to make him feel better. Concoct a plot and characters to illustrate a husband's longing . . . a self-centered yet fearful wife," she murmured.

Rex's ears pointed skyward. His shining eyes coaxed her to go on.

Feeling better—having a purpose again—Solace hugged her dog close and let her ideas take shape. Grace would *not* ruin a perfectly honorable situation with her accusations! Positive solutions could arise from even the most questionable circumstances—and she was just the woman to make that happen!

Chapter Eleven

Gabe's hands shook as he opened a telegram the next morning. Would he ever understand women? Bad enough that Grace was holding his "indiscretion" over his head, to be revealed when it would cause the worst stir. Solace had been lost in thought at breakfast, and had avoided him ever since she'd run from his room yesterday. Eve Bristol now watched him with the intensity of a cat focused on a plump mouse: her brown hair was pulled up into a haphazard knot and she wore a paint-smeared smock that smelled of turpentine.

"We so seldom get telegrams delivered here," she explained. She glanced toward the stairway, to be sure the children hadn't heard the front bell. "Usually they relay unfortunate news, so I hope that isn't the case."

Gabe laughed softly. "What worse can befall me after Letitia's passing? I'm curious about who it's from since so few people know I'm here."

"Everything all right, Mister Gabe?" Beulah Mae peered out from the dining room, where she was brushing crumbs from the tablecloth.

"I'm sure it is. Thank you!" he replied with forced cheerfulness. Everything he did or said here was subject to the scrutiny—and comment—of the household. It took some getting used to.

As he glanced down, the name at the end of the telegram made him smile: Michael Malloy! Now there was a man who could handle a houseful of women!

WANTED YOU TO KNOW ABOUT AN OPPORTUNITY IN
ABILENE. A JUDGE HAS DIED, QUITE SUDDENLY, AND
YOUR LEGAL EXPERIENCE IN A LARGER CITY WOULD
MAKE YOU A CHOICE CANDIDATE FOR HIS REPLACEMENT.
YOU COULD LIVE WITH US AS LONG AS YOU NEED TO. LET
US KNOW. WE'LL ARRANGE INTERVIEWS.

HOPE YOU'RE DOING WELL, SON. WE PRAY FOR YOU
EVERY DAY!

MICHAEL MALLOY

Gabe grinned like a little kid. His mind was spinning with
this unexpected news, and he adjusted his glasses to read the
telegram again.

"What is it? Who's it from?" Eve asked eagerly.

"Mike Malloy," he murmured. When he looked at Billy's
wife, he suddenly knew how she'd endured so many
personal tragedies: she'd remained true to her calling.
Though Eve Bristol was a devoted mother and wife, she was
also a gifted painter. She had a *purpose*, and it gave her a
reason to get up each morning . . . to greet each day
knowing what she intended to accomplish.

Letitia never had an inkling of such things. He'd been
falling prey to his inner darkness, as well, but this message
from Mike Malloy felt like a directive from God himself.

"A judge has died in Abilene," Gabe continued. Was that
really his voice, thrumming with excitement again? "Malloy
thinks I'd be well suited to the position."

"But your wife has just died!" Furrows appeared on Eve's
pretty forehead. "Surely you need time to—"

"How long was it after you buried those little babies
before you picked up your brushes again?" he asked,
gesturing toward the cemetery plot outside. He gazed into
Eve's green eyes, which appeared serene despite her
rumpled attire. She looked like the classic scatterbrained
artist, but she looked happy. Deeply satisfied with her life.

She blinked. "My portraits had to wait during those dark days, and yet—" Eve smiled then, understanding his point. "I was sneaking back to my studio before Billy ever knew, those nights I couldn't sleep. The only way I kept my sorrow and guilt from burying me alive was to paint. It's what I do. It's who I am, down deep."

"Exactly." In his excitement, Gabe curled the telegram into a scroll and tapped his palm with it. "This is an opportunity I wouldn't have been offered if I were still in St. Louis. And practicing the law—ferreting out legalities and details to defend my clients—is what *I* do."

Eve's expression remained doubtful, but she reached for his hand. "You're welcome to stay here as long as—"

"And I appreciate your kindness," he murmured, already heading to town in his mind. "You and Billy have helped me sort things out more than you know."

Eve chuckled slyly. "I suspect Solace has been the biggest help in that regard. Are you taking her with you?"

Point-blank she'd asked him that! Before he'd even sent Malloy his reply. Gabe cleared his throat, carefully wording his reply. "Solace has always made her own decisions. Far be it from me—or any other man—to tell her what to do."

What a perfect answer! It got him out of a conversation with Eve and on the seat of a buckboard beside Billy within fifteen minutes.

Billy glanced sideways as he clapped the reins across the horse's back. "So you really want that job, bein' a judge?"

"They haven't appointed me yet. I'll have to interview with several lawyers and the other judges before—"

"In Abilene?" Billy waved him off with a snicker. "You're a shoo-in, Gabe. 'Specially if Mike talks to 'em first, 'cause the locals trust his judgment, no questions asked. And he's right—your bein' a lawyer in St. Louis makes their other judges look lackin' by comparison."

He hadn't thought that. Hadn't had a chance to think of *anything* in the short time since he'd received Mike's note, and the Bristols already had him robed, with a gavel in his hand. "I might not accept the offer. It's not like I'm destitute, or willing to take any job that comes—"

"But you're ready to move on. My kids're makin' you crazy."

No, it's the kid sister who takes the cake there. "Well, you do have a very active household," he admitted, "and Owen thinks I'm his best buddy—not that I mind that!"

Billy chuckled knowingly. "He told me you and Solace were smoochin' in his room."

"How'd he know *that*?" Gabe blurted. "And besides, it's not true! Solace and I were talking about—"

"You don't have to tell *me*. It's been written all over your face since you first laid eyes on her. The day you came here." Billy halted the horse in front of Richmond's telegraph office, his tanned face alight with glee. "My boy's figured out all the ways and places to listen in on things—same way Wesley, Christine, and I eavesdropped on Mama and Daddy when we were kids."

Gabe's stomach churned. "The heat grate? Does sound pass through the ceiling from Owen's room into . . . the classroom upstairs?"

"You get a gold star, Mr. Getty."

So that's how Grace had known when to walk in on them! Nothing he'd ever say in that house would remain confidential . . . which meant Solace—maybe everyone else—had heard him crying over Letitia's journal, too. Though he wasn't ashamed of his emotions, Gabe sensed that if anything was to develop between him and Miss Monroe here—and that was a very big, very distant *if*—the entire Bristol household would know about it before she did.

He smiled at Billy, his decision made. "You're the best friend a guy ever had, Billy. I hope you won't feel offended if I'm on the train to Abilene tomorrow."

That crinkle-eyed grin eased his mind. "Hey, you were always the one to chase after the far-flung prize while I stayed home. You'll be in good hands, though—Mercy and Mike're no strangers to takin' in the souls of the road. I reckon they'll be glad to have Solace home, too. Must be mighty quiet around there with all the kids gone."

There it was again: the foregone conclusion that Solace would follow him to Abilene.

Would she? As Gabe stepped inside the little office to reply to Malloy's telegram, his heart fluttered. He imagined her eyes, soft and dewy-brown, widening at the prospect of returning to Kansas by his side. Solace wasn't pretty in a conventional, fussy way, but she seemed to seek him out, and he enjoyed her company and her conversation . . . .

You want a lot more than talk, so stop kidding yourself. You want to see where this might lead, without a houseful of people second-guessing your every move.

What a difference a day made! He took a slip of paper from the front counter to write his reply, feeling lighter and happier than he had in months:

THANKS, MIKE. I'LL ARRIVE ON TOMORROW AFTER-NOON'S TRAIN. BLESS YOU FOR THINKING OF ME. GABE.

Chapter Twelve

Solace heard the buckboard coming down the driveway and stepped outside the barn to watch it. She'd been riding hard this morning, chasing her demons—first on Lee and then on Lincoln. With Rex sitting at her feet, panting, and her shirt and pants clinging to her warm, damp body, she felt more sure of herself now.

No more sulking because she'd been caught in Gabe's room doing nothing wrong. If Saint Grace was worried about her soul, fine. She'd found her absolution in riding hellbent-for-leather across a green pasture straight out of the Twenty-Third Psalm, and she felt closer to God now: in His world, in her own way.

At the sight of Gabriel Getty smiling beside Billy, her heart lurched. He looked *happy*! He'd made a decision and it was the right thing for him. In her mind's eye, Solace saw herself running to him, scrambling onto the buckboard as he clutched her around the waist and then . . .

Then he kissed her! Like he *meant* it. Like he thought she was the most beautiful, desirable woman in the world.

Of course, in this split-second fantasy Billy had disappeared, so she and Gabe were free to enjoy their first kiss. His mouth made her giddy, moving so confidently on hers, promising more affection in the days to come.

But then reality settled in: as Billy steered the horse in her direction, Gabe fastened his gaze on her. What did he see, that illustrious lawyer? And why did he seem so much happier now? The way he looked at her was almost as potent as that imaginary kiss, and her anticipation rose like colorful balloons straining to be free of their strings.

"You two made an early trip to town," she remarked when the buckboard stopped in front of her.

"Takin' care of business," Billy remarked cryptically. "You coulda ridden along, but you were just a fast-movin' speck flyin' in the distance."

His teasing tone bespoke good news, just like Gabe's cheerful expression. Curiosity was burning a hole in her patience. Especially since both men seemed determined to make her *ask* what they'd been doing.

"I got a telegram from Michael this morning," Gabe began.

Were his eyes actually sparkling behind his spectacles? He looked ten years younger than when he'd come here. Infinitely more alluring, with his chestnut waves tousled by the breeze. The shadows were gone from his face, too.

"Obviously good news," Solace prodded.

Why didn't he just blurt it out? Why was he searching her face, weighing his words before he spoke? She gripped the curry comb, grinning when Rex woofed at the tall man who dressed in finer clothing than anyone from around here. With his collar open and his jacket unbuttoned, Gabe looked more like a prosperous gentleman farmer than a big city barrister. And she liked the way he looked.

The lanky lawyer swung down from the buckboard and then leaned over to stroke Rex's head. "A judge from the Dickinson County court has passed on. Michael thinks I'd make a good replacement if I care to interview for the position, and live at the Triple M until I find my own place."

Her heart stuttered. "*And*?"

Her impatience made his eyes dance. "Why not? It's an opportunity I wouldn't have been offered in St. Louis."

Billy nodded emphatically. "Better to be a big fish in a small pond sometimes. You were down to nothin', and that always means God's up to somethin'," he declared. "Knew He'd steer you in a new direction, when the time was right."

And what else was the time right for? Solace's heart was pounding so hard, she couldn't swallow. Here was the perfect opportunity to escape all these eyes and ears who made her business their own. After all, why should Gabe rattle around in that spacious house outside of Abilene with only her parents for company? What would they ever find to talk about?

"When do you leave?" she asked in a tight voice.

"Tomorrow. First train west."

"I'm coming with you."

Early in the morning they left for the train station in Lexington with Gabe's boxes and trunks loaded alongside hers. Lincoln and Lee were tethered to the buckboard, while Rex sat regally behind the seat, facing backwards, to be sure the carriage behind them kept up. It was like a parade, with Asa driving Mercy, Grace and the children in the larger vehicle while Billy held the reins beside her. The wooden seat was barely wide enough for the three of them, but Solace didn't mind. Gabe sat angled sideways with his arm draped behind her on the creaking seat, and she could imagine Grace glaring at this bodily contact.

But it was a beautiful spring morning, ripe with promise, and she wouldn't waste a second of it worrying about appearances. On the train, they could finally talk without others spying and eavesdropping. In her excitement last night, she'd written the last segment of her desperado story; maybe Gabe would advise her on how to improve it.

What a fine life it would be at home again: tending the horses and livestock . . . getting to know Gabe better, when he returned from his days in the courtroom. She had no doubt whatsoever he'd get the position. Mr. Getty, with his quiet wisdom and confident, bespectacled gaze, would impress anyone who interviewed him. Abilene had come a long way from being a backward, lawless cow town but even its most educated citizens lacked this man's polish and professionalism.

"What are you smiling about?" he asked in a low voice. "You look like the cat that swallowed the canary. A mighty pleased cat."

Solace gazed into his face and was struck by something. "If you grew a beard—trimmed it along the line of your jaw—you'd look a *lot* like Abraham Lincoln. Except younger and much more dashing!" she added quickly. "You're going to get that appointment, I just know it! But if you looked like Mr. Lincoln, well—"

"I think your wild imagination's talkin', Solace," Billy said with a chuckle. "But I s'pose a woman looks at such things from a different angle."

She nipped back a quick retort: Billy had called her a woman! Now *that* was new.

"Actually, I've considered growing a beard. Just for a change in appearance." Gabe shifted slightly, which brought his hip into contact with hers. "They say it adds a look of maturity and wisdom, and jurors and lawyers would respond better to a judge with such qualities. I'll try that—after the interviews."

Solace's pulse shot up. He would consider a beard! Not a flicker of an eyelash suggested Gabe found her idea silly or trite. And he liked her writing . . . took comfort in her presence and her touch . . . hadn't been afraid to show his dark emotions the other day. Most men acted stoic and unfeeling rather than reveal their tears, and Solace felt honored that he'd entrusted them—and Letitia's diary—to her without apology.

She found everything about Gabriel Getty very appealing right now, mostly because he encouraged a Solace Monroe no one else even knew about. His interest in her raised her a notch closer to his level, and she liked that feeling. A lot.

When they arrived at the train station, Billy and Gabe

carried the large camelback trunks and boxes to the platform, where the porters would load them on the train. The carriage had caught up with them, so Asa and Beulah Mae, plus Gracie, Eve, and her brood of redheads watched the proceedings eagerly.

"I *love* to ride the train!" Owen announced hopefully. "I wanna see the ranch where Daddy grew up!"

"So many people!" Olivia sang out as she watched the railway workers and passengers in rapt fascination.

"Oh, the station in St. Louis is truly huge," Grace joined in. "With so many tracks and trains coming from all over the nation, it's quite an experience."

Solace nodded, not really paying attention to her sister as Billy led her two horses and Rex into the livestock car. It wasn't fair that her dog couldn't sit in the seat beside her, she thought. He'd never misbehave. Rex loved to ride and look out the window—and he loved it even more when folks stopped to admire his unusual markings.

When she felt a tug on her skirt, she looked down to see Bernadette gazing up at her with a stricken expression. Solace swung the little girl to her shoulder, and when those chubby arms and legs wrapped around her, she hugged the toddler close.

"I love you, too, sweetheart," she murmured against that downy cheek. Bernadette's rust-colored curls felt like silky feathers against her face. "Where I'm going, there aren't any little girls anymore. I'm going to miss you so much—"

"*Nooooo.* Don't go! Don't *gooooo.*"

Solace's eyes widened, while Eve and Grace and the other children crowded around. "What did you say, Bernadette?" she rasped. "You-you're talking!"

That impish face, only inches from hers, turned bright pink as tears streamed from Bernadette's crystal blue eyes.

"It-it's a miracle!" Grace proclaimed.

"What did she say? What did she say!" Olivia demanded.

"Don't go, Solace," Bernadette begged again. Her voice

sounded husky but the words were perfectly clear. "Stay and play—with *me*!"

Eve was now peering into her youngest daughter's face, clearly astonished. "Are you telling me, young lady, that you've known how to talk all along?" she demanded.

The little girl watched for Solace's reaction. Then she nodded gleefully.

Beulah Mae laughed richly. "Why's I not surprised? That'n, she's had the look of a sly fox since the day she's borned!" the cook exclaimed. "Just bidin' her time 'til she had somethin' worthwhile to say. Weren't ya, missy?"

Bernadette laughed despite her tears. "I's sly!" she mimicked.

"I figured you for a trickster all along," Solace teased quietly. She rubbed the tip of her nose to Bernadette's, pulled between staying at this little girl's special request, and going along with Gabe.

"Why *Solace*?" Grace asked pointedly. "All this time, you could've been talking to—"

"We believed she couldn't respond with words, so we talked *for* her," Eve mused aloud. Her green eyes shone with tears of joy, yet she appeared perturbed. "You let everyone else pander to you—baby you along!—because—Billy!" she called across the busy platform. "Billy, come here!"

His wife's urgent cry brought Billy trotting over to them, followed closely by Gabe. "Everything all right? We're almost finished loadin'—"

"Bernadette's talking!" Olivia piped up. "She told Solace not to go! It's like Solace knows magic, because her horses and Rex—and now the baby—all do what they're supposed to when she's around!"

Solace laughed, but her heart swelled. Billy stood beside her now, gawking raptly at his youngest child, while Gabe . . . Gabe Getty was gazing straight at *her*. Looking into her eyes with a wonder his glasses magnified.

"Maybe Olivia has a point," Billy replied. "If Solace can

coax this pixie to talk, maybe we could persuade her to stay with us and train more horses. What do you say, Solace?"

She was still caught up in Gabe's rapt expression—until she saw her sister's fallen face. Solace breathed deeply and framed a diplomatic answer. "That's why you have *Grace* with you," she said firmly. She looked at Owen and Olivia, to instill some respect for their new teacher. "Miss Malloy is a lot smarter than I am, and trained as a teacher. And now that Bernadette's talking, she'll devote more time to *you* two."

Billy chuckled. "We'd love to have you, if you care to stay, Solace."

"I appreciate that, Billy. And Eve, I thank you for opening your home, and for sharing your children with me," she added. "But I have other things to—"

"You're chasing after Gabe," Grace muttered. "He's your latest, greatest novelty, and when you've tired of him, you'll move on. You flit like a bee, from flower to flower, Solace. Without regard for anyone else's feelings."

A stunned silence rang around the family circle.

Solace's first inclination was to snap back at her little sister for being such a know-it-all—jealous because someone like Gabe Getty had shown an interest in *her*! But the quiver of Gracie's lower lip stopped her.

More than envy played over Grace's delicate, pretty features: she had greatly anticipated teaching Bernadette sign language, and now her thunder had been stolen. Her studies were for naught.

Although Solace hadn't deliberately done this—who could have known about Bernadette's knack for keeping silent?—she understood the sting of being upstaged by her sisters. Reminding herself to remain patient, and to redirect everyone's attention, Solace stepped toward her younger sister.

"Bernadette, did you know Miss Malloy is my little sister? That means she's a lot like me, so I know you'll love her, too. And guess what!" she continued, smiling into the child's inquisitive eyes. "Your new governess *adores* little girls like you! She'll be the most wonderful teacher you could ever have, sweetie. I promise I'll come see you again real soon, all right?"

"No!" the littlest Bristol blurted. "I want *you*, Solace! I wanna ride your horses and teach Rex tricks and—"

"Would you listen at that little angel a-talkin'?" Asa murmured. "*Years* I's gone, prayin' to hear that little voice. I think we's due for a big celebration back at the house! Cake and ice cream—just like for a birthday, don't you s'pose, Beulah Mae?"

"And don't we know how this little imp loves a lemon puddin' cake?" the old cook cooed at Bernadette. "I wanna hear you tell about your paintin's, too. 'Bout how those bright ideas goes from your head into them tiny fingers holdin' the paintbrush. You reckon you could tell ole Beulah Mae 'bout your special talent when we get home?"

When the old woman opened her stout arms, Bernadette reluctantly loosened her hold on Solace. And once the child had rested her freckled cheek against Beulah Mae's coffee-colored one, Solace knew not to tarry too long.

"We'd best find our seats," she said, hugging Olivia and Eve. She squeezed Billy, too, and rumpled his son's thick cinnamon hair. "Thank you all for making a place for me, and—and Gracie, I'm *so* proud you've taken up your life's work now. You're a born teacher, and these kids are lucky to have you."

She wrapped an arm around her sister's slender shoulders, not surprised that Grace's hug was lackluster. Best to be going, before she unwittingly rubbed more salt in her sister's wounded feelings.

As she stepped up into the coach car, the Bristols' good-byes followed her. Solace swallowed a knot. It was difficult to leave this family behind. She'd grown up with Billy and Asa encouraging her every day, and life at home just wasn't the same without them.

When Gabe took his seat beside her, however, her excitement returned. "I-I hope you don't mind my inviting myself to Abilene," she gushed. "But it's so deadly dull at the Triple M these days, I thought I'd spare you those evenings when Mama and Papa will close in on you for conversation."

As the train lurched away from the platform, Solace waved from the window. The cluster of dear people waving back made her sad.

Gabe leaned across her to wave at them—and then he moved to sit in the seat opposite hers. They both waved then, until the Bristols and her sister were specks obscured by distance and the steam coming from the engine.

And then darned if Gabe didn't stay over there, watching her with an odd look on his face.

"I-I finished my story about the little boy whose daddy was an outlaw," Solace said, reaching for her valise. "Would you read it and tell me where it needs fixing?"

"I'll be happy to." He stiffened . . . almost as if he were digging his boot heels into the floor to keep from sliding toward her. "But first you need to understand how things will have to be between us, before you jump to any . . . romantic conclusions."

Solace blinked. What on earth did he mean by that?

Chapter Thirteen

Gabe felt her pain as though it were his own—all the more reason to set Solace Monroe straight before she assumed things about their relationship. And yes, before he fell head over heels for her.

She was eighteen but sheltered; Solace probably hadn't entertained many beaux, because the Triple M was about three miles from town—and because she suffered no fools. Most men her age would be completely baffled by her talents and insights. When he'd been eighteen, he was socially inept despite his academic talents, and he would have acted like an idiot in her presence, too.

But how could he tell her she was the most extraordinary young woman he'd ever met, without making her think he shared her giddy excitement about traveling with him? He was older and had just lost his wife. The intense joy Solace Monroe stirred in him felt totally inappropriate.

Liar, liar, pants on fire!

That was Billy Bristol's voice in his mind, remembered from childhood. Billy clearly knew what was going on between him and Solace: there'd been no mistaking the twinkle in his brilliant blue eyes. That look was his most compelling reason to have this difficult discussion on the train. Once she got home, Miss Monroe would have the emotional advantage over him.

"Solace, you and I have shared some . . . remarkable insights these past few days," he began, wishing he sounded more confident. "I truly appreciate your comfort and compassion . . . your astute observations about my wife, after you read her diary."

"Don't beat around the bush, Gabe." She crossed her arms, already disappointed in him. It took all his strength not to sit beside her again and grab her hand . . . not to say things just to bring the sunshine back to those sparkling brown eyes.

"Fair enough," he said with a sigh. Several people were seated within earshot, so he leaned his elbows on his knees. "You and I have become confidants in a very short time, sweetheart, so it's only fair to tell you I'm not ready to court another woman. It'll take my heart some time to heal. And meanwhile, it's not fair to keep you from meeting other men who—"

"That's horse hockey. Did you learn how to dress it up and take the stink out of it while you were practicing law?"

Gabe's jaw dropped. Solace wasn't smiling one little bit, yet a dimple winked at him from the side of her mouth.

He had the sudden urge to kiss it. Where had *that* come from?

"Gabe, we've been over this." She, too, leaned her elbows on her knees, which brought her face down to his level, about a foot away. "I *know* you've been married and have practiced a profession for several years now—and I should *hope* so, since you're nine years older than I. And I *know* you wanted to do right by your wife. And it'll take a while to recover from what loving her cost you."

She sighed, lowering her voice when a few passengers glanced their way. "You enjoy talking to me and watching me ride, and making me feel special—because you *do* that, Gabe," she whispered beneath the rhythmic clatter of the train. "You let me be myself—a woman who could be the other half of *you*, and heal your wounds. Everybody else in this world thinks I'm too outspoken, or too much the tomboy, or too wrapped up in my animals, but I never got that feeling about you. Guess I was wrong, huh?"

His mouth went dry. He felt two inches tall. How had this trick-riding sharpshooter of a cowgirl reduced him to a flea, when he could face any high-powered lawyer in any courtroom while defending a client who'd broken the law?

"This isn't easy for me, Solace," he protested. "Please try to understand when I say—"

"I don't believe in *trying*, Mr. Getty. I either do things full-on, or I don't." She leveled that gaze at him again, and when her eyes lingered on his lips, he sensed she wanted to kiss him despite her tough talk. "I understand what you've been saying, but my feelings for you are real, Gabe. I'm not some gawky little girl chasing after you because I don't know any better. I'm all grown-up now. And I've made up my mind."

Solace straightened then. Her voice carried with quiet clarity, straight into his soul. "I'm going after you with the same determination I use to train a new horse. And you've never seen a horse I couldn't convince, have you?"

Gabe let out a helpless laugh. "You're very persistent."

"I don't take *no* for an answer," she whispered intently. "And just like I felt Bernadette was holding out on us— because she's too bright for her little britches—I know you need me in your life, Gabe Getty. I know you love me, too," she added in a voice he could barely hear. "And just as I've persuaded my horses and Rex to trust me completely, by taking away their fear, I'll have you eating out of my hand, too. Once you believe that, you'll be a mighty happy man, Gabe. Mark my words."

Where did she get this ability to twist him like a ribbon and tie him into a knot? Where did such confidence come from? Such savvy? Lord, but he wanted to grab her and kiss her silly—to shock some sense into her, the way she'd smacked him with her simple truth.

But if he gave in to that urge, if he lost control of his feelings now, he'd be doing them both a disfavor. Wouldn't he? He couldn't properly court her while he was about to throw himself into a new career that would require nights of deep reading and his full concentration.

He'd lost his heart to one woman, and he still ached from the false hopes he'd strung himself along with. What if he was just as wrong about Solace?

"You have your opinion and I have mine," he murmured. "Time will tell who's right, won't it?"

She chortled, making that dimple wink again. "I've got all the time in the world, Gabe. It's not like other men are beating my door down, and my horses and Rex aren't going anywhere, either. I would ask you one favor, though."

He raised an eyebrow. "What's that?"

"Don't tell anybody about my writing. We're keeping that between you and me."

"But your family would be proud—"

"Mama might not take it so well that I twisted Daddy's name around," she pointed out. "And, frankly, I don't want everybody fussing over me, like they had no idea I could put pen to paper. You understand that kind of stuff better than they do."

"It's your place to break that kind of news, anyway," he agreed. "But don't underestimate your parents. Your mother was educated at Miss Vanderbilt's academy, after all, and—"

"Please, Gabe. Let's handle it my way."

He smiled. Then he realized she'd spun another gossamer web: Solace's talent would be one more thing she shared with him and no one else. A secret like that gave her even more power over him; it made him the guardian of an important part of her life, which linked her more closely to him. They had little in common when it came to training animals—or riding and shooting—but the interplay of words and ideas was a powerful connecting point. Something he'd never shared with Letitia.

The remainder of the train ride was quiet. He read "Daddy Was a Desperado" and sincerely enjoyed it. Solace showed amazing insight, speaking through a boy who grew up among the outlaws his father ran with, but who led a law-abiding life after his father was killed during a bank robbery. Gabe recognized details from Wesley Bristol's career, but the undefiled voice of honesty belonged to Billy. Not surprising, considering how Solace had idolized his best friend since she'd been big enough to sit a horse in front of him.

This thought brought back images from this morning, when Solace was holding Bernadette while the child begged her to stay. The moment had held great power, even from across the busy platform: Solace's love for that little girl had radiated like the morning sun. She talked to Billy's children straight on, too, without condescending to them. She *expected* things from those children; she presented ideals and challenges for them to live up to, without withholding her love when they went astray. She would make a wonderful mother someday.

Admit it. You want Solace to raise your children with the same unconditional love she gives to the Bristol kids.

Gabe sighed and gazed out his window. Everything led him back to the young lady sitting across from him. Solace had studied him while he read—watching for reactions to her story, yes, but also sizing him up as a man.

And he liked that. If an amazing woman like Solace Monroe found him interesting enough to admire, maybe he was a worthwhile man, after all. A desirable man, perhaps.

He glanced sideways, to see that Solace sat with her nose pressed to her window. She looked like an eager child as she gazed toward the outskirts of Abilene.

"What do you see?" he murmured.

She giggled. "Off in the distance, toward the fairgrounds, some big tents are going up, Gabe. Do you suppose the circus has come to town?"

He peered out again, but the sun's glare in his spectacles obscured his view. "No doubt you'll head that direction at the earliest possible moment."

"Will you come with me?" Her face enthralled him when she lit up this way. Such a special beauty she had—such a passion, which was lacking in most people.

"We'll go after my interview, all right?"

As the train approached the Abilene station, Gabe prepared himself for another emotional onslaught. The Malloys were people of deep faith who considered him more family than friend. Their sympathy over Letitia's death would be sincere, but all the more difficult to bear. While living among the Bancrofts, he'd forgotten how some families supported each other and talked things out. He'd become accustomed to silence, or to conversations that only skimmed the surface—except, of course, when Henrietta had informed him of his many shortcomings.

The sight of Mercy and Michael Malloy standing on the platform—waving eagerly and keeping pace with him when they spotted him in the window—made him realize how much he'd missed out on when he moved to St. Louis. Had it not been for Agatha Vanderbilt's special affection while he studied under Arthur Bancroft, he'd have existed in an emotional vacuum.

He'd never realized, until he stepped down from the train into Mike and Mercy's embrace, how insulated his life had been these past eleven years. How isolated he'd truly felt.

"Welcome back, Gabe! We're so glad to see you!" Mercy cried as she hugged him hard.

Michael's face, more weathered now but still a beacon, lit up as he wrapped an arm around Gabe's waist. "We've missed you, son. Good to have you back."

Son. The simplest of words, yet it brought back a flood of feelings he hadn't known since he was a boy. Michael had called Billy his son, too—at a time when both of them had been left to grow up without their parents. This steadfast man and his wife had filled in a lot of important gaps.

Gabe stepped back to help Solace descend the metal stairs, blinking away the dampness in his eyes. She grasped his hand as she greeted her mildly surprised parents, and he didn't let go of her. Instead, he gazed briefly at the small, familiar train station—at people dressed in simple, hardworking denim and calico—and drank in the two loving faces he'd missed more than he knew.

"Thank you," he breathed. "It's good to be home."

Chapter Fourteen

"Whatever you did to bring Solace home, I thank you for it."

Gabe turned from his box of books to look at Mercy Malloy. She wore her brown hair in a simple upsweep now, with a few silver strands shining at her temples. Her clothing looked more stylish than when she'd been a homesteader's wife, but she still radiated the same solid, sincere warmth he'd always felt in her presence.

He grinned, following her gaze out the window. The young lady in question was carrying water to the trough in the corral, while Lincoln and Lee followed her every move. Rex was at her heels, his whole body wagging with the happiness of returning to his own turf.

"I had little to do with her decision," he replied. "No one really convinces Solace to do anything."

Mercy's laughter rang in the small room that had once been Billy and Joel's. "You've hit the nail on the head, Gabe! Solace has always marched to her own unique cadence—not that she's wrong to do that."

Gabe cut the box's string with his penknife, waiting for the rest of this subject to present itself. Mercy, perhaps because she missed her children and the ones she'd raised as her own, yearned for more conversation. Or was she fishing for information? Things her unusual daughter might not mention to her parents?

"I'm a bit concerned for her, though. She seems eager to marry and have a family, yet she rejects—or repels—every young man who makes overtures." Mercy smiled at him, as though she trusted him to keep these thoughts in confidence.

"While Lily and Grace probably dismissed more young men than we'll ever know, they at least have the . . . social graces most men look for in a mate."

She shook her head, although she was smiling. "Poor Solace! She feels like a fish out of water when her sisters shine at what they do, yet she swims upstream to avoid conforming to the norm. She chooses to go against the tide."

"She's her own woman," Gabe agreed. He slipped a few of his books into the shelf Mercy had emptied for him, wondering how much to reveal. After all, Solace had stated her case very clearly on the train. And while part of him was thrilled that she'd chosen *him*, he wanted her declarations to remain a secret—something that would have a chance to germinate and grow between the two of them before anyone else drew conclusions about their affection.

"Lily and Grace probably appear more popular because they *do* go with the flow," he remarked quietly. "And both have clear visions of their missions right now. But so does Solace."

He glanced outside again, to where that sturdy figure in denim pants put her geldings through their paces. Rex watched for her signal, and then at precisely the right moment, he leaped up to ride the inside horse. "She's good with animals, but do you know of her way with children? Bernadette Bristol *talked* this morning, begging her to stay!"

Mercy's eyes widened and she clapped her hands together. "No! You mean she just blurted out—"

"Fully formed sentences, yes. She spoke quite clearly and made her point with childlike eloquence," he went on, happy for this conversational side trip. "Solace had suspected all along that the little dodger could talk, but she didn't *want* to."

He sighed at the memory of that moment at the train station. "It was a sight to behold. Solace was hugging Billy's little girl to her hip . . . having a matter-of-fact conversation," he murmured. "Now they consider Solace a miracle worker, yet Solace—and Beulah Mae—weren't amazed at all."

"How relieved Eve must've been, after all the doctors they've seen these past few years." Mercy paused, assessing what he'd just said. "Your reason for remaining mute after your family died was different, of course, but I imagine you rejoiced in a special way when Bernadette began to speak. We were all so thrilled when that fur-ball of a puppy brought you out of your silence!"

Gabe's heart stilled for a moment. How like this woman, to understand his childhood grief as no one else had. "I was so happy to see Billy's little girl was normal—not to mention extremely intelligent. And I was delighted that it was Solace who got Bernadette talking."

"And how did Gracie react to that?" Mercy asked pensively. "She's studied a great deal, hoping to bring language to a child we assumed was mute."

Gabe smiled at the memory of Solace's going-away speech. "Solace praised Grace's teaching ability and love of little children, as though her younger sister possessed far greater skills than she. It's not true," he added pointedly, "but she made a convincing case that put Grace in a positive light."

He grinned, and then proceeded carefully. "I can't say Grace was as diplomatic about lifting up Solace's abilities."

"We've seen some catfights that would curl your hair." Mercy tugged playfully on his waves, as though he were still a kid. "With three girls only a year apart in their ages, and with such different temperaments, perfectly polite dinner conversations could escalate into clawing matches in the blink of an eye. Poor Michael!" she exclaimed with a laugh. "He knew when the fur was about to fly, but couldn't stop it. It was much easier with Billy and Joel—even though Joel's remained a vagabond."

Gabe recalled Michael's young son . . . the dark cloud that

had hovered around him even when he was a child. "He was only ten when he ran off, wasn't he? And you never hear from him?"

She shrugged, and her eyes lost their sparkle. "He drops in now and again. Stays until his father asks what he wants to *do* with his life, and then goes on his way."

"I'm sorry," Gabe murmured. "That must worry you."

Mercy smiled bravely at him. "Joel's twenty-one now. If he's survived this long without begging for money or shelter or forgiveness, he's figured out how to take care of himself, I guess."

"Yes, I guess he has." Gabe tried to picture the wiry, wary man Joel Malloy must have become. But he was twenty-one now? It was one more way life on the Kansas prairie had moved on without him while he'd lived in St. Louis.

Yet returning to this ranch . . . being here in the home Michael Malloy had built as Mercy's wedding present, brought back a rush of emotions he hadn't anticipated. Because he'd grown up with his Aunt Rachel and Uncle George on the neighboring homestead, after his family was slaughtered in Colorado, he'd never really felt he *belonged* anywhere. He'd felt beholden for every meal, every article of clothing the Clarks had provided. Visiting Billy and playing with the four dogs had been the highlights of his childhood. Judd Monroe and Michael Malloy stood out as monumental men in his early life, and Mercy . . . well, Mercy was a woman like no other.

"Thanks to you and Mike—and your Aunt Agatha—I've never had to go begging, either," he said quietly. "It seems like a lifetime ago when I became Arthur Bancroft's apprentice. I owe you so much for encouraging me beyond the possibilities I had as a kid on the Clark's farm, and now you've found me another potential position. Saying thank you will never be enough."

"Oh, Gabe, we were happy to." Mercy opened her arms and he entered an embrace that warmed and enfolded him.

She hugged him hard, as though she needed this moment as much as he did, and he wrapped his arms around her with a sense of utter love that he hadn't felt in years. *Years*.

Mercy exhaled, smiling up at him with shiny brown eyes. "We don't want to upset you or dredge up uncomfortable feelings, but Michael and I hope you'll unburden yourself about your wife and her . . . untimely demise."

Did they sense that Letitia had brought about her own death? Or was this Mercy's intuition talking? Either way, she'd probably read him like a book if he brought up the subject of his difficult marriage.

"Thank you," he rasped. "Letitia's parents never issued me that invitation. They blamed me for her decline in health and spirits, and—well, thank goodness for Billy and his family. And where would I be without you and Michael?"

"I suspected as much," she murmured. Then she eased herself from his embrace. "I should let you unpack and collect your thoughts before your meetings tomorrow. Whether or not you're appointed, Gabe, I want you to know how proud I am! You've come so far, and it's almost like my own son is interviewing for this honor."

I want you to know how proud I am . . . almost like my own son. . . .

Had his heart ever felt this full? As Mercy left the room, Gabe looked out the window again, overcome with emotion. Solace was standing barefoot on one of her bays, balanced gracefully as it cantered around the corral; her smile looked absolutely ethereal as her hair drifted behind her in the breeze, as though she were floating effortlessly.

Just as effortlessly as she rode into my life . . . into my soul, he realized. And though it was a wondrous thing to be here among the Malloys, where their love warmed and uplifted him, Gabe felt a twinge of apprehension.

Things were happening awfully fast. What if this happy bubble burst? What if he didn't meet unspoken expectations this family—especially Solace—had? Where could he go from here?

Solace tried her best not to fidget as Papa opened the well-thumbed Bible after supper that night. She'd barely tasted Mama's stew, made from beef, potatoes, and lots of carrots—thick with gravy, the way she liked it. Who could eat, with Gabe Getty seated across the table? He'd stolen several glances at her . . . maybe because she'd changed into a clean dress? Or because she'd pulled her hair up? Ordinarily she didn't care how she looked at dinner, except that her hands were clean. But tonight, without noisy distractions from children or the tale-telling her sisters had often engaged in, Solace felt more inclined to present herself well.

After all, Gabe expected the woman in his life to be a lady, didn't he? He might admire her skills with horses and a gun, but no ordinary cowgirl would do for a man about to take his place on the bench in the Dickinson County courthouse.

Papa cleared his throat and gave her a knowing look. "It seems right to recall a couple of important points Jesus made about who we were created to be, on this evening before Gabe interviews." He ran his finger down the page to find the verse—and Solace took that spare second to glance across the table.

Gabe was looking at her, too. Maybe he'd take her to the fairgrounds after their devotions. The circular at the train station said it was Apache Pete's Wild West Extravaganza she'd seen in the distance. From the looks of all those tents, it was a show such as Abilene hadn't hosted in years.

" 'Ye are the salt of the earth,' " her papa began—

I can taste those salted peanuts they'll be selling. . . .

" 'But if the salt have lost his savour, wherewith shall it be salted? It is thenceforth good for nothing, but to be cast out, and trodden under foot of men.' "

Or horses. Or buffalo—might be some of those at the show, too!

" 'And ye are the light of the world,' " he continued with a lift in his voice. " 'A city that is set on a hill cannot be hid—' "

Neither can all those tents! What a spectacular event this'll be!

" 'Neither do men light a candle, and put it under a bushel, but on a candlestick; and it giveth light unto all that are in the house.' "

I can see those flickering torches . . . . smell their burning oil, and the scents of manure and horses being worked into a lather . . .

" 'Let your light so shine before men, that they may see your good works, and glorify your Father which is in Heaven.' "

Does he see the light in my eyes? I feel them glowing whenever he—

"And how do you interpret that passage, Solace? What do you think Christ would expect of Gabe, if he becomes a judge?"

She blinked, and then blurted, "Seems to me Jesus is saying that life's a lot like a-a Wild West show!"

Why was everyone staring at her? Her parents wore odd expressions and Temple Gates, the Negro teacher she'd known since childhood, looked downright flummoxed.

"A Wild West show, Solace?" Her dark pink lips lifted as she laid a conversational trap for her former student.

Solace cleared her throat as heat rushed into her cheeks. "Why, yes! God created those, too, you know! As a way for horses and sharpshooters and other performers to show off the *glories* of the West—as a part of His handiwork."

Gabe chortled. "You're digging yourself a deeper pit," he said lightly. "Michael was exhorting me to use my gifts. To shine as an example of how Christ would listen to cases and come to decisions."

"Which would be a blessing indeed, considering how . . . uninspired Hannibal Prescott, our other judge, has proven to be," her mother chimed in.

"I'm a shining example, too," Solace countered staunchly. "In the arena, and right here where I can make the rest of you look so good for *listening* to the scripture passage. Please excuse me for letting my mind wander. I stand humbled and corrected."

She smiled at Mama, Papa, and Temple in turn. Her teasing speech didn't pardon her wandering attention, but at least she hadn't given away the true nature of her thoughts. She focused intently on the man who'd raised her, a demurely penitent expression fixed on her face. Being raised with two paragon sisters had taught her plenty about how to appear angelic, and this little slip wasn't going to upset her. Not much of *anything* would upset her, now that she'd have time to convince Gabe Getty he loved her.

"I suggested that the committee who will appoint our new judge convene tomorrow afternoon at two," Papa said, "thinking you'll have time to prepare yourself for their questions by then, Gabe."

"Thanks, Michael. I can certainly do that."

Gabe's expression turned pensive, as though considering what he'd say . . . how he'd present himself for this meeting. Once again Solace recalled those pictures of Abraham Lincoln in her school books. More than twenty years after his assassination, this influential president was held up as the example of compassion and honor all public figures should aspire to. She was about to point out this resemblance to her parents, when the doorbell rang.

Temple sprang from her chair, her dark face alight with curiosity. "Now who could that be? Good thing we made a fresh peach cobbler."

"Yes, invite them in!" Mama bustled toward the kitchen to prepare dessert, while her papa placed the Bible back on its stand on the sideboard. As always, he left it open to the passage he'd read, in case anyone wanted to consult that scripture further.

But the familiar laughter coming from the front hall made

Solace forget all about the sweetness of peach cobbler and her romantic notions. Temple's surprised greeting rang out, and at the sound of the visitor's voice, Mama and Papa rushed to the foyer, too.

Gabe appeared as astounded as she did. Gentleman that he was, he rose from his place at the table and looked toward the doorway. Solace stood up, too. She crossed her arms, reminding herself to be a candle on a candlestick rather than a torch tossed on a haystack—if only because Gabe should see how mature she could be. But she hadn't counted on this intrusion, and she wouldn't take it sitting down!

"When I heard Gabriel was to interview in Abilene," the guest gushed, "I packed and came home as soon as I could! He's going to need encouragement and guidance and—" Lily rushed into the dining room, and then halted with her mouth hanging open. "Solace! What are *you* doing here?"

Solace took in her sister's perfectly coifed golden hair, the skin as fair as fresh cream, and the fashionable fuchsia traveling suit that displayed her womanly figure to perfection. "This is home, remember?" she replied in a coiled voice. "It's nice to see you, too, Lily. What a fine surprise."

Chapter Fifteen

"Maybe you should ride into town with me," Gabe teased the next morning. "Might be your best chance for peace and quiet today."

Mike chuckled, but went pensive as he tested the girth strap on the Morgan he'd just saddled. "When they were younger, Lily and Solace were so close—despite their differences in temperament—they shared that bedroom without a squabble."

"Now they can't occupy the same *house* without tearing into each other," Gabe said with a sigh. "I'm seeing a different Solace than I found at Billy's. The sharp-edged Lily we heard last night never showed her face at Miss Vanderbilt's academy, either."

"Aunt Agatha would tolerate none of it. Just as I don't intend to." Malloy's face looked older. His two grown-up daughters had battled bitterly over the least little things last night, until Mercy had marched into their room to silence them. "While you're away, the girls and I are going to have a chat. I assure you things will be different—and we'll be celebrating your success—when you return."

Gabe swung into the saddle, shaking his head. "I'm truly sorry—I never intended to be the reason those two turned into—"

"What fellow doesn't dream of being fought over by two wonderful women?" Michael laughed and patted the horse's rump. "Believe me, Gabe, you did nothing to cause this uproar. For the first time in their lives, Solace and Lily want the same thing. I wouldn't blame you a bit if you took a room in town, although you're welcome to stay at the Triple M as long as you want."

"Thanks, Michael."

"Good luck and Godspeed today." Malloy watched the young lawyer ride toward the road, dressed in a fresh suit and shirt that would surely impress the men he talked with. His two daughters had noticed Gabriel Getty's fine attire, as well . . . he wasn't surprised to see the curtains flutter in that upstairs bedroom—and in the dining room—as Gabe rode off.

And now, while visions of that lonely lawyer danced in their heads, it was time for him to temper their thoughts—or at least their tongues. Mercy had always provided guidance into the feminine graces, but she had better ways to spend her day than mediating their daughters' arguments. It was a far cry from the past weeks when the house had echoed with stillness, and he and Mercy had talked constantly about having their brood back.

Michael stepped in through the kitchen door, listening . . . gauging the mood of his home. Temple Gates turned from the sink, where she was washing the breakfast dishes.

"Hey there, Mister Michael. I can see what you're about, and I've asked God to put love on everyone's tongues," she remarked with a sad smile. "Guess we thought our girls were above the squabbles other families talk about."

"I grew up with a raft of sisters, so I'm no stranger to catfights," he reminded her quietly. "That doesn't mean I'll let them wreak havoc in my home, however."

"Yes, sir. We all must learn how to get along. How to share—although that's not the solution we're after here."

"Nope. Not when two eager hearts are out to win the same man." He passed through the dining room then, where Lily stood at the sideboard, thumbing through the big family Bible.

"It's good to have you home, sweetheart. I think—"

"Is it?" she challenged. Her strained face told of a tearful night and a troubled heart. "Then why don't you tell Solace to behave herself? She has no right to—no idea what Gabriel needs, now that he's lost his wife! He's starting a whole new life, moving into a new profession—"

"And he can make his decisions without you hovering over him!" Solace clattered down the stairs dressed in pants and a plaid shirt that she'd worn a time or two. She'd stepped in something out in the corral.

Lily wrinkled her nose. "Why would he want *you* around, horrid as you smell? Go back to the barn where you belong, so—"

"Sit down, girls. I've had enough." Michael pointed to chairs on opposite sides of the dining room table. "You've both forgotten a lot more than manners. You've forgotten who you are, and *whose* you are."

In the past, such a stern warning would have been enough: Solace and Lily knew when they'd stepped over the line. Yet each sat simmering in her own purpose . . . her own narrow, selfish, competitive purpose. Since neither daughter was really listening to him, Michael took the Bible from its stand and placed it in front of Lily.

"Let's review what the apostle Paul taught us about Christlike living, shall we?" he asked quietly. "Maybe you won't take *my* advice, but I've never known you to turn away from the ultimate source of wisdom and direction."

Lily exhaled impatiently. "Papa, it's all well and good to go quoting the Bible, but I don't recall a single passage that recommends a woman—or a *girl*—spend her time at manly activities, and then expect somebody like Gabriel to pay her any attention!"

Solace slapped the tabletop. "That's the most ludicrous— if you weren't so holier-than-thou—"

"Enough!" Michael sat down so he was on their level—so they couldn't miss a single flicker of his disappointment. "Lily, since you've made the Lord's work your own, I want you to turn to the passage in first Corinthians—or its sister passage in Romans—and refresh our memories about how God created us with different gifts."

Lily raised her eyebrow at her sister. Her fingers danced over the crisp pages, making swift, proud music until she found the book and chapter she searched for.

"Romans twelve," she huffed. "Beginning at verse six. 'Having then gifts differing according to the grace that is given to us, whether prophecy, let us prophesy according to the proportion of faith; or ministry, let us wait on our ministering: or he that teacheth on teaching; or he that exhorteth, on exhortation: he that giveth, let him do it with simplicity; he that ruleth, with diligence; he that sheweth mercy, with cheerfulness.' "

Lily looked across the table triumphantly. "Is that the passage you referred to, Papa? While I see many fine gifts listed in Paul's verses, none of them mentions training for a dog and pony show, when we should aspire to—"

"Let me see that!" Solace stretched across the table to pull the Bible toward her. As she ran her finger over the page, Michael smiled. Watching his girls outdo each other in their biblical knowledge pleased him—and it gave them something better to bicker about.

"Same chapter, but the verses right before that!" Solace crowed. "Seems you left this part out, Princess Lily! 'For I say, through the grace given unto me, to every man that is among you, not to think *of himself* more highly than he ought to think; but to think soberly, according as God hath dealt to every man the measure of faith. For as we have many members in one body, and all members have not the same office: so we *being* many, are one body in Christ, and every one members of another.'

"So *there*! In black and white—directly inspired by God— it says not to think of yourself so doggone highly, dear sister!" Solace's nostrils narrowed as she drew in a fortifying breath. "Maybe you *do* have better book learning and spiritual skills than I do. And maybe you were cut out to be a preacher and a teacher and a seer of angels, but I have my faith, too! I was given the gift of physical strength—a different kind of grace—" she added staunchly, "and I've made myself into the best dang horse trainer—and rider!—I can be.

"And meanwhile," she continued, "I believe I have every bit as much to offer Gabe as *you* do, smarty-pants!"

"And while we're in this chapter, where Paul is telling the Romans not to fight among themselves," Michael cut in pointedly, "I'd like you to continue a little further on, Solace. This part follows what Lily read, about behaving like a Christian."

Sighing, Solace scanned the long page.

Across from her, Lily drummed the table with impatient fingers. "Do I need to find it for you?" she asked archly. "If you spent more time reading and writing—"

Solace flashed her a look that should have left burn holes in Lily's pink blouse. "Careful there, sister. You have no idea how much time I spend reading. And writing. And here it is—the guidance we've all been waiting for—"

She cleared her throat ceremoniously. " 'Let love be without dissimulation. Abhor that which is evil; cleave to that which is good'—which does *not* mean that because Gabe's a good man, he needs you *clinging* to him!" Solace added. " 'Be kindly affectioned one to another with brotherly love; in honor preferring one another'—which means you should allow me to get better acquainted with Gabe, without butting in to—"

"That's it. Hand me the Bible." Michael reached for the beloved old book, feeling older but by no means defeated. "Lily, when Christ was quizzed by the Pharisees about God's commandments, what was the great and first one?"

"You shall love the Lord your God with all your heart and all your mind and all your strength," she fired back.

"And the second one is like it, Solace," he prompted.

"You shall love your neighbor as yourself," she replied tiredly. Then she looked across the table at her sister. "Look,

Lily, I know you have things to offer Gabe, but dang it, so do I! And mark my words, he loves me!"

"He loves me, too!" Lily rasped.

"But you've had opportunities to meet all sorts of nice men who—"

"None as nice as Gabe!" her sister retorted. "And whose fault is it that you stayed home with the animals? You could've gone to school, same as Gracie and I did, and—"

"That's all!" Michael shut the Bible with more force than he intended, and the loud *whump* resounded like a knell in the room. "Until you ladies can make your peace—without wearing the rest of us thin—I insist you separate yourselves. If I were Gabe, I'd move to town and refuse to see either one of you again."

Solace's brown eyes widened. "But Papa, we're sharing the same room, and there aren't any spare—"

"Work it out," Michael insisted. He put the Bible back on the sideboard, praying his girls would see their folly—and soon.

"I get the bedroom!" Lily piped up. "So you can take your things out of it and bunk in the barn, Solace!"

"Fine by me, Princess! At least Rex and I can talk without biting each other's butts off."

He shook his head as he headed for the kitchen. Their voices rose in the stairwell . . . followed by Solace's solid footfalls and Lily's lighter, kid-slippered ones.

"I didn't accomplish a thing," he said with a sigh. "I could've talked myself blue in the face, and they wouldn't have heard a word."

Temple smiled ruefully and pulled the drain plug. "You gave us all a night's sleep, anyway. Maybe tomorrow we'll see things more clearly and think of other ways to talk to those girls. Let me see what I can come up with along that line."

Temple hung her wet towel on the handle of the cookstove and removed her apron. She was no longer the girls' teacher, but she was a fixture in this household and his children respected her aura of love and light. "I'll be upstairs with Mercy. She's going over Gabe's wardrobe, mending a few things and sewing on buttons for him."

Michael nodded mutely. He poured the last of the morning's coffee from the pot on the stove and then grimaced at its bitterness.

Life was like that sometimes: nothing beat a fresh cup of coffee, but when things sat past their prime—got cold and acidic—there was no fixing them. He sincerely hoped this rift over Gabe Getty wouldn't become a permanent wedge between sisters who'd always shared things much more important than a bloodline.

He wasn't surprised to hear Solace's trunk *bump-bump-bump*ing down the back stairway a few minutes later, nor to watch her fetch a two-wheeled cart from the barn to haul the rest of her belongings out there. She'd always taken care of herself and pulled her own weight; he was depending on Solace's solid, unruffled nature to kick in again—to offer Lily an olive branch—because Lily's behavior baffled him.

When he saw Solace gallop off toward town a few minutes later, holding Rex in front of her, he got an uneasy feeling. True enough, she was eighteen—most of her friends were married and had children—but it wasn't like his sturdy, good-natured daughter to take off in a fit of proud anger without telling anyone where she was headed.

Ride with her, Lord, he prayed. *Help her make good decisions none of us will regret.*

Chapter Sixteen

"Holy cow, Rex, would you look at that!"

Solace slowed Lincoln to a halt near the entrance to the Dickinson County fairgrounds, gazing ahead eagerly. Three big tents shimmied in the wind and the whole place buzzed like a hill of ants; burly men with sledge hammers checked the tent pegs while others watered the horses, longhorn cattle, and buffalo that fed from troughs in the corrals. Scents of roasting peanuts, burnt popcorn, and animal droppings came to her on the breeze, but to Solace it smelled like a promise. Here, if folks were quibbling, they would soon set aside their differences for the afternoon performance. Or they'd be soothed by the lullaby of lowing cattle and whickering horses.

A shot rang out—and then another!—yet no one scurried for cover. Then she saw a costumed cowgirl taking target practice with a large bull's-eye painted on canvas and propped against hay bales.

"Well, heck, anybody could hit that!" she murmured to Rex. Nudging her bay into a walk again, she circled the bustling grounds to take in all the excitement: Indians sitting cross-legged while a dandified cowboy painted their faces; a carnival midway lined by small booths, where costumed hustlers prepared for another onslaught of spectators; including a Gypsy fortune-teller who eyed her up and down, as though she knew things she'd never reveal. Somewhere a brass band tuned up and then burst into a spirited march.

Solace smiled and a shiver shot up her spine. What a life it would be, to perform on the road! A different town each week, yet the acts would remain the same. A bantam rooster of a man in a black cowboy hat, wearing a crimson cape over his jeweled ebony suit, strutted to the end of the midway and raised a megaphone to his mouth.

"Sixty minutes and counting!" he called out imperiously. "Have your mounts ready! Prepare for the opening parade! Leave nothing to chance!"

"Whoa, boy," Solace murmured. She took the flyer from her shirt pocket and nodded. "That's Apache Pete himself, Rex! Kind of a pip-squeak, don't you think? Not much of an Injun, either, from what I can see."

Her dog panted in her lap, gawking in every direction. It was a palpable thing, the excitement vibrating around them, and Solace sensed this performance would outdo any wonders she'd witnessed under circus tents as a kid. It featured stagecoach robberies and fancy shooting and Indian attacks—things she planned to write about in upcoming stories. She'd arrived just in time to get a feel for the majestic spectacle to come.

Solace looked around for the ticket booth. No sense in waiting until a line formed. She could be the first one in the grandstand—unless somebody objected to Rex. If anybody did, she'd find another way in, or they'd enter with a cluster of folks, when the ticket-taker was distracted. Rex would behave like the perfect gentleman.

She tied Lincoln in the outer lot, which was intersected by hitching posts and lengths of rope. "Come on, Rex, let's get a good look around before the crowd sets in."

With a confirming yip, the white dog fell into step beside her. He looked up with adoration in his shining eyes.

"Yeah, you're my best friend, too, fella," Solace crooned. "Lily won't follow us out here—might dirty her new kid slippers—so we can do as we please! Don't go wandering off, though. Somebody else might try to take you home, fine pup that you are."

Rex perked up his dark ears, forming the butterfly she

loved. Solace felt perfectly safe, because while he was the gentlest of pets, this loyal dog would jump any roustabout or carny barker who dared lay a hand on her. Rex suffered no fools; he was compact enough to stage sneak attacks, yet large enough to do some real damage if provoked.

In the far corrals cowboys mounted up—men dressed in flashy red shirts with black trim like no real cattleman would be caught dead in. But what a spectacle they made, herding those longhorn steers off the fairgrounds! A stagecoach swung into position ahead of this herd, and its bright yellow sides proclaimed "Apache Pete's Wild West Extravaganza." The brass band was riding on top of this vehicle, and Apache Pete had vaulted up into the seat beside the uniformed driver.

"Well, hot dang! We get to see the parade twice—going and coming!" Solace said with a grin. "Let's just stay right here and look around."

A dozen half-naked Indian braves fell into formation, with tall feathers in their beaded headbands and loincloths that showed off their dark, muscled legs. Then came three magnificent chiefs in full regalia, with ceremonial headdresses that trailed behind them. Solace wondered if the center chief was a white man who'd stained his skin . . . but then, that was part of the show's magic, wasn't it? If the crowd believed he was a redskin, that was all that mattered.

"You want I tell your fortune, brave lady?"

Solace turned to see the Gypsy approaching with a purposeful glint in her eye. Her coal-black hair had beads braided into its front strands, and her bracelets played a seductive song as she swayed in her loose, gauzy skirts. She had a shiny gold tooth—something Solace had never seen—and it flashed in the sunlight when the provocative woman smiled at her.

"Give me hand! I not charge you nothing," the fortune-teller coaxed. "Madame Flambeau, she see something very . . . unusual in you. Come to table! I read your cards!"

It was a bid for money, pure and simple. "No thanks, I'm just watching."

"Somebody here, he watching you, too. He tell me you destined for glory—someday real soon." The Gypsy reached for her with a playful wink. "You not be sorry! It not cost you nothing—and your dog, he like me! He know Faustina, she tell the truth when she read your palm and your cards."

Rex indeed sat mesmerized, watching the woman's skirts and gold bangles glimmer in the breeze. Solace trusted his judgment . . . it would be several minutes before the parade returned to start the show. "Oh, all right! But tell me who's watching me!"

"Perhaps a secret the cards will reveal, no?" the Gypsy teased. She sashayed down the midway toward her tent, her gaudy skirts of purple and gold and red shimmering with every step. When Solace sat in the wooden chair the fortune-teller indicated, Rex hopped into her lap. Everybody knew this card-reading stuff was all for show, so she let him remain there to watch for special attention or perhaps a treat. He had that way with people.

But the Gypsy shuffled her colorful deck, gazing at Solace with unflinching kohl-rimmed eyes. "You have unusual name. Born in . . . a snowstorm, yes?"

Solace blinked. "Yes, ma'am, but how'd you—"

"Faustina Flambeau never reveal her source of wisdom. Bring on a curse, you understand?" The brazen woman grabbed her hand and turned it palm-up on her small table. "Aha! The lifeline, it show a woman of rare strength and courage—dangerous—I see a gun!"

Solace nipped her lip. These fortune-tellers made their living from fools who swallowed their stories and unwittingly gave them more information. "And what do you see that gun doing?" she asked cautiously.

"Shooting, of course!" Madame Faustina's raucous laughter rang inside her tent—and just as dramatically, it ended. "You save a man's life once, yes? With a gun?"

Her insides tightened and she glanced nervously around the midway. How in the world did this tricked-out Gypsy know?

"But you gentle and kind. Madame Faustina see exciting days ahead for you." The Gypsy dropped her hand then, to shuffle the deck again. "Here—you shuffle now, many times. Think of question you want answer for. You know already that I speak the truth about you . . . I know your secrets and can read your heart. Your *destiny*."

Her first impulse was to bolt from the chair, yet curiosity won out. Solace took the worn deck and began a clumsy shuffle with her arms bent around Rex. She hadn't said two words to this woman—hadn't given away a thing in chitchat beforehand—but this queen of the gaudy carnival was too accurate to deny. She shifted the cards into a single pile then and rapped the deck's edges on the table.

"Put out top three cards," the Gypsy instructed. "Past, present, future."

Solace laid them face down on the coarse tablecloth and turned over the first one.

"Queen of Swords reversed . . . someone angry with you—a woman," the seer murmured. "She not thinking straight . . . jealousy over a lover."

Now how could this woman—these paper cards—possibly know I just had a fight with Lily over Gabe? This is too outlandish to—

Solace shifted her dog's weight to the other leg, too entranced to move. "That's in my past, right?"

"Yes. And your eyes tell me cards are correct."

Quickly Solace turned over the middle card. If the Gypsy woman had secrets and didn't answer direct questions, well, she could play that game, too.

"Knight of Wands—you ride triumphant. You know fame, fortune and success—very soon!" Faustina pushed back her coal-black hair to flash Solace a knowing gold-toothed smile. "You will make name for yourself with horses—but maybe not the name you want. And in your future—"

The woman flipped the final card with a shimmy of gold bracelets. Her eyes widened, and she considered the card portraying a crowned, winged woman in white with a sword in one hand and a scale hanging from the other. "Justice. Madame Flambeau see courtroom and much publicity . . . a fair trial. But maybe not in your favor."

"What do you mean by that?" Solace demanded. It was Gabe who'd be in a courtroom soon, not her.

The Gypsy shrugged and gathered her cards. "Faustina, she seldom make mistake. The cards, they never lie."

An upside-down queen of quarrels . . . a knight who would ride high and make her famous . . . a fair trial. What did all this mumbo jumbo really mean? Smiling politely, Solace rose from the rickety chair. "Thank you, Faustina. You've given me a lot to think about."

The Gypsy's eyes, as dark and hard as marbles, followed her from the tent—probably looking for a donation. But those cards were just a parlor game . . . weren't they? If that upside-down, agitated queen fit perfectly with Lily, did it mean the cards about riding high and ending up in a courtroom—maybe not a winner—were accurate, too?

The return of the show's yellow stagecoach and the brass band distracted her from thoughts of her future, however. Who could be concerned about a fake Gypsy's forecast while watching those red-shirted cowboys funnel a herd of longhorns into the nearest corral? Their bawling and that huge cloud of dust sent Solace trotting toward the ticket booth. Folks were riding in by the score, beckoned by the pomp and pageantry of Apache Pete's parade through town. She wanted a seat down front so she wouldn't miss a moment of the excitement.

Rex remained at her feet as she paid, so the fat old woman in the ticket window didn't notice that he followed her in. The musicians had assembled on the bandstand, and when their director tipped his cowboy hat back and raised his baton, the fun began.

Solace sat entranced; a few riders put their mounts through practice paces while those in the crowd took their seats. Rex panted beside her, his eyes and ears alert. At the back entrance flaps, Indian braves gathered, and she heard the impatient snorts of buffalo. Then the band struck up a dramatic introductory fanfare.

"Ladies and gentlemen!" The loud voice echoed in the peaked canvas ceiling. "Prepare yourselves! Keep your arms and legs *out* of the ring because—oh, my stars! It's a buffalo stampede!"

With a crash of the cymbals, more than a dozen woolly, bearded beasts thundered into the tent to circle the arena, chased by Indian braves riding paint ponies. Solace's pulse raced right along with them. When she felt Rex gather himself to leap at one of the buffalo, she slipped her arm around him.

"This isn't our show, fella!" she reminded him. "Those buffalo are pretty tame, but they wouldn't know what to do if a little white dog jumped on their backs!"

As the stampede pounded out the opposite tent exit, Apache Pete began his patter. "In the early days of the West, folks, our homesteaders and settlers had to shoot their food and defend themselves," he crooned over the band's low, patriotic music. "Most often we think of *men* as the hunters and sharpshooting scouts that tamed the wide-open plains, but we have with us today a rare and glorious treat! Please welcome Crack-Shot Cora, our lady sharpshooter!"

Applause rose around her, and Solace joined in. Cora— that woman she'd seen taking target practice—circled the arena with a big grin fixed on her face, holding her Sharps rifle high as she urged her ebony mount into a fancy canter. Red streamers flapped on either side of her, while on the far end of the ring, the roustabouts scurried to set up her props.

"Don't get any ideas about riding with *her*, either," Solace whispered to her quivering dog. "So far I haven't seen a thing you and I don't do, but let's give her a chance to prove herself."

Rex whimpered, wiggling in his place. He was so eager to dash out there and show off, she kept a hand on him—just in case his excitement overrode his training.

Meanwhile, Cora dismounted and made a big show of loading her rifle. Then, as the band played a low, intense tone to quiet the crowd, the lady in the ruffled red skirt took aim . . . shifted her stance . . . and then *ping! ping! ping!* took down the closest three painted cans. Another shot rang out, and then two more—but as applause filled the tent, Solace noticed one of her six targets was still in place.

"We've got her beat, don't you think, Rex?" Solace whispered as she clapped. "Why, I can shoot better than that astride a moving horse!"

Still, it was exciting to watch the colorful performers, and hear the music, and take in the crowd's reaction, and as the extravaganza progressed through a stagecoach holdup and a ceremonial Indian dance, Solace gloried in every moment.

Too soon the show was over. Too soon she had to think about going home. Her fit of temper at Lily was long gone, but it still galled her that her sister had commandeered their bedroom and felt *she* was the answer to Gabe Getty's problems.

And how had Gabe fared at his interview? He'd be headed back to the Triple M by now, and if she wanted to hear his account firsthand, it was time to be on her way. As the crowd mobbed the narrow exit flaps of the huge, poled tent, Solace took a last, longing look at its fluttering walls and the cowboy band, which had finished its final song. She opened her arms, and Rex sprang up into her embrace.

She giggled when he licked her nose—and then noticed a roustabout standing beside a nearby tent pole, watching her intently. He was a tall, lanky fellow with broad shoulders and slim hips; his hat was cocked down so she couldn't see his eyes. That strong chin and the sandy brown hair looked familiar somehow . . . .

Rex began to rumble; the hair stood up on his back, and he seemed ready to lunge out of her arms.

"Easy, Rex," Solace murmured. "Don't go causing a ruckus in this crowd. I see that fellow, too, and he's just looking us over. Just thinks you're pretty special, to be coming to a show like this."

"Your dog Rex is a good judge of character." The man leaned against the thick log pole, still watching her intently from beneath his hat brim. "I wouldn't trust me, either— except you know damn well I'd never lay a hand on you, little sister."

Solace's heart lurched. "Joel?" she breathed. "Joel, I—my Lord, how long's it been since—?"

She broke away from the last stragglers leaving the tent. Rex still bristled in her arms, but when her vagabond brother pushed back his hat and grinned, the dog woofed in recognition.

"Saw you coming into the fairgrounds," he said as he hugged her. "Figured you'd come to see the show sooner or later—"

"Not that I couldn't out-shoot and out-ride anybody who performed here!" she cut in with a laugh. She gazed into his chiseled face, so like Papa's yet tougher. Harder. "You really should come home to see Mama and—"

"Yeah, well, they keep me pretty busy here."

Though Solace didn't fully understand Joel Malloy's aversion to Mercy and his father, she kept her questions to herself. This was the kid who'd slipped away to the cave with her, to help her with target practice when she was only seven, even though they knew such sneaking around with guns was wrong.

"I actually *miss* you, you know that?" she teased. "Now that Lily and Grace have graduated from Aunt Agatha's academy, it gets slow at home. I spent the last couple weeks at Billy's— he gave me a matched pair of bays that'll whip anything

Apache Pete has here! You should see us! I ride them standing up—and Rex rides along—"

"You should be telling this to Pete, not me," Joel teased. His voice had grown lower, manly in a gruff way. "I already *know* you could whip Cora. Haven't seen her hit all her targets yet during a show."

Solace's eyebrows went up. "So why's Apache Pete keep her on? He could surely find a better sharpshooter—"

Joel's expression eased into a foxlike grin. "They're lovers."

Her mouth fell open. Leave it to Joel to tease her with his worldly ways.

After a moment, however, Solace put some pieces into place. "If you saw me coming to the fairgrounds . . . it was *you* who sicced that Gypsy fortune-teller on me, wasn't it? That's how she knew I had an unusual name—and was born in a blizzard and—"

Her brother laughed so hard his whole body shook, but he kept an arm slung around her shoulders, as if he'd missed her companionship as much as she'd missed his. Joel Malloy looked rugged and rough-cut on the outside, yet she still saw a skittish desperation in his eyes . . . a defensive bravado he never dropped, even when it was just the two of them.

"Faustina had you going, did she? Gave you the lowdown on your destiny?" he asked in a voice that bubbled with laughter. "If you went back to her now, you could tell *her* fortune . . . like maybe, if she plays her cards right, a tall, good-lookin' cowboy'll be waiting at her wagon later tonight."

When her jaw dropped again, Joel kept chuckling . . . as though he knew a world of things she'd never have the occasion to learn. "I'll just head on home, thanks," she replied. "Gabe Getty's interviewed for a judge's position on the Dickinson County."

"Got your eye on Gabe? Thought he was married."

Solace glanced around, and saw that they were alone in the tent now. She set Rex on the ground, considering how much to reveal. Knowing Joel, he'd tease her mercilessly if he suspected her romantic notions.

"Long story," she hedged. "His wife died—they lived in St. Louis, you know. When he went to visit Billy's family, I was already there working my horses."

Joel's squint said he was reading way too much between her lines. "Never pictured you with a bookish type like him. Opposites attract, huh?"

How was she supposed to answer that? If she denied her interest in Gabe, Joel would only tease her more. "Guess we'll find out, won't we?" she challenged, looking him straight in the eye. "Shall I tell the folks I saw you? Or do you plan to keep darting in and out of our lives like a dragonfly?"

His jaw hardened. "Look, you know how Pa gets—and you know how I don't cotton to having Bible stories shoved down my throat! Tell them whatever you want, but don't hold your breath about me stopping by the house. It hasn't been home for a long, long time, Solace."

She nodded sadly. Ever since Joel had run away at ten, after learning that his actual mother was a prostitute, he'd had a big chip on his shoulder—and a wagonload of resentment for the man who called him *son*. It was sad, but it was just plain fact that Joel Malloy would probably *never* know a home: he never stayed in one place long enough to make any attachments. Didn't put down any roots.

"Well—it's been good seeing you," she said as she hugged him again. "I'll probably come to another show before you close down here."

"Got another week before we move on to Enterprise," he replied with a nod. Then he gave her a cryptic grin. "I wasn't just whistling Dixie when I said you ought to sign on. You'd outshine Crack-Shot Cora with one hand tied behind your back." He paused then, angling his hat back over his eyes. "I double-dog dare you to show Apache Pete what you can do, little sister."

Electricity raced up her spine. Never had she let a dare go unanswered! Yet Joel was suggesting something far riskier than shooting squirrels or sneaking their papa's pistols out of the case for target practice down by the river.

"Then there'd be *two* black sheep in the family," she finally replied. "You know Mama'd have a fit if I—"

"Got to be your own woman, Solace. Nobody else can live your life for you—and you're certainly old enough to call your own shots now."

She had a quick vision of herself circling this very ring, balancing atop Lincoln and Lee while the crowd cheered her on. She felt that rush of excitement and the steady thrum of the horses' muscles beneath her feet. . . .

Solace sighed and came back to reality. "It's true enough that nobody's ever been able to tell me what to do," she said with a tight smile. "But I've never had your bravado, Joel— and things are different if you're a girl. I'll tell the folks you said hello."

She exited the big tent then, with Rex at her heels. She wasn't upset by Joel's insinuations, exactly . . . more peeved with herself, for denying herself the exciting life he'd dared her to audition for. After all, if she was really to put her skills to work, she'd have to approach a man like Apache Pete someday. Otherwise, she'd be riding around the corral at home forever, imagining how the crowd applauded and adored her and her amazing dog. . . .

But right now, she was hungry for a good supper and she wanted to see how Gabe had fared in town. Her time at the Wild West Extravaganza had settled her temper enough that she could ignore Lily's attempts to steal him away from her. Because yes, she *was* her own woman—and she had spoken for Gabe Getty first!

Chapter Seventeen

Gabe stepped off the sidewalk and into the sunny street wearing the biggest grin he could ever remember. Just like *that*, he was Judge Gabriel Getty!

Michael Malloy must have said some astounding things about him because the committee had hung on his every word—as though they'd decided to hire him before he even walked in. Most of the men remembered him from when he was a kid coming into town with his uncle, George Clark. To a man, they admired his credentials. Through yet another minor miracle, Arthur Bancroft had telegraphed them a sterling reference, as had Miss Agatha Vanderbilt.

"We had a case in progress when Judge Ratcliff passed on, and public sentiment's running high to have it resolved," the mayor informed him. "Since Judge Prescott has a . . . family connection, you'll understand our need for a levelheaded, progressive, and *unbiased* man on the bench for Prescott versus Prescott. Can you start tomorrow?"

Curiosity got the best of him. "What sort of a case is it?" he asked, noting the committee members' taut expressions.

"A building on Texas Street has been reopened as a sporting establishment, after the Missionary Society believed *they* had purchased it," the mayor replied. "Hannibal Prescott has a . . . former wife in both camps."

So Gabe had been sworn in, and he'd come out with a thick sheaf of notes from the court's reporter. He had a new career and a case to hear, and had been treated to dinner, all within twenty hours of arriving in Abilene. Tomorrow he was to set a date for the trial to reconvene.

He was ready to rush back to the Triple M, but the telegraph office beckoned him. Quickly he sent off his appreciation to Miss Vanderbilt, and then a note of thanks to Arthur Bancroft, as well. It pleased him that his former partner and father-in-law had bestowed a blessing on his new life—probably ignoring his wife's strident objections.

Gabe stopped by the bank, too, to open himself an account, and then to cash a check on behalf of Sol Juddson. The bank teller, a wiry fellow with a prominent Adam's apple, already knew he'd been appointed as the new judge. "Nice doin' business with you, sir!" he'd chirped as he passed the money from his window.

Sir! Now if *that* didn't make him feel old!

But he needed to assume an air of wisdom and maturity, didn't he? Gone was Gabe Getty the junior partner and son-in-law. All who entered his courtroom would address him as "Your Honor" now, even though he wasn't yet thirty. His eyeglasses had always given him a scholarly look, but maybe Solace's suggestion about a beard wasn't such a bad idea . . . .

As he rode back to the ranch, he wondered how to deal fairly with the two young women who were vying for his affections—that situation seemed even more complicated than hearing testimony from a madam and a missionary. He wasn't sure he should embark on any romantic relationship so soon. Too many questions had been left unanswered about his wife . . . too many emotions were still left untended.

He unsaddled Michael's Morgan in the barn and led it to a stall with fresh straw and oats . . . savored the scent of the horse's feed as he admired its sleek lines and conformation. Two stalls over, Solace's fine bay—was this Lincoln or Lee?—whickered, as though demanding where his mistress had gone.

Odd that Solace was out on her other gelding without putting this one into the corral to await his training session.

He looked outside for Rex, and the dog's absence made his gut tighten. Did she usually take off with him? Or did his absence signal something more drastic than a jaunt around the pasture?

What do you know about her riding habits, really? Trying to guess what she might be doing is like . . .

Why was her trunk in the back stall, along with her bedding? What could she possibly have done, that she'd been banished to the barn? Gabe picked up his satchel and walked slowly toward the house, not sure what he might find when he stepped inside.

Or was he overreacting? During his marriage any problem meant Letitia would be buried under her bedclothes with Henrietta clucking over her. This family was woven of different fabric—and the sight of Temple Gates and Mercy standing at the pie safe, rolling out dough and fitting it into pans, made him smile in the doorway. All was calm. All was bright. There was a logical explanation for what he'd seen in the barn, and no one here would get hysterical over it.

Mercy's brown eyes lit up. "How was your day, Gabe? We've been wondering if those men grilled you, or—"

"I was a shoo-in, thanks to Michael. I start tomorrow— but why are Solace's things out in the barn?"

The women looked at each other, one face the color of coffee and one the color of cream. Both smiled knowingly. Temple patted a top crust over the apple filling that teased his senses with its cinnamon sweetness.

"Mister Michael separated the two girls until they could quit their bickering. Miss Lily called dibs on the bedroom."

That fit with what he knew about them. Lily would no more sleep in the barn than she would've saddled up and ridden away—which Solace had done to settle her temper, no doubt.

"I don't suppose you saw her in town?" Mercy asked. "She rode off in a huff without telling anyone where she was headed. Not that she can't take care of herself."

Gabe smiled at this valiant effort not to be concerned over her daughter's whereabouts. Henrietta Bancroft would have been wheezing as she reached for her camphor vial. "No, but I bet she went to the Wild West show. It was setting up at the fairgrounds as we came in on the train."

"Miss Solace would go there," Temple agreed with a chuckle. "I've never known her to miss a meal, so I'm thinking she'll be home shortly. She'll be wanting to know *your* news, of course, Mister Gabe. Or should I say, Judge Getty?"

"Doesn't that sound grand? Congratulations!" Mercy clapped the flour from her hands so she could hug him. "I'm just sorry your aunt and uncle and Emma aren't here to see what you've accomplished, Gabe. You were always a puzzle to them, being such a bookish boy, but I figured you'd leave the prairie and *make* something of yourself. Good for you!"

Once again his heart did that funny little dance because someone had sincerely praised him. So seldom he'd heard that, except from this woman and Agatha Vanderbilt.

And Solace. She was a nurturer—an encourager—by nature, too. He couldn't wait to see her grin. It had been a special moment when she'd shared her writing success with him, and he wanted to share this with her.

He blushed when Mercy bussed his cheek. "I'm going upstairs to change out of this suit. After dinner, I have a *lot* of reading to do. I need to catch up on a controversial case that was left open at Judge Ratcliff's death."

"We'll feed you a good meal, then, Mister Gabe. Fortify you for the new opportunities coming your way!" Temple's melodic voice followed him from the kitchen through the dining room, where the table was set with the good china. What a joy it was to be back among these people, who celebrated everyone's successes!

Gabe started up the stairway with a feeling of deep satisfaction . . . a sense that his life was turning itself around to head—no, to soar!—in a fresh direction. Once he got this

Prescott case underway, he'd look for an apartment in town. He wanted to be his own man before . . .

He stopped on the landing. Lily Malloy sat on the top stair above him, with her pale pink skirts wrapped around her ankles. Her eyes were closed and her face raised toward the beam of sunshine pouring through the skylight. With her blonde hair aglow in this heavenly radiance and her serene expression, she looked like an angel come down for a visitation. She sat motionless, apparently unaware of him. Deep in prayer, perhaps.

He hated to interrupt her meditative state, so he started downstairs.

"No, Gabriel. Wait," she murmured. Her eyes remained closed as her lovely smile lit up the entire stairwell. "I wanted to tell you that I'm not chasing after you like Solace thinks. I understand how lost you feel—how you need time to establish your new life. I came home because God told me to."

He didn't dare argue with that . . . but what could he say? Lily had always radiated an aura of grace and truth, yet this conversation was headed down a road he'd rather not take.

"And . . . what else has God told you about this situation?" he asked quietly. It couldn't hurt to hear what one of His emissaries said on that subject, could it? He greatly respected Lily's connection to the angelic realm.

She opened her eyes, to fix him in her crystal gaze. "The angels and God assure me that my feelings for you are right and holy. The dreams I have—the inner visions—show you and me together, Gabriel. I've come to clarify the confusion you felt in your marriage to Letitia . . . to release you from the guilt written in the premature lines on your beautiful face."

Gabe shifted. "What about your calling to assist Miss Vanderbilt? Your unique spirituality leads her girls along the higher way, so I assumed you would—"

"Don't you see?" Her face glowed with a flirtatious yet

girlish innocence. "I was at the academy, doing God's will, and He directed you there, as well. When the time was right."

"Lily, I—" He sucked in a long breath. "You have my best interests at—you've always been patient and kind and—but I have to tell you—"

"You don't have to say a word, Gabriel." Lily stood up slowly, smoothing her pretty pink dress. She looked as fresh as a spring flower, basking in the light. So fragile and angelic it tore at Gabe's heart.

"Let me hold you. There's a power in the laying on of hands," she continued tranquilly. "God has blessed me with the ability to heal you. To balance your mind and body and spirit. Please—" She opened her arms, beckoning from the top of the stairway.

Gabe inhaled again to quiet the riot in his heart. It was wonderful to have a beautiful young woman blessing him as a direct order from God, but he still felt uneasy.

"Please, Gabe," she implored, gazing down with a beneficent smile. "I'm not trying to control you, or to steer you in a direction you don't want to go. That would be contrary to God's wishes."

How long since he'd been invited to share affection? With the sunlight making a halo around her golden hair, and her lips parted in a lovely smile, Lily looked so much like his wife when they'd first met . . . when Letitia was happy and playful and sweet. How he longed to erase his painful memories of these past months . . . to retain his mental portrait of Letitia before her fall into perdition, flask in hand.

He took one step, and then another. Lily encouraged him with a saintly silence, inviting him to lay aside his burdens, like a baptismal immersion, to signify his freedom from the past.

When he stopped just beneath her, Lily slipped her arms around his shoulders and rested her head against his. They exhaled together, standing in this suspended state with the soft light enveloping them.

Gabe felt awkward about not embracing her, yet he sensed a stirring within Lily as she lifted her face to study him. So flawless she looked, so lovely as her lips parted. . . . He had to state his case quickly, before she got ahead of his intentions. She'd revealed her mission and purpose—restoring his soul after he'd walked through the valley of the shadow—so he couldn't, in all fairness, let her believe he felt the same way right now.

"Lily, I appreciate—you should know that—"

Were those footsteps? If someone was coming, he needed to set her straight right now! "Lily, please understand why I can't return your—"

"Oh, but you can!" she breathed. Her blue eyes widened and she stood on tiptoe. "We have all the time in the—"

"I hear someone—"

Her lips brushed his and Gabe's heart leaped into his throat. He placed his hands at her waist, easing away from her well-intended . . .

"Oh, *fine*!" Solace's protest rang in the paneled stairwell. "I was coming to congratulate Judge Getty, but I see we're moving at the speed of *angels* here!"

"Solace, please don't—" Gabe lowered himself a step, but Lily refused to let him go. "This isn't what it seems!"

"Oh, yes it is." She glared up at them with betrayed brown eyes. Her face was ruddy from more than a horseback ride home. Solace looked stricken, as if she'd lost her last friend. "I heard your little 'sacred mission' speech, Lily. You're dealing Gabe a very low blow to—"

"Every word I said was true," her sister refuted. "You're just jealous because you were out galavanting around. Not here to welcome him—"

"I'm *appalled*," Solace countered, clenching her fists at her sides. "You've used that angel story to get what you wanted before, Lily. But this takes the cake!"

Lily drew herself up, stiffening against Gabe. "How dare you insinuate that I've used my faith to—"

"And how dare you talk like I don't have any!" When Solace shook her windblown hair back from her face, her tear tracks shone in the sunlight. "Just because I don't gaze into space—speaking to beings I can't see—doesn't mean I'm not connected to God! I'm tired of you looking down your nose at me, Lily! It's arrogant and rude, and Jesus isn't one bit happy with you right now."

"You have no idea how Jesus feels! How presumptuous, to—"

"Yeah, well, at least I'm stating my case without angelic assistance! And I don't need anybody's help telling me how I feel about Gabe, either!" Solace turned, and her boots thumped sharply against the stairs.

When Lily exhaled it sounded almost like a purr. "Some girls just can't handle it when—"

"This isn't right! Let me go!" Gabe pried her arms from his shoulders. "We'll finish our discussion after dinner."

He rushed down the stairs, wondering how he'd wedged himself between two sisters who'd never acted so much like hissing, scratching cats. Voices came from the kitchen— Mercy's and her daughter's—so he stopped outside the door. He didn't want to eavesdrop, but he couldn't let Solace stay angry with him. And he wouldn't let her leave before he set some things straight.

"I've *had* it, Mama! This house is only big enough for one of us, so if Lily has laid claim to—"

"Your sister has a *room*, Solace. You both have my heart— and you're tearing it in two! Now *stop*!" Mercy insisted in a strained voice. "And please tell me where you're off to this time. You may be eighteen, but I'm your mother and I still worry about—"

"Well, worry no more! I refuse to listen to Lily's claptrap about—"

"Careful there, young lady." Michael Malloy came in through the kitchen door and removed his hat. "In this house, we respect each other's beliefs—and we respect our parents' wishes. You're about to run off again, aren't you? It reminds me of Joel when he was a little boy."

"And it's Joel's idea that I audition for the Wild West show!" Solace piped up. "He was there today. I talked to him—invited him home. But of course he made excuses about how busy they keep him."

Gabe nipped his lip. There it was again, that unerring knack for sidetracking a conversation when it wasn't going her way. Curiosity and anguish—and maybe guilt—took hold of Michael and Mercy's expressions.

"Did he look well? Is he holding down a good job?"

"What's he talked you into now?" Mike asked quietly. His smile looked resigned.

Solace let out her breath. She couldn't dodge the man who'd blocked her retreat in more ways than one. "After the show, when I remarked that Crack-Shot Cora wasn't much good—that I could hit more targets from a moving horse than she had from solid ground—Joel suggested I take Rex and Lincoln and Lee to show Apache Pete what I can do.

"So it's not like I'm running off," she continued in a more biddable voice. "Joel will be there. And now that you know my intentions, you can check up on me by coming to the show. It moves to Enterprise next, and I'll let you know where we'll be traveling after that."

Gabe felt sorry for the two parents facing their formidable daughter. Solace wasn't a troublemaker, but she *had* defied them in ornery little ways all her life. She stood in that sunny kitchen wearing her denim pants and a homespun shirt, with her wild waves hanging in disarray around a sun-kissed face that reminded him so much of Judd Monroe, he sensed it was her best weapon when dealing with her mother.

But at least she talks to them—handles their challenges by presenting her own. Letitia wouldn't have lasted two minutes in this situation, and Henrietta would be sobbing.

From behind him came the quiet rustling of skirts. Lily stopped beside him—except she peered openly through the doorway. "If Solace wants to perform in the Wild West show, I say let her. She'll be living out her dream, using her God-given talents," the blonde remarked coolly. "She'll be riding the road to perdition, but at least she'll be straddling two fine horses, thundering out in a blaze of glory."

Solace's jaw dropped. She turned to see Gabe in the doorway—again with Lily leaning against him. "I can't believe you—"

"That's enough from you, Lily," Michael muttered. "You'll have to wait your turn."

"No, she won't. I've seen all I need to." Solace's face crumpled for a moment, but then she faced her parents again. "Look, I know you don't like this much, but I'm going to audition for that show. If I don't try it, I'll always wonder what I might've missed. I've been practicing for this all my life. It looks like my best chance to be happy—to be myself."

She stepped resolutely out the door, heading toward the barn. Gabe freed his hand from Lily's and trotted after her. "Solace! We need to talk about—"

"Ever heard that old saying, about how actions speak louder than words?" she asked over her shoulder. "You've made your choice, so I'm making mine, Gabe. Joel's right—I'm my own woman. Nobody can live my life for me."

"But, here—I've got your money!" Gabe hurried past her so he could stop her in her tracks. His heart was pounding painfully, and it wasn't from keeping step with this hard-headed young woman. "You might need this," he said, reaching inside his jacket. "And *promise* me that if you need—if anything goes wrong—you'll send for me."

"You remembered to—thanks, Gabe." Solace's expression wavered. She lowered her gaze, but held tight to the money. "Busy as you were landing your seat on the bench today, you still found time to—"

"And what might *that* be for?"

Lily stood a few feet away, her arms crossed and a catlike expression on her face. The look didn't become her. And because he had a perfectly legitimate answer to her question—an answer that would set Miss Malloy straight about her sister's other talents—Gabe almost blurted out the truth. The truth might set them all free right now.

But Solace's budding career as a writer was *her* secret. So Gabe gazed at her, the silent question in his eyes.

Solace had been derided one time too many. She mirrored Lily's feline smile as she folded the stack of bills into her shirt pocket. "I guess this money's none of your business, is it, sister?"

With her blue eyes wide and her cheeks ablaze, the blonde looked ready to go up in smoke. "Solace, if you've been— why would Gabe be giving you money, unless he was paying you for—for—"

"Not one word more, Lily. You've gone too far." Gabe turned then, so Lily was on one side of him and Solace on the other. This was even uglier and more upsetting than the confrontations he'd had with Letitia over her tippling.

"Solace earned that money in a perfectly honorable way, and I can understand why she doesn't wish to discuss it right now." Gabe inhaled deeply, praying for the negotiating skills King Solomon had called upon when two women had claimed the same baby.

"Lily, I hate to be blunt, but I-I was trying to tell you, on the stairway—" He closed his eyes, feeling her panic. But he couldn't stop now. "I'm sorry if you misinterpreted anything I said or did, but I-I can't return your affections. It's not your fault, but you . . . you look too much like Letitia. I could never love you for who you are."

Gabe thought his chest might cave in, but he could leave nothing unsaid. "Find someone else to share your life, Lily. I-I'm sorry I had to say it this way."

He retreated to the house, feeling whipped and vulgar and

crude. Behind him, Solace had the last word—but she didn't sound any more triumphant than he did.

"Happy now, Princess?" she demanded. "You've driven away two of the people who loved you most. So now you can go to your room and *rule*!"

Chapter Eighteen

Closing her eyes, Solace clenched her teeth—and then jerked away from Joel's scissors. "You're *sure* this is the best way? Once you whack off my hair, there's no putting it back, and—"

"If Crack-Shot Cora or Pete suspect you're a girl, you don't stand a chance. The show doesn't have room for two female sharpshooters—"

"Not that Cora's any good," she muttered.

"—and even if Pete hired one, there'd be nothing but trouble from the start. Trust me on this." Her brother leaned over her shoulder to nod convincingly.

As if to voice his agreement, Rex whimpered. He leaned against her leg, gazing into her face as Solace stroked his silky ear. Was he edgy about this setup, too? Should she walk away—tuck her tail between her legs and go home?

"If you want a chance at the big time, a male disguise is your ticket, Solace. I wondered if you were half boy when we were growing up anyway," Joel continued with a chuckle. "You could out-ride and out-shoot me—and every man I knew—before you were ten years old. Shot Wesley Bristol's horse out from under him when you were only seven! Sure wish I'd stuck around to see *that* happen!"

Solace sighed. She'd caught a lot of grief from Mama and Papa that night. And she'd endured her share of guilt and nightmares after bringing down the outlaw Bristol brother, even if a Pinkerton operative's bullet had actually killed him.

"Guess I should understand about having too many hens in one nest," she finally agreed. "It's partly why I'm here. Once Lily gets on her high horse—"

"See there? Lily always did think she was better than the rest of us," Joel pointed out with a flourish of his scissors. "If she's got ideas about latching on to Gabe, it won't be settled 'til only one of you's left standing. Or left at home, anyway."

Sighing ruefully, Solace sat straighter. It was one thing to wear old pants and shirts the hired hands left behind; it was another matter entirely to sacrifice her mane of thick, wavy hair. What if Pete didn't take her on? How would she explain her boyish appearance to her parents—and to Gabe?

And what if life on the road wasn't everything her maverick brother made it out to be?

But these doubts only stood between her and what her heart had always longed to do. And the longer she wavered, the more Joel would believe she didn't have the guts to carry out his double-dog dare—much less to perform in front of hundreds of people.

"All right. Cut it off."

With the lifting of the first hank of her hair and the brutal *sniiiiip* of those scissors, her fate was sealed. Like it or not, she sat in a cheap, dingy hotel room in a dubious part of town—at Joel's insistence—turning herself into the Sol Juddson she'd become with the sale of her first story. She *had* acted half like a boy all her life, but this . . . this shearing ceremony brought everything into stark focus. She felt like a sacrificial lamb in more ways than she cared to think about . . . because if she was sacrificing her chances with Gabe, what would it matter if she became the sharpshooting champion of the world?

Snip. Snip.

She couldn't look at the hair landing on the floor. Couldn't imagine justifying her actions to Gabe or anyone else, because frankly, this felt like a deeper, dirtier deception than sneaking out to the cave with Papa's pistols when she and Joel were kids. Then, she'd put the guns back in their case and slipped back up to her room. Now, she'd face this decision in the mirror every day. And this drastic haircut was only the first of many details to keep up with if she was to truly pass herself off as a young man.

A cockroach darted from under the rug and got tangled in a brown curl. Rex pounced on it, which sent long, loose strands of hair flying all over the dirty wood floor.

"You could've picked a nicer place to do this," she remarked in a tight voice. "I've got the money to pay for it. And Mama would be having a tantrum—"

"But Mama's not here, is she?" her brother challenged. He took a big handful of hair above her left ear and snipped it gleefully. "And you're what? Eighteen now? Most girls your age are hitched, with two or three brats hanging on to them . . . looking worn out before their time. Wondering what happened to their romantic notions."

He stepped to her other side then and clipped quickly. "You, on the other hand, are sidestepping the matrimonial trap because you've always had a more exciting vision. A passion for riding and shooting."

Joel wasn't lying. But was he the example of what it meant to grab life by the horns and live it his way? She remembered the nights when she'd lain awake wondering if her brother were still alive, whether his family mattered to him at all.

At least he was here with her now. She would've approached her audition all wrong, had Joel not given her such important pointers. Maybe it was more than fate. Maybe it was God's way of looking after her as she tried on a new set of wings—even though her parents objected to it.

Solace recalled the fear in their faces as they'd hugged her good-bye. But she'd have run off anyway, had they forbidden her to try this, and that knowledge was reflected in their eyes, too. She'd never found an easy way to be herself. . . .

"What's your name going to be again?" Joel cut into her thoughts. "I need some practice saying it, so I don't call you your real name by mistake. Especially not in front of Cora or Pete."

"Sol," she breathed, wondering how it felt to be a Sol. "Sol Juddson."

"And where'd you come up with that?"

"Doesn't matter, does it?" she snapped. He was certainly smart enough to figure *that* out.

"Well, Sol, you're in luck, buddy," Joel teased, "because I found you a decent shirt and pants, and a fabric band to tie real tight around your, uh, chest. Now answer me back in your best manly man voice."

Solace swallowed and concentrated on a male sound. "That's right kindly of ya, Malloy. Comes a time I can ever do ya a favor, you let me know, hear?"

Her older brother stepped in front of her. He raised her chin to assess his barbering. "You sound like a sickly cow, Sol. First rule of the road is never be too nice."

His grip tightened, and he looked downright dangerous . . . hardened beyond redemption. "You *trust* too much, Juddson," he grunted. "This is a rough bunch we're running with—mostly folks who can't find other jobs, and Injuns who'll work for the liquor and the chow every night after the show."

"So why're *you* here?" she challenged in a lower, rougher voice. "Seems to me you coulda done better for yourself if—"

"Don't go judging me or you're on your own." Joel stooped so his eyes were level with hers . . . eyes as hard and dark as indigo marbles. "And don't forget—you never saw me before, understand? If Pete suspects we're related, he'll find another roustabout with a snap of his fingers."

Joel didn't have to say another word about the future of their relationship if her mistakes cost him his job. The long, thin fingers that *snapped* in front of her eyes drove his point home with a force that made her flinch.

"That's a girlie way to react," he muttered. "Come on, Sol—toughen it up. Act like a man, dammit!"

It was another double-dog dare in thin disguise, and when she impulsively spat in his face, Rex took over. The dog lunged for Joel's leg, as though he intended to remove it at the knee.

Joel swore, teetering sideways with the force of the dog's attack. "Hey! Call off your mutt before—"

"You asked for that!" she muttered in Sol's low, gravelly voice. "Leave me be, Malloy, or Rex'll be havin' fresh meat for dinner. Got it?" With a snap of her fingers and a short, harsh whistle, she signaled Rex to sit down.

The Border collie obeyed her, but when he crouched nearby, Rex's intense eyes never left the man she was glaring at.

Footsteps thundered in the hallway and somebody pounded on the door. "What's goin' on in there? We don't allow no animals in this establishment."

"Then why'd ya rent a room to Malloy?" Solace hollered gruffly. "And if that's the case, ya better see to these cockroaches, too! Why, I could *ride* one them suckers!"

The man muttered something and went on his way, while Joel gathered his hat from the chest of drawers. He was watching her dog very closely—and Rex was returning the favor.

"You're getting the hang of this, so I'll be getting on back now—"

"Somethin' about waitin' for Faustina at her wagon, as I recall?" Solace stood up, consciously squaring her shoulders and hooking her thumbs through her belt loops. "Thanks, Malloy. In spite of spittin' in your face, I really am glad to see ya. Glad you're helpin' me out with this, too. I owe ya one."

Joel's lean face softened, and just for an instant Solace saw the lost little boy who'd never felt he fit in with the rest of them. She missed that kid.

"Stop it right there," he muttered. "You were the only one who ever mattered to me when we were growing up. Don't go mushy on me."

He hooked an elbow loosely around her shoulders. It was a short, brusque hug, but at least he would still touch her. At least Joel's heart hadn't gone totally wild and unreachable in these years he'd been gone.

He put on his dusty hat, and with a nod he stepped out into the hall.

The solid *thud* of the door sounded awfully final. She was alone, in a strange, dirty hotel room with only Rex and the roaches for company.

The sight of all that long brown hair strewn on the floor was suddenly more than she could take. Solace snuffled back tears and double-dog dared herself to look in the splotchy mirror above the pitcher and bowl.

"My Lord, he didn't leave me—I hardly have any hair at all!" she wailed. "But I don't look any more like a man than I look like—"

A nudge at her knee made her lean down to hug Rex, and the dog nuzzled her damp face. He'd always been a worrier when anything made her cry. He sniffed eagerly at her head, searching for the Solace-scent that mingled with the smells of Joel's hands and the scissors. Then he sneezed so hard he shook all over.

Solace laughed sadly. "Got little hairs up your nose, fella? Maybe if I rinsed this rat's nest and combed my fingers through it, I wouldn't look so pathetic. Never thought to ask Joel if he'd cut hair before."

She poured water into the bowl, doused her head, and then rubbed it briskly with the ragged towel on the wall peg. When she faced the mirror again, a sense of purpose took over— and so did the natural waves that had always defied her efforts to tame them. Maybe Joel was a better barber than she'd given him credit for: the layers fell evenly into place, and she gave thanks for the thick mop of hair she'd gotten from . . .

Daddy.

Solace blinked. Those distinctive eyebrows . . . the strong nose, and that dimple in the corner of her mouth. Every one of those features held her attention whenever she gazed at the picture Mama had given her years ago. She still carried it with her whenever she left home, like a good luck charm— and if she'd ever been in need of some luck, it was now. While Michael Malloy had been the best father any girl could've asked for, it was good to have another one to fall back on when times got tough.

Solace lifted the framed likeness from her carpet bag and gazed at it. She looked in the mirror, and then back at the man whose presence she'd always felt, even though he had died before she was born.

"Well, I've gone and done it now, Daddy," she murmured as she gazed at his faded face. "I-I hope it's not something you'll think was wrong or—I didn't do this to hurt anybody, you know. I just . . . had to try it out."

She sighed, feeling very alone. But then, this was the first night she'd ever spent entirely by herself.

"Why is it so dang hard to live out the life I've always felt best about?" she asked him. "Why have I always been so different from—"

A soft whimper . . . a pawing at her leg . . .

Solace glanced down at Rex. His ears were peaked to form that brown butterfly she loved, and he gazed up at her with so much love she scooped him into her arms.

"Yeah, it's you and me now, buddy," she whispered against his silky hair. "I know you won't let me down, and I'll try to hold up my end of that bargain, too. We'll have Lincoln and Lee with us—and Daddy, and God. That's the best anybody can hope for, isn't it?"

Rex rested his head on her shoulder as though he didn't have a worry in the world. She wished that same peace would come as easily to her.

Lord, if this is meant to be, she prayed, *I'll do my very best to glorify You with the skills You've given me. And if it doesn't work, well—give me the grace to bow out before I make a total mess of things, all right?*

Chapter Nineteen

"Well, Mr. Juddson, I don't really need another sharpshooter." Apache Pete looked her over with a doubtful expression—and he watched Rex, too, because the dog was staring him down. "But you've got a couple of fine-looking bays here. And you say this pooch rides along with you?"

"Yessir. Rex, he loves to show off for an audience," Solace replied in Sol's best low voice. "Guarantee ya I'll hit whatever targets ya got, standin' still or ridin'. And for my big finish, I'll be straddlin' both bays, circlin' the ring at full gallop."

Apache Pete twirled his handlebar mustache around a finger, assessing how many extra dollars this might bring in. He didn't look nearly as impressive without his ringmaster's red coat; he resembled a bantam rooster as he circled her horses again. "Won't cost me a cent to see if you're as good as your word," he murmured. "Let me get somebody to toss your targets. And since the band's practicing, I'll have them strike up a real pulse-pounding song once you've got both horses under you."

"Thank you, sir. I appreciate this chance to show you what we can do."

Had Apache Pete seen through her disguise? Would he take a chance on a total stranger?

"Time to find out what we're made of," she whispered to Rex as they led Lincoln and Lee into the ring. The huge tent looked shabby without a crowd in it, and the air smelled hot and stale. Here came Crack-Shot Cora and Faustina Flambeau, along with Joel. The two women sat a few feet apart in the second row, as though it wasn't their idea to be here. But Solace couldn't let that distract her.

Her brother shot the pair a quick glance before turning his back to them. "You got a big trick for the end—a real show-stopper—if Pete asks you?"

Solace fought the urge to adjust the tight band under her new black shirt. "I can shoot an apple off Rex's head," she replied cautiously. "But I'm not going to show him that one. Somebody sneezes or throws a wadded-up peanut sack, and I've lost my best friend."

Joel nodded, thinking. "I'll toss some random targets as you circle the center ring. You can show how much better you are than Cora."

"But what if I hit *you*?" Solace's heart was rattling her ribcage, now that the hard, cold reality of this audition was hitting home.

Joel lowered his hat brim over those unflinching eyes. "You won't miss, Sol. I wouldn't take that chance for anybody else in this world—so don't prove me wrong!"

He trotted toward a wooden trunk near the bandstand, to fish out some colorful whirligigs. With a deep breath and a prayer, Solace mounted Lincoln's bare back and instructed Lee to stay put. As the band struck up a loosely woven waltz, she urged her mount forward to accustom him to the music and the arena. Once Apache Pete joined the two ladies on the bench, she sprang up to stand on the gelding's firmly muscled back . . . found the beat . . . let her trusty bay find his gait as though he'd been born for this moment.

She slipped into a half-trance, a state where her body relaxed to flow with her horse while her mind remained alert. It kept her from thinking too hard or making a misstep. When she felt herself ease into perfect, effortless rhythm with Lincoln, she gave a short whistle.

Rex loped alongside them and leaped, then landed behind her with a triumphant little *woof*! As she cantered past her observers, she caught the sparkle in their eyes. Crack-Shot

Cora looked a little bristly, but she followed every nuance and move.

Solace flashed Joel the thumbs-up then, and slipped her pistol from her waistband. It seemed fitting to audition with the pearl-handled set Billy had given her, and at the flutter of a shiny metal whirligig high above her, Solace shot without really taking aim.

A *ping* echoed in the tent's high ceiling, and then another and another. *Ping! Ping!*

She didn't check Apache Pete's reaction or think about what she was doing. Total relaxation was the only way to carry this off—and after five more moving targets, she signaled for Joel to stop. Then she waved to the bandmaster.

The music accelerated into a flashy show march, and as she circled toward Lee, she clapped her hands twice. The gelding tossed his black mane in anticipation and fell into step with them. Then she nimbly hopped over to his back to establish the pulse—the heartbeat that kept both horses moving beneath her in perfect harmony. She squatted, taking both their reins in her hands.

"All right, boys, here we go." A moment later she eased over to stand with a foot on each cantering horse and the floor going by beneath her. Solace leaned into the turns around the arena . . . let herself float and fly as their magnificent black manes fluttered in the breeze they created. If there was any finer, more exhilarating sensation on God's earth, she didn't know what it would be.

As the music subtly accelerated, Lincoln and Lee responded in perfect precision. When she reached her upper limit, Solace cleared her throat.

"Up, Rex. Give 'em a wave, boy," she commanded.

She could only feel him, balanced on Lincoln's back, facing backward. But she knew when the dog had done his trick.

"Bravo! Brav-*oh*!" Apache Pete called out. He stood up as they passed him, clapping wildly and grinning like a kid.

She knew when to quit. Solace sidestepped to stand on Lee, and then raised her arm in a ceremonial salute to the empty benches. Instinctively the two geldings slowed their pace until they came to an easy halt in front of Pete, Cora, and the Gypsy fortune-teller.

"Well done! The crowd's going to eat this up!" the show's owner crowed. "Let's get you a costume. You start tonight, Sol!"

The Extravaganza's other performers grudgingly changed the order of their appearances to give Sol Juddson the spot after the stagecoach robbery—long after Crack-Shot Cora had performed—but they watched in awe as she and Rex and the two bays cantered smoothly around the ring. They were impressed, too, by her marksmanship as the spinning whirligigs splintered one after the other—*ping*! *ping*! *ping*!—in the high tent top.

The showstopper, of course, was when Rex sat up to wave his paw at everyone. With the long fringe on her buckskin shirt drifting on her breeze, and hundreds of eyes following her every flex and balance adjustment, Solace raised both arms triumphantly during her final trip around the ring. As she slowed the two bays to exit the tent, Joel was there to lead them to the corral.

"See there?" he whispered when no one else was around. "You're a natural, Sol! A boy wonder with his trick dog! Better think of some other stunts you can do, little sister. Pete knows a crowd-pleaser when he sees one."

Sweet words, from a man who seldom showed his emotions. "Did I convince them I was a boy?"

"The buckskins help. You'll have to be careful come time to strip down and hit the hay for the night, though."

"You don't really think I'm going to take off my shirt in front of—"

"All the men'll want to hear your story—where you're from, and where you got these fine matched bays," he remarked. He sloshed water into the trough for Lincoln and Lee, glancing around for eavesdroppers. "The ladies'll check you out, too. Most of them are old enough to be—well, not your mother, but they've been on the circuit awhile. You're a fresh piece of meat, Juddson, and they'll all want a taste."

Her jaw dropped. She'd never considered this. Never thought about bunking in circus wagons and tents with men who probably slept in the altogether.

"Watch out for Faustina especially," he added. "Can't say her card readings are genuine, but she sizes folks up pretty fast. And accurately."

"She's seen my face close up, too. Before you cut my hair," Solace mused. "Thanks for letting me in on all this. I'll groom the horses and feed Rex now. Tend to my personal business where nobody'll see me."

"Yeah, if Sol squats to pee, it's all over, little sister."

For the next week, Solace led a charmed life: she triumphed during two daily performances, tended her horses, and practiced some new tricks in between. After Joel's warning about how everyone would want to know Sol's story, she played Juddson as the quiet type who kept to himself. It was a proud moment when an artist from *The Chronicle* sketched her and Rex atop Lee. SOL JUDDSON STEALS THE SHOW!! the article's headline proclaimed, and beside it there was another sketch of her sighting down her pistol at the reader, looking poised and pleased.

Joel bought her a couple copies of the issue in town, so she could stash them in her trunk. "Something to look back on when you're old and gray," he teased.

But the pride in his eyes made her feel ten feet tall. She wondered how her parents and Gabe would take it, when they saw her short curls and fringed buckskins in the newspaper. Would they understand that she was living out her dream? And that Lily's ungracious behavior hadn't chased her away from home forever?

Sunday at breakfast, Apache Pete announced they'd be extending their stay in Abilene because the crowds were eager for more of Sol Juddson before the show moved on to Enterprise. Solace felt elated, but things got tricky after the matinee performance: Madame Flambeau and Cora had time to spare then. Time to come sniffing around while Sol helped Joel feed the livestock.

"You're a damn fine rider, kid." Cora bit off the end of a cigar and then moistened it with her tongue before lighting up. "Luckiest shot I ever saw. Don't think you missed a target all week."

Sol flashed her a shy smile. "Thanks, ma'am. That's a mighty high compliment."

"And me, I'd like to set you down at my table for a . . . reading sometime," Faustina purred. She sashayed between Solace and Joel as they loaded hay bales into the stock wagon, and then the Gypsy gripped Sol's upper arm in a suggestive squeeze. "Don't you just want to run your fingers through those thick curls, Cora?"

The sharpshooter snorted behind her haze of cigar smoke. "I know who butters my bread, but that won't stop me from sayin' this straight out, Juddson. You oughtta *miss* once in a while. If you get what I'm sayin'."

Solace composed her face carefully. "And why would I wanna do that?"

"You gals better move along, so's we can get the buffalo fed," Joel cut in pointedly. "Pete'll be around to rag on us if we're not done by—."

"You let the women handle Pete," Faustina said with a flirtatious grin. "Cora's just pointing out that since she's the *star*, it would be polite for young Sol not to steal her thunder."

"'Specially since you got that dog and those fine horses in your act," Cora cut in. Her tone had turned edgy. Her expression was speculative as she studied Solace's reaction. "There's only so much to go around, kid. Only so far I'll be

pushed, before somethin' happens to that cute pooch. That'd
be a real shame, wouldn't it?"

The color rose into Solace's face. Joel's warning glance
made her bite back a retort. How would Sol Juddson handle
two women trying to get a rise out of him? How should he
set Cora straight, firmly but politely? Rex, meanwhile, sat
very stiffly, following this conversation with his instincts as
much as his eyes.

"I'm not tryin' to show you up, ma'am," Solace said in a
tight voice. "Just doin' my act and mindin' my own business.
If you want me to help you practice—"

"I want you to understand *one thing*, buster," Cora replied
gruffly. "I don't care if you *did* make the show go an extra
week in Abilene—you'd better *miss* once in a while—or fall
off your horse, maybe. I don't cotton to playin' second fiddle,
or havin' a damn *dog* get more applause than I do!"

The stocky little woman turned abruptly and stalked off,
leaving a trail of harsh-smelling smoke in her wake. Joel
laughed, distracting Faustina by slipping his arm around her
waist to kiss her. But that didn't stop the Gypsy from
looking Solace over very closely.

"I see a Six of Wands reversed," she whispered ominously.
"A man who was once riding high gets laid low. Better do as
Cora says. She packs a lot of punch around here."

With a sway of her gauzy skirts and a mysterious jingle of
bracelets, Madame Flambeau left Solace and her brother.
Rex followed the fortune-teller's retreat with a low growl.

"Anybody touches my dog, I'll be shooting at more than
whirligigs!" Solace said with a hiss. "I don't care *who* she is,
she can't tell me to—"

"Those gals pull a lot of weight, and they lead Apache Pete
around by the—ear," he added quickly. "It's always a sign
Faustina's claws are out when she loses her Gypsy accent."

"Why does *she* care how well I shoot? It's not like her
fortune-telling business is affected by—"

"No, but she and Cora always unite when the chips are

down. Birds of a feather gotta flock together." Joel tossed the
last two hay bales up to the wagon, his expression pensive.
"You might want an excuse to leave the show before we roll
on to Enterprise. From there we go to Nebraska and parts
north—a lot farther from home if mischief kicks up."

"But I just got started! We're a *hit*!" she protested.
"Apache Pete said there'd be a pay raise if I can come up
with a really fantastic trick where Rex rides one of the
horses and—"

"You won't *have* an act, much less the heart to keep
performing, if your dog meets up with a so-called 'accident.'
Cora means to practice on a moving target, if you don't do
like she says."

Stunned, Solace hugged her dog when he leaped into her
arms. She'd worried about Lincoln or Lee getting out of step
while she shot, or about somebody whistling to Rex, but
never had she imagined somebody threatening her dog
because he'd outperformed her in a show! That cigar-
chomping not-so-Crack-Shot Cora had better watch her own
back, if she kept talking like that!

"Be careful, little sister," Joel warned as she turned to go.
"When you get hot under the collar, you look way too pretty
to be a boy."

Easier said than done in the world of the Wild West, where
performers came and went at all hours, playing cards and
carousing from one wagon to the next with their whiskey
bottles.

While she'd practiced riding and shooting at home all
those years, dreaming of the day she could perform for a
tentful of amazed spectators, Solace hadn't considered the
seamier side of this world she'd only watched from the
grandstands. Theatrical makeup and costumes covered a
lot . . . created illusions as alluring as Faustina's Gypsy
personality, for impressionable audiences that came to be
astounded and entertained. She'd learned things she didn't
really want to know about some of these folks, and she had a

lot of thinking to do. Any more visits from Cora and Madame Flambeau—especially if they cornered her when Joel wasn't around—and there would be trouble. She didn't have to be a fortune-teller to predict that.

Trouble struck the next day, without warning.

Solace had decided to ride along the Smoky Hill River before breakfast, to clear her head of Cora's threats and enjoy some time away from prying eyes. With Rex in her lap and Lee following obediently behind, she steered Lincoln to a secluded spot upstream from the back corrals. She tethered the horses to graze on the lush shoreline grass, and then slipped out of her clothes. Quickly she ducked under the cool water and then rubbed herself with soap she'd brought along.

Rex joined her, eager to splash and play—but when he let out three sharp barks, Solace turned around before she thought about it.

Cora was laughing slyly, holding not only Sol's pants and homespun shirt, but the long strip of fabric Solace bound her breasts with.

"I *knew* it! I knew, soon as I laid eyes on you, there was somethin' not right about our spectacular new sharpshooter!" she jeered. "Wait till Pete sees *this*!"

"No—I—you've got to understand—"

"Oh, I understand perfectly," the little woman snapped. "You intended to horn in on my act! Maybe steal my spot completely, and then reveal yourself to Pete to attract *his* attentions, too! Anybody who'd trick herself out like a boy can't be trusted for a single minute!"

Off she stomped, triumphantly waving Sol Juddson's clothing in front of her.

"Wait! You can't just march off with my clothes! I—"

Rex bounded from the water, barking fiercely. He grabbed a leg of Solace's pants to snatch them away, but Cora turned to glare at him.

"Get away from me, mutt!" she cried. Then she hollered

toward the corrals and show wagons. "Boys! Pete! Help me! Mad dog! *Mad dog!*"

Apache Pete came running, and so did Joel and a few others, while Solace could only watch, helpless and naked, from the stream.

It was all over. Sol Juddson had just gotten off to a wonderful start as the star of this Wild West Extravaganza, and now the secret was out.

"Rex! Easy, boy!" she hollered. She'd have even more trouble if her protective dog attacked somebody.

By then Cora was surrounded by curious men, and she was in her glory. "Would you look at what I just uncovered!" she cried. "Seems our Sol Juddson is a *girl*, passin' herself off as a young man! She's gotta come outta that water sometime, and you'll see it for yourselves!"

The men buzzed like bumblebees and hurried toward the riverbank, where Rex had positioned himself to protect Solace. Joel broke away from the group, shrugging out of his shirt.

"Better put this on and come clean," he said as he tossed it to her. "Your riding and shooting speak for themselves in the ring, but Cora's stirring up a whole new nest of snakes. It'll be up to Pete now, whether you stay with the show or leave."

Nodding sadly, Solace stepped out of the river. Joel's old shirt covered her breasts and bare backside but not much else. It was better than returning to the wagons naked, though. "Thanks," she gasped. "I should've been more careful."

"Those two biddies've been waiting for just such a moment. Would've happened sooner or later." He walked ahead of her, to where Apache Pete stood with Cora ranting on one side of him and Faustina Flambeau crowing on the other.

"No surprise to me that something wasn't right about our new *boy*," the raven-haired Gypsy exclaimed. "Wrong walk, wrong gestures. Way too graceful, standing on those horses to perform. I saw it right off!"

Apache Pete took in the way Joel stepped to the side, shirtless, as she and Rex approached. Still soaking wet, with rivulets of water streaming down from her cropped curls, Solace had never felt more at a disadvantage. But if she didn't defend herself, who would?

"Malloy, I've got to ask this straight out," the showman said. "If you're in cahoots with Juddson, or whoever he—she—is—"

"She's my sister." Joel looked his boss in the eye without a flicker of apology. "And she's the best damn performer I've ever seen—the best one *you've* ever seen, too, isn't she?" he challenged. "Before you go thinking the wrong things about her, *I'm* the one who suggested she disguise herself. Didn't figure she'd even get to audition if she had to compete against Cora."

Apache Pete twirled an end of his handlebar mustache, looking from Joel to Solace. "And what do you have to say for yourself, missy?"

"I'm sorry," she breathed, clutching the shirt around her wet body. "I've loved to ride and shoot all my life, and I just wanted a chance to perform. If you want me to leave, I'll—"

"Nonsense. Folks *love* you and Rex—and that's the *only* reason I'll tolerate your trickery, young lady. What's your real name?"

"Solace Monroe."

"And where do you live?"

"Just the other side of Abilene, sir. Been training horses and riding since I could walk, practically. Out on my parents' ranch."

Pete's eyes softened, but he was a man in charge of a close-knit troupe and a tight schedule. "You'll continue to appear as Sol Juddson because we've sent our flyers ahead to Enterprise, advertising you and your dog. So I expect—"

"But, Pete! If this upstart's deceived us about her sex, who knows what else she'll pull?" Faustina demanded.

"I don't trust her any farther than I could throw her!" Cora chimed in.

Apache Pete cleared his throat, pondering his dilemma. "Get over your objections, ladies, because from here on out she'll be bunking with you. I can't think you'll mind having a handsome, talented young fellow like Sol as a wagonmate."

Pete glanced around at the crowd that had gathered to follow this little drama. "Now get your breakfast and get ready for the next show! Most of you've got deeper, darker secrets than Miss Monroe, so I don't want to hear another word about this. The Wild West Extravaganza must go on! Bigger and better than ever!"

As the roustabouts turned to do Pete's bidding, Solace gave the show's owner a grateful grin. "Thank you, sir. I truly appreciate being able to stay in the show—"

"Don't speak too soon, missy. Traveling with the likes of Faustina and Crack-Shot Cora might change your mind about that."

Chapter Twenty

That evening's performance was her best ever; Solace rode with more flair, and Rex performed a new trick, dancing with her atop Lee's back as they cantered around the ring. She didn't miss a single shot—and Joel spun her some wide, wild targets as a challenge. The audience cheered so loudly that Apache Pete brought them back into the ring twice, just so folks could adore her with their applause.

She went to the wagon that night with a big grin on her face. It was no secret that Apache Pete played to the crowds—and that Sol Juddson's flamboyant riding and shooting were filling the grandstands during their extended stay in Abilene. The ringmaster had apparently warned Cora and Faustina to behave themselves, because after the show, they went off to drink and play poker with the roustabouts.

She didn't like to perform on a full stomach, so Solace ate the bowl of beans and stew she'd set aside, sitting cross-legged under the wagon with Rex, as she always did. The company cook must've emptied a few odd bottles of sauce into the pot, because it had an off taste. The meals here left a lot to be desired, compared to what she was used to eating at home, but she was too excited about her performance to care. She gave Rex his own piece of leftover corn bread as a reward. "Guess we showed those ladies how it's done," she murmured as she stroked the dog's silky hair.

He woofed softly and licked her hand clean. Then he curled up under the front of the wagon for the night, and Solace crawled into her pallet of blankets inside, on the floor.

She was jolted awake by loud pounding on the door. Had she just fallen asleep, or was it hours into the night? She felt too groggy to tell.

"Sol Juddson, you in there?" a gruff male voice demanded. The door flew open just as Solace grabbed her bedding up around her, and two burly fellows in broad-brimmed hats stepped inside. Apache Pete peered through the door behind them.

"What the—what do you want?" she protested. The men were coming at her as though she'd done something horrible!

"You know anything about Cora's whereabouts?" Pete asked. His voice sounded thin and he looked shaken. Much more humble and cautious than she'd ever seen him.

"Last thing I knew, she was playing cards with—I went to bed after the show, so I have no idea—" Solace glanced at the two bunks, which were empty. Where were Faustina and Cora? And where was Rex? He should've been barking and charging at these intruders.

"You'd better come along with us and straighten some things out, missy," the taller fellow insisted. "We get enough extra trouble when you circus types come in, and I'm not puttin' up with it. Not in *my* town."

Solace's mouth went dry and she shook herself awake. She didn't recognize this man's voice, and she couldn't seem to focus her eyes. "I still have no idea—"

"Better check your pistols, Miss Monroe. There's been an . . . unfortunate incident." Pete cleared his throat nervously. He peered around, as though he might find Cora hidden in the armoire or under her bed.

"Never mind about my pistols! Where's Rex? My dog should be—"

"Ain't seen hide nor hair of no dog," the shorter, stockier fellow replied. "But you're in a heap of trouble if you don't answer to us pretty dang quick."

Trouble? Head spinning, Solace crawled to the corner of the wagon where Faustina and Cora had cleared a small space for her to stash her carpetbag and pistol case.

"I *told* you, I've been sleeping like the dead—or I'd know where my dog's gone!" Tin stars glinted on their chests as the two men watched her like hungry hawks. She knew Sheriff Draper and any lawmen who came from Abilene, yet she couldn't put names to these two shadowy faces. "I cleaned my pistols after the evening show, like always. Stored them in this case to—"

The bottom dropped out of her stomach. Only one pistol rested in its velvet casing.

"You sure you didn't leave it in your buckskins?" Pete asked in an agitated voice. "If you can't put your hand on it, the sheriff'll have to—"

"I *know* what I did with my pistols, Pete. Now where's the other one?" she demanded, willing her body not to shake. "Why don't you fellows just tell me what's going on here, instead of scaring the stuffing out of me?"

The taller man—the one in charge—raised a bushy eyebrow at his partner. "Better come with us, Miss Malloy. You've got some explaining to do."

"I've got nothing to explain until you tell me where—"

"Don't argue," Pete rasped. "Cora's been shot. They-they found her body in the trees along the river."

The blood drained from her head. This whole scenario felt like a nightmare gone terribly wrong, and as she was escorted from the stuffy wagon into the half-light of early morning, Solace noticed the other members of the Wild West show milling about like ants in a hill that had been raked away. When they caught sight of her and pointed, the dryness in her mouth turned to a coppery tang. She stumbled. Her head felt muzzy, and she had trouble walking.

Do NOT vomit! Do NOT complicate things by puking on this lawman's boots, she warned herself.

"There she is! There's the low-down snake who killed Cora!"

Solace stopped to stare. Faustina Flambeau was rushing toward her like a rabid dog. This was all so bizarre. Details faded in and out, as though she were shrouded in a haze she couldn't see through.

"Wasn't enough that you showed her up in the ring again!" the fortune-teller cried. "You had to yell her down and get her riled up, when she *nicely* asked you to—"

"I don't know what you're talking about," Solace mumbled. "I've been asleep."

"Oh, shut up! There goes my best friend on that stretcher—and you shot her dead!" Faustina swiped at tears, pointing to the figure slung on a sheet between two of the roustabouts. "I knew you were trouble from the start. Get that lousy traitor out of here, Sheriff!"

The lawmen grabbed her arms when Solace bolted forward, toward the fake Gypsy whose accusations made absolutely no sense. "You're lying and you know it!" she rasped. "You and Cora have had it in for me—"

"Don't say another word." The shorter fellow cleared his throat pointedly. From his back waistband he pulled the pearl-handled pistol that hadn't been in its case. "We found this near the body, Miss Monroe. It's your word against everybody else's, but none of 'em saw or heard anything unusual—till one of the fellows tripped over Miss Cora about an hour ago."

"We're arresting you for her murder," the other one chimed in. "Every person we asked had an alibi—and mentioned you as the one most likely to pick a bone with her. Let's go."

Her head was spinning as the lawman's words swam in her ears. *Murder*? When someone had obviously swiped her gun? And her dog? And what about Lincoln and Lee? If the horses were gone, too . . .

Her vision grew patchy and Solace felt the last of her resolve give way as she wilted to the ground in a heap.

A few miles from the fairgrounds, Joel Malloy stopped on the bank of the Smoky Hill River to rinse the blood from his tooth-marked arm. He let out a short laugh when Rex crouched into pouncing position, on the back of one of the bays he'd led behind his own horse.

"I'm taking you home," he assured the feisty white Border collie. "Solace needs more help than we can give her back there. And she needs you alive, you feisty mutt."

The dog followed his every word with those bright, beadlike eyes and the rise of those dark ears. Joel stuck his arm into the cool water and rubbed it where the bites still bled a little; it hadn't been easy, snatching Solace's protective dog out of harm's way, and Rex still wasn't his willing hostage. But he'd smelled trouble brewing after the show, when Faustina hadn't spared him a glance. She went whispering to Apache Pete instead, and then she'd hung thick with Cora and a couple bottles of cheap whiskey.

"Should've known something would happen after Cora told Solace to miss some shots, but I never figured on *this*," he explained to the bright-eyed dog. "Never should've talked her into trying out for the show—even though there was no keeping her away from it. Come on, Rex. We're almost at the ranch."

Joel followed the river for another twenty minutes. He felt shady approaching the Triple M from behind the barns rather than through its white arched entryway, but he'd taken cover under the cottonwoods in case Pete sent somebody after him. He'd done the right thing by his sister. Yet his gut tightened with something he couldn't name.

Mercy and Malloy would blame him for what had happened to Solace, and he didn't intend to hang around for their tongue-lashing. Just wanted to deliver her horses and dog, and the message that she was in trouble for a crime she didn't commit. Then he'd head west again; it was a sure bet Apache Pete wanted nothing more to do with him.

He nudged his horse forward with his heels. The two-story house shone like a white diamond in the morning sun. Except for the green patch of yard inside the picket fence, the Triple M farmstead rolled off into corn and wheat fields as far as he could see in any direction. It was the most prosperous spread in the county, and he could claim his birthright any time he chose. As Malloy's only son, he'd be welcomed and celebrated just like that prodigal runaway in the Bible story.

But this wasn't the life for him. It reeked of rules and do-gooding.

He smelled bacon and biscuits; warned himself not to sit down to the breakfast they'd be serving up with a heavy dose of Biblical wisdom, even though a home-cooked meal would soothe his soul. Maybe he'd just slip the bays into the corral and keep riding . . . let Rex kick up a fuss, until everybody realized Solace was in trouble because she wasn't with her trusty dog.

As though the mutt had read his thoughts, Rex hopped nimbly off his horse and ran for the house, barking like the barn was on fire.

Joel led the horses to the paddock, watching for whomever answered the dog's summons. He wasn't surprised when Temple Gates came out the kitchen door, even though the children she'd tutored were grown up and gone. The coffee-skinned caretaker glanced around the yard, and when she spotted him . . . gave him a long look . . . Joel waved at her.

"Rex, you hush now!" Temple cried as the dog circled her frantically. "Mister Joel, is that really you? Miss Mercy— Mister Michael! You'd better come see who's here!"

He hooked the corral gate, and as he strode toward the house, Mercy and his father stepped outside. Their usual joy at seeing him would be tempered by disappointment once the initial surprise of his visit wore off. Usually took about two minutes.

"Joel! Solace said you were traveling with the Wild West show—"

"And we were so hoping to see you!" Mercy finished his father's welcome.

"Wish I had better news for you, but Solace found herself some trouble with the law." Never one for small talk, Joel endured Mercy's embrace and shook his pa's outstretched hand. "She'll no doubt be charged with killing Cora Walsh, even though she didn't do it."

"Killing who?"

"You can't possibly mean—"

"So where is she? Why didn't you bring her home?" There it was already, Pa's accusation that he hadn't done enough.

"I heard two shots out behind the wagons, and some whispered insinuations. Figured I'd better bring Rex and her horses back here," he explained impatiently. "Last thing I saw was the sheriff and his deputy walking toward the wagon where Solace bunked. Ever since Cora exposed Sol Juddson as a girl in a man's clothes and haircut, Solace has run short of luck."

"Sol Juddson?" Mercy's face creased with an uncomprehending frown.

Temple, too, looked doubtful about this news. "Why on earth would Solace cut off all her hair?"

His father's face grew solemn. He looked a little more lined from the weather and the years, but those hazel eyes still shone with a fierce love for the girl he'd delivered during a blizzard; another man's daughter he'd loved as his own. "And all this happened where?" he asked quietly. He laid his hands on Mercy's shoulders to settle her agitation.

"Just the other side of town, at the fairgrounds."

"We'd best be on our way then." His dad glanced at the shocked female faces on either side of him, and then leveled his gaze at Joel. "Let me get a few things together, and we can leave—"

"Not going with you," Joel insisted with a sharp shake of his head. "Apache Pete'll see this as my doing. I talked Solace into auditioning, so it's my fault the law came down on his show, after his lady friend got herself shot. I want no part of that."

Joel eased out of Mercy's embrace. Better to break up this little reunion before anybody got ideas about how long it should last.

"We're just setting breakfast on the table. Surely you can stay long enough to eat a bite—to put some meat on those bones," Temple insisted. She, too, had a few silvery streaks in her hair, but those coffee-colored eyes still watched for signs he was fibbing, like they had when he was a kid.

He planted a quick kiss on Mercy's forehead. "You know me. Once I accomplish what I set out to do, there's no home like the road. Take care, now."

Chapter Twenty-one

Solace jerked awake and was immediately sorry; every muscle in her body cried out, and her head was pounding so hard all rational thought was driven away. She was vaguely aware of being on a narrow cot, which she fell out of when she tried to sit up.

I've died and gone to hell. But how did I get here?

As she curled in to hold her knees, still lying on the dirty floor, Solace caught a whiff of sour vomit. She was wearing the long underwear she'd been sleeping in when . . .

What happened? Why are those iron bars in front of me like a . . .

"Mornin'," a male voice said. "You've got visitors, Miss Monroe."

She winced. Why would anyone want to see her when she smelled so vile and probably looked even worse? At the sound of footsteps, she opened one eye.

"Here she is, Malloy," that same male voice said. "There was some confusion last night with the two new deputies on duty, but even so, I can't think this is your girl they brought here."

"Thanks, Harry, but I'm hoping it is. I understand there's been trouble at the fairgrounds."

"Yep. Lady sharpshooter from the Wild West show was found dead, around sunup."

Solace trembled and couldn't stop. Fragments of dialogue came back to her . . . two men barging into the wagon . . . one pistol missing from its case. . . .

"Solace? Solace, can you hear me, honey?" A familiar,

worried face swam before her eyes—and then the woman turned toward the outer room where the men were talking. "Harry Draper, you unlock this cell! My daughter will *not* lie here like a-a caged animal!"

Solace's eyes flew open. "Mama? Lord, I don't know how—and Gabe? Is that you? Or . . . or are you angels come to save me from—"

"Darn right we are. I don't know what's going on here, but we'll figure it out, sweetheart. You're going to be all right now."

Gabe Getty's voice cut through the fear and confusion in her mind, and when her hand shot forward, he grabbed it between the bars. The next few moments went fuzzy again, but she heard jangling keys and the snick of a lock. Strong arms scooped her gently from the floor . . . she overheard her mother's muffled disgust and saw dearly familiar faces that looked . . . confused. And very, very worried.

"Let's set you right here and get you a glass of water," Papa said as he helped her into a chair. "You can tell us what you know when you're ready, honey."

Solace gulped greedily from the cup they held to her lips, gazing from her mother's tear-streaked face to her papa's concerned hazel eyes, to that bespectacled figure she'd seen in her dreams. Although she sensed her problems weren't solved, she felt the supreme relief of knowing she wouldn't be sorting them out alone.

"I don't know what to say," she rasped. "I just remember bits and pieces. Must've passed out when the deputy grabbed me—and I never do that!"

Gabe scowled, gently lifting her chin with his finger. "Follow this with your eyes," he said. Then he moved his other hand back and forth.

She obeyed as best she could. Why was everyone staring at her as though they weren't sure who she was? "Wh-what's wrong?" she mumbled. "What's happened to me?"

His expression wavered between concern and pain. "Your

eyes look glassy. Your pupils have shrunk to pinpoints, like Letitia's did when she'd taken too much laudanum. You were arrested for shooting a woman in the Wild West show—"

Solace's breath caught. "You know I'd never do that!"

"—and from what little the sheriff can tell us, I believe you've been accused of this murder to cover someone else's crime."

He straightened to his full lanky height then. "Mr. Draper, I suggest we ride out to the fairgrounds and question Apache Pete and members of his show before they move on. We might find some details that'll be helpful if this goes to trial."

"And we'll be taking Solace home," her mother insisted. "You can't possibly believe she killed anyone!"

"Nope, I don't. But Solace is feistier than most—and a better shot, too." Harry Draper reached for his hat on the peg by the door. "You folks better be ready for the gossip. When word gets 'round about this shooting—and when they see your daughter with her hair all chopped off—folks'll have a lot to talk about."

Why did his words have such an ominous ring? Solace watched the sheriff stride out the door behind Gabe, wondering how so many nasty things could have happened during her short career with the Wild West Extravaganza.

"Where's Rex?" she demanded in a faltering voice. "And what about Lee and Lincoln and—"

"Joel brought them home, honey," her father explained. "Let's get you there, too, and we'll sort things out when you feel better."

"And smell better," Mama added with a grimace. "Then you'll tell us why on earth you pretended to be a young man, and why you cut off all your hair. You have a lot to account for!"

"Joel!" she rasped. "I've felt so lightheaded—so worried about Rex and the horses—I haven't even wondered where he is. Why didn't he stay with me when all this trouble broke loose?"

Her mother's smile looked sad and resigned. "Will we ever know why Joel acts the way he does? He headed out before we could even talk him into breakfast. Who knows when or where he'll turn up next?"

Solace sagged as they walked her toward the door. Life felt a whole lot trickier now that her memory was floating back. Too many pieces missing from this puzzle . . . questions she might never have answers for, if her one ally from Apache Pete's troupe had disappeared.

Why would Joel leave me? What did they do to me—to Rex!—while he wasn't there?

What if he'd run off because *he'd* killed Crack-Shot Cora? Framed his sister for his crime, figuring nobody would try her in court because she was a girl? And if she'd been drugged with laudanum, as Gabe suggested, who had done that to her? And why?

"You'd better see that justice is done, Sheriff Draper. And soon!" Apache Pete spouted. "Because with Cora dead and Sol Juddson out of the show—and now a roustabout gone missing—this incident's cost me way too much!"

Gabe had listened very carefully, with his eyes as much as his ears, while various people from the Wild West Extravaganza gave Harry Draper their accounts of Cora's murder. None of this was adding up: not the way Solace's pistol had been found near her rival's body, nor the way Faustina the fortune-teller insisted Solace and the dead woman had come to blows. In his mind he still saw her glassy brown eyes punctuated by such tiny black pupils . . . heard the fear and uncertainty in her voice. It was obvious to him that Solace Monroe had *not* killed Cora Walsh, but who had?

"We'll need to take the pistol with us, Sheriff," Gabe said when he saw they'd get nothing further from these performers. "And I'll stop by the undertaker's when we get back to town."

He faced Apache Pete then, taking in the little man's

pompous waxed mustache and his puffed-up presence while he again insisted that the sheriff saw justice was done immediately.

"That means you and your troupe will need to remain in town," Gabe pointed out, "because Miss Monroe has the right to a trial by a jury of her peers."

Pete's eyes widened. "But we're moving on to Enterprise—reorganizing the show, now that Sol and the dog aren't—"

"If you want justice, sir, you must cooperate with the same law you're invoking against my client," Gabe pointed out. "If you leave town, you'll be taking all the witnesses with you and I will be forced to drop the charges for lack of evidence. Is that what you want?"

"Drop the charges?" The raven-haired fortune-teller raised her black lace veil to glare at him. "You're insinuating that a killer would run free."

"Not at all." As he leveled his gaze at the Gypsy, tricked out in that black veil and layers of flowing fabric and jewelry, Gabe saw a flicker of something in those brazen eyes. "I'm just saying the justice you seek is as much your responsibility as mine. I suggest you hire a lawyer to present your case when it goes to court."

"A lawyer?" The ringmaster scowled. "Why should I put out good money—waste more of our time—when all the evidence points to Miss Monroe?"

"Ah, but it doesn't," Gabe said mysteriously, gazing steadily at the showman and mustering the stern demeanor he'd used so effectively in St. Louis courtrooms. "Good day, sir. Feel free to let us know if you've reconsidered the charges. Ask for Judge Gabriel Getty."

When Harry had fetched the pistol, they returned to town on the lawman's buckboard, riding in thoughtful silence for a while. "Not doubting your word, Mr. Getty, but I don't see how you can act as Solace's lawyer if you're presiding over her trial."

"You've thought about that, but our man Pete hasn't," Gabe pointed out. "Before my court appointment, I'd have taken Solace's case and run with it. But I'll be finishing a trial my predecessor, Judge Ratcliff, began . . . and in the meantime, looking for evidence in Solace's behalf while I find ways to discredit Apache Pete and Faustina Flambeau's stories."

The sheriff chuckled. "You sound like a man who enjoys his work."

"It's my mission to prove people innocent when they've been falsely accused," he said. "The challenges of gathering evidence and quizzing witnesses . . . ferreting out the holes in a criminal's alibis. Those things make the tedium of research and record-keeping worthwhile. They elevate the law to a calling, above an ordinary job."

Viewing lifeless bodies had never been his favorite part of that calling. But as he studied the evidence Gabe focused on finding a way to acquit Solace, instead of on how grisly this murder had been.

Miss Walsh had a bullet hole through her shoulder and she'd been gut-shot, as well. Gabe clenched his jaw to keep from gagging at the dark damage done to her fleshy white body. Her eyes stared sightlessly at the ceiling of the undertaker's workroom; her air of mild surprise suggested secrets that might never be revealed . . . unless he figured them out before she was buried.

"Would you mind turning her over?"

Roland Markham scowled. "Don't see what good that would do, especially since you're not family."

"Humor me. I have a theory."

With an impatient sigh, the lugubrious little man placed his hands on Cora's shoulder and hip to roll her onto her stomach. "And?"

Gabe's pulse pounded faster as his hunch proved correct. "Don't you see it?" he asked quietly. "How the bullet holes are smaller and cleaner from this side? It means that Miss

Walsh—a sharpshooter by trade—was shot from behind. Which also means her killer was a coward. Too weak, for whatever reason, to face her when they pulled the trigger—even though she wasn't armed herself."

Markham's pale blue eyes widened. "Word around town's that the Malloy girl killed her. Was trying for more fame and fortune in that Wild West show by getting rid of the competition. They say she cut her hair to—"

"What they say and what we see don't match up then, do they?" Gabe countered with a purposeful gaze. "Thank you for your time and cooperation, sir. When's the funeral?"

"Tomorrow morning. Ten-thirty."

With a nod Gabe left the stuffy room in the back of Markham's Furniture Emporium. He had a lot to think about between now and tomorrow, and establishing Solace as a victim whose naivete was used against her would be his biggest contribution to this case. It was more of a challenge than he'd faced with previous cases . . . more of a personal mission than dealing with clients in whom he had nothing invested.

But Solace? How he craved her faith in him! How would he ever face her again if he failed to set her free?

Chapter Twenty-two

Solace paused beside the buckboard, assessing those who had gathered around the open grave. She knew them all—or did she? They'd been friendly enough to her—or to Sol Juddson, anyway—as she learned the ropes of performing in the Wild West show. But one of them had killed Crack-Shot Cora.

"So why are we making this appearance?" she whispered. "Won't they think it odd that I've shown up when they believe I'm the killer?"

Gabe tucked her hand in the crook of his elbow and led her sedately toward the small graveside gathering. "You're showing them what you're made of, Solace. Proving you have nothing to hide, and that you're a decent human being come to pay your respects.

"And meanwhile," he added, "I'm watching their every move and reaction. Cora's killer is here, and may well distinguish himself—or *her*self—during the funeral service."

They stopped slightly behind the handful of mourners. Solace didn't like it one bit that Hannibal Prescott would preside over her case . . . wondered whether Gabe couldn't arrange to be the judge if he really wanted to. He dropped her hand to stand a proper distance from her. It was the professional thing to do, yet she yearned for more personal reassurance of his feelings for her.

"Good morning," she murmured when Apache Pete widened his eyes at her.

The woman beside Pete, swathed from head to toe in black bombazine and lace, gasped indignantly behind her veil. "How dare you show up and taint our purpose here?" Faustina blurted. "Isn't it enough that you shot—"

"Hush, dear. You're upsetting yourself needlessly." The ringmaster slipped an arm around her, coaxing her to face forward as Roland Markham stepped to the head of the grave. "God is watching. Judgment—and justice—are in His hands, and we trust Him to carry them out for poor Cora."

Solace blinked. While he was absolutely correct, she'd never heard the swaggering Apache Pete invoke the name of the Lord . . . noticed how the words didn't ring quite true coming from his lips—just as she realized the fortune-teller was a totally different character without her Gypsy accent and clothing. Faustina Flambeau was as much a fictional character as Sol Juddson, weaving her illusion of mystery and romance whenever it would pay.

Gabe leaned toward the ringmaster. "Your case has been scheduled for two weeks from today," he said in a dignified voice. "That should give you ample time to arrange for legal counsel and—"

"We'll take care of ourselves, thank you!" Pete's gaze flicked from the lawyer's face to Solace's, making silent assumptions about her and Gabe Getty. "God—and the law—are on our side, after all."

Solace nearly blurted a retort, but Roland Markham had opened his prayer book and seemed impatient to begin. At Gabe's warning glance, she composed her face, stood demurely with her hands clasped in front of her.

"We gather today to remember Cora Walsh and to commit her earthly body to the ground, whence she came," the undertaker intoned in a dreary voice. "Ashes to ashes, dust to dust . . ."

Solace's mind wandered during the brief and uninspiring service. In front of her, the dozen or so folks from the Wild West show bowed their heads, but she felt their glances . . . sensed their discomfort because a lawyer—a judge—had accompanied her here. Gabriel Getty returned their gazes with straightforward solemnity.

"Amen," the undertaker said, and everyone echoed him.

Faustina wailed mournfully and turned away from the open grave, bawling into her handkerchief. It sounded overdramatic to Solace—as did Pete's gallant response.

"She's in a better place now, Faustina," he soothed as he escorted her toward the waiting wagons. "Cora would want the Extravaganza to go on—just as she's counting on us to avenge her death! We must all be strong."

"We must live for the moment my best friend's killer is convicted!" Faustina turned, and even though Solace couldn't see the fortune-teller's eyes, she felt the sting of a daggerlike glare. "We must carry on so Cora's life and death will not have been for naught!"

Apache Pete followed Faustina into the undertaker's black carriage with the air of a man determined to prevail . . . and perhaps to profit from this tragedy.

"I don't like this one little bit." Solace ran her hand through her short curls, acutely aware that the show's performers and roustabouts followed her every move. They treated her differently now that she wore a simple gown of dark brown faille . . . as though they thought Sol Juddson looked mighty odd in a dress.

"Forget their theatrics. Focus on being your straightforward, unshakable self, Solace." Gabe walked her to the buckboard without touching her. "When a jury convicts the innocent, it's often because the accused behave as though they *are* guilty. Or they feel intimidated by the threats and accusations leveled at them and cave in. I've seen folks admit to crimes they didn't commit because they couldn't handle cross-examination."

He stopped beside the buckboard, weaving his fingers together to give her a step up—but then he straightened to his full height again. "Be aware that for some folks, a trial is a game—and they love to play it from all possible sides," he said softly. "Just because they *can*."

Solace's stomach clenched at this remark. Gabe made it sound as if she was a duck decoy at a carnival stand, waiting to be shot at for a prize. "I hate to sound . . . desperate," she breathed, "but I'd feel so much better if *you* were trying my case, Gabe. I-I'm no good at fending off threats, or standing up to accusations. Especially now that people will be staring at me—at my short hair—and thinking—"

Gabe grabbed her head gently between his hands. His dark eyes widened behind his lenses as his fingers sifted her soft curls. He gazed at her face as though he might never see her again—might never . . .

His kiss made her heart lurch, and then gallop like a filly set free! He was telling her he loved her. Expressing what he couldn't put into words: that everything would work out. And after he made sure she won her case, they'd ride off into that magical, mystical sunset of her daydreams.

Solace slipped her arms around his waist, holding tightly to this vision . . . kissing Gabe with all the love her heart held, now that she finally had the chance. His lips were urgent; he was seeking completion, just as she was.

He pulled away too soon. Looked as flummoxed as she felt. "I-I've taken a room in town, for both our sakes," he rasped. "This case is all about your credibility, Solace. If I were presiding as the judge, Apache Pete would have reason to declare a mistrial because I'm a friend of your family. We can't take any chances right now."

We can't take any chances? She inhaled sharply. He might as well have gut-punched her. Was Gabriel Getty hiding behind his judicial robe for her benefit, or his own? "I understand what you're saying. I guess."

He looked away as though he couldn't bear to watch her cry. Because she was going to. "I would drive you home, but—"

"You have a job to show up for. Important things to do and people to see," she murmured. She hated to sound so pathetic, but this was not the way she'd pictured things while he was kissing her. "Thanks for all your help, Gabe. It's not like I can't find my way home. I-I'll see you again before the trial, I hope."

Truth be told, Solace saw Gabe Getty every time she climbed the stairs the next two weeks . . . Gabe standing in her sister's embrace, while the sunshine beamed down on them like a blessing Lily had arranged with her angels. Small consolation that she had her room back; her sister had returned to Miss Vanderbilt's Academy for Young Ladies while she'd been performing in the Extravaganza.

On the surface, her life seemed the same as before she'd reunited with Gabe at Billy's house, but everything that mattered had changed.

At least Lily hadn't wrangled Gabe away from her, but the fights with her sister shrouded her days like a dark cloud. It wasn't her way to bicker—not with the sister who'd been her closest friend as they'd grown up. Gracie was probably still peeved at her, too, because Bernadette had spoken to her first. And now that she awaited her day in court, her parents' faces tightened every time they looked at her.

Was it her imagination, or did Mama and Papa look older? More vulnerable than she'd ever imagined them? They weren't saying it straight out, but Solace suspected they were worried sick . . . all because she'd ridden off in a huff and joined up with Apache Pete's Wild West Extravaganza on a dare, to *prove* herself.

Well, what had she proven, really? A few days of glory, riding her horses and showing off in buckskins with Rex, had cost her more than she'd bargained for.

Tongues were wagging in town, about how she'd ridden to hell in a handbasket, disguising herself as a boy to ride and shoot. Solace didn't feel comfortable showing herself in public—especially not in church, where people she'd known all her life stared at her hair. These same friends treated her parents differently, too. They stopped whispering when Mama and Papa approached—or they lectured about how to deal with a daughter gone wrong.

So Solace divided her days between riding Lincoln and Lee with Rex, and moping in her room. Each glance in her mirror was a reminder of her foolish, impulsive decision to perform as a boy, so she stopped looking there. But she couldn't miss the direct gaze her father gave her from his frame on her night stand . . . couldn't dodge the fact that she'd made her choices, and everyone was paying for them now.

One afternoon when she felt particularly bleak, she picked up the picture of Daddy that had been her guide and mainstay ever since Mama gave it to her. Again she studied his dark eyebrows and curls, which resembled her own now.

Judd Monroe's face shone with strength and integrity . . . surely this man had never done anything foolish, as she had! Her father knew the Bible backward and forward. Had devoted himself to serving others and raising fine Morgan horses for the stagecoaches that connected East with West. He'd remained true to his faith. And he'd died defending his home—her mother and Billy and Asa—from attacking Indians. Judd Monroe had made the ultimate sacrifice so she would survive in Mama's womb.

"And what have *I* sacrificed?" she whispered sadly. "Oh, Daddy, you must be so disappointed with the mess I've gotten myself into! I've fallen so far short of everyone's expectations—"

"No, Solace. You've thrown us a few curves," a voice replied from the doorway, "but we've always admired your strength; the way you insist on being the stalwart trailblazer God created you to be. We couldn't stop loving you if we tried."

She looked up, gripping the picture. She knew Mama was aware that she spoke with her father's spirit, but having Papa find her this way felt . . . awkward. "You must think it's pretty silly for me to talk to—"

He crossed the room in two strides to sit beside her on the bed. His arms were lean but corded from physical labor, and his embrace enveloped her in a love so fierce it made her gasp.

"Honey, your father was a man to be admired, but you know what?" His mustache curved with a grin that held a secret. "Judd Monroe felt he fell short. Constantly wondered if he'd asked too much of your mother, bringing her here to homestead in a log house where they had to scratch out a living."

Michael Malloy's face took on a pensive glow, lit by those golden-brown eyes. "It *hurt* him, that Mercy cooked for hours so the passengers on my stagecoaches could gulp their meals and then leave her with a huge mess twenty minutes later."

Solace sniffled into the red handkerchief he'd handed her. "But that was different! He hadn't run away to follow a shallow, impossible dream—"

"Your mama's parents—and his—thought he had." Papa thumbed a tear from her cheek, smiling tenderly. "His family owned a carriage factory and your mother's people were quite well off. Judd refused to fit himself into their mold. Knew he was created for something other than running a business, so he left a secure future to raise horses out here on the untamed prairie.

"And he raised the finest horses in Kansas, honey," Papa insisted in a low voice. "Your mother believed in his dream and worked alongside him to make it come true. It's why I respected them both so much."

Again that grin flickered as the man who raised her recalled his past. "Judd Monroe's example inspired me to settle down and help your mama raise all the children God sent her way. Before that I was a nomad without a cause. Just like Joel."

"Still sounds a lot more . . . *noble* than anything I've ever done," Solace said with a sigh. "And now I've made things harder for Gabe, when he's starting his new job as a judge. It was a kick in the gut when he took a room in town. But then, why would he want to be seen with me, when—"

Papa's soft laughter shook the mattress. "He's going through a time of testing, to be sure. But it has nothing to do with your hair, honey! Gabe Getty's establishing himself again so he can make the right impression . . . so he can be worthy of the woman who takes his breath away."

Solace raised a doubtful eyebrow. "*Now* who's talking silly?"

"Love is never silly, Solace. It's the reason we were created."

She swallowed hard. Papa's hazel eyes had softened but he didn't drop his gaze. He gently took the picture from her hands and smiled at the image behind the glass.

"Your father knew that. Your mother knows it, too." His voice was so soft, she had to listen carefully. "And I've seen that same ability to love—to share and serve, to dare and trust—in *you*, Solace, since the first time you laid those big brown eyes on me, honey. Gabe's a lucky man."

Papa sighed, rubbing her knuckles. "He knew better than to fall for Lily, although her affection's sincere. But he's scared that he'll relive the pain he went through with Letitia—afraid he won't measure up, in your eyes. Once this court case is behind us, Gabe will soar with the strength of his purpose and convictions. He'll devote his whole heart and soul to winning you then."

Though Papa's words stirred something deep within her, they still sounded too good to be true. "But Pete and Faustina will convince the jury that I'm deceitful! They'll say such awful things—"

"'Sticks and stones may break my bones, but words will never hurt me,'" Papa reminded her quietly. He squeezed her hands between his strong fingers. "You feel like you're in the valley of the shadow now, Solace, but never forget—it's only a valley, and it's only a shadow. Fear no evil, just like David wrote in his Psalm. David was far from perfect—as we all are—but the Lord loved him and blessed him. He's blessing you, too, Solace."

As he pressed a kiss to her temple, tears trickled from her eyes. She badly wanted to believe what Papa had said: he was another man who never lied, or did anything thoughtless or stupid.

Was it true, that Gabe was working to be worthy of her?

Do I really take his breath away?

Chapter Twenty-three

Gabe paused over the telegram he was composing. The last thing he intended was to bring his best friend running when Billy was so busy raising his children and his horses. . . .

> *Keep us in your prayers. Solace goes to trial for a trumped-up murder next week. Got my seat on the bench, but can't try her case. Lily returned to the academy, peeved that I can't marry her. HOW DO YOU HANDLE ALL THOSE WOMEN?? Gabe.*

The message sounded silly and self-serving, but he had no time to think up another one. He tossed the paper to the telegrapher along with a few coins. "That goes to Billy Bristol in Richmond, Missouri, please."

"Yes sir, Your Honor. Fine man, Billy is," the fellow remarked from beneath his green visor. "We could use more like him in Abilene these days."

"You've got that right. Thanks." Gabe strode out the door, turning his thoughts to the high-backed chair and impressive wooden desk he'd occupy again today . . . a dream he could scarcely believe he'd achieved. He'd known several judges in the St. Louis courts, but he'd never imagined the responsibility that came with sitting in such a lofty courtroom seat. Life and death were in his hands. He had the power to change lives. . . .

So why can't you change your own? Leave Letitia behind and hitch your wagon to Solace's star? You know she loves you.

"Morning, Getty. Break your razor?"

Gabe blinked at the short, rotund man entering the office beside his own. He'd seen very little of Hannibal Prescott, and wasn't sure how to respond to him.

Maybe the truth is your best bet, his thoughts challenged, but the voice was Solace's. Color crept into his cheeks. "I'm growing a beard. Maybe if folks associate me with Abraham Lincoln, they won't wonder if I'm old enough to—"

"*Lincoln?*" Prescott's laughter echoed in the paneled hallway. "Trying to get yourself assassinated, kid? From what I hear, that gal they arrested at the Wild West show might use you for target practice!"

Gabe stopped in his doorway to study this man before he replied to such an outrageous remark. What he'd heard about "Hanging Hannibal" rang true, not because this judge was so hard on outlaws, but because he shot off his mouth before his brain was engaged.

"I doubt that, sir," he replied coolly. "I've known Solace Monroe all her life. And I know she did *not* kill Cora Walsh."

"So *that's* why I got stuck with this case? Because you're sweet on the accused?" Prescott looked him up and down with a jaundiced eye. "No matter what you know—or don't know—I promise you this, Getty: the gavel's coming down hard on anyone who makes a mockery of justice in *my* courtroom! At the first sign of a circus, Miss Monroe's dog-and-pony show'll be tossed in the calaboose—or we'll string her up. Don't go thinking I'll be lenient, just because she's a girl—or because she's *your* girl!"

"I never said—"

"You don't have to," the portly barrister jeered. "It's written all over your face, little man."

As Prescott slammed his office door behind him, Gabe entered his own sanctum with bumblebees in his belly. Did his face reveal so much? Or was Hanging Hannibal full of bluster—seeing what he wanted to see? Though his first case had often felt like a comedy of errors, Gabe gave the two previous Prescott wives credit: opposite as they were, they'd both had the sense to leave him.

But he had more important matters to consider.

He let his satchel drop to the floor beside his desk . . . unlocked his bottom drawer and, using his handkerchief, took out the pearl-handled pistol that had killed Crack-Shot Cora. His thoughts wandered back to her pale body . . . to the two bullet holes that had made him queasy at the undertaker's.

What didn't set right? Why had his gut told him something didn't add up, when it came to the lady sharp-shooter's wounds?

Gabe looked at the pistol again, noting the smudged grime on its barrel . . . the dust that had stuck after it was fired and tossed aside. The answers were staring him in the face if he could only recognize them.

He glanced at the clock. In an hour he'd hear the final testimony of two cowboys who denied rustling prime cattle from the ranch adjacent to their boss's. He predicted the wronged rancher's lawyer would rip their stories to shreds and the jury would reach a verdict quickly. Nobody wanted to deliberate in a musty courtroom when a pretty spring day beckoned. Justice was often a matter of such timing. . . .

And timing might determine the verdict in Solace's case.

On impulse, Gabe went to his bookshelf and ran his finger over the volumes crammed there . . . took out his newest title about methods of criminal detection. Hanging Hannibal could poke fun at his fledgling beard, but *nobody* bested Gabriel Getty when it came to researching his facts and hunches.

Knowledge was power. He intended to show Judge Prescott a thing or two about what he—and Solace Monroe—were made of. And how powerfully persuasive they'd be when they joined forces.

"You must let go of the sadness in your past!" young Betsy insisted. "You're walking in the valley of the shadow, and you must believe you can reach the light at the end!"

Will gave her a rueful smile. "Easier said than done. Losing my dear wife, Lorena, has stripped me of the will to love again. She was so despondent at the end, and try as I might, I couldn't console her."

"Maybe she chose to be inconsolable. Just as she chose to truss herself too tightly in corsets, which rendered her unable to conceive your child." Betsy paused, aware she was treading on dangerous, sacred ground. "You didn't tip that laudanum bottle to her lips, Will. If you let your guilt overshadow your chances for happiness now, the opiate will have claimed two lives."

Solace reread her hastily scribbled pages, shaking her head. Her story about a frontier lawyer grieving his deceased wife seemed melodramatic, but it had been the best way to pass the unbearable days until her trial—and to express her deep feelings for the lawyer her hero, Will Motlow, was modeled after.

Twice Gabe had declined Mama's invitations to dinner, claiming he was working late on a troublesome case. And twice she'd sensed he was avoiding her company. Ever since he'd taken her face between his hands and kissed her, following his heart instead of his head, Solace sensed that Judge Getty was *afraid* of her. Afraid of what they could share, if only he'd let go of Letitia.

Solace glanced out her window. The sun's evening rays made the green, growing wheat shimmer as it rolled over the gentle hills. Out by the pasture gate, where Lincoln and Lee grazed, Rex sat surveying his domain. So orderly and perfect this picture looked . . . why couldn't her life follow the same effortless pattern? One little mistake—one slip of her better judgment—had thrown her whole world into chaos.

"Oh, stop the weeping and wailing and gnashing of teeth," she muttered. She took fresh paper from the back of her portfolio and went to her desk. Better to write the final copy of this story than to mope away another evening. Work and Win might not buy this one, emotional as it was, but Solace felt better for getting her frustrations in writing. Things always clarified in her mind after she put pen to paper.

Lost in thought, focused on improving her phrases and pacing, she didn't hear her mother come upstairs.

"Honey, let's have our devotions now," Mama murmured. "With the trial tomorrow, you'll benefit from . . ."

As Solace scrambled to cover what she'd been writing, Mama raised a curious eyebrow.

"Just some notes on strategy," she fibbed, hoping her smile didn't give too much away. "A way to organize my thoughts so I'll speak clearly tomorrow if Apache Pete or the judge try to intimidate me."

Her mother's knowing smile spoke volumes. "That's a fine idea, dear. There's still time if you'd like us to hire a lawyer for—"

"No need for that. If Pete and Faustina can state their cases, I can, too." Covering her story with the portfolio as she stood up, Solace smiled more confidently. "As you and Papa have said, I've done nothing illegal or immoral. The truth is on my side. I slept through the entire crime, probably because someone stirred laudanum into my supper. I can't lie about what I don't know."

Would her confidence sustain her tomorrow? It was her word against Pete's and Faustina's, and anyone else from the troupe who might testify. Solace took her seat in the front parlor; with only four of them at home now, it seemed cozier to gather here than at the dining room table, where the empty chairs reminded them of who no longer shared this ritual.

Temple Gates reached over to squeeze her hand. "I've prayed for you all day, Miss Solace," the governess assured her. Her dark eyes shone with a faith that never wavered.

"I've asked Saint Michael the Archangel to protect you in the courtroom. And of course, the Lord will be there, as well."

"Thanks," she murmured. Talk of archangels was nothing new to the family's housekeeper. Solace didn't always know how to respond to Temple's visions of the invisible, but it couldn't hurt to accept such powerful help in court, could it?

As Mama sat down beside her on the love seat, Papa riffled the pages of the big family Bible. He smiled when he found the scripture he wanted to share. "I thought we'd return to the Psalms tonight, to passages that remind us where our strength comes from—and that God never abandons or forsakes us, even when we forget how powerful He is. Hear now the words of the ancient poet in the Forty-Sixth Psalm."

Solace shifted. Even though everyone here had assured her things would go well tomorrow—or at least according to God's plan—their confidence-building made her nervous. How she wished Lily were here, shining with her innate faith and angels! And Billy! If ever there was a time she needed her dearest friend—or even Joel, the vagabond who'd shared some of her deepest, darkest secrets . . .

"'God is our refuge and strength, a very present help in trouble, '" her papa recited clearly and calmly. "'Therefore will not we fear, though the earth be removed, and though the mountains be carried into the midst of the sea; though the waters thereof roar and be troubled, though the mountains shake with the swelling thereof. Selah.'"

"Amen to that!" Temple murmured, while Mama took her hand.

"'There is a river, the streams whereof shall make glad the city of God, the holy place of the tabernacles of the most High. God is in the midst of her; she shall not be moved: God shall help, and that right early.'" Papa looked up at her with a special smile that made his new reading glasses catch the lamp's light like a starburst. He continued in a voice that grew more expressive with each declaration of the Lord's power.

"'The heathen raged, the kingdoms were moved: he uttered his voice, the earth melted. The Lord of hosts is with us; the God of Jacob is our refuge. Selah.'" he declared. "'Come, behold the works of the Lord, what desolations he hath made in the earth. He maketh wars to cease unto the end of the earth: he breaketh the bow, and cutteth the spear in sunder; he burneth the chariot in the fire. Be still, and know that I am God!'"

The parlor rang with stillness, indeed, as they pondered that profound statement. Solace had heard it all her life . . . mostly when she was being reminded that she wasn't in charge of anyone else's business, and that she wasn't as all-fired powerful as she liked to believe.

Was she strong enough to withstand whatever they'd shoot at her in Hannibal Prescott's courtroom?

"'I am exalted among the nations. I am exalted in the earth,'" came the final phrases she'd heard since childhood. "'The Lord of hosts is with us; the God of Jacob is our refuge.'"

As he folded his hands on the open Bible, he smiled at each of them. "Pretty marvelous, isn't it? That the God of Jacob is still our refuge today? That while He rules His universe, He prevails in each of our lives, as well? We should remember this if the case doesn't go as we'd—"

Rex's barking drifted through the open window, growing more insistent as he approached the house. Hoof beats then . . . and by the time Temple had gone into the kitchen, they heard loud pounding on that door.

"Well, now! If you're coming to supper, you're a little late!" she said with a chuckle. "But for *you*, I'd scare up a plate of chicken and noodles, or . . ."

"Thanks, Temple, but I'm here to see Solace."

"Everyone's in the parlor," Temple replied, "and they'd welcome a visit from the angel Gabriel!"

Solace's heart kicked her ribcage. Gabe had ridden all the way from town—to see *her*! He'd set aside his excuses, or whatever he'd been doing, for a surprise visit the night before her trial.

As he stepped through the parlor's arched entryway, however, Gabe Getty's expression dashed any hopes for romance. His cheeks shone with evening dew and a high color that bespoke his urgency. The wind had whipped his sorrel curls into an unruly nest, and the top button of his white shirt was undone.

He was the handsomest man she'd ever seen . . . even if an irregular band of hair bristled along his jaw. She nipped her lip to keep from teasing him about it, because the newspaper he was unfolding had obviously brought him here on serious business.

"Have you folks seen the *Chronicle*?" he asked breathlessly. "I can't believe they'd print—this smacks of planting misinformation to influence—to taint any chance that the jury selected will remain unbiased."

Her parents' expressions made her hold her breath. She had no trouble telling which article had inspired Judge Getty's wrath: SHARPSHOOTER CAUGHT IN LOVER'S TRIANGLE, its headline proclaimed. It sat about halfway down the front page, but whose eye wouldn't fly to *that* tidbit rather than to the piece posted at the top?

"We did see it," Mama replied quietly. "And we felt it was such an utterly ridiculous article that we—"

"It started a real nice fire in the cookstove. So I could fix dinner." Temple slipped an arm around Solace's waist, her brown eyes brimming with compassion. "We know you don't need protection from such claptrap, honey. But stupidity isn't something our family wastes time on, is it?"

Solace heard her, but her mind was already mired in the muck of an article so false she felt like spitting. "Where did anyone come up with—I was *not* trying for Pete's affections! I didn't even *like* the man, except that—"

Gabe lowered the paper by grasping her hands. He gazed steadily into her eyes to silence her. "The most damaging lies start with a whisper of truth, Solace. Tell me what you know about Apache Pete—how he treated Cora and that Gypsy fortune-teller—"

"Faustina?" Solace exhaled, thinking back. "I can't swear to this because I didn't join their late-night poker games or carousing, but Joel said Crack-Shot Cora wouldn't want me shouldering in on her act, not to mention her affections for Pete, because . . . well, he said they were lovers. That's why he thought I should audition as a boy."

Her mother sucked air. "That was *not* something your brother needed to tell you about."

Papa took Mama's arm, sighing grimly. "Propriety aside, such things go on. And it might have a bearing on how those Wild West performers present their side of the story tomorrow."

"The reporter makes it sound like Solace wore the buckskin disguise and short hair to make her shooting and riding more credible to the audience, but also to deceive Apache Pete," Gabe said in a tight voice. "While that's partly true, it's a blatant attempt to discredit your character, Solace, to tamper with justice. I intend to find out who convinced— or bribed—the editor to publish it."

He was on a crusade, and Solace adored the fire in his eyes and the ring of authority in his voice. It didn't bode well, however, that this article had come out the night before the trial—and that she would have *no* one in the courtroom to back up her story. "Are you sure you can't hear this case? I'm not guilty, but—"

"That's precisely what we're going to prove. So I've come here for your help."

His eyes widened beneath a stray lock of wavy brown hair; he pushed up his glasses as much to command her attention as to see her more clearly. "I regret not coming to any of your performances, Solace. I'm wondering . . . how did they go? How did Apache Pete and the others respond to your act?"

"I didn't miss a single shot, but Rex was the show-stopper!" she replied eagerly. "After the first night, Apache Pete was promising a raise in my pay if I'd work up a few encore tricks with Rex—"

"Yes? What're you thinking now?"

Solace cleared her throat. "There *was* a tense moment when Cora suggested I miss a shot now and then—or fall off a horse. Green-eyed envy, pure and simple. But I told Cora if she messed with Rex, like she hinted—"

"She threatened to hurt your dog?" Papa asked incredulously. "What could Rex possibly do to—"

"He got more applause than she did. And because I rode a fine pair of matched bays, and Lincoln and Lee performed so flawlessly, I guess Cora thought Pete might take her act out of the show altogether."

Gabe was nodding, taking all this in. "How did Cora and Faustina get along?" he queried. His eyes narrowed in thought. "From what we saw at the funeral, Cora should've been concerned about Madame Flambeau jeopardizing her place with Pete, rather than a tomboy trick rider."

"Those ladies were thick as thieves. Especially after Sol Juddson was exposed as a girl," Solace mused aloud. "Cora snatched my clothes from the riverbank while I was taking a quick bath. Got everybody all stirred up."

"Solace! You should've come right home."

"That's not her way, Mercy," Papa said with a grin. "She had to stick it out. Had to stand up for her talent—let her performance speak for itself, no matter what clothes she wore. A lot of words describe our daughter, but *coward* isn't one of them."

Her cheeks tingled with heat. "Thank you for understanding that, Papa. When I apologized to Pete for causing such a ruckus—for being exposed as a girl—I told him all I wanted was to play to an audience. What good are my shooting and riding skills if nobody else ever sees them?"

Gabe sighed then, nodding. "So it was your expertise—your perfection—that got them stirred up. Now tell me this." He paused, thinking about how to word his question. "After your last performance—before you got taken to jail—did you clean your pistols, honey?"

"Of course I did!" she blurted. "Any sharpshooter with a scrap of sense checks her equipment every day. But those pistols belonged to Billy and his daddy before that. I'm too proud—too picky—to show off with guns that don't sparkle and shine."

He caught hold of her hands again, his face a mask of earnest concern and . . . maybe a little love. "That's how you should answer them all day tomorrow, Solace! Leave no doubt in anyone's mind about your intentions and your integrity. Then leave the rest to me."

Chapter Twenty-four

"Order! I will have *order* in my courtroom!" *Whack! Whack! Whack!*

Solace winced each time Judge Prescott's gavel banged the desk beside her. The trial had been a circus since it began three hours ago, and her head was throbbing. Apache Pete and Faustina had already testified, led along a sensationalized, dramatic path by the lawyer they'd chosen to represent them at the last minute. Mr. Dorling's shrewd questions had elicited their outrage and their tears, as they described the betrayal of their trust by the young sharpshooter who'd drawn such crowds with an extraordinary talent.

By the time the two performers had told how Sol Juddson stole into the show like a thief in the night, using Rex and the matched bays as diversions, the crowd in the courtroom had been whipped into a frenzy. The jurors sat wide-eyed, as though watching a stage play crafted to shock them into convicting her. Between Percival Dorling's theatrics and Hanging Hannibal's gavel-whacking, she hadn't uttered a complete sentence on her own behalf since she'd taken the stand.

"Miss Monroe," the lawyer intoned, staring her down with his beady eyes. He reminded her of a crow waiting to peck an emerging worm. "Miss Monroe, would you please repeat what you just said, about why you auditioned in men's clothing after having your hair cut off?"

Solace looked him in the eye as best she could, considering

he was such a weasel. "I auditioned as a male on the advice of Joel Malloy, my brother, who was a roustabout for the Wild West Extrava—"

"And is he in this courtroom right now?"

She choked on the rest of her sentence—again. "No, sir. We've already established that Joel—"

"Do *not* tell *me* what we have established, young lady!" Mr. Dorling's slender body quivered as though she'd wrung him like a rag and then released him. "Please just answer the question!"

"Which one?" she demanded in a coiled voice. "You interrupted my first answer with a second question. I believe you're trying to upset me, sir."

Whack! went the gavel. "Watch your tongue, Miss Monroe, or I'll remove you for contempt of court!"

She closed her eyes, praying for the strength to get through her testimony without bursting into tears—which was exactly what they were after. In the front row, Mama clutched her handkerchief while Papa's expression grew stormy with a rage she'd seldom seen. Temple Gates had closed her eyes; her lips moved silently, probably pleading for the angels to swoop down and rescue them all from this blatant miscarriage of justice.

And where's Gabe? What about his promise to make everything turn out all right?

She couldn't think about that right now. The courtroom had finally gotten silent, and Dorling stood before her with a fist against his hip. He waited, as though she should know which ridiculous question to answer next.

"All right then, let's move on to another area of concern about your *character*," he said with a disgusted toss of his head. "Is it true that when you were seven years old, you shot a man's horse out from under him? And that he, too, died of gunshot wounds?"

Solace's jaw dropped. Not only had this incident happened

more than ten years ago, but the question also implied that she'd killed Wesley Bristol! If she gave an honest response, she'd be hanging herself without Judge Prescott's help. But if she didn't answer . . .

"Your Honor, I was there right after that happened! If Solace won't tell you about it, I will!"

The crowd sucked in its collective breath and all eyes focused on a man who stood up in the jury box. Solace had known Newt Billings all her life . . . he'd helped them round up the livestock that strayed after Wes set the barns afire that awful night, but he had *not* witnessed the shooting.

Solace sat straighter in her hard wooden chair, focusing intently on the conniving lawyer. "I did shoot Wesley Bristol's horse—while he was charging at his twin brother, Billy, and shooting at *him*," she clarified in a quavering voice. "But a Pinkerton operative's bullet killed Wesley—"

"And what were you doing with a *gun*? When you were only seven years old?" Dorling demanded tersely. "Seems to me—"

"This is an outrage!" Papa shot up from the bench, pointing his finger at Dorling. "You cannot imply that my daughter—"

"Don't try to cover it over, Malloy!" Newt Billings cried. "It was your gun she shot him with. All of us neighbors were horrified to hear we had a—a *killer* in our midst! And she wasn't even taken to task for it. Well, it's come full circle now and by God, we'll get to the bottom of it!"

Pandemonium erupted as friends stood up to shout Billings down. The jurors buzzed among themselves and meanwhile Judge Prescott tried to out-shout them all, pounding his gavel like a madman.

A madman who's enjoying himself too much. You were convicted before you set foot in this courtroom.

Indeed, Pete and Faustina sat at the table in front of her

wearing foxlike grins—as though they'd orchestrated this mayhem with the same sleight of hand and showmanship that kept Madame Faustina reading her cards while people streamed in for the Wild West Extravaganza.

Always one to play to the crowd, Joel had said of Apache Pete. And as he sat twirling that waxed handlebar mustache, Solace saw him for the self-serving rabble-rouser he was . . . already counting the profits his newfound notoriety would bring to the show.

Whack! Whack! Whack! "Order, I say! Silence! Or I'll call in the sheriff to clear the courtroom!"

As the chaos continued, Solace closed her eyes and held her head. *Please, Lord, deliver us from this uproar before something catastrophic. . . .*

"Counsel requests permission to approach the bench."

Whack! Whack! "Why are *you* here, Mr. Getty? This is not your case."

"I'm acting as counsel for Miss Monroe. At her earlier request."

As the crowd became hushed—straining to hear every word of a surprise they hadn't anticipated—Solace's heart sped up. Gabe stood a respectful distance from the bench, wearing his best pinstriped suit and carrying a fine leather satchel. He appeared polished and professional—and clean-shaven—just as he must have looked during his days in St. Louis. His calm demeanor made her heart swell with pride. And hope.

His dignity had a settling effect on the unruly crowd, maybe because he radiated the earnest integrity that had gotten him appointed to the bench a few weeks earlier. Gabriel Getty stood tall, looking at Judge Prescott, as they both awaited the full attention of everyone in the room. An electric current of curiosity charged the air, and they were both playing it to best advantage.

"This is highly irregular, Mr. Getty."

"Everything I've seen and heard this morning has been irregular, Your Honor," he answered wryly. "I intend to rectify that, by presenting evidence that proves Solace Monroe could not possibly have shot Cora Walsh. I can also prove, beyond reasonable doubt, who *did* commit the murder."

"Objection!" Mr. Dorling cried. "The court has no reason to allow Mr. Getty's participation in this case now that it's in progress!"

"My presence here—my stepping in to restore some semblance of truth and order—is not nearly so unreasonable as the circumstances of *your* being here, Mr. Dorling. When the sheriff heard what was going on, he decided it behooved him to appear, as well."

A murmur hissed through the crowd. Necks craned to see Harry Draper's intimidating figure filling the doorway, with a deputy on either side of him. None of the lawmen was smiling.

Hannibal Prescott stiffened . . . glanced at Mr. Dorling with an expression Solace couldn't interpret. "While you are licensed to practice law, Mr. Getty, I believe your appointment to the Dickinson County bench precludes—"

"I resigned this morning, Your Honor."

"*Resigned*?" The judge hammered with his gavel to silence the surprised outburst that echoed around the courtroom. "But Mr. Getty, a man of your relative youth seldom earns the opportunity to—"

"I have learned—and verified—that Mr. Dorling related that ludicrous story on yesterday's front page to the editor of the *Chronicle*," Gabe replied with an edge to his voice. "While I will have other opportunities to practice the law, Miss Monroe might never have the chance to clear her name—her reputation as a respected resident of Abilene—unless I assist her. *Right now*."

The courtroom buzzed like a hive of storm-struck bees. Solace gazed at Gabe, willing him to look at her, but he kept his focus on Hannibal Prescott.

Mr. Dorling's fist flew toward the ceiling. "You cannot prove—I don't know why you'd fabricate such a flagrant misrepresentation of the truth, but—"

"Sheriff Draper has also received a telegraph, just this morning, verifying that Mr. Dorling has never studied the law," Gabe announced above the noise. "He is, in fact, a shoe salesman from Kansas City."

Solace sucked in her breath, along with everyone else. Then somebody snickered, and the laughter became contagious.

Whack! Whack! "Order, I say!" Judge Prescott bellowed, and with an impatient wiggle of his finger he muttered, "Approach the bench, gentlemen. Let's settle this once and for all."

Solace nipped her lip, bursting with the curiosity that had those in the jury box and the benches leaning forward to catch every detail. *If this case was a circus before, it'll become even more entertaining now!* their expressions said. She exchanged tentative smiles with her parents . . . noted that Pete had stopped twirling his mustache and Faustina had grown pale beneath her witch-black hair and heavy cosmetics.

Hanging Hannibal cleared his throat ominously as he leaned low over his desk. "Mr. Dorling, is there any truth to what Mr. Getty has said? Don't lead me astray with any more bluster! Sheriff Draper is waiting to set us all straight, and I refuse to compromise my own credibility in this courtroom."

Dorling went limp, like a rag doll. "It's true, Your Honor. I sell shoes," he rasped. A drop of sweat trickled down his nose to plop on his shirt.

"Then why in the blue blazes—? Why have you led us all to believe—?"

"She's my sister."

"*Who* is?" Hanging Hannibal looked ready to live up to his name, while all around them, the courtroom resounded with hushed anticipation.

The waspish little man turned and pointed. "Ernestine. Faustina Flambeau, the fortune-teller."

Whack! went the gavel and Judge Prescott stood up. "Court is recessed until one o'clock. Getty, I'll see you in my chambers immediately."

Chapter Twenty-five

"Please state your name for the record."

"Solace Monroe."

She placed her hand on the Bible again, calmly this time. The strength of that book seemed to seep up into her body and settle her, just as Gabriel Getty's steady gaze did. He watched from a few feet away, in front of Judge Prescott, and his professional detachment served as a model for her own responses. After all the shenanigans and disruptions during the morning's session, she wanted nothing to jeopardize her chance to set the record straight.

"Do you swear to tell the truth, the whole truth, and nothing but the truth, so help you God?"

"Yes, sir, I do."

As the bailiff sat down, Gabe approached her with his hands folded loosely in front of him. If Hanging Hannibal had lectured or threatened him over the noon recess, he showed no sign of it: his face looked composed and serenely confident. "Miss Monroe, will you please tell us what happened on the night you were accused of killing Cora Walsh?"

She exhaled, collecting her thoughts. "The first thing I recall was a pounding on the door of the wagon. I was asleep on the floor—"

"Why weren't you in a bed, Miss Monroe?" His question hinted at an irregularity . . . a point she might make in her favor.

"The wagon was quarters for Crack-Shot Cora and Faustina Flambeau, sir. I had only slept there a couple of nights because Apache Pete told them to make room for me."

"And were Cora and Faustina there, when somebody pounded on the door?"

"No, sir. I was alone."

"Go on from there, please."

Solace relaxed. Although everyone in the courtroom was watching her closely, no doubt assessing her boy-short hair and simple blue dress, she sensed they would at least listen to her this time—even if they didn't believe her story. "Two men threw open the door, and Apache Pete followed them inside. They talked like I was in some sort of trouble—which seemed crazy, since I'd been sound asleep—but I knew something was out of kilter when they asked to see my pistols."

"Which pistols, Miss Monroe?"

"The ones I used in my act."

Gabe went to a table on the other side of the judge, and then carried over a pistol positioned on a folded towel. "Is this the gun you're referring to?"

"Yes, sir. And when it wasn't in its case with the other one—when I noticed the tin stars the men were wearing," she continued in a hesitant voice, "Pete said there'd been some trouble. Said Cora had been shot."

"Let the record show as evidence one Colt .45 caliber Peacemaker with a mother-of-pearl grip," Gabe said as he approached the jury. "And I'd like you gentlemen to note the condition of its barrel . . . the presence of fingerprints and dust, most likely from being tossed aside at the scene of the murder, as Sheriff Draper can confirm."

Gabe carried the pistol to the judge's stand and then carefully laid it in front of Hannibal Prescott. "Had you performed that evening, Miss Monroe?" he asked her.

"Yes, sir, I did."

"And do you usually clean your pistols before a performance, or afterwards?"

"Anybody with any respect for a nice gun like that would *never* put it away dirty!" Solace exclaimed. "Those pistols were a gift from Billy—"

"Please just answer the question, Miss Monroe," Judge Prescott warned. He was following her story intently—probably looking for loopholes to hang her with. But at least he was listening . . . eyeing her pistol with an air of anticipation.

Solace smiled demurely, knowing not to push her luck. "I clean them after every performance, without exception. Sir."

Gabe nodded, glancing toward the jury. "Which tells us that, since you were sound asleep in those early morning hours when the two lawmen and Pete came to the wagon, *you* had not handled the weapon that killed Cora Walsh."

"That's right."

"Be careful, Mr. Getty. You're leading the witness—asking us to draw conclusions." Judge Prescott leaned forward on his desk, as though to ride herd on any stray questions, while Pete, Faustina and Mr. Dorling sat very still at their table.

"Thank you, Your Honor. I'll be more careful." Gabe's lips flickered in a grin. He then cleared his face as though it were a slate that could be wiped clean of emotion. "While we're on the subject of that pistol and its condition, I would ask the court's indulgence—and Miss Monroe's—to pursue the subject of those fingerprints we've seen."

As he looked around for expressions of objection on the fascinated faces in that room, Gabe pulled a small piece of paper and something else from his suit pocket. "Perhaps you've heard about recent innovations in criminal identification, based upon years of study by William James Herschel and others, that have established fingerprinting as an almost infallible way to confirm—or eliminate—who has handled something."

He placed the piece of paper on the stand in front of her, and then opened a flat tin box, which contained an ink pad. "Miss Monroe, would you be willing to roll the thumb of your shooting hand on this ink and make a print on this paper for me, please?"

Her eyes widened. Was this some sort of a trick? Even though she'd wiped and cleaned her pistols painstakingly, there was a chance some of her fingerprints remained on her guns simply from cleaning them—wasn't there?

Gabe gazed steadily at her, his smile patient.

Solace felt the sincere affection in his brown eyes. She chided herself for doubting his intentions. "Of course I will," she replied, and quickly rolled her thumb across the damp, black pad.

"Thank you. And now—if the court will continue to indulge me—we'll compare your print to a very prominent thumbprint preserved in the dust on your pistol." He took Solace's print over to Judge Prescott and then pointed out the one he'd just referred to. "Even though this print is on the barrel—far above where one would grip the pistol to shoot it—it proves that someone other than the defendant last handled this gun. We don't have to be seasoned detectives to see that whoever held this weapon, presumably to shoot Cora Walsh, had a much larger hand and a distinctly different pattern of loops and whorls."

Solace held her breath. Would Hanging Hannibal go along with this? Was it enough evidence to set her free?

"You make a convincing point, Mr. Getty. Bailiff, please allow the jurors to compare these thumbprints, as well," the judge instructed. "But first show them to our two plaintiffs, so they'll be apprised, as well. Then you may continue with your line of questioning, Mr. Getty."

"Thank you, Your Honor." With the subtlest of smiles, Gabe glanced at Solace and then stepped aside as the bailiff gingerly carried the pistol and the piece of paper over to where Apache Pete and Faustina sat. The owner of the Wild West show gave the evidence a cursory glance, but the woman beside him turned her head as though she had no need to see it.

Or can she not bear to face the evidence?

Solace blinked. This voice in her head made her sit up

straighter—and then glance at the judge to see *his* reaction. Prescott's expression remained as bland as milk toast, yet the way his gaze lingered on Faustina made Solace's heart flutter.

"Tell the court, Miss Monroe, how you came to be sharing a wagon with Cora and the fortune-teller, if everyone believed you were Sol Juddson, a young man."

She took a settling breath. No sense jumping to any wild conclusions about Faustina—or sounding apologetic when she wasn't. Gabe was trying to prove her innocence, so she didn't want to raise any new suspicions about her character. "A day or two before I was accused of her murder, Cora Walsh exposed me as a girl by swiping my clothes while I was bathing in the river."

A quiet chorus of "ohh!" whispered around the room.

"And how did Apache Pete react to this revelation?"

Solace thought for a moment. "He didn't act all that surprised. But since he'd already sent flyers ahead to Enterprise about Sol Juddson's fine riding and shooting—and he'd extended the show's stay here in Abilene—he didn't dismiss me, either."

Gabe nodded. "And how did Cora and Faustina react to this?"

Glancing at the fortune-teller, Solace cleared her throat. "Faustina, fortune-teller that she is, said she'd known I was a girl all along. Cora didn't seem too happy about having another roommate, but she didn't kick up any fuss. At least not to Pete."

"So . . . if we were to speculate about who might be angry enough to shoot somebody," Gabe said in a thoughtful voice, "it seems reasonable that *you* would've been the victim, rather than the killer."

"No more speculation, Mr. Getty. Please make your point." Prescott's fingernails drummed his desk.

"Yes, Your Honor. I'm establishing that Miss Monroe still had her spot in the show and a place to stay—no reason to kill anyone," Gabe explained. "Also, she would not have left her prized pistol so grimy after a performance—*or,* had she indeed shot Cora Walsh, I doubt Miss Monroe would've been foolish enough to leave her pistol at the scene of the crime. And it's plain to see that someone else has handled her gun."

Hanging Hannibal shifted impatiently. "Fine, then. I suggest you call another witness—"

"With all due respect, Your Honor, it's Solace who's on trial here, and I'm providing the jury with a more complete picture of the night of the crime, as well as her character."

Gabe faced the jury then. "Before Miss Monroe steps down, I wish to discuss her skill as a sharpshooter because it directly relates to the fact that Cora Walsh's body had *two* gunshot wounds. I saw them myself, when I examined her at the undertaker's. May I continue this line of questioning, Your Honor?"

Judge Prescott settled back in his seat as though he knew no one would be leaving any time soon. "Yes, Mr. Getty. I'd appreciate your explanation."

Gabe nodded. A quiet smile lit his eyes as he addressed Solace again. "Was there a reason Crack-Shot Cora resented your presence in the Wild West Extravaganza, Miss Monroe? Besides the way you passed yourself off as a young man?"

Solace sat straighter. She knew where this was going now, and she was starting to enjoy herself. "Yes, sir, there was. Even before she stole my clothes, she took me aside and insisted I start *missing* some shots!"

"And why would she do that? You, as Sol Juddson, were bringing in a *lot* of paying customers."

"She was jealous. She said if I didn't miss now and then— or fall off my horse during a performance—something might just happen to my dog, Rex."

"She threatened your *dog*?" Gabe looked at the jury with an expression of utter disbelief, which was reflected on faces all over the courtroom.

"Yes, sir. She said she didn't like playing second fiddle—getting less applause—than Rex did."

Somebody snickered. Then somebody else joined in—and within seconds the entire courtroom was abuzz with chuckling and whispering and the shaking of heads.

Whack, whack! "Order, I say! You in the back!" Judge Prescott called out. "If you continue to disrupt these proceedings, I'll have Sheriff Draper remove the lot of you!"

"Didn't mean to cause a ruckus, Judge. It's been a long trip from Missouri, and the kids are fidgety—"

Solace's eyes widened.

"—but I helped bring that young lady into this world, and I'll be double-dog *danged* if I'm gonna let anybody convict her!" Billy Bristol flashed her a reassuring grin as he kept a hand on Owen's shoulder and stepped aside for Eve and Olivia to squeeze between the people standing in the back aisle. And then her sister Grace slipped in, holding tightly to white-haired Asa's hand as he led Beulah Mae in behind him.

How on God's green earth did they know?

However You did this, Lord—and Daddy, I'm sure you helped—thank you, thank you, THANK YOU! Her heart skipped into triple-time and she looked at Gabe for an explanation. But his eyes were as wide as hers.

The courtroom again resembled a hive of busybody bees as folks craned to see what the commotion was about, and who had made such a profound pronouncement. *Billy Bristol!* was the name on everyone's lips, followed by a buzz of whispers.

"Isn't that the old darkie fellow who—?"

"Would you look at those redheaded children! My goodness—"

"Could that be little Gracie Malloy? What's *she* doing with—?"

Whack! Whack! "Order! Silence, I say!" Judge Prescott cried. "You folks who just came in will have to find places to stand—quietly! And immediately! I won't tolerate any more disruptions in my courtroom."

Billy steered his wife and son toward the corner while the rest of his household followed. Despite the judge's orders, the other people in the back were still greeting the Bristols and making room for them—and then a small figure darted down the side aisle, beating a path to the witness stand with rapid footsteps.

"Aunt Solace! Aunt Solace! I knew you were here, 'cause Rex is sittin' out on the front steps, waitin' for ya! Papa wouldn't let me bring him in!"

Solace's heart shot up into her throat and she leaped to her feet. Never mind that her dog had mysteriously made it into town—or that this freckle-faced pixie was talking so fluently. "Bernadette! Honey, you shouldn't be—"

Gentle laughter and yet another wave of whispers followed the little girl's progress. Her flounced frock of sky blue set off her brilliant eyes and matched the huge bow that bounced atop her mop of coppery curls. She stopped at the end of the first row of benches, gazing eagerly at Solace. Then she clasped her chubby hands and lit the entire room with her little-girl smile.

"Oh, Aunt Solace!" she gushed. "You've got twirly-gig curls! *Just like mine!*"

Chapter Twenty-six

The world stood still as Solace's heart filled with so much love she thought she might explode. She stepped down from the stand, opening her arms. Bernadette Bristol rushed into her embrace with a squeal that set loose her own childlike laughter. She hefted the little girl to her shoulder and rocked her side-to-side, lost in the delight of her warm weight and her rustling petticoats and the arms that squeezed her so hard she could barely breathe.

Then Bernadette leaned back to stare into her eyes. With a shriek of pure joy, she rumpled Solace's hair into a wild frenzy—which had them both giggling so hard tears streamed down her face.

"I'll get you for this, little girl!"

"You already got me, Aunt Solace! Now what're ya gonna *do* with me?"

She was aware then of quiet laughter all around her . . . a jury box of men whose expressions looked awestruck, as though they saw her in a whole new light now. As Gabe walked up to her, Solace feared she'd allowed this display to get too far out of hand, and yet . . .

Gabe couldn't take his eyes from the pair of them—carrot curls and chestnut, smiles like rainbows sent from heaven after a storm had passed. Here was a love he envied like nothing else he'd ever witnessed; it struck him in the gut like a lightning bolt. He realized that the mood of the room had just swung completely in Solace Monroe's favor. Her love, given without hesitation or reserve, had struck every one of them in

the courtroom with its grace. She was a madonna in their
midst, embracing a beloved child.

And Gabe suddenly longed for it to be *his* child.

Her eyes, as round and soft and brown as a doe's, widened
to let him into the circle of that love. He exhaled; felt himself
go helpless in her gaze. No one had *ever* looked at him that
way and he didn't want it to end.

"Mr. Getty, I believe we're settled now. Would you please
continue questioning the witness?"

Solace blinked and broke their eye contact. Since
Bernadette showed no sign of letting her go—and since
every person in the courtroom was now beaming at her—she
returned to the witness stand and set Billy's redheaded
daughter facing forward in her lap. "You've got to be quiet,
Punkin, or we're in big trouble," she murmured.
"Understand me?"

Bernadette's head bobbed. She looked out over the huge
roomful of people like a queen surveying her subjects.

"Miss Monroe, it's highly irregular for a witness to hold a
child while—"

"Yes, sir, I realize that. But it's a long way back to her
mama—and we don't want another disruption, getting her
back there—do we?" She widened her eyes at Hanging
Hannibal, aware that her messy hair was *almost* making him
laugh. "Unless, of course, *you* would like to hold her, sir.
This is Bernadette Bristol—Billy's daughter—by the way.
Bernadette, say hello to Judge Prescott."

The little girl grinned coyly at him. "How do you do, kind
sir? It's such a pleasure to meet you!"

"Likewise, Miss Bristol." When chuckles erupted, the
judge reached for his gavel, but he refrained from using it. "I
believe we'll proceed. Now, Mr. Getty, you were saying—"

Gabe clasped his hands in front of him and felt his face go
hot. "Your Honor, I apologize, but I've forgotten where I was
in my argument."

Snickers rose around them, but they were kind, friendly snickers.

The judge cleared his throat ceremoniously. "You were discussing the fact that Cora Walsh's body had two bullet holes. Establishing Miss Monroe's skill as a sharpshooter."

"Thank you, Your Honor!" Gabe reminded himself that even though things had miraculously turned around during these past few minutes, he hadn't won Solace's acquittal yet. He'd been ready to request another *highly* unusual display of evidence before the Bristols walked in, and he wasn't sure now if he should push for that.

"I believe we can follow the logic presented thus far, that because of the condition of the murder weapon—including a large thumbprint that couldn't possibly be Miss Monroe's—and other circumstances of that evening, the defendant is most likely innocent of Cora Walsh's murder," Gabe went on in his professional tone. "But what struck me as I saw the bullet holes in Crack-Shot Cora's body was that she'd been shot from behind—"

Whispers hissed again, but then the room went quiet so no one would miss a word Gabe Getty had to say.

"—and that the killer had shot her *twice*. Once in a shoulder, and once through the lower back," he said gingerly. "Gentlemen of the jury, you may believe me when I say I've witnessed Miss Monroe's unerring accuracy with her pistols, or you may request a quick demonstration of her skills, behind the courthouse. My point being that Solace Monroe would've killed Cora Walsh with *one* shot. Probably through the heart."

The crowd came to life again, murmuring, and Solace sat straighter in her wooden chair. What did he mean by *demonstration*? If Gabe was suggesting she would—

"Rex is right outside!" Bernadette crowed, pointing toward the back doors. "Aunt Solace could shoot an apple off his head! He *loves* that trick!"

Judge Prescott raised the gavel, but silence suddenly rang in the room. Eyes were wide, focused on Hanging Hannibal ... wondering how he'd respond to such an outrageous idea.

A display of her marksmanship—right outside the courthouse! It would mean getting an apple, and loading her pistol, and getting Rex to concentrate with so many curious, whispering witnesses watching them. And how could they be sure no one got hit by a ricocheting bullet? And what would she be firing into, that would absorb her shot? She never practiced or performed near buildings, or where onlookers might be endangered—and Gabriel Getty, without knowledge of such things, perhaps hadn't considered these hazards before he'd so boldly proposed showing off her skills.

Solace tightened her arm around Bernadette and whispered in her ear. "Sweetie, you really do need to keep quiet so the judge doesn't get mad at—"

"I believe we all have the image in our minds, of that apple shattering. No further proof of Miss Monroe's skills will be required." The magistrate leaned forward with a purposeful look in his eye. "If there are no further questions for your client, do you wish to call anyone else to the stand, Mr. Getty?"

Gabe knew a hint when he heard one. "Yes, Your Honor. I would like to question Faustina Flambeau, please. Thank you, Miss Monroe."

Solace slid her redheaded good luck charm from her lap, but kept a firm grip on the chubby hand that reached for hers. As she steered Bernadette to the table opposite the one Pete and Faustina's slumping brother occupied, she flashed a guarded grin: Mama, Papa, and Temple were leaning forward to grasp her free hand, relief written all over their faces. If they believed she'd won her case, did she dare believe it herself?

As she settled Bernadette sideways in her lap, Solace watched the bailiff hold the Bible for Faustina. Although she wore a fashionable suit of magenta taffeta, with her hair tucked up into a matching plumed hat, the fortune-teller looked older . . . less confident about charming her way through her testimony this time, as she placed her gloved hand on the Good Book. After the formalities were complete, Gabe stepped in front of the witness.

"Miss Flambeau, would you please state your full legal name for the record?"

Faustina frowned. "I just did. My name's Ernestine Dorling."

"Never married?"

The fortune-teller's nose rose into the air. "All right, then—my full legal name is Ernestine Lorena Dorling."

"You're under oath, ma'am," Gabe reminded her gravely. "And while it's understandable you'd have a stage name to maintain your Gypsy image for the Wild West show—"

"What do you want, for crying out loud?" she blurted. "All right, so my name is Ernestine Lorena Dorling Schumacher!"

As a buzz rose around them, Gabe pressed on. Solace had never seen him look so . . . intent. And ruthless. His boyish features had hardened into the mask he must have worn while trying complicated cases in St. Louis. She was glad he hadn't looked at *her* that way.

"And is your husband in the courtroom, Mrs. Schumacher?"

"Why do you want to know?"

Whack! went the gavel. "Please answer the question, ma'am. Mr. Getty has a reason for asking it, because we've just established that Mr. Dorling allowed your real names—pertinent information—to go unstated this morning as you were sworn in. You're dangerously close to perjury." Judge Prescott's expression had gone somber and tight . . . as though he'd already figured out the path Gabe's interrogation would take. "*Is* your husband in the courtroom?"

The woman's face puckered as she pointed. "He's right there! So what does this have to do with Solace Monroe shooting Cora?"

Gabe's expression turned downright predatory as his head turned to where Faustina had pointed. "Let the record show the witness has indicated the gentleman known as Apache Pete, earlier sworn in as Peter Redman. So is his real name Peter Schumacher, then?"

"So what if it is?"

"Did anyone in your troupe know you and Pete were married, ma'am?"

"No, because it was none of their damn business!"

Whack! "Watch your tone and your language, madam!" the judge said, and he stood up to emphasize his point. "I'd throw you out for contempt of court, but that's precisely what you're trying for, isn't it?"

The loud whispering around her hushed and Solace sat up straighter. If Faustina and Apache Pete were married . . . if Faustina and Cora had been wagon mates, and the fortune-teller had never resided in Pete's quarters . . . then maybe Cora Walsh hadn't realized . . .

"We've established that you and the victim shared a wagon before Miss Monroe was told to bunk with you," Gabe continued coolly. "How would you describe your relationship with Cora Walsh?"

Faustina sneered. "We were the only two women—besides the married ticket-taker—traveling with the show. So it only made sense—"

"Did you *like* Crack-Shot Cora?" Gabe pressed on. "When Sheriff Draper and I were on the grounds the morning after she was shot, there was talk among the other performers about Cora having . . . *relations* with Apache Pete—"

"What's *relations*?" Bernadette whispered. "Does that mean they were a family?"

Solace's face flared. She pulled the little girl closer and whispered, "Something like that. Now be quiet, so we don't distract Gabe."

Faustina suddenly stood up, looking agitated enough to— well, to shoot someone. "All right, look—Pete and I had our reasons for keeping our marriage quiet, but then Cora signed on and—she had *ideas* about how to get more pay out of him, among other things. So I decided to keep a closer eye on her!"

"So you two ladies became bunkmates," Gabe summarized aloud, "and when Cora revealed Sol Juddson as a female, your husband declared she would share your wagon. How did Cora react to this? She'd already threatened Miss Monroe—and her dog—after all."

Faustina rolled her kohled eyes at the jury. "Cora went pouting to Apache Pete, pleading with him to get rid of Sol Juddson altogether. Promised she'd fancy up her act if he'd help her train some sort of monkey or—or steal the Monroe girl's dog and horses when he sent her packing."

Solace stiffened. She'd had no idea that Cora Walsh's hatred for her had run so deep. But then, Cora was a fool to believe Rex or Lincoln and Lee would perform for anyone but her.

"So you killed Cora Walsh because you were tired of her meddling with your man. And by making it appear that Solace Monroe had fired those shots, you were getting Sol Juddson out of your hair, as well. Correct?"

The onlookers sucked in their collective breath.

Solace felt the blood drain from her face. She held Bernadette so tightly the little girl squirmed, but she didn't take her eyes off the woman in the witness stand. Gabe had just accused Faustina of killing her closest friend!

But then . . . that companionship had been an act, hadn't it? A way to keep the rest of the troupe in the dark about what was really going on—and to keep Cora in Faustina's sight at all times.

"You can't prove that, Mr. Getty!" the fortune-teller jeered. "And besides, *I'm* not on trial here! We're deciding Miss Monroe's fate, so don't expect a dramatic confession from *me*!"

"Miss Monroe is indeed on trial . . . but isn't it interesting how testimony from other witnesses often points the way toward the truth?" Gabe's smile grew foxlike as he reached into his suit pocket. He walked forward slowly, until he was standing directly in front of the witness stand. "Does anyone else from the Wild West Extravaganza tell fortunes with a tarot deck, Mrs. Schumacher?"

Faustina's expression curdled. "Of course not! Madame Flambeau's the only—"

"Did you notice a couple of your cards were missing? Or notice a hole in the skirt you were wearing when you shot Cora Walsh?" He held up two cards so she could see them.

Faustina snatched them. "This proves nothing! The wind could've blown them from my table."

"And dropped them at the edge of the woods where Cora's body had been dragged? That's where the sheriff and I found them." Gabe gripped the railing, leaning toward her as he held her gaze. He was tall enough that they were eye-to-eye—and not a soul in the crowded room dared to cough or shift. "If you pressed your thumb into this ink pad and gave us a print, as Miss Monroe did, we'd know without a doubt who was gripping that pistol when—"

"I have no reason to do that!" she rasped. "Because again, Mr. Getty, *I* am not on trial."

"And you have no need to do it, Mrs. Schumacher," he said in a low voice that carried to the far corners of the courtroom, "because the sheriff and I found thumbprints on these two fortune-telling cards which match the ones on the pistol."

Gabe backed away just in time to avoid getting slapped— *hard*. "Thank you, ma'am. No further questions, Your Honor."

Chaos erupted around her, and Solace didn't know whether to laugh or cry. Hannibal Prescott was banging his gavel, and as Faustina stepped from the witness stand she broke into a trot down the side aisle . . . .

But Sheriff Draper blocked her escape.

"Aunt Solace, let me *go*!" Bernadette whined. "What's goin' on? Why is everybody talkin' and—"

Solace exhaled a sigh of huge relief as hands behind her grabbed her shoulders.

"See there? We knew it would work out!" Mama rasped.

"Fine job, Miss Solace!" Temple's voice thrummed. "The Lord knew the truth and He made sure everyone else heard it, too."

"Gabe Getty has done us a huge favor today," Papa declared, "and has insured himself a sure future as a—"

Whack! Whack! Whack! "Order, I say! Order in this court!" Judge Prescott cried. "You will resume your seats immediately!"

Solace was aware that the din gradually died down, and that the jury was being instructed about how to reach its decision, but all she really knew was that Gabe was gazing at her. As though in a trance, he came to the table and took the wooden chair beside hers.

She wanted to throw her arms around him, but, of course, that wouldn't be the proper thing to do, right here in the front of the courtroom. The jury hadn't yet reached its verdict, and Gabe had a professional reputation to uphold.

"Gabriel Getty, that was the most magnificent—most *brilliant*—performance I've ever seen," she whispered.

His eyes softened and he adjusted his spectacles. "All in a day's work," he murmured happily. "Circumstances were on my side, and during the recess I uh, laid out my cards for the judge so he'd allow me some legal leeway when I cornered Faustina. Arguing cases like this sure beats sitting on that bench."

Solace blinked. Was Gabe saying he'd resigned his seat on the bench for good? Not just so he could defend her case? She'd never known him to behave so impulsively or—

But then, she'd never seen such a flush of professional pleasure on his face, either. He was dressed to the nines, looking so much more sophisticated than these Kansas cow town folk. He looked dapper yet intelligent. *Successful*— because he'd obviously found the purpose he'd been created to carry out. The excitement shining in Gabe's eyes had come from outwitting his opponent with facts and a flair for subtle drama that had almost made her bite her nails!

No, little girl, it's YOU making him glow this way.

Solace blinked. That was clearly Daddy's voice in her ear again. . . .

"Silence, please!" Hannibal Prescott banged his gavel once as the jurors took their seats with expectant expressions. "Mr. Chairman, have you reached a verdict?"

"We have, Your Honor." Clyde Fergus, their longtime neighbor, gazed at her, and then at Gabe, with a solemnity only a Scotsman's eyes could muster. He'd been the first man to the ranch the morning after she'd shot Wesley Bristol's horse. He'd homesteaded alongside her father, Judd Monroe, as well.

Does he feel I've betrayed Daddy, behaving this way?

Solace held her breath. She hadn't even realized the jury had returned—and so soon after they'd filed out. She'd known several of those men all her life, yet for the past couple of days the entire town of Abilene had cussed and discussed her riding and sharpshooting and . . . *unusual* skills as though she was a stranger in their midst. A brazen woman who'd cut her hair to pass herself off as a man so she could ride and shoot in a Wild West—

"We find the defendant, Solace Monroe, not guilty."

"Thank you, sir! We are adjourned!" *Whack!*

The courtroom rang with shouts and cheers and applause. Bernadette sprang to the tabletop to do a little dance as Solace stood up, her heart hammering in time to the child's feet. Mama, Papa, and Temple filed quickly out of their bench to hug her, while Hannibal Prescott surged through the crowd to congratulate her, as well.

Then the judge grabbed Gabe's hand and shook it gleefully. "Good *show*, Mr. Getty! By golly, Dickinson County's lucky to have you on the judiciary—"

"No, sir, when I resigned, I meant it." Gabe spoke confidently, with no sign of apology or regret. "Two weeks on the bench showed me that I'll be much happier trying cases as a lawyer and—"

"And a darn *fine* lawyer, too!" Papa piped up.

"—getting back to my legal roots—than rendering decisions from on high. Thanks for your patience and your help today, Your Honor."

Hannibal Prescott sighed. "My pleasure, Gabriel. Best of luck to you."

Once again Solace caught Gabe's eye . . . saw an inexplicable something on his face. Was he returning to St. Louis, then? Going back to his *roots*—to where he'd established a reputation and a clientele?

Back to where Lily lives?

The thought tied itself in a knot, right where her heart was.

Billy Bristol's family was clamoring around them now, and Mama was inviting everyone to the Triple M for a celebration, but all Solace heard was a soft, lonely sigh deep within herself. Had she won her case but lost the man who'd make her life worthwhile?

Chapter Twenty-seven

"It is *so* good to have you all here!" Mama said for the dozenth time. "I couldn't believe my eyes when I saw the lot of you coming through that courtroom door!"

"It was like the cavalry came in!" Temple exclaimed. "Like Joshua and his armies had arrived to fight the battle of Jericho! Once I saw you folks, I knew we couldn't lose!"

Solace stood out of the way, watching Asa and Beulah Mae working side by side at the pie safe—the old Negro was weaving a lattice crust over a peach cobbler while his larger, more energetic wife kneaded warm, fragrant dough for dinner rolls. Temple chopped cabbage for slaw, and her mother stirred two mason jars of sweet corn into batter for her favorite corn pudding. Eve sat at the table dicing hard-cooked eggs and celery into a large bowl that would hold a *lot* of potato salad.

How their faces beamed . . . how their voices harmonized and danced as they caught each other up on family doings— and all to celebrate her victory in court today. She'd known this kitchen rhythm her entire life, from the time Mama and Asa had put their meals on the table through Temple Gates's taking over as the family's housekeeper. Once her mother had come by more children than she had hands, Mercy Malloy had shared her love of cooking and her home with the Negroes who'd become members of their patchwork family, too.

That was Mama's purpose: to nourish and nurture. Young and old, dark and light alike had flourished in the sunshine of her soul.

Yet while Solace felt blessed by the special love in this kitchen, it really wasn't her place. She could put together an acceptable meal because she and Lily and Grace had always helped with the cooking, but none of them cherished that calling the way their mother did.

Smiling, Solace slipped out the back door and onto the porch, listening to the their voices that carried through the screen door. Moments later Rex showed up to accept a head-scratching, as he always did. From here she saw her sister, Grace, holding Olivia and Bernadette's hands, showing Billy's daughters her childhood home. Gracie was a born teacher, and her delight in those girls was mirrored on their young, freckled faces as they gazed up at her.

Out by the barns, the men talked with their hands in constant motion, as though Billy had never left his post as Papa's horse trainer. Young Owen shadowed his daddy, looking just the way she remembered Billy Bristol when he was that age. Gabe, in more comfortable clothing now, completed the quartet that leaned on the corral, facing fields that bristled with bright green wheat.

Each of them, too, had found the life path God had meant him to follow: paths they'd recognized from early childhood. Michael Malloy knew ranching; Billy Bristol knew horses; Gabe Getty's bookish ways had led him to the law. And they'd pursued these occupations as though their fathers had led them by the hands and given them the keys to the kingdom.

And yet they'd all lost their fathers early on. Just as she had.

How had they known what they were called to do in this life?

It was a mystery that intrigued yet agitated her as she stood on the porch, looking out over the world as she'd always known it. If Gabe went his way without her—if her life as a trick-shot artist had already run its course—how was she to spend her days? In her heart, she knew she'd never raise another dog like Rex or own other horses as magnificent as

Lincoln and Lee, just as she now understood that life with a traveling show wasn't nearly as glorious or glamorous as she'd imagined.

She was only eighteen, yet she'd accomplished all she felt called to do. It was a scary . . . lonely thought.

"I guess it's just you and me now, Rex," she murmured as the Border collie nuzzled her leg.

You are never alone, Solace.

She sighed, smiling sadly. "All right, Daddy, so you'll always be in the picture, too. And thank you for seeing me through the trial today . . . but I have no idea what to do next! Where to go or—"

He holds your hand, Solace. That's all you need to know.

Even as she knew her father was referring to God, her gaze fell on Gabe Getty. Would *he* ever hold her hand again? Was she wrong to want him so badly? Silly to believe he could love a short-haired tomboy who thrived on the thrill of a trick no one else could perform.

He knows you better than that. Better than he knows himself.

Solace raised an eyebrow. When she turned and saw that Gabe had dropped his satchel on the porch to hug her mother, she knew what to do next. It was a baby step, a long shot, a casting out of a net that might not catch anything. . . .

But it was now or never.

Solace passed purposefully through the kitchen so no one would sidetrack her. Up the stairs she clambered, two at a time, until she reached her room. She pulled out the carpetbag under her bed, where she kept her portfolio and the story she'd completed late last night after everyone else was asleep. It had kept her sane while she awaited her trial, and now it would either convince Gabe Getty of how much she loved him, or it would drive him away for good.

She unbuttoned her bodice and tucked the sheaf of papers inside it. If she went down the service stairs and out the back door . . . walked around the house as though taking in the lovely sunset . . . slipped the story about the prairie lawyer and his brave-hearted heroine into Gabe's satchel, well—he couldn't miss her message, could he? Would her writing convince him to let go of Letitia and give her a chance to win his heart?

Her plan went perfectly—until someone came up behind her as she slipped the story into the satchel. "Solace? I—can we talk for a moment?"

The color of getting caught was red, and when she quickly stood up, Solace felt her face giving away her secret. "Gracie! Yes, of course, we can—"

Her sister's gaze drifted south. "Maybe you'd like to fasten up first?" she asked with a grin.

Solace fumbled with her buttons, knowing darn well she'd better explain this situation . . . or give a simplified version of it, anyway. By now, Grace had worked with Billy's children enough to see through fibs and fabrications. "I uh, wrote a little something for Gabe. So he could think about it later, when there aren't so many people around."

When had Grace Malloy grown into such a pretty young woman, with Papa's light in her eyes and Mama's sweet smile? Her simple frock of yellow dimity reflected a soul filled with childlike sunshine, yet her curves bespoke a womanly strength. Solace stood awestruck for a moment, caught up in the emotions she saw at work on Grace's face: a strong sense of duty and devotion, mingled with doubt right now. "I have a confession," her little sister murmured.

Solace straightened. What on earth could Saint Grace have done that warranted such a furrow between her brows? A quick glance told her the children were romping with their father, and behind them, the committee of cooks still sounded busy in the kitchen. "All right, I'm listening. But I can't imagine—" She took hold of Grace's hands to stop her fidgeting, and her sister sighed as though she bore a heavy load indeed.

"I—when I saw you today on that witness stand—on trial for *murder*!" she rasped, gripping Solace's fingers. "Well, I *knew* you hadn't shot that Walsh woman. But when I realized you might go to jail for—that I might not see you for a long time—"

"Oh, Gracie, Gabe took care of that," Solace whispered. "This whole Wild West misadventure is behind us now."

"But you *loved* riding and shooting and—and you looked so magnificent and so—so fearless! Like you were flying with invisible wings when you stood up on your horses," Grace blurted. "I just wanted to apologize for the rotten, rude things I said to you at Billy's. I was on a high horse myself, full of my sophisticated schooling. But you saw the Bristol children for the challenges they'd present, and—"

Solace slung an arm around her sister's quivering shoulders. "Are they giving you trouble, Gracie? I'll smack their butts and set them straight if—"

"No! They're just—well, they're kids!" she said with an exasperated shrug. "I have so much to learn. We thank God Bernadette has started talking, but now she's never quiet. I couldn't possibly keep Owen on task—and keep Olivia from tattling all the time—if I were teaching that little imp to speak. And—"

"You're the perfect governess for them, Gracie," she said, trying not to laugh. "You have quite a mix of personalities to mold and make into something, but you'll do it. From where I stand, training Rex and my horses was a snap, compared to what you've undertaken."

Grace let out a long sigh and rested her head on Solace's shoulder. "I didn't intend to carry on this way," she said quietly. "I'm making progress with them, actually. I just wanted you to know that I'm sorry I was so mean-spirited about your clothes and your dare-devilish ways."

She looked up with wide hazel eyes. "I just wish I had half your heart and spirit, Solace. I'm so glad you're my sister."

A huge lump blocked her throat. Solace blinked repeatedly. She hugged Gracie hard, grateful for such an unexpected blessing—and just when she'd thought she didn't have many of those! "All right, and I'm sorry, too. For calling you Saint Grace," she admitted. "We need more people who naturally behave the right way and do what needs doing."

Her sister dabbed at her eyes with her lace handkerchief. Then she grinned. "Actually, I deserve that name ... because I *am* the perfect servant, you know! Come on—let's set the table. It'll be just like old times."

Indeed, as Solace gazed around the table at these beloved faces, it was like all the best dinners in her memory rolled into one. It was more than the savory ham and the soft, buttery rolls that made her close her eyes in bliss as she chewed; more than Mama's salty-sweet corn pudding, baked just for her, and the tang of the slaw's vinegar dressing—not to mention the promise of Asa's incomparable peach cobbler awaiting them on the sideboard. It was the smiles ... the voices ... the *presence* of the people she loved best.

It occurred to Solace as she buttered another of Beulah Mae's rolls that this celebration wouldn't have happened, had she not been accused of a crime. Yes, her patchwork family would have found another time to come together, but today it was for *her*. The thirteen of them had crowded around this table because they loved her and wanted the best for her.

At this moment, even though she felt her life was at loose ends, Solace knew how very blessed she was.

She set aside her woolgathering to follow Gabe's account of events leading up to his surprise appearance today ... to watch his eyes and face and gestures. He talked as though he'd always been a part of this family.

"How'd you find out about the Gypsy fortune-teller being married to Pistol Pete?" Billy asked. His ruddy face was alight with fascination—and admiration—as he helped himself to more ham.

"*Apache* Pete," Olivia corrected. "Although he looks nothing like a redskin to me!"

Gabe laughed. "It's those stage names you've got to watch," he replied, lavishing apple butter on his roll. "While every troupe features performers with fictitious identities, it can also be a way to disguise lives they don't want us to discover."

Sol Juddson knows something about this, Solace mused. She followed the cadence and timbre of Gabe Getty's polished voice, partly to determine if her own assumed identity had affected his feelings for her. He had admired Sol's stories, as well as the riding and shooting, but it wasn't Sol who so badly wanted him to *love* her. His face might reveal what she needed to know, for he hadn't talked to her since he'd arrived this evening, except to say hello. He'd stayed beside Billy, mostly . . .

"I went downstairs for dinner at the hotel earlier this week," he continued confidently, "and I saw a man sitting alone. I was going to ask if I might join him—except then a handsome couple came in and sat with him. I realized it was Pete and Faustina from the Wild West show, dressed in everyday clothing, but the other man called her *Ernestine,* and kissed her cheek. So I sat in the nearest corner with my back to them."

"Talk about timing!" Eve exclaimed. "And luck! You could hear *everything*, but they had no idea!"

"Weren't no coincidence," Asa asserted. His gnarled fingers closed around another roll before he passed the basket along. "That was God workin' things out, so's Mister Gabe could do his job for our Miss Solace! He prepared a table in the presence of your enemies—there in the hotel, and again in that courtroom—and then He anointed your head. Couldn't nobody's evil touch you then!"

Solace smiled gratefully at the old man across the table. How like Asa to put things in a Biblical perspective that set things straight in her heart . . . reminded her that yes, her cup really had run over with God's goodness and mercy today.

"You're exactly right!" Gabe smiled as he recalled how these details had dovetailed so perfectly. "During the meal, I overheard Percy and Ernestine discussing a brother who *is* a lawyer, but he wanted nothing to do with their case. Then they decided to whip up adverse publicity, so sentiment would run against Solace—which alerted me that the jury might hang her before Hannibal had the chance.

"And as I stole glances at them, it struck me that Pete and Faustina acted like a *couple*," he mused aloud. "Made me think back to their little drama at Cora's graveside—which was all a ruse. Falsified grief at its finest."

Gabe gazed at her straight on then. Though it was clear he was fond of her—as everyone in the family had insisted at one time or another—Solace saw no overwhelming spark of love in those dark brown eyes. He was a lawyer reliving his victory: a professional who'd accomplished his goal.

"After that, it was a matter of asking a few questions and sending some telegrams," he said nonchalantly. "I verified, this morning, that Dorling had instigated that front-page story in the *Chronicle*. Then I notified Harry Draper, and stood outside the courtroom, peering through the crack in the doors, at the circus Prescott was presiding over."

Solace couldn't help grinning at him, even if her expression gave away her outright adoration . . . even if her heart was laid open for him—and everyone else here—to see. "So how did Rex end up at the courthouse—just in case I had to shoot an apple off his head?"

"That was me!" Owen piped up proudly. "Since I could ride the fastest—and since Rex would hop onto my horse with me—I went after him."

"And the rest of us got to eat dinner in the restaurant!" Olivia said.

"*And* we got ice cream!" Bernadette crowed. Then she speared her fingers into her coppery curls, a gesture of sheer joy. "I wasn't s'posed to go down front, but when Olivia turned loose of my hand—"

"Some fat old lady tromped on my toe!" her sister protested.

"—I just had to come see ya, Aunt Solace. You looked awful lonely up there."

"Perfect timing once again," Gabe said, shaking his head with the wonder of it. "Billy, I didn't intend for my telegram to haul you away from your work, but I was never so glad to see anybody in my life."

Billy raised a russet eyebrow, his fork poised with a bite of ham. "You couldn't think I'd stay home when my best girl was in trouble," he teased. "I knew a cry for help when I saw one, old buddy. It's what blood brothers *do*."

Where else would she find a roomful of people so intent on her safety? People to light her way through the valley of the shadow when she insisted on riding hellbent through its darkness.

"I b'lieve we'd better be passin' that peach cobbler to celebrate Miss Solace's victory!" Beulah Mae announced with a wide grin. She'd seated herself closest to the sideboard so she could hold the warm pan, while Mama dished up portions for everyone to pass around.

As Solace cut into the latticework of flaky pastry, down through the thick, sweet layer of golden peaches, Asa grinned at Owen.

"You wanna run out to the springhouse and fetch that fresh ice cream, Mister Owen?" he asked. "Nothin' but the best for Miss Solace, ya know. And for Mister Gabe, our miracle worker."

Bernadette sucked in her breath, her blue eyes sparkling. "Ice cream again? Twice in one day? Now *that's* a miracle!"

Solace smiled around her first mouthful of warm cobbler, and then again when Asa spooned fresh, cold ice cream over it for her. The real miracle, she mused, would be Gabriel Getty staying to practice law in Abilene. Considering how impressed everyone was—how national newspapers would carry the story of his fingerprinting wizardry and his polished professionalism in the courtroom—he was destined to go a long, long way as a lawyer.

Would he take her with him?

Chapter Twenty-eight

Unfinished business . . . missed opportunities . . . *unrequited love*. That was what bit into his heart the next morning as Gabe gazed out the window of his lonely room. The rain didn't help any. After getting back late last night—politely declining Michael's invitation to stay over—he felt a black, bleak mood settling over him.

No job. He'd resigned.

No home. He'd come here instead, to this spartan hotel.

No life. No . . .

If you didn't say no to the invitation in Solace's eyes, you'd be sharing a happiness like you can't imagine.

His heart knew this, and his head knew it. So why couldn't he *believe*?

When Bernadette Bristol threw her arms around Solace in the courtroom yesterday . . . rumpled her hair with that childlike glee, he'd lost his heart again to the woman in the simple blue dress and boy-short curls. Somehow, her bobbed-off hair only made her more endearing. More genuine. With Solace Monroe, the goodness so visible on the outside was amplified by the radiance of a simple soul. A soul born to love and serve and give.

Letitia would've dropped that child and escaped to the nearest powder room. Her mother would've followed, with the smelling salts, and it would've taken them an hour to make your wife presentable again.

Thoughts of his tormented wife made Gabe rake his uncombed hair with desperate fingers. The disappointment on Solace's face last night—even though he'd won her case in a grand way—spoke volumes about how he'd let her down when it counted . . . how he'd used her family's presence as an excuse not to address her needs. Her feelings.

Your needs. Your feelings. It's you who has trouble loving, not Solace.

Desperate for something—anything—to occupy his thoughts, Gabe reached for his leather satchel. Perhaps the notes he'd scribbled to prepare Solace's defense would provide a lead, an idea . . . a guide to what he'd done best, so he'd know what sort of job to search for, or where to . . .

Gabe pulled out an unfamiliar sheaf of pages and stared at it. *Her Shadow, by Solace Monroe,* was written in two lines across the top, and he knew immediately that he was in no mood to read this story. Yet the simple script and unpretentious language drew him in . . . led him quickly along every line, down the entire first page.

How had she done this? How had Solace recounted his life story—the one he'd been so careful not to reveal to anyone else—in a tale about a frontier lawyer and a forthright young woman who loved him, but couldn't compete with his deceased wife's shadow? He read faster, his eyes blurring during the second page . . . the third . . . until a huge teardrop splattered on the paper and the ink ran.

"This is not . . . *fair!*" He threw the pages against the wall. What did Solace know about guilt? Addiction? About watching someone he'd loved wither away and hide behind excuses? The nerve of that girl, saying Letitia had made her choices—had put the flask to her own lips and . . .

His reflection in the shaving mirror scared him. Gabe blinked, and then stared hard at the man who'd done exactly as the story said . . . the man who'd blamed himself for whatever had been lacking in his wife's makeup. The husband who believed himself responsible for a failed marriage, even though he'd never really felt married.

Were these red-rimmed eyes to be his future? Were torment and shame and unrealized dreams to be his life partners?

Has Solace sent this to her publisher? What if this story shows up on every magazine rack in the country?

While few readers would recognize his life's fictionalized circumstances, and fewer would associate Solace's characters with the real people involved, Gabe suddenly had to know if she'd shown this piece to anyone else.

But he couldn't go to the Triple M looking so . . . shipwrecked. It wouldn't benefit either one of them, if—

Gabe let out a ragged breath and turned from the washstand. If he let her, Solace could set him free—just as he'd acquitted her of murder. She was telling him, in no uncertain terms, that his guilt had to go. Or she would.

Despite the rain, he hurried out of the room and down the stairs, wiping his face on his sleeve before anyone could see him.

"Good morning, Mr. Getty!" said the young fellow at the desk.

"Same to you, sir!"

"And congratulations on your monumental success in court. It's all over town, how you outfoxed that fortune-teller."

Gabe stopped and turned in the hotel doorway. The clerk wasn't old enough to understand it was *he* who'd been outfoxed, by Solace Monroe's big brown eyes and bigger heart. "Thank you," he replied in a more thoughtful tone. "The pleasure comes from a job well done. From knowing one's life purpose and pursuing it."

It sounded like something Solace would say. Her words and gestures during the trial came back to him . . . her gentle but direct voice filled his head as he strode along Abilene's streets. He wasn't sure what he was looking for, but he had to follow his gut. Had to seek until he found . . .

"Mornin', Mr. Getty, sir! Fine job yesterday!" someone called from the mercantile.

Not two doors farther down, a woman hailed him with a wave of her handkerchief. "Oh, Mr. Getty, you were *brilliant*!"

she gushed. "As I watched you present your case, why—I just knew you'd be the man to untangle some unfortunate financial affairs my nephew's gotten me into!"

"Thank you, ma'am. When I've opened my law office, I hope you'll come in."

Law office? Where had *that* come from?

Gabe shook his head and followed his feet away from the business district, toward streets lined with trees and neat picket fences ... modest, but tidy homes he hadn't noticed before. Why was he feeling so urgent? So driven to gaze at white houses with lace curtains and lamps in the windows ... as though he were being guided by unseen hands?

Or the beating of wings ...

He slowed down, paying closer attention to the sensations that prodded him along. Gabe had no idea where he was— except, of course, that he'd followed a side street into this residential area. Now that the homes were two stories, with larger yards, his heart beat faster. The last thing he wanted was another mausoleum of a mansion like ...

Step away from your past. Find your heart's desire.

Who would be talking to him this way? The voice in his head was perfectly clear, yet he'd never conversed with angels or invited their presence. He slowed his pace, spying into the garden behind a red brick home with a gallery porch across the back. Its iron fence needed blacking. The trumpet vines and morning glories had run amok, and the place had a sad air of neglect that ... reminded him of himself.

Then he spotted the white wooden swing, secluded among lilac bushes that were in full bloom.

Gabe inhaled their fragrance on the breeze that caressed his cheek. For several moments he stood at the fence, gazing at the overgrown yard, yet always returning to the swing ... so much like the one at Billy's, where Solace had slipped away to write her stories ... where he'd first realized she was a writer, and a woman who made his heart beat hard, the way it hammered now.

"Why are you showing me this?" he murmured.

Figure it out.

Slowly he walked to the corner, and then turned to pass in front of the house. Here he saw pillars that needed paint . . . symmetrical front windows on the second story that peered at him like eyes. Empty, forlorn eyes. Then he noticed the little boy on the front steps, sitting with his elbows on his knees and his chin between his fists.

"You from the orphanage, mister? Come to fetch me back?"

Gabe's chest tightened. Somehow his hand had found the latch on the gate and he was stepping through it. "No. Why would I do that?" he asked carefully.

"'Cause I runned away again. 'Cause my mama and daddy, they went to heaven awhile back and they didn't take me."

He stopped on the walk, blinking rapidly. That little voice, so lonely . . . that small heart-shaped face with the huge brown eyes that studied him so intently . . . the ache in that pint-size heart that took him back to Colorado, to the log house the Indians had set afire after they'd butchered his parents and sisters . . . .

"This is your house, isn't it?" he asked quietly.

"Yup. That's my room, right up there." He pointed to the window at his left, above the porch roof. "'Cept I can't get in 'cause they locked the door."

In two long strides Gabe reached the top of the wooden stairs to sit beside the boy, whose blond hair framed his face as though someone had put a bowl on his head to cut it. "My name's Gabe. What's yours?"

"Charlie."

He offered his hand, and felt a distinct jolt when Charlie's small palm met his own. "Does anyone live here now, Charlie?"

"Don't think so. Don't look like it to me, does it to you?"

"Nope. Not that I can tell."

What was going on here? Why was his breathing so

shallow, and why did it feel as if he'd been sent on this walk at this exact time to end up on this porch with runaway Charlie? And why did it feel so right to be sitting here—as though this was already home?

And when had it stopped raining? When he'd left his room, the drizzle was soaking his shirt, yet now the sky shone bright blue. The whole world felt fresh and new again. Washed clean.

Figure it out.

He cleared his throat, realized the boy was still hanging on to him. The sight of that small hand on top of his did crazy things to him. For a moment he swore he saw Solace sitting on the other side of Charlie, and imagined they all lived here in this cozy house and . . .

Had he just found his heart's desire?

"Was you gonna say somethin', Gabe?"

Charlie's expectant expression left him no excuses and nowhere to hide. "What do you say we walk into town and find some breakfast?" he suggested. "If it's all right with you, we can let the orphanage know you won't be going back there—"

Oh, those eyes got wide! And something made Gabe want to keep this look on Charlie's precious face forever—or at least until they worked out a plan and the reality of the details settled in. Then it would be Solace's turn to make him smile.

"—and we can see about getting a key. I know a lady who would love to live here—if you'd be willing to share your house with us."

"Can I have a dog?"

Gabe blinked. The solemnity of the question made it sound like a *no* might negate the entire plan—the future— that had just fallen so neatly into place. "Matter of fact, this lady has a dog named Rex. And he rides horses!"

Charlie hopped to his feet, bringing Gabe with him. "Can he sleep in my room with me? In my bed?"

The images were streaming through his mind so fast Gabe couldn't keep up with them. Charlie was leading him down the walk, gazing up at him as though the whole world depended on the answer to those two simple questions. He chuckled so hard he could barely talk. "I think Rex will be real glad I came past your house today, young man. Rex's mama, too."

As they swung the gate open, the boy turned and looked up at the window—his window—and waved. "Bye, Mama! I'll be back. You did real good today!"

Gabe's gaze followed Charlie's, to where the ivy and trumpet vine, entwined on the downspout, fluttered in the spring breeze. Try as he might, he couldn't see anybody in the bedroom window, or any sign of whom this boy might be talking to.

"She's an angel, ya know," Charlie said matter-of-factly. "She promised to find me a family, and Mama always keeps her promises."

Had there ever been a morning like this one? Gabe had orchestrated many a dazzling courtroom defense, but never had the details fallen into place with such ease. Such grace.

Surely goodness and mercy shall follow me all the days of my life. . . .

In the time it took to order and eat their pancakes and eggs, he found out whom to contact at the orphanage—a Miss Wilkes, who also had the key to Charlie's house. And the woman who'd waved her handkerchief at him knew of a storefront office for rent. Then, when they went to the dry goods emporium to buy Charlie some longer pants and a clean shirt, Gabe spotted three unexpected treats on the magazine rack.

On the higher shelf sat a dime novel with a drawing of two masked men peering out of a cave, entitled "Smoky Hill Hide-Out." On a row beneath it, with red-bannered mastheads that said Work and Win, An Interesting Weekly for Young America, he saw "Captured by the Comanches" and "She Ran Her Daddy's Ranch." But it was the very small, very discreet byline that made his lips quiver in a grin. *Sol Juddson!* Right there for the whole world to see.

Gabe glanced around, and then snatched up all the copies of all three publications. It seemed fitting that *he* should present these to the author, before word got around that Juddson was more than just a Wild West performer who'd gained notoriety in court. It would give Solace a chance to explain these stories to her parents before anyone else asked about them.

"You gonna read *alla* those dimers, Gabe?" Charlie asked as they left the store. He had a hint of a swagger now. Nearly ran into somebody because he was gazing down at his stiff new pants.

Gabe considered his response. Decided to take a chance, and see what the kid was made of. "Can you keep a big, *huge* secret, Charlie?"

His blond hair fell softly back from his eyes as he looked up. "What? You don't want *your* mama to know you read them dimers, neither? My favorites are the ones about Buffalo Bill."

Gabe swallowed hard, because his heart was in his throat. When his hand landed on the boy's head, he marveled at the warm silk of that straw-colored hair . . . at the way Charlie pressed against his palm instead of pulling away.

"The lady I told you about, who has the dog named Rex?" he asked tentatively. "She *wrote* these stories! But you can't tell a soul. It'll be a surprise to everybody there at the ranch, so I want *her* to break the news. All right?"

Charlie's eyes widened as he thought about all those details. Then he grinned, revealing a dimple at one side of his mouth. "Cross my heart, I won't tell a soul," he said, making an X on his chest with his fingertip. "But only if ya let me read the one about the Injuns while we're ridin' out there."

Chapter Twenty-nine

Dear Solace, dearest sister,

Though I wouldn't blame you for not wanting to read anything I write to you, I hope you'll understand my need to apologize . . . my need for your forgiveness.

"Well, *here's* a surprise! Princess Lily—Princess Perfect—baring her soul to *me*!" Solace murmured. She stroked the soft hair at Rex's ear as he pressed his head against her hand. "I sure hope she's not up to something sneaky. I've had enough of that."

Solace held the pages of pretty stationery in both hands to keep them from quivering. A glance toward the house told her she had a little more time before Billy's kids came looking for her, so she settled back against the cottonwood tree. Kicked off her shoes to fully enjoy the cool seclusion of the shady riverbank.

The way I've treated you—my callous disregard for your feelings—is inexcusable. It's a perfect example of what goes awry when I listen to my own wants, my own selfish desires, rather than following God's voice and His will for me.

I realize now that your love for Gabriel Getty is sincere—as his is for you—and that I was just plain jealous. I'd helped him first, after Letitia passed, and I assumed that gave me more reason—more right—to love him than to let him follow his own course. I was too arrogant to believe you could be the answer to his prayers.

I was sadly mistaken.

"Oh, Rex, can you believe this?" Solace said between sniffles. "I was calling Lily a holier-than-thou, but bless her frilly pink frocks, last night's celebration just wasn't the same without her."

The Border collie fixed his bright brown eyes on her, following every word.

Solace sighed, picturing her older sister's elegant blond upsweep and her soft, glowing smile. "Can't blame her for setting her heart on Gabe, though, can we? I-I sure hope she won't end up an old maid school marm like Aunt Agatha. Lily's—well, Lily's just too special for that."

> *It was horrid of me to make you move your things to the barn, as well. And when I heard about the upcoming trial—how those underhanded Wild West people have treated you so badly—I realized I haven't behaved much better. I was so relieved when Papa sent word to say Gabe would be helping with your defense, if only from the sidelines.*
>
> *Can you forgive me, dear Solace? You're the last person in this world I ever intended to hurt. I feel horrible that I've been so blind to your unique radiance and spirit. In a world of darkness and despair like Gabe has known, you're the perfect antidote to his grief.*

"I wish somebody'd tell *him* that," she murmured. Yet she was chuckling as she swiped at her eyes. "Real nice of everybody to point out how perfect we are for each other . . . like I needed their permission to have feelings for him!"

Rex rolled over to wiggle and twist in the grass. He was scratching his back, but with his tongue lolling out and the low, blissful grunts that escaped him, he appeared to be laughing. Probably at her!

Again, please accept my apologies on paper until we
can be together. My prayers are with you as you go to
trial—and prevail!—Solace. How wonderfully you've
lived up to your name! What a comfort and joy you are
to all who know you! The next time I come home . . .

The clatter of wagon wheels brought Rex to his feet with a protective *woof*, prompting Solace to gaze around the trunk of the tree. "Who is it, fella?"

The dog's tail wagged happily and he sprinted toward the yard—until he saw she wasn't following him. Then he gave her the what-for, an unmistakable lecture in bark-talk that brought three redheaded kids out the kitchen door. Owen and Bernadette dashed into the yard, because greeting a guest was the high point of their day, while Olivia followed more sedately, like the ten-year-old model of decorum she was.

"Gabe! Gabe!" Owen crowed as they ran. "We thought you'd be—"

"Who's *that*?"

Bernadette stopped to point at a smaller figure on the buckboard seat, perfectly expressing Solace's own curiosity. She remained behind a tree, watching the scene in the yard. Her pulse pounded. Her entire body had gone tight. It was good that Gabe had come back sooner than she'd anticipated, but where had he come up with a little boy? And why?

"Where's your Aunt Solace?" Gabe asked as he peered toward the house. "Charlie's come to meet her and—"

Rex's barking made Gabe turn his head in her direction, but it was the boy she watched; he didn't look very old or very strong, yet he had no trouble clambering down from the buckboard to greet her dog. And he knew enough to approach slowly, instead of running at him. Then he crouched and opened his arms.

Her loyal Rex ran at him, so excited and exuberant he knocked the boy back onto his haunches. Then he began licking his face!

Charlie's high, childlike laughter called to her heart as nothing ever had: it invited her soul out to play, as though he knew how desperately she needed to have some fun. Rex licked his face and nudged him up to play and . . .

Though she adored being among Billy's kids, playing their games and settling their squabbles as only a tomboy aunt can do, this little boy's husky voice suggested a deep sadness bubbling up within him. His laughter sounded out of practice, as though he longed for the kind of unquestioning love only a dog could provide.

Only a dog? You know better, Solace.

She blinked. She should go up there and meet this little boy, yet she hesitated. "What's happening, Daddy?" she whispered. "Gabe's got something up his sleeve—"

An arm to hold you, and another one to hold this boy. How do you think your own patchwork family got pieced together, honey?

As though she'd heard Judd Monroe's voice, her mother stepped outside, followed by Papa and Temple. Soon everyone in the house would be finding out about Gabe's guest, wondering where she was hiding herself.

Hiding has never been your way. The boy's mother and I had a hand in getting him here, so don't mess with heavenly intervention!

Now there was no way out! No way to deny that this mystery child already tugged at her. Solace folded her sister's letter and grabbed her shoes. Despite her attempt to remain dignified—to make a somewhat ladylike first impression—her legs insisted on long, urgent strides and her free hand lifted her calico skirt so she could move faster. By the time she reached the yard, the little boy had gotten up to politely shake hands with Papa.

"Charlie Carpenter? That's a fine name, son," he said. He crouched, so he could gaze up into the boy's face with an unabashed grin. "Jesus was a carpenter, you know. Can't go wrong there."

"Yeah!" Bernadette crowed. "Carpenters build peoples' houses."

"Yes, sugar, they surely do." Beulah Mae sidled up beside Papa to flash their guest her finest grin. "And I b'lieve this little fella's already started him a new home."

Solace's heart stopped at the old cook's declaration. How long could Gabe have been keeping—? Where would he have found—?

And why does everyone else already know how this'll turn out? Somehow, she kept a smile on her face. It wasn't Charlie's doing that the Malloy family took in lost kids like some families latched on to stray cats.

"And this is Olivia, and Owen, and Bernadette—and their daddy, Billy Bristol," Mama said as she gestured to their smiling, expectant faces. "And *this* is my daughter, Solace."

Charlie's head swiveled. His eyes drank her in, starting with the short curls she hadn't combed yet . . . following the faded red calico sleeves she'd rolled to her elbows, to the old shoes she gripped. He gazed at her bare ankles and feet, and then at Rex, who sat beside her and leaned into her leg.

How long did she have to hold her breath before he said something?

But then, she was the adult. It was her place to . . .

"Solace?" He lingered over her name, as though rolling it around his tongue to get the taste and texture of it. "I've heard that somewhere . . . in a song! A song 'bout Jesus bein' our friend," he said in a rising, excited voice. "Mama used to sing that while she played the piano! Do *you* sing and play the piano, Solace?"

Dear Lord, how his brown eyes sparkled! As if he already knew her well enough to tease her. How she wished she'd practiced the way Lily and Grace had! "Not very well, I'm afraid," she admitted with a sigh.

"Me, neither! Mama tried to teach me, but every time she left me to practice, I snuck off."

"Me, too," Owen chimed in. "Piano playin' is for *girls*! Or sissies!"

"That ain't me! I'm no sissy!" Charlie gawked happily at the Bristol kids then, as though he'd found a whole new world in their coppery hair and twinkling blue eyes.

"You like caves? And catchin' frogs?" Billy's son asked with a conspiratorial lift of an eyebrow. When he leaned over and whispered something in Charlie's ear, Solace caught the words "ice cream in the springhouse." The little boy's face lit up with the joy of finding this new friend . . . and maybe something else, as well.

"Excuse me. I'll be right back." Pausing only to widen her eyes at Gabe Getty, Solace strode toward the house. She felt the weight of the questioning gazes that followed her, but by golly, she'd show those boys a little something about . . . how she couldn't help loving them.

By the time she came out of the kitchen again, a redhead and a blond were walking toward the river with a quick gait, glancing back to see if anyone noticed they were about to take a detour.

Mama was a-flutter with anticipation, as excited as she'd been when the Bristol household had arrived at the trial. "Well, Gabe, this is certainly a fine surprise."

"Owen Bristol! I need a word with you, young man!" Solace called after him. She took off across the yard, doing her best to keep a straight face. She longed to follow the boys to the springhouse, but Billy's son was providing a diversion for the adult business that needed tending.

Owen stopped short, his expression wary. "What'd I do *now*? You surely won't make me cut a switch for takin' Charlie to catch frogs? We were just—"

When they met in the middle of the yard, Solace turned her back toward the group who stood near the buckboard. She slipped two spoons from her skirt pocket. "A little something to uh, catch those frogs with," she whispered. "But if you don't bring these back, you're in deep trouble, understand me?"

Owen grinned at Charlie. "Keep the girls away, willya, Aunt Solace? They'll ruin everything and tattle on us for—"

"Scoot! Be sure to wipe your mouths good, or there'll be no living with your sisters."

Charlie's giggle made her heart tip sideways. When he looked into her eyes again, the sky lit up around her. Then he took off toward the river. "C'mon, Owen! C'mon Rex!" he called. "I betcha there's Injuns—or pirates!—in that cave you's talkin' about! Who knows what kinda treasure we might find?"

What was it about the sight of two boys skedaddling across the lawn with a dog trotting between them? As she turned toward the others, a big, silly grin lit her face but she didn't fight it. That smile belonged there—just like the one that was slowly curving Gabe's lips. He adjusted his eyeglasses, a move she'd seen a hundred times, yet now it hinted at more secrets. Maybe some answers.

And maybe one very important question.

"Is there something you'd like to talk about, Mr. Getty?" she asked.

Chapter Thirty

"What on earth did you tell those boys? They looked like you handed them the keys to—"

"Nope. Just spoons." As they reached the road, Solace scooted toward the center of the buckboard seat so she could command Gabe's full attention. "But we're not talking about two boys sneaking ice cream here, Mr. Getty. We're going to discuss Charlie Carpenter. And then you're going to tell me—"

Like lightning his arm slipped around her shoulders, and then his lips found hers. Gabe kissed her with everything he had: all the wonder and joy and anticipation of her reaction. He turned it loose, now that they were finally alone. She tasted like spring and fresh promises he longed to keep with her. She felt like *hope,* and all the answers he'd been seeking suddenly fell into place. Effortlessly.

Solace slipped her hand behind his head, into those thick, warm curls, so he couldn't pull away until she was good and ready. Her eyes fluttered shut and she marveled at how their mouths could say so much without uttering a word— even if Gabe *had* interrupted an important . . . topic of . . . conversation. . . .

But what could possibly be more important—or more revealing—than this kiss? She relaxed into it . . . allowed Gabe's lips to teach her what she'd never known. A few fellows had caught her in a clinch, but she'd failed to see the attraction—the whole point of kissing—until Gabe Getty gave himself over to the emotion of the moment.

Best of all, he gave himself without reservation. No hint

of past sadness lingered on his lips. Something had finally freed this man from a marriage he'd endured rather than enjoyed, and Solace sensed Letitia would no longer haunt them. When their lips finally parted, they shared a sigh.

"I love you, Solace," he whispered. "I—"

"High time!" she teased—and then immediately regretted it. Gabriel Getty deserved a woman who would do him proud and build him up. A lady who would take him seriously. "I'm sorry. That was a rude—"

"Sorry I love you?" Gabe's eyes glimmered like dark, strong coffee.

Solace sighed, impatient with herself. Now that he was saying all the right things, she was not! "I could never be sorry about that, Gabe! But maybe we should talk about Charlie—"

"Maybe." He clapped the reins against the horse's back again, smiling, eager to see her reaction to so many things, now that this miraculous day had cleared the right path for him. "You'll never guess whom I saw in town this morning."

She raised an eyebrow. "Your diversionary tactics might work in the courtroom, Gabe, but this is *me* you're talking to! And if you think you can just show up at my parents' ranch with—if you think Charlie Carpenter's big brown eyes will win me over *for* you—"

He chuckled and reached beneath the seat. "Took me all of two seconds to fall for that forlorn little face, sweetheart. Don't let his appearance deceive you, though. Charlie's advanced for his age and more capable than his size suggests. He thinks Sol Juddson writes a fine Injun story, too."

With quaking hands, Solace reached into the flat sack he'd handed her. The sight of these dime novels from the mercantile was nothing out of the ordinary, because she'd bought stacks of them over the years, but . . .

"Oh, my—oh, my Lord, it's—these are *my* stories!" she gasped. Her eyes couldn't get enough of the Work and Win banner, and the Beadle Dime Novel masthead she'd seen dozens of times—except there she was! Sol Juddson! Right on the front, beneath the bold black titles, "She Ran Her Daddy's Ranch," "Smoky Hill Hide-Out," and "Captured By the Comanches."

She flipped open the front covers, breathless at the sight of her own words set in type on the pulpy pages. "Gabe, I can't thank you enough for—where'd you find these?"

Her change in tone told him the consequences of writing these might be sinking in. "Right there in front of God and everybody, on the mercantile's magazine shelves!" he said lightly. "So I bought every copy. I figured you might want to show them to your family before someone else did."

Her mouth fell open. "I . . . thank you," she breathed.

"You're welcome, Solace." He smiled, finally letting his eyes linger on those tousled curls and her distinctive face for as long as he wanted to. "Not only are you astute and intelligent in so many ways, my dear, but you're now Charlie Carpenter's favorite author. He read the story about the Comanches to me on our way to the Triple M."

"Really? He doesn't look old enough to—"

"I was an early bookworm, too. A good story was my way to live other lives . . . to escape the nightmare of my family's massacre, when I was too lost inside myself to talk about it." Gabe gazed thoughtfully at the road, amazed at how comfortable he felt with the sorrows in his past now . . . possibly because he felt so absolutely happy with the woman beside him. "Never underestimate the power of your pen, Solace. Not only do you entertain, you . . . you change lives."

Solace swallowed hard. Maybe she shouldn't have slipped the prairie lawyer story into his valise. She'd presumed to tell Gabe how to mend his broken heart, when she'd had no idea how to fix her own.

"I was impressed with your rendering of the Comanche attack . . . the details of setting and character," he continued softly. "You wrote the scenes so vividly, I saw them in my mind as Charlie read to me. You were *born* to write."

An odd flutter tickled her stomach. "That's probably good, since my career as a trick-shot artist is over, and—"

"Maybe not," he asserted, grabbing her hand. "You're a natural teacher, too. You'd train riders as well as you've trained your horses and dogs, I bet. When I told Charlie about your riding and shooting in the Wild West show, he got so excited! He wants a horse, and to learn to ride. The main reason he agreed to come along with me was that I told him about Rex, and . . . promised him Rex could sleep in his room. In his bed."

Gabe's sheepish grin made her giggle. "You two gentlemen must've had quite a talk. So is that where you're taking me?"

"To his room. And his bed?" His smile turned downright devilish. "Before we go down that road, I have to clear away some details about Letitia."

"Ah. I'm not surprised," she breathed. "It-it really hasn't been all that long since she—if you need more time to—"

"Solace." Gabe stopped the wagon. Wrapped the reins around the brake so he could take her hands in his. "When I found your story early this morning, I-I got so upset I had to leave my room. I took a walk, not knowing or caring where. And yet, as I passed houses I'd never seen, I felt as though I were being led. *Steered* is more like it."

She gripped his fingers, remaining silent so he'd finish his story.

"And when I passed beside a fenced yard with a garden in the back and a wooden swing among the lilac bushes, like the ones at Billy's, I-I saw you there so clearly, Solace."

Gabe paused for breath. He couldn't stop gazing at her face. He'd made some monumental decisions today in a very short time—without consulting the woman he wanted to share them with. "Next thing I knew, I spotted a lonely little boy sitting on the front steps, and I was going through the gate to sit by him. He-he asked me if I was from the orphanage, come to fetch him because he'd run away again, Solace. I-I just couldn't leave him there."

He cleared his throat, moved again by the emotions of that moment . . . the timing that was too perfect to be coincidence. "Nor could I take him back to the orphanage when I learned the house had been his home. I hope you don't feel I've been misguided or presumptuous."

Her arms flew around his neck. "You did exactly the right thing, Gabe! That's the most incredible—"

"No, what's incredible is that his mama had promised to take care of him—and then *I* showed up! He waved to her spirit as we went to get some breakfast," Gabe continued in a breathy voice. "He thanked her, and . . . said he'd be back."

Solace swiped at a tear, following every word with a heart that swelled in her chest. "And to think my story upset you enough to leave your room, and—"

"Your story set things straight in no uncertain terms. Not only were you *right*, but I knew if I didn't pay attention to the warning between those lines, I'd lose you," he said hoarsely. "And I-I can't imagine how bleak my world would be if that happened."

She hugged him hard. Felt him shudder as he held her close. "Want to hear the rest of this story, Gabe?"

"You mean there's more?"

"Uh-huh. I heard Daddy telling me not to mess up what he and Charlie's mama have brought about," she murmured. "As though the decision to . . . to make him part of our family had already been made. By angels."

His sigh released the tightness in his body. Gabe looked at her, noting how her eyes had the same depth and sparkle Charlie Carpenter's did. He wanted to spend years sitting close to her, so he could gaze at her this way. "They've been working on you, too? Conspiring against us?"

She laughed softly, and the sound warmed his soul. "Oh, it's more than a conspiracy, dear man. It's destiny," she declared. "Papa and Asa would say God's working His purpose out—and maybe Lily would, too. She—she wrote me a letter to apologize last week. I was reading it when you and Charlie arrived."

"I'm glad. I didn't want to become a wedge between you two. I never intended to hurt her by rejecting her affections."

"She knows now that it wasn't meant to be." Solace considered this for a moment. "Could be Lily's angels caught her before she wandered any farther down the wrong path. Maybe they even dictated that letter. In spite of her saintly ways, Lily can be . . . headstrong at times, unless someone higher up gives her backside a boot. If you know what I mean."

Chuckling, Gabe picked up the reins again. All this talk of spirit involvement was a bit beyond him, yet the Malloys and the Bristols accepted it as a part of their everyday lives. The faith in these two families certainly felt a lot warmer, a lot more welcoming and—right, than tiptoeing around Letitia's addiction and her mother's confrontations.

"I'm a different man because of your story, Solace. And because you persisted in telling it." He glanced over at her, noting the wet tracks on her cheeks. "Thank you, sweetheart. You saved my life."

"And you saved my backside in that courtroom!" she replied lightly. "So that makes us even, right? Starting out on level ground and ready to . . . gallop out of the valley of the shadow."

"I hope you'll feel that way when you see the house. It . . . needs some work."

As he steered the horse down the street he'd followed this morning, he sensed that heavenly guidance again, like the rush of wings blowing him along on a gentle breeze. "Charlie told me his daddy died about five years ago, after an outbreak of smallpox at the factory where he worked. His mother took on cooking and cleaning for people, but it wasn't enough and . . . she wore herself out, I suspect. He . . . he was holding her hand when she passed."

"Oh, Gabe," she murmured. "What a difficult thing for a small boy—"

"He sounded peaceful about it. Said she'd been coughing so hard she'd brought up blood the last couple of weeks—"

"Consumption, probably."

"—so he understood that she was out of her pain. He talks to her. Feels her presence very clearly, especially when he's there at the house." He sighed when he caught sight of the two-story structure; it didn't look any more inspiring in the afternoon sunlight than it had this morning, shrouded by clouds. "I got the key from the director of the orphanage. If-if you don't feel comfortable here, I'll understand. I know a move into town will be difficult, after spending your life at the—"

"Let's go in," she whispered. "No sense in second-guessing our doubts, is there?"

"You're right." He smiled wryly and put on the brake. "But then, that's usually the case, isn't it?"

The careworn furnishings in the Carpenter house might have been second-hand before they came here. Solace walked slowly through the downstairs rooms, looking beyond the dust and cobwebs . . . allowing herself to imagine how Charlie's childhood must have been, especially after his daddy died. Amelia and Steven Carpenter had lived so modestly . . . so meagerly, she wondered how they'd afforded this large home. But she sensed they'd been happy here. Blessed by Charlie's birth.

Had he been left alone while his mother worked? Had he been scared of monsters beneath that sideboard with the griffins carved into its legs? Was this the rocking chair where his mama sang him to sleep? The lamp he'd learned to read by?

The table in the dining room had odds and ends piled on it . . . the carpet runner was worn through to the plank floor in spots. Dishes in the kitchen's dry sink suggested Charlie might've spent a few days here by himself before the undertaker informed the orphanage about him. As her hand trailed up the banister dulled with dust, Solace felt very attuned to others who'd climbed these stairs . . . those who'd once loved Charlie dearly and had hated to leave him behind.

"Oh, my," she murmured as she entered the room at the top of the steps. "Amelia died here. I can *feel* it."

"Me, too." Gabe let out the breath he'd been holding, looked around at the crowded bookshelves . . . a wooden Chinese checker board set up on the floor, left unplayed. The bed was unmade and the top sheet was bloodstained. "Do you suppose she was in his bed, and he was caring for her? This is the room he pointed to as his."

"No doubt about it," Solace whispered.

"I—it's entirely up to you, whether we live here. I'll think of a way to explain it to Charlie, if you feel uncomfortable or—" He raked his hand through his hair. Was it the stuffiness of a house too long unaired, or were memories of too much death closing in on him? Gabe felt compelled to leave, to go outside immediately, yet he didn't want to rush Solace. He felt silly, having this sudden sensation come over him.

"Take all the time you need," he said in a tight voice. "I'll be outside checking the porches. Thought I saw some rotten wood in the stairs."

"I'll be down in a minute. I really want to see that swing in the garden, you know." Solace smiled at him. The curls he'd rumpled stuck straight up, as though he'd seen a ghost.

And maybe he had.

She waited for the sound of his retreating footsteps to fade at the bottom of the stairs. "What are you saying, Daddy? That after all these years of our little talks, you've shown yourself to Gabe but not to me?"

Soft laughter echoed in the small bedroom, but it sounded gentle. Like a father reassuring his child there were no spooks in the armoire. *I never had to show myself, honey. You believed without seeing.*

"I felt your presence," she replied with a nod. "I knew you were my father from the time you first came to my cradle."

And I'm about to leave you. At least in the way you've known me.

Air rushed from her lungs and Solace glanced frantically around the dim room. It seemed to spin with an energy she couldn't describe. She had the urge to throw open a window, to get some air—except that would bring Gabe running to see what was wrong. "What do you mean, you're about to— but I've always depended on your guidance, Daddy! Where would I be without it?"

Right here. Carrying out your purpose with a child who longs to share his heart and soul with you. It was the same way for me when Billy and his sister showed up, and for your mother when Lily was left at her door in a basket. He paused to let these new concepts sink in. *Nice story about running your daddy's ranch, by the way. Charlie loved it.*

"But—but I don't understand why you can't keep on—"

Sometimes we aren't meant to understand. Sometimes we must simply believe. "Trust and obey, for there's no other way"—like the hymn says.

"But who'll I talk to when—"

Figure it out.

Solace stuck her clenched fist onto her hip. "Now what kind of answer is that? It's not like you have other daughters to—"

It's your turn to care for the children, Solace, and I've brought you one. If you look closely into his eyes—if you love Charlie the way I love you—you'll know what to do. You can always go to God for help. Or to Michael, who's been a wonderful father in my place.

The whirling of the room's invisible cyclone slowed until the sensation of movement ceased. She once again stood alone in a little boy's bedroom. A room that bespoke heartache and loss, but a never-ending love, as well. Was it the room that held special power because Amelia Carpenter had passed on here? Or had these revelations come from Daddy through her because their time had arrived?

No wonder that little boy insisted on living here. . . .

And if Charlie Carpenter was attuned to his deceased mama the way she'd known Daddy, dead before she was even born, well . . . she and that little boy shared something very special. A miracle—a guiding love light—like most folks never knew.

"We haven't met yet, Amelia, but I promise to take good care of your boy," she whispered as she gazed at the ceiling.

A warmth surrounded her. She felt someone smile.

Twinkling with her new purpose, Solace went downstairs to get a *yes* out of Gabe.

Chapter Thirty-one

When Gabe settled into the swing, he knew everything would work out. Its white paint had faded, but the wood remained strong, and the chains made a comforting creak each time he swung forward. The fragrance of lilacs, both lavender and white, enveloped him in a sweet dream in which he saw Solace sitting here with him of an evening to share her day's events and listen to his.

Life would be good here. Fresh paint and rugs and curtains would bring this home to life again. . . .

But what's taking her so long? Maybe she's torn between accepting this home and crushing Charlie's hopes . . . or she can't leave her horses behind . . . or she resents the way I presented this as an open-and-shut case.

Gabe's heart fluttered anxiously—or were those her footsteps? Before he could think up a rebuttal to her protests, Solace appeared on the back porch. She paused there, leaning against a white pillar to take in the garden and the fenced backyard. Her eyes looked wide and her expression held an ethereal otherworldliness he'd never seen before.

Did she see problems, or possibilities? Had he made a huge mistake, assuming she'd look at this place through the eyes of love—through Charlie Carpenter's eyes?

Solace stepped down from the porch as though the swing drew her like a magnet. She pinched off a white lilac bloom and twirled it in front of her nose . . . inhaled deeply as she closed her eyes.

She was stunning, and completely unaware of it. So fresh: elegant in her simplicity. Again Gabe studied her whimsical curls; Solace Monroe wore such an unconventional style to great advantage. She had a talent for turning the unfashionable into a positive attribute.

When she opened her eyes to gaze at him above the white flower, she looked for all the world like a bride with her bouquet. Pure and virginal. Yet when she settled against the far end of the swing to bat her long lashes at him, she became the world's biggest flirt.

Gabe knew he'd better navigate this tricky situation before she refuted all his best points. Solace Monroe loved a good contest of wits and wills, and she could corner him with her insightful logic—or, failing that, with a kiss. If she tried *that* tactic, he was a goner.

"What's your honest opinion of this place, Solace?" he asked as his hand stole toward hers. "I know it needs some attention, but—"

"Oh, that doesn't bother me!" she replied serenely. "The Malloys and the Bristols would make short work of the painting and repairs, like we did when Billy reclaimed his home place. They'd consider it a wedding present. If there is one."

Gabe's throat went dry. "A wedding or a present?"

One expressive eyebrow rose. "Figure it out."

Figure it out? How did she know about his earlier conversation . . . which may or may not have been real? He licked his lips, knowing what should happen next. It wasn't as though he'd never done this. Wasn't as though he didn't *mean* what he needed to say to this woman. And this was the perfect time, the perfect place. . . .

He was perfectly mute. Speechless.

Solace eyed him sideways. "What do you suppose Charlie's doing?" she asked coyly.

"Charlie! How can you talk about Charlie at a time like this?"

"Like you insisted on talking about him all the way into town?" Her lips gave a funny little smile. "So what do you . . . *propose* we talk about, Gabe?"

Oh, she was asking for it! He slid to the center of the swing but stopped short of touching her—physically, at least. His eyes burned into hers. "It was one thing to tell me how to deal with Letitia's memory—"

"Let's not talk about her, either."

"—but if you think you can have *all* the say-so about when—"

Solace silenced him with the tip of her lilac blossom. It tickled his lips and teased him with a heady scent that made him inhale deeply.

"Will you marry me, Gabe?" she whispered.

Just like that. No fuss or flurry.

He released his breath, marveling at those steadfast brown eyes . . . at the dimple that twinkled beside her lips. He wove his fingers between hers. Moved the lilac away from his mouth.

"I should tell you no, out of principle and propriety," he murmured, "but I don't have the heart to tease you that way."

"You find me bullheaded, yet irresistible."

"Yes, I do, Solace."

"You've found me a home and a special child, so—"

Gabe slipped his fingers into her soft curls and kissed her until they both surrendered to elemental need . . . the physical and emotional connection of lips. She giggled, pressing harder to torment him, but Gabe held steady. He moved his mouth slowly and surely until Solace surrendered to his rhythm . . . followed his lead as willingly as he would always follow hers.

"You're the lady I can't live without," he whispered. "So yes, sweet Solace, we'll make this our home, and Charlie will be the start of our family—if you'll marry *me*, that is."

Her grin did indescribable things to him. "Couldn't have said it better myself," she quipped. Her fingertip traced his lips. "I-I'm not used to handing over the reins, but for you, I'll do my best—once in a while, anyway. I fell in love with you at your first wedding, you know . . . when you asked me to dance. When you made me feel special for who I was."

He sighed at the memory of that day, and that dance. Gabe said good-bye to the woman who'd been a slave to convention and a silver flask as he again kissed Solace, the most unconventional woman he'd ever met. Not a single doubt lingered this time. She made him *so* happy!

It was a match made in heaven and sanctified by angels. Who was he to defy celestial intervention?

Chapter Thirty-two

October, 1886.

"Something old, something new," Grace chanted happily.

"Something borrowed, something blue," Lily chimed in. "Just look at you, Solace! Mama's gown is perfect for you. Simple and sophisticated."

"And with the new veil, and the blue ribbon laced in the bodice—and Lily's pearls—you're the picture of wedding perfection!" Her little sister sighed wistfully. "I hope I'll get married someday soon. May I wear your dress, too, Mama?"

Mercy Malloy seldom denied her three girls anything, yet her smile, bracketed by gentle lines, was diplomatic. "I've saved you the gown I wore when I married *your* father, dear. Billy's sister Christine designed it—made it of ivory silk, with a lace overlay. She wore it when she married Tucker, too—out in the yard where Solace will say her vows. Not many gowns have graced three beautiful brides."

Lily's expression softened. "Christine," she murmured. "Now *there's* somebody I miss!"

Solace was too busy gazing at the stranger in the mirror to enter into this sentimental chatter. Who would have believed the difference a bridal gown could make? The sky blue ribbons had been Mama's idea, to gather the scooped neckline into a better fit for her smaller bosom. And frankly, a touch of her favorite color made the gown—the entire occasion—much less daunting. Less prissy, too.

Her mother was circling her slowly, nipping her lip. "You do that dress justice, honey. Even though I was thin as a bride, I was so corseted I had to breathe and move very carefully. The church was crowded, and I was so nervous I nearly keeled over before Daddy walked me to the altar."

"Thank you for letting me wear it, Mama. It's a special honor." Solace suddenly recalled Letitia Bancroft fainting in Gabe's arms at their wedding, and it gave her great satisfaction to draw a deep breath without popping any seams. None of those nasty whalebone stays for her today! Nor ever! Training ten new horses for Obadiah Jones, one of Papa's longtime buyers—and teaching Charlie to ride on weekends—had kept her body firm and fit over the summer. And she was thankful for that.

"Judd would be so proud." Mama's steady brown eyes glistened with unshed tears, but then she smiled brightly. "And Michael's downstairs pacing a rut in the carpet, he's so excited. We're overjoyed that you and Gabe found each other, and Charlie. Clearly, it was God's plan for you!"

Solace grinned. It had turned out that her parents were impressed by Sol Juddson's stories and had encouraged her to keep writing, but they were far more ecstatic about Charlie making them grandparents.

From the first day Gabe had brought him here, he'd fit like a hand in the family glove. He was all boy—loved the riverbank and romping with Rex—yet he listened attentively during devotions, and was minding the manners Temple Gates and Mama had instilled in them all. Charlie adored Michael Malloy—loved his stories about being a stagecoach driver and a soldier in the war. And Papa was so happy having a shadow again, his grin lasted from the time Charlie arrived until Gabe took him home.

"I can't thank you all enough for the way the house glows now." This time, it was her turn to get misty-eyed. "I was concerned about moving in where Charlie's parents had lived and died—and just as worried that changing his home would upset him. But he loves his blue room, and the whole place has taken on another life. What a difference new colors and carpet and curtains have made!"

"Takes more than paint and new parents to scare Charlie!" Lily remarked.

New parents. That was the part that made Solace nervous. She and Charlie shared a special bond, to be sure, yet raising a seven-year-old boy felt like a monumental responsibility. No chance to back out—no reverting to the days when she'd spent all her time with her dog and her horses, or had hidden herself away to write.

Gabe already had a good feel for fatherhood, because he'd moved into the house the week they became betrothed. Charlie had helped him set up his new law office and then returned to school in town. He did his homework while Gabe saw his last clients each day, and then the two of them went to dinner before strolling home.

How would she fit herself into their tidy routine? Could she cook decent meals and keep the house clean? And how would she possibly make time for all the things she felt called to do? She marveled that Mama had handled Billy, two baby girls, and Joel when she'd married Papa—and then delivered baby Grace a year later. How had she stayed sane?

"Look at Charlie out there! Determined not to fall under Bernadette's spell, while she refuses to be ignored!"

Grace joined Lily at the window, chuckling. "Miss B's sketchbook already contains several rough drawings of Charlie. In the back, where she thinks Owen and Olivia won't see them."

"But *you* looked!" Solace pointed out. She held very still as Mama slid the beaded headpiece into her hair, just behind her ears. Her curls were trimmed short again, because Gabe liked them that way—which was all the reason she needed.

"I'm her teacher. It's my responsibility to know what my students are writing and drawing," Grace replied loftily. Then she chuckled. "It was her mother who gave me the hint, however. Eve has seen a small canvas of a boy with dark blond hair tucked behind some others. Apparently Bernadette sneaks up to the studio to work on it."

"Ah, young love," their mother teased. Then she grinned at Solace. "It was Billy *you* idolized, sweetheart. Poor kid couldn't go anywhere or do anything without you. There— see if you like these ribbons."

Solace was about to reply, but once again her reflection caught her by surprise. Gossamer layers of tulle cascaded past her shoulders, and three strands of gently curled blue ribbon hung from each side of the headpiece. It was a small detail she'd not seen on any of the veils they'd looked at in town, and it set her apart from brides who wore white on white.

"Oh, Solace. How pretty you look!" her little sister cooed as she came from the window.

Lily, too, lit up as she took in Solace's completed ensemble. "It's nearly time to go downstairs, so let's bring this layer over your face—"

"No, thank you!" Solace grabbed her sister's hands, once again aware that Lily's soft palms bore no calluses from carrying water or roping foals.

But that was as it should be: this regal blonde dressed in rose silk would always reign as the prettiest princess of the family. "I intend to walk under the bridal arch with both eyes open and nothing clouding my vision. And Gabe might as well see what he's getting full-on, while he has one last chance to escape!"

"Hah!" Gracie retorted. "Like you wouldn't ride after him and rope him with your lariat."

"He knows you're good with a gun, too. Poor man doesn't stand a chance," Lily joined in. She slipped into her elegant pink gloves and then picked up her sheet music. "Are we ready, Gracie? Guests are arriving, so it's almost time for our song."

She turned toward the door, but then pivoted quickly on

her heel. Before Solace realized what was happening, Lily's silken arm was hooked around her neck and they were hugging each other.

"Be happy, Solace!" she whispered. "If anyone deserves a wonderful man like Gabe Getty, it's you! You're the best sister in the world, and I'm honored to attend you today."

With a flurry of silks and satins, deep rose and sage green, her sisters hurried out the door. As their happy chatter descended the stairway, Mama smiled. "Forgiveness is a fine thing among sisters. It's so good to have all three of you girls at home, without any hissing and bickering!" she said with a chuckle. "But we'll miss you. This house'll feel awfully empty with just Temple and your papa and me."

"So you'll have to come into town to see us. Often," Solace insisted. And she was only half-joking when she added, "I'll need your help to keep us fed and dressed, Mama. Housekeeping has never been my best trick."

"You'll do fine, dear. But perhaps we'll come now and again . . . to see Charlie," she clarified with a sparkle in her eyes. "Now scoot! A bride should never be late for her big day. Aunt Agatha will be checking her watch."

Nodding, Solace gestured for Mama to precede her. She gazed at her mother's elegant posture and trim figure . . . followed the flow of her simple blue gown trimmed in the same ribbon that adorned her own veil.

How would she would ever live up to the example this woman had set? The meals she'd cooked, the tears she'd dried, and the calm sense of control she exuded, no matter how trying the circumstances? She was a rock, Mama was. Yet even with some silver in her hair and gentle creases in her skin, Mercedes Malloy never seemed to tire or age.

As she stepped out of the room she'd grown up in, Solace glanced back into it . . . smiled at the way the sun shone between the blue calico curtains Mama had made years ago. When she set foot here again, she'd be a married woman. Her world would have tilted in a different direction in the time it took to repeat her vows and taste Asa's magnificent wedding cake.

"Solace! The music's started!"

"Coming, Mama." With a giggle and a tingle of sheer joy, she started down the stairs. Gabe would be waiting—for *her*! And she couldn't wait to see him.

Gabe smiled at the familiar faces in the crowd without really seeing them. He chuckled as Owen Bristol and Charlie unrolled a runner of midnight blue velvet down the aisle, under the white bridal arch adorned with ribbons and chrysanthemums from the garden . . . sighed as Grace Malloy played the new pump organ while Lily sang "O Love That Wilt Not Let Me Go." He returned Agatha Vanderbilt's proud smile from the front row, and then watched Mercy Malloy take the aisle seat beside her . . . almost got teary-eyed when Billy kissed her cheek and came forward to join him beside Reverend Larsen. It was sheer joy to watch Olivia and Bernadette Bristol strewing rose petals in their fancy new frocks of lavender and lace.

But when the organ crescendoed into the bridal march, and Solace appeared at the end of the aisle, Gabe Getty could only gape. That woman in white, with her gossamer veil floating behind her and her smile shining forth like the sun, made his breath come out in a rush.

Beside him, Billy chuckled. "Don't tell me it'll be *you* I pick up off the floor this time, ole buddy," he whispered.

"I'm fine," Gabe rasped. "Just stunned. Utterly stunned. And to think she wants the likes of *me*."

"Must be Abe Lincoln's beard. I can't think of another single thing you have to offer."

Gabe grinned again, because Solace was focused on him . . . challenging him with her sparkling eyes. For a fleeting moment he recalled the ordeal of his first wedding. Prayed for a better day and a smoother future—and then apologized to God for being so silly. Solace Monroe was bold and brave and yes, she was beautiful—in ways that required no cosmetic assistance. Her walk was steady as she held her proud papa's arm and smiled at her friends and family. She was having the time of her life.

So why shouldn't *he*?

Gabe reached for her, and she released Michael Malloy's arm to grab his hand. No gloves. Just warm, strong fingers gripping his as though she'd never let go. He kissed her knuckles before tucking her hand into the crook of his elbow—didn't take his eyes from hers until they faced the preacher. Lily and Grace came down to assume their places beside Solace while Charlie grinned up at Billy as he stepped into place as well. When he wiggled his finger, Rex came out from under a front chair to sit proudly beside him.

"Dearly beloved, we are gathered here today, in the sight of God Almighty, to witness the joining of Solace Monroe and Gabriel Getty in holy matrimony," Reverend Larsen intoned. His voice had mellowed over the years, but his Norwegian accent had not. "Marriage is a sacred state, not to be entered into lightly or with reservation. If anyone here knows a reason why this man and this woman should not be joined as one, let him speak now or forever hold his peace!"

For a long, expectant moment they waited. Beside him, Billy shifted, no doubt recalling how Eve had cried out in the throes of labor when he'd stood in this place beside Emma Clark. On the other side of Solace, Lily turned her head to glance at the crowd.

Please, Lord, don't let her change her mind! Gabe pleaded silently.

But Lily smiled prettily at him, and then at the minister. "I think it's safe to proceed," she whispered, elbowing Solace.

Reverend Larsen's dark robe quivered with held-in laughter. "Who gives this woman in marriage?"

"Her mother and I."

It was all Solace could do to look into Papa's stricken

face. Though Michael Malloy had given his blessing to this union even before she had, he looked oddly fragile. Ready to cry. Those hazel eyes loomed large in a face tanned from days in the sun, and he kissed her quickly. "We love you, honey," he whispered. "Be joyful. Be the woman God created you to be."

Gabe blinked rapidly. Never had he felt so blessed . . . so enveloped by the love the Malloys shared as though they were all blood kin. What a difference these people had made in his life, even before he chose Solace! And what a difference, to be standing here among them, *with* them, rather than wondering if he'd always be the outsider. For the first time since he'd been a kid, the word *family* wrapped itself around his heart and hugged him tightly.

He repeated the initial intentions after Reverend Larsen . . . so engrossed in Solace, he hoped he got the words right. He heard her do the same, yet was following the movement of her pretty lips rather than the meaning of the text.

Then Billy Bristol stepped to the lectern on the dais to read the scripture he'd chosen.

"It's an honor to stand here where we're used to seein' Mike Malloy," he said with a grin. He smoothed his auburn hair, composing himself in a moment of emotion that shone like crystal in his blue eyes. "If it hadn't been for Michael, and Judd Monroe before him, I wouldn't've had any idea what passage to pick . . . or how to read from the Good Book and put any meanin' to it. I chose verses from the Forty-Fifth Psalm, about the Messiah and His bride, to honor Solace Monroe—who I helped to birth—and my lifetime friend, Gabe Getty. Listen now to the word of the Lord."

Gabe smiled at his bride. She leaned into him, never dropping his gaze.

"'I recite my composition concerning the King,'" Billy read. "'My tongue is the pen of a ready writer.'"

"Like you," Gabe whispered, and Solace blushed.

"'Grace is poured upon your lips. Therefore God has

blessed You forever . . . in Your majesty ride prosperously because of truth, humility, and righteousness.'"

"Like *you*," she whispered back, and his heart laughed with hers.

Billy's Psalm stretched into forever, yet Gabe felt only patience . . . spent those moments breathing with Solace and adoring the way those blue ribbons curled around her radiant, sun-kissed face. Healthy and ripe and ready, she was her own woman, and soon to be his! What a blessing she'd be. What glorious children she'd give him . . . .

"The Twenty-Third Psalm has become our family's favorite," Billy was saying. "It reminds me how Solace and Gabe have each gone through their own valleys to meet on the other side and restore each other's souls. I'm pleased my daughter Olivia wants to lead us in reciting it."

Solace's heart swelled as the slender ten-year-old stepped up beside Billy. How grown-up she looked in her gown of lilac satin, with her auburn hair pulled back in a bow. Olivia's smile looked anxious, yet she clasped her hands demurely and gazed out over the crowd. "'The Lord is my shepherd; I shall not want,'" she began in a clear voice.

As they were embraced by the reverent voices around them, Solace joined in with Gabe, sharing the ancient verses she'd known since childhood. "'He maketh me to lie down in green pastures . . . he leadeth me beside the still waters . . . He restoreth my soul.'"

Gabe squeezed her hands. "'Yea, though I walk through the valley of the shadow of death, I will fear no evil: for *thou art with me*,'" he emphasized.

"'. . . thy rod and thy staff they comfort me,'" she replied softly. His pulse thrummed through her fingers and she gazed steadily at him, letting memory and the guests carry them along through the rest of the passage. All she knew was that Gabriel Getty wanted to make a home—a new life—with her. With *her*! That was all she needed to know.

"'Surely goodness and mercy shall follow me all the days

of my life: and I will dwell in the house of the Lord for ever.' "

A collective sigh served as an amen. Then they exchanged their vows and their rings. The little band of gold circled her finger like a sparkling promise. . . .

"I now pronounce you man and wife," Reverend Larsen proclaimed. "You may kiss your beautiful bride, Mr. Getty."

For just a moment those words called up a different vision. Yet when Gabe blinked, Solace stood before him with her lovely young face uplifted. Her breathing sounded fast and shallow, but it was expectant joy flushing her cheeks: her sense of adventure rather than fear.

He couldn't recall what Letitia looked like.

A surge of hope drove his lips toward his bride's as she rose to meet them. They'd kissed dozens of times over the summer, but *this*! This was a coming together of mouths and minds—man and wife—that felt like nothing he'd ever known! Gabe held her tightly and she kissed him back with an eagerness that made all things new and right. So he kissed her again!

Gentle laughter and throat-clearing finally eased them apart. The pastor raised his arms happily. "Congratulations, Gabe and Solace! Ladies and gentlemen, may I introduce Mr. and Mrs. Gabriel Getty!"

The applause was warm as everyone stood up. She and Gabe turned, beaming at those who loved them. Lily, Grace, and Billy slipped behind them to recess down the aisle.

"Hey, wait a minute! We ain't finished yet!"

The urgent voice was Charlie's, and as everyone came to a stunned silence, Solace gaped at him. He looked so handsome in his navy blue suit and red bow tie, he might have been the son of a cattle baron or a railroad tycoon. His blond hair caught the afternoon sunlight and held it—just as he held their total attention.

"You gotta do that part about Mr. Getty kissin' his bride again," the boy informed Reverend Larsen. " 'Cept *this* time,

I'm gonna be in on it! It'll mean we're a real family, 'cause we're sealed with a kiss!"

When Charlie grinned and raised his arms, Gabe grabbed him, laughing. He swung the boy to his shoulder as Solace had seen dozens of times, and the sight of it filled her with a special blessing. Charlie slung an arm around her neck and Gabe's . . . arms that were so short the three of them went cheek-to-cheek-to-cheek immediately.

"Mr. Getty, Mrs. Getty," Reverend Larsen sang out, "you may kiss your son, Charles Carpenter, and may God bless your family forever and ever!"

"Amen!" everybody chorused.

As her lips met Charlie's soft cheek, and as Gabe pressed into him from the other side, Solace felt a surge of pure, boundless power. Pure, boundless *love*. It was no surprise to hear some sniffles and "ahhhs" from those in the front rows, but then Papa spoke up with such reverence she had to open her eyes.

"Look! It's a sign!"

Solace watched in awe; the largest monarch butterfly she'd ever seen was circling slowly above them, to land on Charlie's hair.

As the sun's rays caught the brilliant orange and gold of its magnificent wings, the butterfly lingered to bestow its special benediction. It fluttered slowly, resting on his head, while Charlie held his breath. His eyes sparkled as if he'd just heard the world's most wonderful secret.

Solace swallowed hard. It seemed the most special guest of all had waited until the last minute to appear, but he was no mystery to her.

"Thank you, Daddy," she whispered. "We love you, too."

MARION COUNTY PUBLIC LIBRARY